CAIRO BY NIGHTFALL

Romantic Suspense Among the Ruins

Book 5

Deborah L. Cannon

ISBN-13: 979-8680327654

Cover design by Aubrey Cannon

FRESCO NIGHTS SAGA

Fresco Nights

Pompeii at Dusk

Midnight in Palmyra

Baghdad before Dawn

Cairo by Nightfall

For
My friends and neighbors in Westdale

CHAPTER 1

"Do not scream when you see the mummy."

What on earth could that possibly mean? The message was cryptic. I read it again for clarification but the second reading made no more sense than the first.

My eyeballs slowly slanted skyward, away from the text and the cellphone in my hand. My vision moved sideways to the banner on the left side of the museum's heritage entrance. In large red letters shadowed in black, one word in bold uppercase had been printed vertically down the cloth banner that now snapped in the gusting breeze. The material of the banner was weatherproof Sports Mesh, and resisted tearing. An answering flap came from high above the other side of the triple revolving glass doors. This was its twin, another banner, lettered identically. Below the metal grommets that fastened the banners to studs on the outside walls the word ran like an accusation:

M
U
M
M
Y!

The message was a warning, but a warning against what? The museum was advertising a special exhibition. So what? The curatorial staff was busily making preparations for opening day. This was normal.

A planeload of Egyptian artifacts had arrived from Cairo last week along with one of their curators. This shipment included the body of Prince Pentawere, the homicidal son of Pharaoh Ramses III.

Wow, did that bring back memories! Memories long forgotten. I had seen more than a couple of mummies in my profession. In fact, my career in museum illustration had begun with a mummy. So—why would I scream at the sight of one?

My cellphone dinged. Aras had not waited for me to respond before a follow-up text appeared.

"Tell no one that we've been in touch. It's essential that no one know. It is a matter of national security."

I frowned. Tell no one? Not even Luke? Why was Aras even texting me instead of Luke? I am just a friend. Well, maybe more than a friend. I like to take credit for reuniting the estranged brothers. But why trust me and not Luke?

I sat on the limestone steps of the heritage entrance to the Royal Ontario Museum, dressed in designer jeans and lightweight wool sweater beneath a navy blue blazer, basking in the late autumn sunshine, feeling guilty as hell. It was strange. Aras and I were hardly besties, although I liked to think we were friends. I know the billionaire archaeologist, on occasion, still had doubts when it came to his younger sibling. But Aras had shown me the strength of his character more times than I could count.

A grey dialogue balloon immediately followed the message on my screen. *"NOT even Luke."*

It was like he had read my mind.

"What about Norman? I have to tell Norman. We don't have secrets from each other." I clicked send. My own dialogue balloon, in green, appeared.

"A matter of NATIONAL SECURITY, Lucy." This time

he had capitalized the words.

Which nation? His nation or mine? If I were to hazard a guess I would say *his*. Canada is a peaceful nation. A small nation. We don't get into international conflicts. And unlike our American neighbors our national security is not worth threatening. On the world stage we are peacekeepers not aggressors. Aras, on the other hand, lives in Syria, a place where people are fighting for their lives—for land, religion and freedom. Need I go on? We all know what happened there. Innocents were killed, and history was bought and sold like so many slices of bread. Our job (and I cannot repeat this often enough) as members of the International Save Our Ruins Effort is to save those pieces of history: the frescos, statues, gold and silver and painted art from the war mongers who wish to destroy them—or sell them to fund their conflicts.

How did Aras fit into this? He worked outside our organization as a freedom fighter, the leader of the Resistance. He was not a terrorist; nor did he kill innocent people, but he was also far from a pacifist. The corrupt government he was trying to overthrow had slowly regained ground. They had recovered most of the territory captured by the rebels, and consequently succeeded in driving Aras and his followers underground.

No one had heard from the resistance leader in weeks. The last time we saw him was at the ancient archaeological site of Nineveh on the outskirts of Mosel in Iraq. He had stolen a pair of colossal statues worth millions. Then—unexpectedly and to everyone's surprise—he had surrendered the treasure.

Perhaps a little refresher on how I am acquainted with Aras is necessary.

We met outside a terrorist camp. He was under the command of the Islamic militant extremist Nizar Tarek. Don't get me started on Tarek. One part of my brain shuts down when I hear that name. He had detonated a grenade, collapsed a tunnel on top of my Norman, and left him for dead. The clever bodyguard had managed to save himself in time to follow the treasure to Baghdad and rescue a hapless American girl the terrorist had recruited as a war bride.

Meanwhile it was I who had shot him. To be quite clear the act was in self-defense. Regrettably for me I was inexperienced and a horrible shot. He had survived.

He had gone underground, and currently we were all safe—for now. Except for Alessa. Tarek, that evil murderer, that demon with nine lives had kidnapped my friend and mentor, Alessandra Piero.

I cut off my musings to avoid a well of emotion, but it seemed Aras had remotely tracked my line of thought.

"What is ISORE doing about Piero?" was his next question.

Alessandra Piero was one of ISORE's premiere operatives. Everything I knew about guns and survival I owed to Piero. Everything I knew about handling myself in a world of artillery and men I attributed to Piero. And now she was gone. She had made the ultimate sacrifice. I checked the rain of emotion as I relived the chain of events that had led me to this day. A few weeks ago, she was voluntarily kidnapped by the notorious Islamic extremist Nizar Tarek. I say 'voluntarily' because she had sacrificed herself to save my pregnant sister Colleen. Alessandra had disguised herself as Colleen, and Tarek had fallen for the bait. What had happened afterward was no one's fault.

I hesitated before I responded to the text. My fingers felt cold poised over the keypad, the chilly sun beating down on my unprotected head. My eyes lifted to the scene across the street.

The traffic raced across Queen's Park Avenue and came to a bottleneck at Bloor Street West. Pedestrians scurried towards the subway. Despite the lazy sun, temperatures were dropping. Some of these people—inappropriately dressed according to the brightness of the sun rather than the calendar—hugged themselves as they rushed off to wherever they were going. Everyone seemed to have someplace to go—and in a hurry. Their lives were wrapped up in personal concerns like where to have lunch, how long before they had to pick up the kids from school, what was the boss going to say if they got back to work late. Did the boys have soccer practice tonight or was it tomorrow night. And what about ballet for the girl?

That was my sister's life. Not mine. Would I ever have that life?

I glanced down at my ringless finger and wiggled the gradually stiffening tip. I tried to force my mind from drifting so seriously in random directions.

No—that was not my life. Did I wish it were? Sometimes. Maybe. I don't know. Until I met Norman I had never thought too much about it. And he hadn't asked me, had he? So no, that was not my life. That was a no-brainer.

Colleen on the other hand was a different story. She was born to that life. And it was because of Alessandra Piero that Colleen was going to *have* that life. So—to get back to the million-dollar question: what was ISORE doing about Piero? Nada. Nothing. I felt my heart skip a beat and my stomach do a tiny flip. This I knew was adrenaline. Induced by emotion. What that emotion was exactly I couldn't say. Was I angry? Yes. Frustrated? Most definitely. But primarily I felt helpless. I hated feeling helpless. Alessandra had taught me never to give in to helplessness. What was it she used to say to me when I found myself in a fix, and things couldn't get any worse? *Life is like being dumped in the middle of the ocean. Keep swimming or you sink. It's the only way to keep moving forward. No matter if the current steers you in a different direction or out of the race altogether. Keep stroking.*

But what could I do? I had defied ISORE once. I had been warned. *Do it again—and you're out.*

It was strange that our boss Arianna Chase had not enlightened any of us on the intrepid ex-Interpol agent's situation. Not even Arianna's ex-husband billionaire archaeologist Luke Trevanian had a clue. Because if she had confided in him at all, he was keeping a solid lid on it, and that just wasn't the man I knew. He and his bodyguard were tight. Everything *he* knew Norman knew. And everything Norman knew, *I* knew. My question now was—why did Aras care? What was Alessandra Piero to him?

I texted back, *"Nothing is being done about Alessa. Why?"*

Maybe I had waited too long and Aras thought I'd signed out. Whatever he thought, my screen remained blank.

Then unexpectedly a voice spoke into my ear. Traffic roared from the road. I could be mistaken. Was I hearing things? I pressed the cellphone up to the side of my head. The device was silent, so Aras had not switched from texting to phone. I turned away from the shade and shielded my eyes against the sun. I blinked and saw that it was Norman hovering over me and casting that shade.

"Who are you texting?" he demanded.

I clicked off my device and hoped my red face was perceived as pleasure rather than guilt. I quickly hid my phone away into a deep pocket of my navy blue, tweed blazer. I answered, flustered.

"Colleen. That was Colleen." My voice came small, almost squeaky. Did he see? Did he know that I was lying? I hated lying to him. Simply hated it. How could Aras ask me to do this? I rolled light-brown, puppy-dog eyes at him.

Exactly what Norman knew he expertly disguised. He made a puzzled face, which turned into a tantalizing grin. "Hmmm. Are you cheating on me, Lucy my sweet? Are you having an affair?"

That put me into a fit of giggles. *After all I went through for you?* Ha. In my wildest fantasies I would never even consider it. "Yeah, I'm having smokin' hot sex with the security guard in the lobby. We were just sexting."

I pulled up a seductive shot of myself, semi dressed in red-lace undies. I had meant to send this to him just before Aras contacted me (And by 'him' I mean Norman, not the security guard).

"Oh yeah? Let me see. I wanna get in on some of that."

But the real thing was far better than anything I could have texted him. I dropped the phone onto my lap, reached up and pulled his head down to my lips. He was standing three steps below me and had been on his way up the stairs when he saw me. When I opened my eyes I could see that Luke was behind him. He smiled. "Hi, sweetheart."

"Hi Luke."

He glanced at the Breitling Chronospace watch on his wrist (prices started at a startling 6K). I am branding his wristwatch to get across the idea of just how wealthy Luke is. In our line of work, as agents of ISORE, unlimited cash flow can sometimes mean the difference between a successful mission and a disaster.

"Did you get Arianna's summons?" Luke asked.

I had. Luke had called the text a 'summons' because every request made by the director of the Royal Ontario Museum seemed like a command.

I flashed him the message on my phone.

Emergency, mandatory meeting in Prep Lab.
1:00pm sharp

He extended a hand, and I shoved my phone into my purse. Norman also thrust out a hand. Together they pulled me to my feet. The three of us went up the remaining steps to the museum—me—a mere five-foot, six-inches tall skinny girl—sandwiched between these two six-foot plus giants whom over the past few months I had grown to love.

I ask you. Does life get any better than that?

CHAPTER 2

It never ceased to amaze me, as we entered the rotunda through the whirling glass doors single file, the marvel that domed over our heads. Millions of gleaming tiles—tiny squares of colored Venetian glass in reds, blues, purples and gold—plastered the ceiling and formed a predominately gold-hued, ornate mosaic of symbols and icons replicated from a diversity of human cultures. An enormous four-sided knot encompassed the central motif above us where an inscription from the Bible read:

THAT ALL MEN MAY KNOW HIS WORK

Stretching out to each corner of the rotunda below this were icons from the Americas, the Ancient World, Europe and Asia. There was the Bison of North American cave art, the Winged Lion of Venice, an Indian Elephant, a Northwest Coast Eagle and the Inca Thunder God proffering up bolts of lightning in the form of snakes. I felt a sharp twinge at the sight of the Egyptian Vulture grasping a *shen* sign and quickly glanced over to see the Sea Horse of Greek myth, Roman mythology's Romulus and Remus, the Gothic Heraldic Griffin, the Japanese Three-clawed Dragon, and the

Fountain Lions of Islamic Spain. What really struck my eye was the Winged Bull of Assyria.

Why had I never noticed that icon before?

My eye swung reluctantly from the Bull back to the Egyptian Vulture.

No one else was looking. Norman and Luke had hurried past the crowd to collect their visitor passes from the museum's VIP desk. A pass was unnecessary for me because I had my employee ID hanging from a royal blue lanyard.

More and more people gathered in the rotunda while my eye idled on the panel above the rotunda's arches. The architectural features there reflected that of the Mayan temple, the Greek temple, the Mesopotamian ziggurat and the Egyptian pylon.

I focused uncomfortably on the Egyptian motifs. The Winged Bulls were a memory from a past adventure. And yet I had this strange, tingling sensation at the pit of my stomach that the museum's upcoming Egyptian display and the Winged Bull of ancient Assyria were intricately connected.

The boys were waiting at the elevator. Norman was just about to come and look for me. I caught the quizzical lift of an almost perfect left eyebrow.

"Hey. Where'd you disappear to? Still sexting with Security?" He sent a sly glance at the two bulging uniformed officers stationed at opposite ends of the three revolving doors that formed the heritage entrance. Of course, they had nothing on him. Norman was built like a brick firehouse and was just as pretty. "Which one is he?"

I poked a finger into Norman's chest, teasing back. "Check your phone."

A bell dinged. The elevator arrived and a group of tourists exited. We got into the empty elevator car and Norman drew his phone out of his rear pants pocket. He opened it and accessed his messages. A mischievous smile spread across his nonconventional but handsome face before he tucked the phone away. My—my—my. Was there just a hint of a blush on his cheeks?

Luke made to grab it. "Let me see."

Norman slapped a hand over his pocket to prevent Luke from stealing his phone. "It's private."

"Nothing you haven't seen before," I joked to Luke.

I am not going to elaborate on what I meant by that. Let's just say that if you know me, you know that I had my time with Luke before I ever hooked up with Norman. So you get what I mean.

Luke grinned. The elevator door opened and we stepped out. We were in the basement of the ROM, a very familiar place for me since I spent many an hour to-ing and fro-ing from my comfortable upstairs studio to the frigid basement labs. It was here that the artifacts were received and catalogued before transitioning to permanent or temporary storage depending on whether they were meant for an upcoming exhibit. Today Arianna had summoned us to the lab. That was where the Egyptian artifacts were being curated.

"What's this all about, do you know?" I asked. Our footsteps thudded on the concrete floors of the familiar maze of corridors. We turned one corner and then another, my body instinctively knowing the way.

Norman shook his head. Luke shrugged. "There was a last minute substitute for the Egyptian curator," Luke said. "Yasmine Lim the original curator got sick. It's serious I believe. Heart issues from what I hear. Not something she's going to recover from anytime soon. The exhibition is scheduled to open in a few days. So in effect, it *is* an emergency."

I was aware that she was the guest curator. The news sent a jolt into my bloodstream. The mention of Egypt always did. But more than that, it was the reference to Yasmine Lim. A sinking sensation in my stomach followed at hearing her name spoken out loud. I squashed the feeling deliberately, did that *la-la-la-la* thing in my head to ensure that the unwanted emotions remained submerged. I forced myself to focus on Yasmine. *She* was who mattered. *She* was the one I cared about. Not that other thing that her name had triggered. I had worked with her one year—eons ago—when I was doing a summer internship as an undergrad.

I turned to consult with Luke. Yasmine Lim was currently one of the youngest Egyptologists in the discipline. I commented on this. "Although you know, when I first met her she was a prop master for a movie company."

Yasmine and I had lost touch over the years. Back then we were good friends. She worked for a Cairo production company as well as served a short stint with the History Channel researching, acquiring and setting up props and locations before switching full-time into her studies. I remembered being quite envious of her and wondering why she had given up a career in film and television to get a PhD.

"No Kidding?" Norman cut in. His voice jolted me out of my thoughts. He scratched at an almost perfectly shaped ear that rose out of his close-clipped brown hair. I had an urge to place my teeth on that juicy lobe. Or maybe I was just trying to distract myself from those other feelings that were threatening to surface.

"Yeah," I replied, clenching my teeth and deliberately focusing on Norman. "She played prop master between degrees to earn money. Her parents are in the business."

"You went to school with her? I thought she'd be a lot older than you, given her position."

Luke nodded; interrupted him. "Actually, she's not all that much older than Lucy. I met her once, at a conference in New York City. Nice woman. Super smart. Probably not much younger than you, Depardieu."

That made her mid thirties now—if my calculations were accurate.

"Well, it's too bad." The mention of her was stirring up all sorts of memories, some good, some not so much. I tried to keep all of that off my sleeve as I continued the conversation. "Heart issues. Geez. That's awful. Isn't she kind of young to have a heart condition?"

"Not if it's congenital." That was Norman.

"When I knew her she was as healthy as an ox. She could climb mountains. I should get her current email address from Arianna. We lost touch. She and I and another friend—" Dammit, I was babbling. And my voice cracked as I bit off my sentence. For no good reason mind you. Except that the other friend had sort of—kind of—been more than just a friend. And it was the association with *him*, and not the mention of Yasmine that had me babbling like an idiot.

Double damn. I was losing my struggle against the past.

I made a scrambled effort at recovery: "Yas and I and this other friend (oh crap, why was I even mentioning him?) used to hang out when we were working on that internship. We were at the Cairo Museum on student visas. I was nineteen. Yasmine was twenty-three. I believe the—our other friend—was the oldest, twenty-five or something like that. All in grad school, except for me. We came from different universities."

Norman was watching me curiously. I was coloring up—or should I say my face was coloring up—incriminatingly.

"He was a *guy!*" Luke said with enthusiasm. The look on his face was that of a person who had just located the last piece of a jigsaw puzzle.

All sorts of pretty muscles in Norman's face bunched up into an expression of roguish amusement. "Lucy, *ma petite*, what did you do with this dude that was so embarrassing?"

"I didn't do anything with him."

"What was his name?"

"I don't remember."

Norman laughed, and the sound came out in a French-accented rumble.

Luke echoed the sentiment.

It was clear they were both ganging up on me. How was this all coming to the surface? I thought I had buried the memory of the man into the deepest darkest recesses of my brain. *Please leave well enough alone.* It was not my finest hour.

They refused to relent. Luke grabbed me from behind

and pinned my arms back while Norman tickled me under my breasts. They continued to razz me. And when I still resisted, Norman lifted up my sweater. I glanced frantically around. What if my boss stepped out of the lab at this moment and moseyed down the corridor?

"All right." I finally broke, tittering helplessly. "You two are incorrigible. I'll *tell* you. But you have to *stop* it. You're acting like teenagers." Norman gave my belly a wet lick, dipping the tip of his tongue into my navel, and I stifled a shriek. I twisted free from Luke and grabbed Norman by the ears tearing his lips away from my wet flesh when he refused to cease and desist. "Stop that!"

"Yeah, stop it, Depardieu. I don't want to have to witness you two going at it like monkeys."

I jerked around, slapped Luke on the arm. "It's *your* fault. *You* started it."

He was still standing half behind me, laughing, when I turned my head to make the accusation. His right arm looped around me like an iron hook trapping my arms to my sides; his lips touched my temple, pressing my back to his chest. By now Norman had stopped his ravaging of my frontal parts.

Norman kissed me on the mouth. Just to remind Luke that the switch from Luke's bed into his was complete. The billionaire graciously released me into the bodyguard's arms.

I shoved Norman back. "I mean it, you guys. Grow up. What if Arianna appeared just now."

"We'd do the same to her," Luke said.

"Fat chance." Norman snorted.

Fat chance was right. More likely she would give them a look that would freeze their man parts.

I straightened my clothes. I turned a corner and the boys followed me.

"What was his name?" Norman demanded.

Oh, not this again.

Norman shared a mocking glance with Luke. "Come on. Or do you want another tickle fest?"

I shook my head. Seriously, these guys were so juvenile

sometimes. They had me flanked between them; I couldn't get away. The lab was only a few paces further. Norman raised his hands like tiger's paws and threatened to use them.

"*Okay,*" I said, chuckling. "His name was Chas."

I paused. Wow. Why did I suddenly feel so relieved that I had spit it out?

"His name was Chas—something." I lingered over the hissing sound of the S. "Happy now? I told you I don't remember him much. It was a long time ago."

And it was. I was almost thirty-one. That would make him somewhere in the vicinity of Norman's age. Thirty-sevenish.

Norman snorted. Luke guffawed. "Chas?" They spat out the syllable simultaneously.

"*Merde*, Lucy, not Chas. What kind of a name is that?"

"Definitely something out of a sizzling romance novel," Luke sniggered.

The guys saw the opening and took full advantage. "Ooh, now we're getting somewhere," Norman tormented. "Friends with *Benefits*?"

"Or just benefits?" Luke piped in.

"Neither," I said, blushing to my eyeballs. "Stop it. You're making up stuff."

"Are we?" Norman probed. "If we're just making it up, why is your face the color of a beet?"

"I was nine-*teen*," I whined. It was a limp attempt at reminding them of their own foibles at that age.

Norman saw that I was getting really uneasy. He stopped teasing me. He sent me a gentle look that I knew meant 'I'm sorry.'

Luke had his eye on both of us. Ever since he and Arianna had decided against signing the divorce papers we had all been wondering if they would finally come to their senses and get back together. This new and improved Luke made him a little more sensitive to other people's feelings. Not a *lot* more sensitive, but enough to let him know when to shut up.

I no longer wished to talk about this and they both knew it.

Then something dawned on Norman. I could see it as clearly as if a light bulb had gone off inside his head. But before he could pose another question I switched the subject and asked, “So who is replacing Yasmine?”

“Ramy Basseem,” Luke replied.

Who now? The name rang a tiny bell inside some miniscule compartment of my brain. I guess my confusion showed because both men were eying me with incredulous amusement. I paused, muddled it over. Yes, Basseem. I had heard the name before. He was an archaeologist wasn’t he, an Egyptian archaeologist? Had I met him at the Cairo museum in my student days, all those years ago?

“Lucy, Lucy, Lucy,” Luke taunted. “Don’t tell me you’re unfamiliar with Ramy Basseem?”

I scrambled for composure. Shrugged. “Should I know him? Is he somebody important?”

“Haven’t you been following the Egyptian media? Don’t you watch National Geographic?”

“Not everyone has cable,” I said. “I stream.” And mostly I streamed romance movies and sitcoms. Pardon my parochial preferences. However, I wasn’t about to reveal my guilty pleasures to these two. Besides, Egyptian archaeology was no longer my thing. I had reason to shun it, like a rabbit running from a tornado.

“Surely, you’ve seen him in the media?”

News Flash. I don’t watch the news. Except when I have to. Lately, I had been *living* it. I was part of ISORE, the International Save Our Ruins Effort. In the past four months I had helped solve the case of a stolen Black Madonna, cracked open a smuggling ring, rescued a dead museum curator’s kids from terrorists and saved the Winged Bulls of Nineveh from annihilation. So, no, I was a poor excuse for a media hound. I did not read the news. I was not one of those people who were constantly glued to their cellphone. I was living my life, not watching other people live theirs.

"Fine—fine. I give up," I said. "Who is Ramy Basseem and is he really someone I should know?"

"Ramy Basseem is the Indiana Jones of Egyptian archaeology," Luke explained, bending the subject away from my relationship with Chas. His voice sounded somewhat stiff. At the time I barely noticed. I was fully concentrating on burying my feelings.

"I thought *you* were," I teased. Around these parts Luke was known as the real life Indiana Jones. I was surprised he was so casual about the label.

"Not in Egypt. In Egypt they barely acknowledge my name."

"Basseem has a network series called *The Astonishing Adventures of Ramy Basseem*," Norman elaborated. "Surely you must have seen it? It started last year and was an instant hit in Egypt and overseas. In the US and Canada it has millions of viewers. Rumor has it one of the future episodes has him chasing down Cleopatra's tomb. He's also written a bestselling book based on it."

Was it my imagination or had Norman's voice changed. There was a harsh, sarcastic edge to it.

"And let's not forget his line of outdoor clothing." It was Luke that made the comment. "Haven't you heard of it? The Basseem label?" He pointed to a pair of young techs who strolled down the hallway, gave us nervous starry-eyed grins, and then hurriedly passed us. "See those stylish khakis on that girl?"—He added a sardonic curl of the lip—"Basseem label. That safari jacket on the dude? Same label. As a matter of fact"—he glanced at Norman's feet—"Your boy is wearing *his* running shoes as we speak."

This time I think Norman *did* blush. He looked like he wanted to toss his footwear in the garbage.

"How was I to know these were his brand? They were a gift. From my sister."

My eyebrows lurched. How could I be so thick? Where was I when all of this was happening? But then, after my stint in Cairo, I had avoided Egyptology. I had wanted to squash time out of mind that episode of my life. New things had come along to grab my attention. Sure the pyramids were cool. But my job was to draw artifacts; there were few requests to illustrate pyramids—or mummies for that matter. In fact, the one and only time I had drawn a mummy was during that internship.

Egypt had not crossed my mind in a very long time. *And yes, I still want to pretend* 'he' *never existed.*

"I guess you don't know about the rest of Basseem's history either."

I turned back to Luke after twisting my neck to gape at the two student technicians in their Basseem duds. Over a decade had past since I had taken an interest in Egyptian archaeology. What sort of history was he talking about?

"Basseem is the youngest individual to ever land the job of Egyptian Supreme Inspector of Antiquities."

This was a government job. It meant that he was responsible for all of the valuable monuments including the pyramids of Giza and those of the Valley of the Kings and the Valley of the Queens. Everyone had to report to him. Sadly, a year and a half ago, Basseem was accused of helping some Islamic extremists to steal an Egyptian cartouche and some other artifacts. The cartouche was chipped from rare, black onyx. It was postulated that it was part of an obelisk. And that made it very distinctive because most obelisks are carved from red granite. The cartouche was never found. Lucky for him he was exonerated.

"I believe he was fired from his position during the investigation and not rehired even after the case was closed," Luke explained. "That's when he went full force into becoming a headline-chasing megalomaniac. He morphed into a media darling. The public adores him. He even *looks* like a young Indiana Jones."

Even more than you? The question remained firmly unspoken. Luke acted indifferent to the comparison and yet secretly I think he embraced it.

"Apparently the ladies love him," he added.

Okay, I had heard enough. Some of this was vaguely familiar. I had my own reasons for not following the Egyptian archaeologist's career. After all, maybe he knew Chas. It was hard for me to even look at a picture of a pyramid without cringing. I had lost touch with Chas for good reason, *and* with Yasmine—probably because she reminded me of those days.

"So, my dear. It seems we are not the only ones with secrets." The remark had come from Luke.

I punched Luke in the arm. "I was not thinking about Chas!"

Lying. When I first met Luke and Norman they were full of secrets. Incredibly, I was now partner to most of them. The scowl I gave the boys said it all. It was *my* turn to be cryptic.

I zipped my lips and walked to the laboratory door. A sign to its left read:

Authorized Personnel Only

Norman reached out. He opened the right side of the double doorway, and single file with me at the lead, we walked in.

At the far side of the room three people were gathered around one of the counters where an opened sarcophagus sat.

The sight of one of those individuals caught me by surprise. Otherwise I would have rushed over to see what all the fuss was concerning the mummy. Aras' warning lingered on the edge of my thoughts.

But it wasn't the mummy that had caught my eye.

CHAPTER 3

The occupants of the lab were unaware of us yet. One of them, immaculately dressed in a dark grey, red-piped, Fall Chanel suit, streaky blonde hair caught up in a fashionable up-do was Arianna Chase, director of the museum. The other was Johnny Sayid, one of ISORE's debonair and very talented Middle Eastern operatives. Their faces were bloodless like they had seen a ghost, something I would have commented on immediately had it not been for the third man—

My mouth dropped open. *Speak of the devil.*

I saw him only in profile. His face could have been behind a mask; I would still recognize him. Luke and Norman, being men, noticed nothing. This person, whose back was all I saw except for the strong line of nose and jaw, sent a ripple of familiarity throughout my system. All of that talk about khakis and fedoras, the references to Indiana Jones, oh yeah, I knew who he was—I would know him anywhere.

Not tall, but not short. Not thin and not fat. Perfectly toned muscles with broad shoulders and strong, sturdy legs. Time had been kind; he looked exactly the same. At least from the back.

Arianna noticed us now. She and Johnny were facing in our direction. Johnny glanced up, too. And then the man in the bush hat turned to look as well. He tilted his head, studied me, and raised the brim to his mushroom-colored chapeau; a smile spreading across his ridiculously chiseled features.

We locked eyes. There was a pleased expression in his warm mocha-complexioned face, and a predatory, slightly mocking nod he reserved for subordinates.

So *he* was the guest curator sitting in for Yasmine? Oh crap. Talk about coincidence. Irony.

I felt Norman stiffen at my side; Luke became uncharacteristically attentive as well. Briefly I wondered why.

"You know each other?" Arianna inquired as she noticed me staring.

"I don't believe so," her guest replied. His eyes smiled. I gave him an incredulous frown. He studied me from head to toe, making a quick assessment in two seconds flat. "Pretty certain we've never met. A pleasure." He extended his hand.

Heat flooded my face as I tried to squash the emotion. I did a double take. Could I be wrong?

"Dr. Ramy Basseem, this is Lucy Racine. Lucy, you will be Dr. Basseem's go-to person while he is here."

My eyes refused to leave his face. The last part of her comment went in one ear and out the other. If this wasn't Chas then swat me with a tennis racket, it was his clone.

"Nice to meet you, Ms. Racine. You're the ROM's head illustrator?"

"Yes. Lu-cy Ra-cine," I enunciated, thinking repeating my name would make him admit to knowing me.

I dropped his hand. Not that I wished to remind him that he damn well *did* know me in front of my friends, but holy crap, did my name not ring a single bell? He used to call me Racine. He used to call Yasmine Yas and me Racine.

Eleven years had past. Had it never occurred to him to do an online search to see what had become of me? Had he once even thought about me? Clearly not. I know that soon after we parted in Cairo I kept waiting to hear from him, and during that first year I searched for every reference I could find that mentioned his name.

I almost slapped myself. Of course! Chas was his middle name. He used to go by his middle name. But his full name was Ramy Chas Basseem. I had followed his career through to the end of his PhD, and then his postdoc, and then his first job at the Alexandria University. That was three years into his career, and then I had stopped. No wonder I had forgotten his other names. There *was* life after Chas.

Oddly, I felt it quite difficult to breathe. Why did he still have this effect on me? *He* never loved me.

And Chas was all about Chas. He had always been about Chas. And from what Luke had recently revealed of his history over that lengthy walk through the museum's basement corridors, in this respect he remained the same. In fact, he was worse. Media darling? Owned his own designer label? Oh my goodness. I wouldn't go so far as to stamp him a narcissist. But what other term was there?

I held my head high, straightened my spine (why? I don't know). And smoothed down the pockets to my jacket.

"Hello—Dr. *Basseem*," I said. I was desperate to reciprocate a cool I hardly felt.

Norman glanced from me to Basseem. Luke smiled a forced smile at the Egyptian archaeologist, and tried to cover his surprise. So, this was Arianna's emergency. She could have told us by text. But even a heads-up would have fallen flat. Nothing could have prepared me for this meeting.

I had no doubt that he was Chas. What I wanted to know was why did he go by the name of Ramy Basseem now?

"I hear you are quite the celebrity," I said.

He flashed me his indomitable grin. Those unnaturally, even white teeth were having the desired effect, at least from *his* point of view. I refused to cooperate and excavated deep into my wits for some cynicism to come to my rescue.

"If it weren't for the fact that Dr. Chase needed me to supervise the installation of this exhibit, I definitely would not be here," he said. "I have other pressing engagements."

Yeah, right. The search for Cleopatra's tomb.

"But this fine lady can be quite convincing." He shot a charismatic glance at the woman of the hour. "And of course the artifacts and their display must always take precedence over any of my public appearances."

Well, la-de-da.

My thoughts were wickedly sarcastic. Not something I normally resorted to—except when I felt threatened. I wondered if I had changed a lot. Was that the reason he thought I was a stranger? *He* certainly had changed. Not physically, but in personality. During our time together, I recalled him being confident and charming, and somewhat self-centered—but definitely more respectful and kind.

A rustling came from Arianna's direction as she shuffled some papers she held in her hands. I was suddenly aware that everyone's interest was focused on us—Norman's particularly. Arianna placed her stack of documents on the countertop beside the sarcophagus. Metadata for the artifact perhaps?

She had successfully diverted our attention, and it seemed she was done with our conversation. She glanced at me and interrupted. "Dr. Basseem. I would like to introduce you to Dr. Luke Trevanian and his associate, Norman Depardieu."

"No introductions necessary," Luke said stiffly. "Ramy Basseem's reputation precedes him. We are acquainted."

"Dr. Trevanian," Basseem nodded, extending his hand. "Always a pleasure."

Liar, I thought. It was clear in his puffed-up peacock attitude that he felt somewhat threatened. After all, the billionaire towered over him by at least six inches.

He turned to Norman who was even taller, and a force to be reckoned with. To his credit he was a gentle giant—unless provoked.

"Depardieu." Basseem shook hands with the bodyguard, before saying derogatorily in a singsong voice: "Can't have *one*—without the *o-ther*."

Norman dropped his hand.

Remarkable restraint, I must say. Norman was a physical man. He could have broken the other's hand, not to mention his face. No one had to tell me that these two men disliked one another. As I noted the passive-aggressive confrontation I felt the tension rise and thicken. The light-heartedness prior to our entrance was struck dead with the snotty remark. A slap in the face was no less than Ramy Basseem deserved, but that of course was out of the question. How I ever thought I had feelings for this arrogant imbecile I will never know.

I lowered my head, the sarcasm dying in my thoughts. Geez, that wasn't fair. It was never his fault.

When we were talking outside the lab earlier, neither Luke nor Norman had let on that there was *this* much animosity between them and the Egyptian archaeologist. Explanations were quite unnecessary however as the latter had said it all. I racked my brain to try to recall if he had always been such a jerk. I think that, maybe, a decade ago I would have said No. What had happened to change him?

It was then that I saw the resemblance that the two archaeologists had to the movie icon Indiana Jones.

Although Luke never wore a fedora, it was unnecessary—for him to claim the title. Luke was handsome and tall, athletic and rugged in a Hollywood sort of way. He exuded masculinity like it was cologne or something. He travelled the world and he was a billionaire, the latter of which Indy was not. So, in that respect, Basseem got points for being more authentic; although as far as looks went, he was also ridiculously handsome, but in a dark aggressive way. He was shorter, less physically imposing but his big personality compensated for that. And he wore the costume well, without reserve. He was not as well-travelled nor nearly as rich as Luke, but he *was* famous.

And while the media hounded Luke because of his wealth and status, the paparazzi stalked Ramy Basseem because of his pyramids. He was the high pharaoh of Egyptian archaeology. He was the star of the National Geographic channel, the History Channel and the Discovery Channel. He had his own US network television series: *The Astonishing Adventures of Ramy Basseem*. These were not accolades Luke could pin to his wallpaper.

While all of this was churning in my brain I suddenly noticed that Johnny Sayid was remarkably silent.

CHAPTER 4

I pushed aside all comparisons between the two archaeologists. It was Johnny's peculiar behavior that held me captive now.

The ashen look on his face had faded, but the concern remained. He was observing me with what I could only interpret as troubled. Or was it pity? Why would he pity me? Did he know of my history with Ramy Basseem? No. Even Basseem didn't remember me. There was no one to tell him.

Then my eye fell to the mummy. When we had entered the lab Johnny had been standing on the far side of the sarcophagus. Arianna on sighting us had walked around it to make introductions. With Basseem on our side of the sarcophagus he only needed to spin around to greet us.

The sarcophagus was beautiful. At least that was my first impression. From where I stood the interior was partially hidden. But the exterior was made from white polished stone and was carved with hieroglyphics and encrusted with faded pigments and faience.

Inside it I caught a glimpse of a wooden coffin. It was painted red and gold. It held what I assumed was the preserved body of the pharaoh's son. What I failed to notice at first was that the coffin and the sarcophagus were a bit oversized for an ancient Egyptian.

This should have been a red flag. In certain periods of Egyptian history sarcophagi were shaped to specification. As I moved in closer I determined that from the style and decoration this was one of those. The coffin and the sarcophagus should have fit exactly the body it was meant to protect, like a piece in a jigsaw puzzle. As well, it should have been carved and painted to resemble the person inside it, and fit his exact angles and curves.

I squeezed myself between Arianna and her Egyptian guest to inspect more closely the contents. There was something about the mummy. Otherwise, why would Aras have warned me?

I was expecting to see the prince, the son of Pharaoh Ramses III or even some other high level nobleman—or perhaps one of the queens. What I saw was a plain mummy swathed in traditional cloth wrappings. The neck portion was unraveled. An unconventional, and clearly modern-day scarf of filmy blue and yellow draped this part of the preserved corpse.

I gulped. My right hand flew to my chest.

Something weird had happened in the vicinity of my heart. Like it had stopped. I felt faint and struggled to regain control.

"What is *that* doing there?" My voice sounded hoarse. I just barely managed to get the words out. "Who *is* she?" My index finger jabbed away while I tried to catch my breath.

Everyone turned to look.

Yes, I had recognized the scarf. As *he* knew I would.

I lunged, my worst fears reeling in my mind.

"Wait, Lucy. It's not what you think." Johnny's hands shot out to intercept me, fingers hooking my wrists to stop me from unraveling the wrappings around her immobile face. I say 'her' because I knew it was a woman.

Then I saw that those strips of fabric were already loose. I was not the first to experience that dart of horror. Someone else had, in a moment of panic, accomplished what I had meant to do.

I met Johnny's eyes with fear and he let me loose, his hands lowering to his sides.

Everyone had gone quiet, and even Ramy Basseem ceased jabbering away. While his normal behavior would be to think of no one but his own self-importance, somehow the gravity of the situation had cut through, and he understood that this was something that had nothing to do with him.

Norman touched my arm to steady me. I indicated to him with a smile that I was steady. The initial shock was fading, and I realized that only Johnny had recognized the scarf—Johnny and I. The others had no reason to remember it.

Luke was appraising Arianna with puzzlement. "What's going on here?"

"That's what Sayid was about to explain to me when the three of you arrived."

Luke glanced over. Luke was not with us when Alessandra wore that veil-like scarf, back in Afrin, as part of her disguise in the terrorist camp, but Johnny was, and so was I. I glanced at Norman. Did he recognize the scarf? I saw light emerge in his darkened eyes. So he *did* recognize it. His hands, too, went to lift the wrappings, but the museum's director prevented him.

"Stop touching it. What is wrong with all of you? Sayid, you have already damaged this artifact. And what does this piece of colored fabric have to do with anything?"

The original curator Yasmine Lim was ill, so contacting her to ask why the scarf was wrapped around the torso was pointless, and Chas—correction—Dr. Ramy Basseem, her last minute stand-in, had no part in the selection of the exhibit's artifacts. He was as clueless as the rest of us. So, how had that scarf become mixed up with the body?

Then I realized something, something that the director should have seen, that surely the Egyptian archaeologist must have noticed straight away.

The cloth wrappings were new. They were only stained sepia to appear old. Furthermore, if—*when*—we removed the wrappings, the corpse inside this shroud would prove to be no more ancient than you or I.

CHAPTER
5

Johnny reached under the counter that held the sarcophagus. He pulled out a drawer, removed a small purple and white cardboard carton from it and set it on the countertop. He plucked a pair of lavender-colored latex gloves from its box and snapped them on. Ramy Basseem reached over, and grabbed the box of surgical gloves from Johnny. "I am the acting curator. I should be the one to do this."

"You don't know what you're looking for," Johnny argued.

The amiable Arab sounded slightly annoyed. Arianna took the box from the guest curator and donned a pair of gloves herself. "Allow me."

She was the boss. It was her prerogative to do the honors.

No one objected, and with a pair of long tweezers she began to remove the strips of cloth from the face of the dead individual. I did a double glance in Johnny's direction while fear once again consumed me.

He shook his head. Was he trying to reassure me I was mistaken? Sweat began to gather on my forehead and the palms of my hands. My mouth was dry. Still terrified by that initial jolt of adrenalin, I was desperate to see who it might be. The warning from Aras echoed in my head.

Do not scream when you see the mummy.

That scarf. It belonged to Alessandra Piero. But with that shake of the head Johnny had implied that Alessa was safe. So who was it? Who did that body belong to? The anticipation was killing me.

I stared at the head. They should have known something was wrong when they unpacked the crate. Now that I was up close and personal I could see all of the details. First of all the sarcophagus was of limestone, not alabaster or marble. The inner coffin was painted wood, not solid gold. The eyes had been revealed and now the nose. As the museum director continued to peel back the strips of cloth the lips appeared—and I *did* almost scream. The mouth was opened in an expression of utter terror.

I shut my eyes, turned and slammed my face into Norman's broad chest. His muscled arms reflexively embraced me, and his heart pounded in tune to my own through his ribcage. I dared not look into Johnny's eyes because I knew he recognized her too, and I could only imagine the mixed but mind-wracking emotion that was breaking his heart. But at least it wasn't Alessandra.

My breath came ragged, in choked gasps. Norman stroked my hair and then released me as I gently broke his grip.

"Do you know her, Lucy?" Arianna asked. It was obvious now that the mummy was no mummy at all but the victim of a murder.

I turned to her, gulped and nodded. It was all I could do not to gag.

"Lucy, maybe you should leave," Norman urged.

"No. No, I won't. I won't leave her. She didn't deserve this."

"Who is she, Lucy?"

Either Johnny or Norman could have answered Luke's question. They chose to fall silent. I was surprised that

Arianna failed to recognize her, but then she was poorly acquainted with the girl when she was alive and had only seen her once, unconscious, in one of the rear seats of Johnny's helicopter. Back then—although the poor thing was suffering from superficial gunshot wounds—she had not looked like this.

She had been injected with just enough embalming fluid to keep her from putrefying. Her once youthfully plump face was shrunken, the eyes hollow, the formerly sensuous lips thin, her skin projecting a grey-olive hue.

It was the wide cheekbones, something about the set of the eyes, and the mouth forming that gruesome O that confirmed to me who she was in life.

Ah, no. There was no doubt in my mind. She was no stranger.

The men deferred to me. Neither spoke. It was I that knew her best, and I started to explain but the sight of her and what had happened to her gripped my imagination, and my stomach jerked. It hit me that I was about to lose my lunch, and I cupped a hand over my mouth and rushed to one of the sinks that lined the long black countertops below the grey subway tiles of the back wall.

Norman followed. He stroked my back as I hung my head over the edge of the industrial depth, stainless steel basin. Thankfully, nothing came out. But how could I trust myself to rejoin the team? I tossed an edgewise glance at our boss. It never ceased to amaze me how she kept her cool even in this situation.

I raised my head. Was I going to be okay? Norman shot me a look of concern, and I managed a weak smile. "Sorry about that. False alarm."

I was trying fiercely to be brave, but my mind wandered back to how the poor girl must have died. Revulsion. Disgust. Loathing—I struggled to churn up the right term to describe the sensations wracking my body. The horror and tragedy of it made my whole being go limp.

My hands were bereft of all feeling as Norman clasped

them in his fists. "It's all right, Lucy. You should not have had to see that. We should have been warned ahead of time."

We were out of earshot and Johnny was unable to answer for himself. "I don't think he knew for sure."

Norman was more confident. "I believe he did. He was just grateful that it wasn't Piero."

"But it *is* Ines?" I posed the statement as a question. The name belonged to the American runaway bride we had rescued from Nizar Tarek in Baghdad.

He nodded. "No doubt about it."

His eyes wandered obliquely to where the others hovered over the sarcophagus.

Why was I such a wussy? Even Arianna could encounter that kind of shock and remain calm, while *my* body threatened to run amuck.

I was relatively new at the game. All of them: Johnny Sayid, Arianna Chase, Luke Trevanian and Norman Depardieu were seasoned veterans when it came to witnessing criminal and terrorist acts. Even Ramy Basseem with his mummy adventures probably had more experience.

Speaking of which, how was *he* taking it? Now that he knew the girl was no ancient Egyptian queen but a modern victim of a heinous crime, what was *his* reaction?

Strangely he seemed composed. From our fragmented conversation he must understand that the mummy was a murder victim, someone that we knew. So why did he show zero signs of shock?

My poor, over-stimulated brain had no answer. This would all have to go into the hands of the police now. Would they hold up opening day of the special exhibition to do the investigation?

Poor Ines. She had always wanted to be important. She had run away from her home in Kansas to marry a Syrian extremist freedom fighter, and had ended up shot and abandoned. We had rescued her. We had left her in the care of a Damascus hospital. Where had she gone from there? I never knew… Ugh. Now that I thought about it, that was no longer true. I *did* know. If she ended up in the sarcophagus with Alessandra Piero's blue and yellow scarf, there was only one person who could have put her there.

It was the man who had tried to kill me. In self-defense, I had shot him. He refused to die. That despicable terrorist who had kidnapped Alessandra in place of my sister was still at large.

And that—that thing there, lying on the laboratory table? It was a warning. If we balked at his demands the same thing would happen to her.

I turned to face the only person who had shared my experience. Was Norman thinking what I was thinking? A chill raced up my spine.

"Tarek knows," I managed to sputter.

Norman nodded. We were still out of earshot and I felt free to speak in low whispers. "He's discovered the deception. He knows Alessandra is not Colleen."

CHAPTER 6

Nizar Tarek and his cousin Cham Nassar had attempted a takedown of the Syrian government and failed. Through terrorist tactics they had tried to set up an extreme Islamic state. People like Johnny Sayid and Aras refused to allow them to hijack their cause. They were resistance fighters and they wanted a peaceful transition to a truer form of democracy. Unfortunately, the current government refused to abdicate peacefully.

The three of us—Johnny, Aras and I—had personal reasons for hating Tarek. The Syrian terrorist had abducted Alessandra. God knows what kind of hell she was being put through even as this notion took hold in my brain. If no one else suspected, *I* did. Johnny Sayid was in love with Alessandra Piero. And there was no stronger motive for wanting her rescued than that.

Aras' motive for hating Tarek was political but just as personal. The terrorists had destroyed his homeland, ordered the murder of his wife, and left his family destitute. And me? I hated Tarek for perpetrating Norman's near-death, and for kidnapping Alessandra who he believed at the time was my sister. Strong motives all of them. So whatever it was that that evil terrorist had in store for us, we were going to have to swallow. It might be the only way to get our friend back.

Arianna was staring hard at the mummy's face. I know I shouldn't call Ines' body a mummy, but that was what Tarek had done to it. He had drained her of all natural bodily fluids and left her dry as leather. If it weren't for the small amount of embalming fluid to preserve her, the smell would have warned us well ahead of time.

It took everything I had to muster up the courage to return to the sarcophagus without gagging. Finally, after regaining confidence in my body, I managed to leave the rear of the lab with Norman. As we approached the others the intense expression on the director's face had me perplexed.

She was pointing at something, and I realized that she was focused on the mummy's opened mouth. I am going to continue to call the unfortunate corpse of the American runaway bride a mummy; it makes it easier for me to accept. I cannot call her by her name or I will implode and have a complete meltdown.

So let me try again. There was something inside the mummy's mouth.

"Arianna, let me do it," Johnny said. His voice was hoarse, low. "I can't let you do it. I mean no disrespect. I know you are as tough as bones. That's why you are the director of this museum and the head of ISORE. But you have to make an exception." His voice caught, and I knew that tough as he was this was having an effect on him. He wrestled with his thoughts and continued. "Surely, you know who she is?" He paused. "Last month… in Baghdad—"

Their eyes locked, and her face changed as comprehension descended. He nodded. "It's too gruesome—even for me."

And that was something—coming from a resistance fighter.

Arianna's shapely lips straightened into a thin line. She made no objection and handed over the tweezers. Basseem who was strangely calm—although he must be totally oblivious to what any of this could possibly mean—stretched out a gloved hand. “You people seem to know the girl?” No attempt was made to hide his presumption. “Perhaps *I* should do the honors.” The bravado was painful to watch. “I’ve seen a lot of mummies, though never one I knew in life. It will be easier for me.”

He had a point, and finally Johnny threw down his macho hat, which Basseem found so easy to raise in others, and passed over the tweezers.

The points of the needle-nosed instrument dived about an inch inside the dead girl’s mouth making me wince. I will never forget that moment, that glint of metal when the tube of paper, about four inches long, was withdrawn, and Basseem separated it from the tweezers to land on the waiting palm of the director’s latex-gloved hand.

“Is it a letter?” Luke asked.

Arianna unrolled the paper. She examined it in silence. Then glanced over. “Dr. Basseem,” she said. “If you don’t mind. None of this concerns you. And I don’t wish to get you involved. I know you want to leave the city as soon as possible after the exhibition opening, so the less you know the better.”

He was about to object, but then he noted the determination in her voice, and decided more would be accomplished if he obeyed, and so he moseyed to the far side of the lab where glass cases of artifacts sat on display, and pretended to engage his attention with those, although I was fairly certain he found them totally pedestrian. I returned my attention to Arianna and the letter, and was grateful that she hadn’t asked me to keep Basseem company. That request I would truly resent.

I leaned over her shoulder so that I could see the script, but to no purpose. It was hand-written in Arabic, and everyone here could read the language except myself. I raised my eyes, an act that Luke noticed, and he borrowed the letter from her and considerately translated it:

Ah, so you thought you could pull one over on me, you

American dogs. (None of us were American except Luke who had duel citizenship) *Your plot has failed. I have your female agent. She is my prisoner. If you do not wish what happened to this charming young lady to happen to HER you will do exactly as I say.*

I have my eye on Prince Pentawere, son of Pharaoh Ramses III. The one they call "The Screaming Mummy." I know you have it. I know it is the highlight of your pagan exhibition. And I want it. Because you are archaeologists I know that you understand how valuable it is. And yes, that was a warning to you I have something that you want—the release of my prisoner.

Send the museum person, Lucy Racine, to the Cairo Museum. I want her to accompany the mummy. I know she is familiar with this mummy and can authenticate it for me. Her name is among those on the documentation forms. If you do not send her I will return your female agent in a box—only this one will not be so pretty.

I will be in touch.

It was unsigned.

I could feel the tension in Norman's body where he stood behind me. "Under no circumstances is Lucy going to Egypt."

The troubled tone of Luke's voice as he answered was unmistakable. He muttered, "At least now we know where he took Piero."

All this time Arianna remained suspiciously quiet.

"She is in Cairo," Johnny said. "And I am going after her whether any of you are coming with me or not."

CHAPTER 7

"None of you are going anywhere without my say-so." The command came from the head of ISORE.

She said nothing more and neither did any of us who belonged to her team. Across the room, Ramy Basseem stared boldly at all of us awaiting an explanation. How much could he hear from where he stood?

No clarification was forthcoming from the director.

She strolled over to where the Egyptian archaeologist waited. She gestured for the rest of us to follow, and when we were assembled, she cleared her throat. She spoke directly to our esteemed colleague. "This unfortunate incident has nothing to do with you, Dr. Basseem."

It seemed to me that the apology had far more behind it than was obvious. Suddenly Arianna's phone dinged. She looked perturbed but pulled the thing out of her jacket pocket and glanced at the text. Whatever it concerned had her even more troubled, although for the moment she ignored it. She shoved the phone back inside her pocket and turned to her ex-husband and his bodyguard.

Her instructions came out hurriedly. "Luke, Depardieu, call the police. Deal with them. They will probably want to speak with you as well, Sayid. Lucy, do me a favor. Please see to Dr. Basseem's comfort. Show him around the museum. We have a mess to clean up here. I will join you shortly in the Special Exhibitions Hall."

I knew better than to contradict my boss, and as it was almost quitting time I hesitantly guided our esteemed colleague (yes, I was being sarcastic), the guest curator up to the main floor of the building. I found it hard to call him Dr. Basseem. In my heart of hearts I knew I was right. How could I possibly have mistaken his identity? On a whim I decided to try again and test him.

"Sorry about all the staring back there—when we first met," I said offhandedly as we stood in the bustling lobby. I was trying to sound super casual, in case I really *was* mistaken. "You remind me of someone I used to know."

"Oh?" His expression revealed nothing. He resisted the bait and answered equally casually, "I've been told that by many women."

So—it was going to be like that, was it? Well, if he refused to own up to knowing me, I certainly wasn't going to be the one to bring up the past. To me he would always be Chas. I squinted at him as though that somehow would shake up his memory.

In some ways I was glad he had forgotten me. It meant I could forget that humiliating episode of my life.... And yet it was so insulting. Was I really that forgettable?

The elevator was crowded with museum visitors and staff, and we chitchatted about nothing. I shied away from mentioning what had happened in the lab because just before our departure Arianna had drawn me aside and forbidden any discussion of it.

What exactly had happened? We had received a threat from Nizar Tarek. There was no doubt in any of our minds that the letter was written by him. He had killed a girl, a young runaway we had rescued on a recent mission, only to have her life end in murder. Oh, there was a backstory, but I wasn't about to disclose it to Chas.

I elbowed my way past two clots of tourists as we exited

the elevator.

"What do you want to see first?" I asked.

Basseem stared at me in disbelief. "Are you kidding me? You think I want an innocent tour of your facilities after what I just witnessed down there?"

"Boss's orders," I answered, lowering my gaze to my feet.

"Ms. Racine. Or may I call you Lucy. What has your museum gotten itself tangled up in?"

"Do you want to see the exhibit or not?" I asked snarkily.

"Not," he said. "I want you to tell me what the devil is going on."

"That is hardly your business. You are here to curate the Mummy exhibit, so *that* is where we are going." Besides, that particular location was where Arianna intended to meet up with us.

I stared at him suspiciously. He was speaking to me rather familiarly, very peculiar—*if* we were indeed strangers. For my part I knew we *weren't*. What were the odds of there being two Egyptian archaeologists from Cairo who looked exactly alike? And that gold eyebrow stud. Chas used to wear a gold eyebrow stud exactly like that. What was his game?

He moved in close to me and I could smell his cologne. Oh, I recognized it. Old Spice. Chas never wore anything else.

I dreaded getting back inside an empty elevator with him because I feared I might lose my cool, so I decided we would take the stairs instead. One thing about these beautiful old museums, even after all the retrofitting, refreshing and refining, a smart architect always retained some portion of the original heritage building out of respect. One of these features was the original wooden staircase with a Northwest Coast totem pole rising to the ceiling.

Most people were lazy and used the elevators, but I preferred the staircase. I hurried up the steps and Basseem had no choice but to follow me. When I arrived on the third floor where the special exhibition was to take place, he had caught up.

Unexpectedly, he grabbed my arm. “Hey,” I said.

Again, very familiar if we *were* indeed strangers.

His cologne was beginning to nauseate me. “Then stop running away,” he ordered. “I want to talk to you.” The sensation of his hard grip sent an unwanted thrill up to my shoulder and down to my wrist. He sensed it and smiled. His fingers remained firmly encasing my elbow.

I shook him off.

“I am *not* running away from you. I am just doing the job I was assigned to do. Conducting you on a personal tour.”

I nudged him out of my way. We had to pass through the Egyptian Gallery to reach the special Mummy exhibit. On either side of me glass cases held ancient Egyptian artifacts. I strode past the Narmer Palette, a touchable reproduction depicting hieroglyphics, some painted wooden carvings of birds and other revered creatures painted in black and gold, and numerous alabaster and slate urns. There was even a hands-on, full-scale, reconstruction of the inner chapel of the Tomb of Kitines further on.

And then we came upon the bust of Cleopatra. Apparently this granite sculpture, owned by the Royal Ontario Museum, was the only statue of Cleopatra ever found. Chas halted abruptly in front of it.

A strange laugh made me turn to seek him out. The laugh had been replaced by a secret smile, a simper. Why?

“You don’t like our bust of Cleopatra?” I asked innocently.

“It’s not yours. It never was yours. It belongs in the Egyptian Museum in Cairo. But the Royal Ontario Museum refuses to negotiate.”

This statue had probably been acquired in the early twentieth century before political awareness, repatriation and reconciliation drove public opinion. I refused to discuss politics with him. I know he had a particular interest in all things Cleopatra, but the museums acquisitions policies had nothing to do with me.

"Besides, that is just as likely to be an image of the goddess Isis," he stated flatly. He walked around the glass cube that encased it. "The back pillar is blank. Normally it would be inscribed. Especially, if she was a queen."

I shrugged. "The display label calls her 'Cleopatra VII, last pharaonic ruler of Egypt'."

"Yeah, and that face could be anyone. It has no identifying features."

I was ready to toss my hands up in the air. Why was he being such a stick-in-the-mud about this? I decided to shut the lid on the topic and moved past the display to the exit. I stood in the open corridor waiting for him to join me. This was what I had wanted to show him anyways. Not that.

A sandwich board with bold letters announced the impending MUMMY! Exhibit, and also warned visitors off. It was my first time inside the forbidden area but we were authorized personnel so the sign only applied to museum guests. I thrust my body more vigorously than necessary between the curtains that were blocking entry into the unfinished installation to see a large, standing sarcophagus with its huge blocky lid propped open beside it.

I swallowed my discomfort and forced myself to focus. This was what all the fuss was about—the Screaming Mummy. How long had it been here? When exactly had it arrived? These questions tumbling about in my mind were firmly held in check. They were merely there to drown out the ones I really wanted to ask. I had no involvement with the curating of exhibits. My job was to illustrate objects so I was about as ignorant as a tourist when it came to the logistics of this artifact.

The whole display was wrapped in an enormous prism of glass to control the interior environment. Mummies would begin to disintegrate once exposed to the air, and this one had been meticulously handled to avoid damage.

The sarcophagus was carved from alabaster and glowed with an ethereal beauty. It was one of the larger exhibits, and was chosen for effect. It was not the original coffin the body was found in. In fact, it was documented—unquestionably—that the mummy of Prince Pentawere was never entombed due to his crimes.

Inside the sarcophagus was the desiccated body. At this moment, my memory of sketching it as a young intern in Cairo loomed large. All my memories of having a serious crush on Chas came back with a vengeance.

"Son of Ramses III," I announced theatrically to squash the humiliating sensations.

The culprit. And the cause of our current troubles. Its mouth was wide open screaming. Something I felt like doing myself right now.

Basseem's eyes darted distractedly for a moment. He ignored the famous artifact and the gruesome expression on its face, and yet there was an undercurrent of acute tension that had no explanation. It was almost as though he thought we were being watched. Which we were. There were security cameras everywhere. In fact, he seemed so preoccupied that I felt I had to comment on it.

"Why don't you want to be here—Dr. Basseem?" I had almost called him Chas and had caught myself just in time.

He looked around the grand hall. There were technicians mounting lighting and plinths to support the various artifacts. Was he worried that the exhibition would not have the expected impact on opening day?

As if on cue his eyes fixed on the opaque, luminescent stone and its notorious, tortured occupant. No matter how often I saw images of this thing (on the internet and in books) its effect on me was the same. Skin crawl. Seeing it in real and positioned upright was grisly beyond belief. I guess he had seen it too many times for it to have the same effect on him. After all, he was affiliated with the institution that owned it. Which meant he had seen it dozens of times. And yet his reaction to the mummy was puzzling.

"Dr. Basseem!"

"Yes?" His dark brown eyes returned to me and I felt a

sensation of sliding.

Damn him for doing this to me.

"What are you thinking about?" I asked before I could succumb to my witlessness.

A change came over his face like he was forcibly refocusing his thoughts.

"What is wrong with you?" I asked. I know my reaction seemed somewhat excessive but, dammit, to me he would always be Chas.

I waved away the smell of his cologne. I was simultaneously drawn and repelled by it.

"With me? Nothing. What could possibly be wrong with me? Except for that gruesome incident in the lab." He exaggerated a shudder, hesitated for a second. "I would think that *you*, on the other hand, would be rather more upset."

"Of course, I'm upset," I snapped. His veiled accusations were screwing with my composure. "A girl was murdered. A girl I knew!"

His eyes jerked up. "You *knew* her. Yeah, I gathered that." Then he collected himself. His tone softened and so did his demeanor. When he spoke next it seemed he was attempting to control every muscle in his face. "Was she a friend?" He made an odd pause before continuing with his questions. "Who *was* she to you? And how are you involved with a terrorist?"

How did he know about Tarek? I stared at him, exhaled. Oh right. He was there. In the lab. He had withdrawn the letter from Ines' mouth with the tweezers. And although the team had kept the contents of the letter secret, perhaps we had mentioned his name aloud?

"What terrorist?" I asked innocently.

The look on his face betrayed the fact that he'd made a mistake.

"Nizar Tarek has been in the news along with his extremist cousin Cham Nassar. It's commonly known that the Syrian government wants those two for trafficking objects stolen from archaeological sites and museums. That's who sent the letter and the body of the dead girl, isn't it?"

"You've met him?" I asked suspiciously.

"I know *of* him. Like I said. He and his cousin are wanted men. There is a bounty on their heads. As a matter of fact, I believe the Syrian government would not only pay for any info regarding them but they would pay for their assassinations."

I hid my feelings of horror while he gave me a soul-piercing gaze. "From your response it is clear you are also acquainted with him. So—how are *you* involved with this terrorist?"

ISORE members—we agents of the International Save Our Ruins rescue organization—were sworn to secrecy. There was nothing I could tell him.

"He hates all archaeologists, historians and museum workers," I replied stiffly. "He thinks we are infidels. What is that Arab word for nonbelievers—?"

"*Kuffar*," Basseem said.

"Yes, *Kuffar*. He hates western interference with all things Middle East. We value their heritage and try to help museums in Syria and Iraq, and other places protect their antiquities."

This was the mandate of *all* museums—to protect the world's artifacts—so I wasn't exactly exposing ISORE's quasi-legal activities.

He looked like he only half believed me. If he was intent on playing this game of mistaken identity, then I owed him nothing.

"It seems rather extreme of him to kill a girl you knew, mummify her body and send it to your museum if it is only that he hates museum people."

You don't know the half of it.

"And why *your* museum? Canada is small potatoes on the world scale. Why not the Smithsonian or the British Museum?"

Why did I feel like he was interrogating me when I should be the one interrogating him?

My answer was short. "Because we happen to be doing a Mummy exhibit."

He made no further comment.

It was just as well because, a second later, Arianna appeared at the entrance.

CHAPTER 8

"I'll take it from here, Lucy," she said. Her eyes flickered briefly at the alabaster enclosed mummy. "Thank you for keeping Dr. Basseem company."

"No problem," I murmured. I waited to see if there was anything else my boss needed from me but she gave me an impatient look so I left the exhibition hall.

Maybe it was just my imagination but something seemed odd about the director's behavior. It might have had something to do with the mummy or it might not. And when I say the 'mummy' I don't mean Ines' preserved remains. I mean *this* one—the one in the display. She should have been more disturbed about the sudden appearance of Ines' body in her prep lab, when instead she seemed more concerned about getting Ramy Basseem alone with the famous artifact.

What on earth could have happened between now and that text she had received in the lab?

I returned to my studio but found it impossible to work after all the excitement. Arianna's behavior was still troubling me. Luke and Norman were busy dealing with the police. The last thing the director had said to me before she dismissed me was that I would be recalled at some point in the day to make my statement to the police.

Right now, all I wanted to do was hear from Aras. Aras knew something—otherwise why the warning? But when I texted him no response was forthcoming.

Then my phone dinged. I removed it from the top of my drafting table and glanced at the text, fully expecting it to be from you-know-who.

It was not. It was from Norman, summoning me to return for questioning by the police. I shoved my phone back into my purse, puzzled over my mixed feelings and left the studio.

As I took the elevator downwards to the basement I decided to make a detour and stop at the café on the main floor to grab a cup of coffee. For all I knew, the police could have me there the rest of the afternoon so I got off at the lobby and went to the modest café that was mostly used by tourists. This time of day it was fairly empty.

I was just about to step into the two person line to order a Mocha Java when I saw in my side vision the distinct Chanel suit, dark grey with stylish red piping beneath the streaky blonde hair caught up in the fashionable up-do.

It was the ROM's director all right. No one else dressed like that. She was seated beside Chas (and yes I know I should call him Ramy Basseem) across from an officious-looking woman. If I were to guess I would say she was Arab. Her complexion was olive and her eyes were dark, as was her hair worn in a tight bun. She was dressed in a navy blue suit with a white and black striped shirt underneath the jacket. Arianna and Basseem's backs were to me but the Arab woman was facing me. She was a foreigner. However, from her demeanor, I would guess that she was some sort of government official, a high level cop or some kind of agent.

On second thought, there was something military appearing about her.

I paid for my coffee and debated on whether I should go or stay. Would the police send people to search for me if I neglected to appear in ten minutes? Ten minutes was all it would take to get a lead on the mysterious visitor.

I told myself there was nothing unusual about Arianna entertaining guests, although this gathering had something sinister about it. I agree I am being dramatic. But when your senses are tingling, your senses are tingling. And oh, how my senses were tingling.

None of this was my business. And yet Arianna (the head honcho of my museum) and Ramy Chas Basseem (a flame from my student days) were not only acquainted, but they were conspiring with this Arab woman. Maybe my prickly feelings would make more sense if I explained it like this. If I was a trusted member of ISORE why leave me, or the rest of the team out of this meeting? Did Luke or Norman know about this? And what *was* this exactly?

I was determined to find out.

I sat down at an empty table with my coffee, behind Arianna and Basseem, about one table back. There was a single man seated at the table between us working on a laptop with his ear buds in.

Ordinarily it was normal to see a colleague having coffee in this modest café. But it seemed to me when the director of the museum had important guests she treated them at the luxurious top-floor Crystal Lounge, an eatery that was by far more impressive than our present location. This was just one more excuse why I lingered when I should be hustling downstairs to make my statement to the police.

There were only two reasons a museum director might be having coffee here. One: she had little respect for her visitor or two: she objected to being seen with her. None of the museum's board of governors or its upper management staff would be caught dead in a place like this. Hence privacy was virtually guaranteed.

The acoustics in the café were sharp. I heard what they were saying almost as though I were seated at their table.

"Is it or isn't it?" the Arab woman asked.

"I can't be sure until I've run some tests," Chas answered.

"It only arrived last week," Arianna attested. "Dr.

Basseem arrived today. There has not been time."

What were they talking about? Tests on what? And why were their heads locked together like accomplices?

"You realize that this artifact is the object of a serious plot?" The question was directed at Arianna.

"Yes. We have our own inside people. They have their eyes on the situation."

"You must keep it safe," the Arab woman said.

"I agree. Believe me, we are fully aware of the danger. That is why it is here. Rest assured I have top security on it."

The Arab woman turned to Chas. "When will you have the proof?"

"As soon as I am able."

"The extremists have been trying to get their hands on it. So far we have thwarted them. But I promise you Dr. Basseem if you help us the Syrian government will do everything in its power to reinstate you as Egyptian Supreme Inspector of Antiquities. In fact if you prove its identity I have no doubt the Egyptian government will be begging to rehire you."

"Thank you, Colonel Abadi."

She nodded. And then turned to his companion.

"And thank *you*, Dr. Chase."

A few seconds of silence dragged as Arianna nodded in turn. Then horror of horrors, the foreign woman's eyes lifted and met mine.

I was staring. Oh why was I staring? And eavesdropping. I should not have been eavesdropping! But that was a bad habit I had picked up from my older sister. Colleen was the gossip queen and although I tried not to emulate her, sometimes I caught myself deliberately listening in. The growing habit had served me well, especially lately. It had helped me to solve four mysteries and even to save my life. I tore my eyes away.

Who was this Abadi person? I got up self-consciously as the Arab woman's eyes followed. I had frightened myself. When she looked at me it was as though I had questioned her identity aloud. Unlucky for me my chair scraped across the faux marble floor making a raw primal scream, causing both Chas and Arianna to turn their heads.

I was too far to their left for them to see me because they had twisted towards their right. I took the opportunity to skedaddle out of their view with my slopping coffee cup in my hand. Unfortunately, in my hurry, I sloshed a third of the contents down the leg of my light blue designer jeans. Whether I intended it or not, that made me stop. *Must make it to the bathroom and get cleaned up.* I forced my muscles to move even though my instinct told me to grab a plastic lid and some napkins from the counter. Again this slowed me down and I felt like I was an actor in a slow motion video.

I cupped my wet coffee-dripping hand overtop the mouth of the cup, grabbed a plastic lid from the countertop where the sugar and milk was, and made my way to the door.

Did Arianna notice? Did Chas see me? *Do not wait to find out.* I scurried out of there fast and went to the public bathroom to clean up.

***

That evening the ROM's director held a reception for the Egyptian guest curator. In my head I still slipped up and called him Chas. I know. I had no proof that he was indeed my Chas. But I didn't need it. My gut told me that he was, and for that reason it was difficult, nay, impossible for me to think of him as Ramy or Dr. Basseem. Besides, the latter term seemed too formal and too arrogant and the former (Ramy) sounded irritatingly casual, and gave an air of something other than what he was—honest.

Arianna had convinced Luke to host the event. It was nothing short of spontaneous and only Luke could possibly host an event of that magnitude on such short notice. It was then that I realized that the billionaire's affection for his ex-wife had never really gone away; in fact it was clear as day. Why else would he give a party in honor of a man he disliked? It was obvious from their interactions this afternoon that he and Chas were mortal rivals. It was equally apparent that Arianna and Chas were not.

I don't truly understand what was going on in the café with Arianna, Chas and the foreigner, Abadi. I had no time to muddle it through. When Norman asked me why my jeans were so wet I told him I had spilled my coffee. But I hadn't told him why. I didn't really know why. I wasn't certain there was anything to tell.

After all, I was eavesdropping. And I had no reason or right to do that. So, I let it drop.

Luke had grudgingly agreed when the museum director suggested the impromptu reception. Ines' body had been turned over to the police. The authorities had advised that there was nothing for us to do but to continue as we were. They would update us after further investigation. As to whether the alleged murder impacted upon the opening of the special Egyptian Exhibition, currently they thought not. Unless other evidence arose implicating the museum, why would it? The museum staff and the other witnesses (Trevanian, Depardieu and Sayid) were free to continue as though nothing had happened. Our statements had been made, and until we were requested for further questioning, our part in the affair was done.

The reception was scheduled to go ahead—and at the Trevanian mansion of all places. You can see why I say this. Luke still loved Arianna, and if he didn't, then he certainly liked and respected and wished to please her. This caused me to smile secretly because—next to having Norman propose to me—there was nothing I desired more than to see Luke happy.

CHAPTER 9

Norman picked me up at my one-bedroom apartment on Oriole Parkway. After a forty-minute drive he parked his Maserati in the enormous cobblestoned courtyard of the Trevanian estate. Norman and I were just exiting the car when a text came from Aras.

He had finally found the opportunity to answer. I sat back, withdrew my foot and eased the car door shut for privacy. As Norman turned towards the house unaware that I did not follow, I opened my phone to view the long awaited response.

My own green dialogue bubble ballooned above his grey one. This was what I had typed:

"Aras. How did you know about Ines?"

His reply? *"Tarek is baiting you, Lucy."*

Quickly before Norman could notice I did not trail behind him I typed. *"That doesn't answer my question. How did you know what happened to Ines?"* I felt a catch in my throat as I added an addendum in a separate dialogue balloon: *"He murdered her!"*

His response was almost instant: *"I am in the loop. You know what I am, Lucy."*

Aras was a rebel leader. Some people considered all

rebels Islamic extremists. But Aras was far from being an extremist. He was a member of the Resistance. And he resisted not only the current Syrian regime but also the terrorists—the latter, secretly. When *they* went underground—after the Syrian government reclaimed the rebel occupied cities—*he* went underground. He was fighting a covert war now and it was dirty. The looting of precious artifacts to fund artillery had not stopped. It was only paused so that the various factions could regroup. Aras and his resistance fighters were losing ground. They refused to kill innocent civilians and they refused to rob archaeological sites to sell on the black market.

And his connections probably stretched across the continent from Europe to Asia. Still, I wanted to know what he knew.

I tapped: *"Tarek doesn't suspect you?"*

One word. *"No."*

"What do you want me to do?"

"Nothing. My reason for contacting you was to warn you when you saw the mummy. I knew you would recognize the girl."

"And you want me to do nothing?"

"Hide the scarf. Keep it to yourself."

"It's too late. The police have the body. And the scarf. They're investigating."

A lengthy pause and then: *"Tell them nothing."*

How could I do that? I had to inform the authorities. Although I had been understandably upset to go into details at the time, the more people who knew about Tarek and his vile activities, the safer we all would be.

I understood the unwillingness of Aras to share the prize. He had a personal vendetta against the terrorist. An extremist militia had targeted his wife's helicopter and shot it down. Tarek was the voice that had issued those orders. She was dead because of him.

"Who else saw the mummy?"

"Everyone. Arianna, Luke, Norman and Johnny. Oh,

and Ramy Basseem."

A knocking came at the car window. Norman, mind preoccupied by the grim events of the day, had headed towards Luke's mansion oblivious to my absence. Then somewhere between the car and the house he had noticed. The car door opened and he poked his head in.

"What are you doing, Lucy?"

The phone in my hand might as well have screamed my guilt. Fortunately the screen faded to black.

"Just fixing my face."

On your phone? But he retracted the accusation before it was spoken.

I shoved the device into my black silk purse and pinched the silver clasp shut.

"As long as you weren't texting Ramy Basseem." The name was said with plain contempt. The door widened fully and a set of wiggling fingers appeared.

I hoped my smile reassured him. Inwardly, though, my body thrilled and chilled. He was only teasing. Because how could he know that Chas and Ramy Basseem were one and the same?

I shook out the skirt to my dark purple halter gown, hugged one side of my matching coat to my chest, and took Norman's hand. *Breathe, be calm. I just have to get through this night.* We walked up the gorgeous, illuminated flagstone path to the gold and blue, stained-glass double front doors.

***

The Trevanian mansion was French chateau style, only modernized. It covered 10,000 square feet of outdoor and indoor space on two acres of land backing onto a river. A three hundred foot, cedar-lined, lamp-lit driveway led to a *porte cochere* entrance that opened to a huge inner cobblestone courtyard where most of the guests had parked. Don't even ask how many garages there were. At a guess I would say ten. These were for the fancy cars.

Party sounds—music, clinking glassware, and

conversation—came from the semi open windows.

We entered through the unlocked front door into a spacious, grey marble foyer with floor to ceiling glass panes. There were sculpture niches with modern pieces and a massive hand-blown crystal and chrome chandelier. The party was taking place in the extraordinary white and black living room that opened out to a formal dining area filled with handmade Spanish-style dining room tables and chairs. From the dining hall French doors led to a spacious stone patio, built overtop a shallow ravine overlooking a quiet river, foliaged with late blooming hibiscus, yews and ferns. Just before the ravine was a vine-covered gazebo and a curved infinity-edge pool illuminated to display the turquoise water.

Only once before had I been inside Luke's house, and as I recalled it had a home gym, a wine cellar and a home theater. It even had a large library with an iron-railed spiral staircase. But my favorite was the spa area. In there was a waterfall feature where I could spend days relaxing to the sound of falling water and the feel of a soft, scented, intimate bath bubbling hot against my skin.

I headed straight for the ultra modern, chrome and white-tiled kitchen past the quartz breakfast bar to see if I could help. I should have known better. There was no one here but the caterer and the young people hired to serve. Someone came and graciously unburdened us of our coats. They indicated where the party was, expecting us to join it.

"I told you, they don't need your help," Norman said when the young man had gone to hang up our coats.

"It's just that it was so short notice, I thought maybe he wouldn't be able to get everything organized."

"Luke has people for everything, Lucy."

I was beginning to realize that.

"Come, let's go in."

"You're being really great about this," I said. I tried to keep the nerves out of my voice. "I know you don't like Basseem."

His broad shoulders heaved. "I don't like a lot of people. That's never stopped me from being civil."

"You wanted to smash his face in."

My grin was audacious (enforced overcompensation) and he grinned too.

"But I didn't, did I?"

No. He did not.

"There's Luke and Arianna. Shall we let them know we're here?" They were outside attending to guests. I could see them quite clearly through the kitchen's enormous picture windows.

"You go ahead. I have to use the little girl's room," I said. I was still feeling a bit uneasy regarding our boss.

I left him heading outdoors via the French doors that opened from the breakfast nook. It was cool but the volume of people inside had made it quite warm and a number of guests including our hosts had meandered onto the patio from the living room to admire the pool and the view.

An infinity pool if you have never seen one is an impressive thing. There are no coping, pavers or decking at the far edge. Instead, the water flows into a narrow, shallow catch basin that then pumps the water back into the pool. Architectural and botanical features cleverly hide the system. Luke's designers had managed to create the impression of a pool without edges, blending in with the landscape and the horizon, which just happened to be a splendid river and the voluminous night sky.

The moon and stars shimmered on the river and some partyers sauntered down the smooth stone steps from the patio flagstones to the wooden dock.

Luke stood out among his guests doing his 'power pose,' legs apart, one hand in his pocket, the other holding a whiskey glass. He had a way of drawing people to him seemingly without effort.

I ducked out of sight and hurried across the foyer to the library. I was making a bad habit of hiding things from Norman. But it wasn't like Luke and Norman hadn't once kept secrets from me.

The roomy library was dimly lit but there was no one here. I dug out my phone and saw that Aras had responded to my message.

"Basseem saw the mummy?" was his question.

"Yes." I resented him calling Ines 'the mummy.' And yet wasn't it I who had labeled her that? That was wrong. The girl deserved respect. I must force myself to call her by her name no matter how gruesome it seemed or how bad it made me feel.

His next text said: *"How did he seem?"*

"Who? Basseem?" I had almost typed 'Chas,' and crushed the twinge. Why should Aras know anything about my past history with him? Nothing but embarrassment could come of that.

"Yes. Basseem the Egyptian curator, did he react?"

"He was horrified like the rest of us."

The library door swung open and the figure of a man entered. I quickly shoved my phone into my handbag. My first inclination was to conceal myself, but it was too late. Whoever it was had already seen me. He left the door wide to allow the light in from the hallway and moved deeper into the room.

"Lucy? What are you doing here by yourself? The party's out there—" The man's arm shot towards the opened doorway.

"Hi Shaun." I had recognized my brother-in-law. "I was—" I hesitated. What the hell could I possibly have been doing in Luke's library? Then it dawned on me. I could say I was researching the Screaming Mummy. Surely by now Shaun who was the ROM's curator of classical collections would have heard about today's unhappy shenanigans in the prep lab.

His voice was gentle when he next spoke. "I'm sorry about the girl, Lucy. I understand you knew her."

"Yes." I looked up at my brother-in-law with new respect. Despite all the stress of impending fatherhood, he was thinking about my feelings. "Where's Colleen?"

"She's looking for you."

"And you thought I would be in here?"

"I *saw* you duck in here. What were you *really* doing?"

"I wanted to see a picture of the Screaming Mummy. I wanted to learn if it's actually as famous as everyone says it is." I crossed my fingers behind my back. Did Shaun remember that I had done a summer internship at the Cairo Museum? Did he recall what my job there was?

It seemed not. Shaun nodded and asked no further questions. "It is."

Before my relief became palpable, another shadow blocked the doorway. This one was small and feminine and pregnant—my sister.

"Oh, there you two are. You've got your heads locked together like Sherlock and Watson. What are you scheming about?"

"Nothing," I said.

I tore my thoughts away from Aras and the dead girl. But extinguishing all thoughts of Alessandra was another matter. Alessa was the reason my sister was standing here right now, big as anything, waiting for her unborn child to signal it was time to make her entry into the world. The big event was supposed to happen sometime in the next two months, so I wasn't too worried. I wanted to be present at the birth because I had promised that I would be. But circumstances had shifted. I needed to go and find the woman who had sacrificed her own life to save Colleen's.

Seeing Colleen now, all glowy and happy was the gift that Alessa had given me. That woman meant as much to me as my real family. If going to Cairo and confronting Tarek was the way to do it, then I *must* do it. But how to convince the rest of the team?

I dared not bring up the idea in front of Colleen. To this day she was still ignorant of the fact that her baby sister *and* her husband worked for a covert organization that rescued endangered antiquities. Shaun and I had made a pact to keep the info from her as long as she was pregnant. That meant I needed to go *and* return before the little one was born.

It was Luke that saved the day. Colleen was ready to go all Big Sister on me when our host popped his head in the door. "Family gathering?" he asked, "Or can anyone join in?"

I rushed over to him and gave him a hug and a kiss, then punched his arm playfully. "You know you're part of my family," I said.

A shadow between one of the bookcases and the iron spiral staircase moved. I almost did a double take but something cautioned me against it. It was a wonder I even noticed as my attention had all been for Luke, but the silhouette was that of a man, and he froze when our eyes met. Although it was too dark for anyone to see him as long as he stood motionless, the slight gleam in the whites of his eyes was sharp—as was the finger that went slowly to his lips. His head nodded ever so slightly, and clearly he wished to keep his presence a secret. Instinct warned me to obey.

At first I thought it was Aras. But that was impossible.

I struggled to regain control of my focus, turned back to my family, and with one hand looped through Luke's arm and the other around my sister's waist I ushered them out of the library and into the grand foyer, chattering about inanities.

Shaun followed. We all headed to the dining room and to the bar that stood at one end where I ordered a martini, and then used my eyes to sweep the entrance for my mysterious visitor from the library.

CHAPTER 10

Luke left us to greet new guests and I sat at the bar with Colleen who settled down with a ginger ale and Shaun who nursed a beer.

"Be back in a minute," I said, setting my untouched martini onto the bar counter. "Nature calls." Instinctively, I waited for a reaction. I had employed this excuse just moments before. My family however was ignorant of the fact.

I left before either could question me. And why would they? Could I have made my purpose any clearer? I slipped out through the expansive dining room and into the foyer. I walked past one of the mansion's twelve bathrooms, and backtracked to the library. A quick search turned up no intruders.

Where had Johnny gone? I must have startled him when I suddenly appeared and he had hidden from me. I racked my brains to explain his odd behavior. Why would he hide from me?

Then it dawned in my cluttered thoughts with crushing clarity. He was planning to rescue Alessandra despite our boss's objections. None of the ISORE team had chimed in and this left Johnny feeling marginalized. He had wanted our support.

But Arianna refused to discuss it. The first item of business she had said was *museum* business, and that meant the reception for Ramy Basseem. She was adamant about it. This was not the time or the place for ISORE concerns. She would schedule a meeting tomorrow.

The decision was unsatisfactory. Especially to Johnny. He had left abruptly. I was surprised given his disappointment and frustration that he had even bothered to make an appearance at the party. And yet I was certain that the person I had glimpsed hidden near those bookcases earlier was none other than Johnny Sayid.

The books on the shelves were undisturbed, and I retraced my steps to the computer on the large mahogany desk.

Just as I thought, it was on. I searched the history and at the top was a link to an article that captured my eye. It concerned the Screaming Mummy. Was this Johnny's search or a search conducted earlier by Luke? I was intimately familiar with every detail of this discovery. Back in the day, when I was an intern at the Egyptian Museum in Cairo—where I first met Chas—my job was to illustrate the famous find.

The preserved prince boasted an unusual past. Criminals had attempted over decades to replicate it and pass off the reproductions as the original. The real mummy was the son and murderer of the pharaoh Ramses III. Legend said that as punishment for his heinous crime the conniving prince was tortured to death and died screaming. Despite his notoriety, his desiccated body today was worth a mere half million dollars on the black market. So why did Tarek want it?

The price tag had me puzzled. To be honest, a half million dollars was a drop in the bucket in the grand scheme of things. It could not bring about the reversal of events that the extremists needed to regain territory and power in Syria. What reason could Tarek possibly have to justify stealing this particular mummy? The plot had to involve more than just the theft and sale of a dead prince. There were many, *many* mummified kings and queens in Egypt—in fact, in the world—more valuable than this. Yes, this particular individual held notoriety because of his famous screaming expression, but as far as priceless antiquities were concerned he fell sadly short as an important historical figure.

The dead prince glared up at me from the screen in a pose that seemed almost alive. The desiccated, leathery body lay inert, but the shoulders were slightly hunched. The ribcage still formed an arch but the flesh overtop it was thin and dried. An old incision in the chest showed where the organs might have been removed, but it was hard to say. In fact the corpse was so desiccated that the gender of it was impossible to discern without DNA testing or an x-ray. The neck was arched, the eyes were closed and the mouth stood open to expose two rows of yellow teeth. I could barely contain a shudder. The scream was almost audible.

Much more was going on here than Aras had divulged. And if he refused to enlighten me, then I would have to work on Sayid.

Which led me back to my original quest. Where *was* Johnny? He would never leave Alessandra in the lurch. The past couple of week's delay had been hard enough. I needed to sniff out his plan.

Where could he be? I abandoned the computer and the library, and returned to the foyer. My heels clicked on the marble floors. Where did a man like that go to think? I hoped he had not gone home.

As I stood hesitating beneath the massive chandelier, my peripheral vision glimpsed the spiral staircase leading upstairs inside the darkened library. I dodged back into the book-filled room and removed my shoes. Clinging to them with one hand I crossed the cold hardwood floor, seized the slippery iron handrail with the other, and ran, hand-over-fist, as soundlessly as a cat, up the twisting staircase.

On the second floor were bedrooms (ten, I believe, each with an *en suite* bathroom) where the staircase opened up to a broad landing of Brazilian walnut wood floors. I wound up one more flight to where the gym and spa were located. More Brazilian walnut floors. And a faint aroma of cherry blossoms and chlorine. I slipped on my shoes and turned a corner. The spa was nearby. Another pleasant whiff of cherry blossom reached me, and I followed the fragrance to a set of polished and steamy glass doors.

Someone must have used the spa recently. I opened the double glass doors to an oasis of tropical plants, palms and birds of paradise, ginger and dripping passionflower vines climbing over trellises and stone walls.

Overhead, a massive dome of bubbled skylights sent moonlight and starlight into the artificial lagoon. Floodlights peeking through the greenery sent lovely verdant luminescence across the polished stone floors. Aquamarine water flowed from one hot gurgling pool to another. I approached the edge of the nearest pool, leaned down and dipped a finger in. Hot. No doubt about it—it was bathwater temperature—and a sensation of peaceful serenity washed over me.

Straightening my posture, I followed the soothing rush of falling water, and negotiated my way through some very tall plants that were almost trees (although potted) until an opening in the small jungle revealed a magnificent waterfall. Green-blue water tumbled from somewhere above, the plumbing hidden by healthy vegetation, mirroring a real-life tropical paradise.

It was warm in here. I was glad I was wearing a halter dress. On a large manmade boulder at the edge of the pool that collected and recycled the water for the waterfall, a dark figure sat waiting.

"Took the scenic route, did you?"

Twenty-five minutes had passed since I'd first glimpsed him behind the iron staircase and the bookshelf. "Hello, Johnny. I thought you were still in the library."

"That, obviously, is a high traffic zone."

So true. Both members of my family *and* our host had

managed to find me there.

"No one will bother us in this place," he assured me.

He had taken off his jacket and wore a dress shirt with the sleeves rolled up. Sayid was like Norman. Neither felt comfortable in dress clothes. They were much more at ease in khakis, t-shirts and combat boots.

I sat down kitty-corner to him on another rock (synthetic of course), our eyes locked in mutual understanding. Before my adventure in the Middle East I had possessed no Arab friends. Now I was close to two very special Arab men. In looks they were similar: each one tall, dark-complexioned and strong. They both had the kind of eyes that seemed to peer into your soul. Was it the deep color or the intensity of the irises that appeared to blend right in with the pupils? Whatever it was, when they looked at you, it was impossible to tell a lie.

Aras and Johnny were similar physical types, but the resemblance ended there. In personality they differed widely because Aras was an idealist while Johnny had a strong streak of pragmatism. "You're coming with me?" he queried.

"You know it."

"Have you told Norman?"

I shook my head. There. You see? I could. Not. Lie.

He stared me hard in the eyes. "I should forbid you to come."

My lips twitched ever so slightly before I said, "Let's say you did that."

He smiled. "I'm serious, Lucy. This is dangerous. We'd be going in blind. I don't know Piero's exact location and Arianna refuses to speak. *If* she knows."

"But you think she's safe?"

He sighed. "To be honest? You know as much as I do."

That reply was infuriatingly inadequate. In the lab when I initially assumed that the mummy was Alessandra (and that was entirely due to the blue and yellow scarf found in the coffin with her), he had insinuated that she was safe. Now he believed he might be wrong? What was he keeping from me?

It was all I could do to prevent myself from reaching over and shaking him by the shoulders. Instead, I remained calm. He was clearly perspiring. Whether from the tropical warmth in the spa or because he was nervous, I do not know. He was at a loss to enlarge on his answer so I asked, "Why were you hiding from us in the library?"

There was silence before he spoke. Perhaps the inability to lie went both ways. "Because I stole something."

My eyes went round. "You *stole* something from Luke?"

It was at that moment I realized he was fiddling with some contraption on his lap. "What did you steal?" I shoved an accusatory finger towards the object, and stopped short of touching it. It was small, about the size of a trade paperback, and oblong, with what appeared to be multiple appendages. It was pale in color.

I tapped it cautiously. "*This* was in his library? What is it?"

"It's a new prototype of an archaeological drone. Luke has a special attachment to this thing. In all his unholy wisdom he's even given it a nickname. *Firefly*."

I extended my hands fully, and plucked the curious gadget off his lap. Interestingly, he allowed me to do this with no objection.

The drone was tiny as far as drones went, and could be launched off the palm of a large man's hand. I turned it from back to front, upside down and sideways. It was a sturdy piece of technology shaped like a quadcopter.

I understand something about the use of drones in archaeological survey. Archaeologists use them to map sites and landscapes, and the ruins of ancient towns and cities. They also use them in surveillance to protect ruins from looters and squatters.

"What's so special about it that you have to take Luke's?" I asked. "Can't you just buy one from a store?"

He laughed out loud. Of course he couldn't buy one from a store. If Luke owned it, it must possess special features, features non-existent in store-bought drones. In addition, the thing must have cost a fortune. Johnny, like me, was no billionaire. Or even a millionaire.

But I still wanted to know.

"So, answer me. Why this one? Why Luke's?" I turned the drone to face me. Well, I thought it was facing me, but to tell the truth it seemed to have neither a front nor a back. I added, "And don't you think he'll miss it?"

"Oh, *he'll* miss it. But not tonight. Maybe not for days. And to answer your other question: why this one? Because it's special." So I was right. "It is not your average run-of-the-mill flying spyware. I don't dare even guess what it cost to build. All I know is that it was designed with the most current nanotechnology and it will do the job that I need it to do—in order to cut down the time required for me to locate Piero."

I flipped the drone over in my hands. *And exactly what might that be?* "How? How does it work?"

"You don't need to know that, Lucy."

Maybe not. But because he was reluctant to tell me made me wary. Johnny Sayid was a Syrian rebel. Not an extremist, but a supporter of the Resistance. He and Aras were tight, tighter than Aras was with his half-brother Luke.

Well, as long as it didn't start randomly firing bullets or self-detonate.

I guess I could live with that. After all, I would trust both men with my life—albeit not with the truth. They were the kings of keeping secrets. I knew with patience however that I could break them. I had done it before.

"Seriously, Johnny. Cairo is an enormous city—almost 20 million people. You can't expect to find Alessa with a drone, especially not with one this size. How would you even begin to look? I know it has a camera but—"

"This drone is equipped with state-of-the-art AI. All I have to do is download a picture of her, and enter search parameters."

Artificial Intelligence? Sure. But without knowing almost exactly where she was located it would be impossible for the drone to succeed. "And you *have* those parameters? You have specific coordinates? You *know* where she is?" I almost leaped off my seat.

"I have a general idea where to search."

My head swung back and forth, almost of its own accord. This was nuts. The drone was tiny. It would take weeks for it to search every neighborhood in the city. "Leave the drone." I glanced up. "You have *me*." I paused to judge his reaction. "Tarek wants *me*. He wants me to bring him the mummy. It's the fastest and most surefire way to find her. I will lead you straight to her." I stopped for breath. "But we *need* the team."

"I spoke to Arianna earlier today, after you all left. She still says no."

I hugged my arms around my chest. I wasn't cold, just agitated. It was so unlike Arianna to abandon one of her people. "I don't understand. We can't leave Alessa in the hands of that terrorist."

"Arianna says she has people on it."

What people—if not us? Who was watching her? A soft sigh escaped me. Arianna was the boss. Her plans were not always clear but they were sound. I came to the only conclusion that I could. We *had* to trust her. "If she says she has people on it, then she does."

"Lucy, I *can't* sit around and wait for other people to bring Alessandra back. If she's okay, why hasn't she gotten in touch?"

Maybe she had. Just not with us. Maybe Arianna *did* know where she was. I placed my hand on Johnny's arm. His muscles were as hard and toned as Norman's. There was no fooling around with these guys when it came to keeping fit.

It was dark. Nonetheless, even in this twilit diorama of a tropical paradise I detected his pained expression. Hard emotion was in his voice, as well as his shadowed face and his body language.

Two seconds was all it took for me to make my decision. I was butting in, like it or not. But if there was one thing I knew for certain it was that Johnny Sayid had it bad for Alessandra Piero.

"It's okay to love her, Johnny," I said.

"I *don't* love her." His face displayed stony denial. "When the terrorists had you in their clutches, we went after you. *Both* times," he said, and paused. "It's the same thing."

I sighed, tried *not* to sound like I was sighing and refocused. "Fine. Whatever you say." It really *was* none of my business. "But we still have to convince the team." There was no way we could attempt this rescue without backup.

Sayid was quick to answer, grateful for the change in subject. "I tried. Luke won't mobilize without a thumb's up from the boss." He waited a modest eye-blink before he continued. "He trusts Arianna. I don't."

"You *have* to trust her, Johnny. When has she ever let you down? You've worked for her for years. She has a plan. I *know* she does."

"My patience is gone, Lucy." He hesitated as he mulled things over. "I'm leaving tonight. And I'm taking this thing with me." He snatched the drone out of my hands as I watched him, helpless. Torn. He gave me a grim smile. "So—looks like we're done here. I have to leave before anyone gets wise to me. I think you should stay. Can't imagine what I was thinking to want you along." I could see his mind doing somersaults as his thoughts took a different jog. "But do me a favor. Cover me for a few hours. Don't let anyone know I'm gone—"

I snagged him by the sleeve. "If you think—for even *one* minute—you're going alone, you're insane. I'm coming with you. And I'll bring backup, too."

He gently disengaged me from his arm. "You mean well, Lucy. But honestly, you're safer here. And Norman will never let you go—for good reason. That terrorist won't allow you to go free even in exchange for the mummy. His offer is a ruse—the mummy *and* your freedom for Piero? Don't you believe it. Not that I would ever allow it to come to that. Nevertheless, your bargain with him is as good as a bargain with a shark. Mark my words. If given the chance, that brute *will* kill you. And not only that but he'll kill Alessandra first—and make you watch."

"Then why did you meet me here, Johnny? You knew I would follow you. And you waited for me. You wanted me to come."

We were both standing by now. He was taller than me by almost a head. If he weren't a friend and a man I could trust, his manner would have been threatening. The sound of falling water crashed in my ears. It seemed louder than it actually was. It was no longer soothing.

"You know the only way you will find Alessandra is if I accompany the mummy. Tarek wants me to verify that it is the original." Although how we were going to get our hands on the Screaming Mummy without the boss's consent was a miracle yet to happen.

He shook his head, studying me with a bewildered expression. "Why? Why you? You aren't an expert on mummies and you're no historian. Nor are you a physical anthropologist with connections to MRI, CT scans or DNA testing. Luke is better equipped to accomplish the job than you."

"Well, thanks for the vote of confidence," I said scornfully. "You forget—or maybe you never knew—but I spent months with that mummy. I don't need all that high-tech stuff. I visually documented the Screaming Mummy for the Cairo Museum as a student intern. I drew that thing from head to toe, at various angles. No one knows that mummy better than I do. I know every wrinkle in his face, every tooth in his screaming mouth. I know how his fingers were clenched, where his muscles were aligned. He was never wrapped in cloth. He was left out in the sun to die—and dry. He was so desiccated, in fact, that you could no longer tell that he was a man. That's how well I know that mummy."

He noted the tears in my eyes. Oh yeah, my imagination had a tendency to go into overdrive. I believed that the living prince had been forcibly restrained when alive, and left to perish in agony in the baking sun.

He grabbed my wrist. "Okay, okay. I believe you." He sighed. "*O-kay*. You're right. I did want you to follow me. I *did* want to meet with you. I think of you as a highly valued, skilled member of ISORE. I know what you are capable of. I've seen you in action. You are brave and resourceful and full of enthusiasm. And sometimes you come up with just the right answers when the rest of us—wiser, more skilled and more experienced—can't. But dammit, Lucy, you're impulsive. You don't think before you act. You act on impulse or intuition—I don't know which. Or maybe they're the same thing. But it gets you into trouble every time. And I don't know if I have the energy to rescue you both.

"When I see you like this in an evening gown and stiletto heels, you just look like a girl—and not a particularly big one. Then, I have my doubts."

"Well, stop doubting."

"The guys will kill me if they know I absconded with you to Egypt."

"Not if we bring Alessa back."

His shoulders heaved. "I don't know."

"Well, I do. What time's our flight?"

"I don't have a ticket for you."

"Then find one. Or we'll have to steal more than just Luke's drone. We'll need one of his planes."

Sayid was an accomplished helicopter pilot. I had no doubt he could fly a jet. I'm pretty certain he thought so too because he bent his head back, and laughed.

CHAPTER 11

Johnny made a quick departure. He told me he was going to leave first so as not to cause undue suspicion. The flight was at midnight. It was just after eight o'clock. The party was close to being fully underway. And if I knew Chas—I mean Ramy Basseem—he was reveling in all the attention, he being the guest of honor.

People might be missing me and yet I remained where I stood amidst trailing bougainvillea vines and hanging frangipani. The fragrance was intoxicating.

I should leave, but I just stood there staring at my reflection in the pool.

Why did I have this strange urge to peel down, and sink into that inviting water? I was well aware that the pool was a giant Jacuzzi. In one of the larger artificial boulders there were shelves stacked with towels. The control panel sat under a sliding lid inside one of the rocks on the pool's edge. At the moment it was not operating. All it would take was a tap on the touch screen to send delicious jets bubbling to the surface.

This Jacuzzi, disguised as a tropical lagoon, could comfortably seat a dozen people. Around the sloping bank just below the surface were smooth white soapstone blocks shaped like river-worn boulders, molded to fit the human form.

I had a huge decision to make. And I had better make it fast. Why did I think I could make it better if I were inside that pool? I grabbed a towel.

It was not like I had consumed one drink too many. In fact, I had barely taken one sip of my martini. And yet my thoughts were heady and my senses dull, while my heart rapid-fired like an engine. If I asked Norman to come with us and he refused, he would try to stop me from joining Johnny. If I just vanished…?

Departing without Norman's approval would have consequences I'd rather leave untested. And there was still the matter of how to get the mummy. If I went with Johnny, I could demand that Luke do something to convince Arianna to release it. The boys could accompany it. If they took one of Luke's private jets—I dropped the towel poolside. I needed something to shock me back to reality.

A dip in the pool wasn't it. But Johnny had not called me impulsive for nothing. Ten minutes just to relax myself. And clear my head.

My gown slithered off my shoulders and over my hips to the floor. There was hardly anything to remove. Beneath the royal purple halter dress I wore red lace panties. That was all.

I was down to my birthday suit when I stepped onto one of the soapstone blocks beneath the water's surface. It was comfortably warm. I felt my way two more blocks down until I was waist deep in water. It was deep enough for me to swim in here.

But this pool wasn't meant for swimming. Besides if I got my hair wet, how would I explain that? I still had to return to the party.

Or did I? If I disappeared without informing Norman or the team, what would happen? And poor Colleen; she would kill me. My thoughts were stuck in a loop like a rigged video.

I sat down on one of the manmade boulders and slid below the wallowing surface until my body conformed to the seat and slope of the pool. It was so amazingly warm and comfortable. This place was designed for pure relaxation. Mustn't allow myself to indulge too long. But it was working. I was calmer, more thoughtful. I had one choice to make and two minutes to make it in. I had already pushed the envelope. People would be questioning my whereabouts, but at least Johnny was safe.

I was still chin deep in water, legs outstretched, when I was rudely interrupted. My back was to the artificial jungle and I was facing the waterfall. The floodlights at the base of the tumbling cascade shimmered up through the curtain of water.

He was as silent as a cougar.

I turned. I smelled him before I saw him. Old Spice.

My heart jerked. I had risen but then realized I was naked and dropped back down until the water covered my breasts. "What are you doing here, Chas?"

Had he followed me? He made no response. Although the reception was a formal affair he was dressed in his own label: Basseem khaki's and shirt, with the ubiquitous bush hat on his head. Did he truly think he was the real life Indiana Jones? His outline contrasted sharply against the twilight glow.

"Aren't you going to say anything?" I demanded.

Apparently not. He wasn't even going to admit to knowing me. "Throw me a towel," I ordered.

I believe he was about to obey when I heard a sound. No one must see us together! My heart shot into high gear and my pulse raced. It was the door opening and closing at the far end of the artificial jungle, barely audible over the sounds of tumbling water.

He stared at me like he wanted to say something. And then he turned and vanished into the dark foliage.

As I stood upright, ready to climb out of the pool Norman appeared out of nowhere.

The light in here was dusky. He said nothing, and neither did I. Had Chas escaped unseen? I hoped so. One thing kept churning in my brain: how to explain this scene? Even though nothing had happened except for my pulse pounding.

Norman stood watching me for a moment. I was waiting for my thoughts to focus and my heart to calm down. He remained silent, undressed and stepped calmly into the water.

His arms reached out and I relaxed. I ran my hands over the taut cords beneath the smooth, damp skin of his iron-muscled biceps. A huge breath of relief escaped my lungs. I was safe. Norman had not seen Chas.

No words passed between us as his hand slid down my rump to pass between my thighs. His other hand rose to fondle my left breast. He lifted it to float cupped in his hand, water beading down. His head dipped and took the tip with his tongue. At the same time a rush of warm water flushed my core. I gasped, lost total control of my body and convulsed, submerging myself to the chin.

I only prayed that Johnny would not return and that Luke would postpone searching for us. Nothing would stop me from fulfilling this irrepressible urge to have sex with my man. Not even a Peeping Tom, and by that I meant Chas. *Please, God, he was gone.*

I almost swallowed a backwash of chorine as Norman lifted me, and roughly cradled my back against the smooth surface of the pool's sloping shoulders. This particular boulder was shaped to fit a reclining body, and mine was spooned like the seat was made from memory foam, rather than some sort of malleable stone.

He fitted himself inside me, forcing the warm water in and then out. It felt amazingly erotic and I opened myself to allow his entry with absolutely no hindrance. He cupped my back and my bottom to protect me from the hard surface and pumped until I was helpless, ready to explode.

The backsplash from his thrusts sent ripples around my bobbing breasts, tickling and teasing just as the action of the jets of water brought the sensation between my legs to a incredible high.

We both collapsed in ecstasy and Norman had to lift me

up to the surface to avoid drowning us both.

He lowered me to my feet waist deep in water. I reached up to plant a wet one on his lips.

"Guess I should have asked permission first." He grinned.

I wrapped my arms around his neck, water streaming down my sides, and strained my lips towards his ear. "That was my answer," I whispered.

He kissed me on the temple.

It was getting seriously late. Time to get a move on. "Come on. Let's get out of this bubble bath before I can't. We need to dry off. Get dressed."

"Why?" he asked. "What's the hurry?"

I darted a glance edgewise at my purse and my phone that sat beside the pool. I leaned towards the rim. I was pathetic when it came to hiding my feelings.

"What's going on, Lucy." It was a demand rather than a question. He repeated it in French when I stayed silent. "*Chérie?*"

No point in pretending that nothing troubled me; he knew me better than that. He grabbed my hand and plowed through the water with me in tow to sit on one of the smooth boulders beneath the steaming ripples. He was either winded from our lovemaking or exasperated by my enigmatic behavior but I swear I could feel his rapid blood beat.

I tried to stand up and he sat me back down with a gentle splash.

"Is it Basseem?"

Shit. Why could he think my urgency to leave had anything to do with Ramy Basseem? And yet he was right.

Our backs were once again to the artificial jungle, faces to the waterfall and shoulders resting against the smooth slope of the pool's edge. When I stayed silent, Norman angled his head behind him and reached for his jacket pocket that lay on the flagstones not too far away. He fished out a pack of cigarettes, tipped one out, and tapped the end on the stone rim of the pool.

"Or does it have something to do with that guy you were talking about earlier, your college sweetheart—what was his name—Chas?"

It was all I could do not to choke. My insides writhed. Chas had materialized out of the mist just moments ago.... Or was it an hour ago? Regret swooped down and enveloped me. How did he have that power over me? Even now! And yet I wasn't even sure he remembered me. Had I ever meant anything to him? And even if I had, what would that accomplish? The reaction my body had to the sight of him had sent a wild tug at my heart. But that had a simple explanation. He had startled me. It was not sexual. No, it was not. He was as dead to me as Ines was.

Norman tapped the cigarette again; then shoved it back inside its pack.

"What's going on, Lucy. How do you and Basseem know each other?"

"What do you mean?" Oh my god. Did he see him? "I *don't* know him. We just met today." *Lying.* Why? Because my time with him was utterly embarrassing.

"Then why are you so uncomfortable around him? I saw the way you looked at him in the lab. If there isn't or *wasn't* something between you two at one time, why are you so twitchy in his presence?"

He reached for his cigarettes again.

I slapped my hand down on top of his. "Stop that."

Norman usually only smoked when he was stressed.

I hung my head, dragged my hand away from his. Dammit. Why had I ever mentioned that name? I regretted more than ever that tease fest in the museum's basement corridors. That was how it had all started. The boys had forced me to tell them.

Now Norman thought Chas was important to me. He thought I had unresolved feelings. He thought that I was fantasizing about the Egyptian archaeologist while I was making love with him.

The decade old memory flooded my mind even as I

fought to squash it. I had run from the scene of the crime (figuratively speaking). I had made an idiot of myself (literally) and had bolted. Wait. That wasn't quite true. I wouldn't have run if Chas hadn't…. Oh why was it so hard to face the memory? If I had to struggle to articulate it to *myself*, how could I explain it to *him?* Besides, it was all ancient history. Why was I even debating the issue?

Norman was watching me and I knew I had to say something. Fast.

My silence was making matters worse. Okay. How about this? I was *nineteen*. It was the best excuse I could come up with.

"I just met Basseem today. And there was *never* anything between Chas and me."

I was sounding awkwardly defensive. I was beginning to perspire and it wasn't just because of the Jacuzzi. I was lying. Why couldn't I stop myself from lying?

How could I tell Norman exactly what had happened. It was *so* stupid and humiliating. *All right, maybe if I just admit it to myself I will feel better.* I had asked a man to marry me who didn't want to marry me—he didn't even love me—and then he had had to chase me off with a tennis racket.

I turned my face away knowing that these thoughts were making me flush. I know. That would have been funny if it had happened to someone else. But it didn't happen to someone else. It happened to me.

Did he notice? I hoped not. One day I would tell him. One day I *must* tell him—but tonight? No. This was a story best saved for when my confidence and my self-esteem wasn't hanging by a thread.

The glow from his cigarette caught my eye. He had lit the end and was smoking it despite my objections.

He nodded. "I see."

What did he see?

"They're both Egyptians. They are both archaeologists. Ramy Basseem reminds you of your ex, Chas. Am I right?"

Not quite.

"Did you sleep with him?" Two feathers of smoke escaped his nostrils.

I shrugged. *Yes. Sort of. Crap.*

"Is he someone I should be worried about?"

I rose from the water, and drops poured down from my bare skin. I'd had enough of this. What had happened between Chas and me was private, and I refused to do this. I did not have to account to him for something that had happened before we met. For the record I did *not* have unresolved feelings….

Then why was I denying it so furiously? Why was I so flummoxed? God, I hated being flummoxed. Was that even the right word? Thank goodness none of this was said out loud.

Norman rose too. He crushed out the cigarette on the trunk of a potted cypress tree. We stood staring at each other oblivious to our nakedness, water raining down our limbs.

"Why are we even talking about Chas?" I demanded.

"Because you act so weird every time his name comes up."

"And just who keeps bringing up his name?" I glared at Norman. "Chas is ancient history. I wish I had never mentioned him."

Then I realized I was wringing my hands. And it wasn't really my hands I was wringing. I was twisting my ring finger—my *empty* ring finger—that *should* have had a diamond on it by now. If I'd had a diamond on it nothing about Chas would bother me.

Oh my god, what was wrong with me. *So what* if I had found that diamond ring in his room back at the base in Aleppo. He had no idea that I knew about it. Not unless Luke had told him because Luke was actually the one who had made the discovery. My thoughts raced, rambled. I had to put a stop to this now!

I reached up and placed my arms around his neck. He would ask me when he was ready. I was being an insecure idiot. And Chas' sudden appearance had set me off balance.

His skin was moist and hot, and my lips planted themselves on his collarbone. He placed his hands on my waist and lifted me into the air before he slammed me against his chest and practically knocked the breath out of me. His arms were wrapped tightly around my back and his mouth found mine. Our bodies smashed together wet and tingling. The heat of his skin melded with the heat of my own.

He released my lips and let my head fall to his shoulder. His cheek found my forehead and rested there. He gently stroked my hair. "I know what happened back then was a long time ago." He raised his head forcing me to lift my eyes. "Are you sure you don't have leftover feelings? One thing I know for sure is that *you* are the woman for me. You made coming to that conclusion obvious. But it still required a leap of faith. You know my history, Lucy. You know that I, more than anyone, have reason to doubt. But with you it's easy. I have no doubts.

"But you? I know this new life that Luke and I have dragged you into is unexplored territory. My life is not simple or stable or safe. Just like love. Sometimes it's wild, and messy and filled with surprises. It's an adventure. What you need to ask yourself is this: Do you feel the same way? Do you have any doubts about me?"

CHAPTER
12

The question was not unreasonable. Except. Was he *crazy?* After all I had gone through for him? Did he not remember how I had entered a terrorist camp to search for him?

And yet, why could I not admit to him that Ramy Basseem was Chas?

The doubts returned with a vengeance. How could I confess to something that might not even be true? Yet in my heart of hearts I knew that it was.

I trapped his gaze, stroked his arm lovingly. What I was about to spill was the truth—at least part of it.

"I asked Chas to marry me."

Panic threatened to paralyze me as the story tumbled out. Me drunk. My erstwhile marriage proposal. Chas rejecting me. Me rejecting his rejection. The tennis racket waving in my face. My having to run under cover of night to hide in my room.

Heat flushed me from head to toe and no matter how I denied it I was still swimming in shame.

Norman did not laugh. For that I was grateful. No judgment or teasing. His smile was gentle and he was considerate enough to ignore the sudden flush of color my whole body had adopted.

"Everyone is an idiot at nineteen," he assured me. "You know what Luke and I did at nineteen.

"So you understand, *now*, why I couldn't talk about it? Why I was acting so weird as you so colorfully put it?"

"It's not so bad."

"Not so *bad?*" I glowered. "Do you know how hard it is to talk about someone who had to chase you off with a piece of sporting equipment? I was just lucky they don't play baseball much in Egypt. He probably would have armed himself with a bat."

Norman pulled me into his arms and kissed my temple. He was doing this so that I wouldn't have to see his face when he asked me the next question. "Did you love him, Lucy?"

Tears of frustration were threatening to surface. Stupid, stupid me. Of course, I did. Why else would I have asked him to marry me?

"Lucy?"

I barely nodded and he felt my confirmation in the reluctant motion of my head. "He didn't love you back?"

I raised my eyes and laughed through a flood of tears. "Clearly not!"

"Lucky for me then. I have your heart."

His warmth enveloped me and I wrapped my arms around him, never wanting to let him go.

"So you don't think I'm an idiot?" I whispered, mopping away the tears.

His lips touched my brow. "*He* was the idiot."

I relaxed into him and let his words absorb the last lingering feelings of regret.

We fell quiet for a moment. It was one of those moments that you wished would never end. Then something caught my attention and my head shot up.

"What's the matter?"

Inconveniently I had spotted Norman's phone that had slipped half out of his jacket pocket (which lay by the side of the pool) when he had removed his cigarettes. The light had been triggered because Norman had accidentally nudged it aside when he hugged me. Now the digits for the clock glared brightly. It was almost ten. A shot of adrenalin hit me. The past disappeared and the present returned with stinging urgency. We had to go if we were to make it to the airport to meet Johnny.

I patted my cheeks where the tears had dried. "How's my face look?"

"Beautiful."

I shoved him playfully. "I'm serious. Am I a mess? Do I have raccoon eyes?"

He ran his thumb under my lower lashes. "There. Now, you're perfect."

Thank goodness for waterproof mascara.

I give him a long lingering kiss and when he acted on it, I gently nudged him away. "We have to get going. People will be missing us."

Swiftly I toweled down, grabbed my underwear and gown, and began to dress.

"Hey, what's the hurry?" Norman teased, removing a towel from the nearby shelf. "My room is just a few minutes away."

I didn't have a few minutes. We had to get out of this place. Stat.

A look of incomprehension settled on his face.

"We'll be missed at the party," I said.

"So?"

I couldn't think of how to explain without telling him the truth. But first we had to get out of this heat.

I quickly helped him to dry off. Then thrust his clothes at him. "I need to talk to you, Norman. Let's go into the hallway. It's too hot in here."

Puzzled, he dressed and followed me out to the corridor, still tucking his shirt in. The cool rush of air after the moist heat of the spa was a welcome relief. I stopped Norman before he went for the stairs.

Norman studied my nervous actions. "What is eating you, honey? If you don't want to go back to the party you don't have to."

I glanced up. I plucked at my damp gown to air dry it. I hated defying his wishes. I hated lying to him. But sometimes his wishes were counterproductive to my own. And that was when lying was the only way to get him to do what I wanted.

This time however a lie would not work.

It was now or never. "I'm going with Johnny to rescue Alessandra."

"NO."

He slapped his hand against the wall to stop me from leaving. I ducked under his arm and twirled to face him. "*Someone* has to go."

"Not you."

"*I* have to go. I was specifically mentioned in that letter. I am the fastest way to finding her. My complying with its demands will keep her alive."

Norman's chest heaved. "I thought by now—after all you have been through—that you would understand how dangerous that machine-gun-toting scum-of-the-earth is. Lucy, the man is a terrorist. A *terrorist!* You know what that means."

He was getting excited. Agitated. No, that was an understatement. I had to say something quickly to pacify his emotion. "Johnny will protect me. And if *you* come, you will protect me, too." My voice softened. "Besides, I'll be safe at the Cairo Museum. I know people there. At least I used to. There are people everywhere in a museum, crowds of tourists and museum curators and staff. He wouldn't dare do anything as long as there are people around me."

"I can't let you go. It's too dangerous."

"You *can't* stop me."

"Lucy—"

I scowled. Surely he must understand. "Alessa sacrificed herself to save my sister."

"Her action was an executive decision," he pointed out.

"She didn't have to do it."

It was his turn to grow livid, and he doubled down on his doubts.

"But she did. She *did* do it," I insisted. Loudly. "And now she needs us. If you don't want to come, then fine. Stay. But I'm going." I stopped to catch my breath. I felt winded. "You *know* that scarf belonged to her. And we don't even *need* the evidence of the scarf to realize she's in danger. The letter said it all. He is going to kill her the same way he killed Ines—if we don't go to find her."

Silence, then, "*Merde*, Lucy. You are going to be the death of me."

Was that why he hadn't asked me to marry him? My brain was in such turmoil. It wasn't the first time he had accused me of that.

He looked like he wanted to punch his fist through the wall. "All right," he finally snarled. "But you are never leaving my sight. Do you hear me?"

I nodded meekly. I had gotten my way. "Now our only problem is stealing the mummy."

"You realize you can't leave tonight and take the mummy with you? There is not enough time."

"I know. That's where you and Luke come in. I need you two to bring the mummy on one of Luke's planes." I paused. "Do you think Luke will help us?" I asked lightly.

I heard the confident tap of footsteps and froze. We were speaking in quiet tones, but apparently not quietly enough. Someone was coming and they might even have overheard some of our conversation.

Then I exhaled in relief as Luke came around the corner in an expensive pair of Stephano Bemer Florentine leather shoes. He stopped and faced us.

"Yes," he said.

Yes? Then he had heard? He understood why I had to go? A feeling of elation overwhelmed me despite the impending terror. That terror would hit me like a fist the moment we boarded the plane. "Oh, Luke, really? You'll help?" I threw myself at his chest and gave him a bear hug. "How much did you hear?"

"All of it. You two fight like cats. It's impossible not to hear." He studied our disheveled appearance but made no comment.

"I'm sorry," I said. "But I have to go. I have to help Johnny. We mean to bring Alessandra home."

Norman and Luke exchanged glances. It wasn't the last time I was going to see those looks of frustration pass between them.

"What about Arianna?" Norman asked. The question was directed at Luke. "How will we get the goods out of the exhibit? It's the star of the show."

"She said she will fire us the next time we defied her orders," I added.

"Leave the mummy to me," Luke said. "As for firing you. She *didn't* last time."

"So—you really intend to help us?"

"Are you kidding me? I can't miss out on all the fun. And you need me. Besides, I can't trust you on your own, can I?" He glanced around—although it was obvious we were alone. "Where's Sayid?"

I grabbed Luke's sleeve and checked his fancy wristwatch. "Probably at the airport by now." I dropped his arm. "Oh hell. I won't have time to pack."

"No worries," Luke said. "I've got stuff for you on the plane."

Of course he did. Luke had a whole wardrobe of men and women's necessities aboard. You never knew when you were going to need a fancy ball gown or a pair of casual chinos.

"We're taking your plane?" I asked.

"Well, we aren't taking my yacht. Oh, by the way,"—his eyes flitted towards the staircase—"Has anyone seen my drone?"

CHAPTER 13

By the time we got downstairs the party was in full swing. Arianna intercepted us as we headed towards the door. "Luke," she said. "Get in there." She indicated the crowded living room. "*This* is your house. *You* are the host."

"I am *not* the host," he refuted. "This was *your* idea."

"Don't argue with me," she said, and tackled his arm.

Oh crap. Now, what to do? How was Luke going to get away from Arianna without telling her the truth? But I had no time to come up with a solution; a new problem was rearing its head in the form of my pregnant sister. "Colleen, shouldn't you be going home. It's kind of late for you to be partying."

"Where've you been?" she demanded. "I was looking for you to tell you—" Then she noticed Norman beside me, and our damp and slight dishevelment. She gave me a sly smile. "Okay. That explains it. You two need to get a room…. Oh, I forgot. You *have* a suite here, don't you, Norman?" The smile spread from her lips to her eyes. "Lucy, your hair is wet. You could be a little more discreet." And then she tittered. "Ah, young love…"

Like *she* was such an old biddy. She and Norman were practically the same age.

He returned the sentiment.

I glanced, mortified, at Shaun for help. I needed to get rid of my sister, I needed to get to the airport, I fussed with the straying locks of my damp hair; I needed to stop blushing like a virgin.

Norman turned to Shaun. "You two want a ride home?"

He was offering? No time for him to play chauffeur. It was just like Norman to offer. He always abstained from alcohol (and if you know Norman you get why) so he was quite capable of driving. However, Colleen wasn't drinking either because of her impending offspring, so even if Shaun had partaken, his wife could safely play chauffeur. Pregnancy was irrelevant to one's ability to operate a motor vehicle.

Shaun thanked the bodyguard and convinced him he was fit to drive. Apparently, except for one beer, he had passed on alcoholic beverages as well. Besides, tomorrow was a workday.

He was carrying their coats and helped his wife struggle into hers.

Colleen kissed me on the cheek, brushed a lock of hair out of my eyes, and ordered me to phone her tomorrow. I watched her wiggle-waggle with her baby bump across the marble lobby. The two departed through the front doors and I wiped the perspiration from my brow, grappled Norman by the hand and went to search for Luke. He was inside a circle of friends regaling them with his wit. I fetched my phone from my purse. It was almost 11:00 pm. We would never catch Johnny before his flight took off.

Norman read my mind. "Forget about meeting Sayid. He's gone."

"I promised him I'd meet him," I insisted. Frustrated, I shoved the phone back inside my black silk handbag.

"Lucy, maybe this is for the best."

The purse swung from my wrist and I almost threw it at him. Too much had happened today. I was an emotional wreck, and this was the last straw. I gripped the purse with my other hand to control the tension in my fist. I glared at him. "How *could* you… how *could* you betray me like that?"

"Betray you? I didn't do anything." His hands reached out to soothe mine but I felt nothing near soothed.

"*Exactly*," I berated him, trembling. "If you hadn't held me up. If you could just have agreed right off to help me, we would have been on our way by now."

I jerked my hand out of his and headed for the door.

"Where are you going?"

"To the airport." I dug out my phone again, and swiped left, searching for the Uber app.

Norman gently removed the device from my grip. "You don't have to do that. The plan hasn't changed. I was just hoping you might have second thoughts. But obviously, you don't. So—I will come with you. But there's no hurry now. We'll take Luke's plane tomorrow." He studied me with a tenderness I didn't deserve. Stay. I'll go fetch your overnight bag from the car."

My eyes roved to the time on the phone. The screen was facing me. Why was he always right? It would have to be tomorrow. *After* this dumb party. Now that I think about it, all of the delay was Basseem's fault. He had stirred up a world of troubled memories. If it weren't for the fact that he was the stand-in curator for Yasmine, none of this would have happened. I would have been on my way to rescue my friend.

***

I spent the night with Norman in the mansion. Our passion had dissipated with the evening's event. I was exhausted from all of the unexpected verbal conflict. High emotion was one of my flaws. After a major disagreement I tended to crash. When at last we collapsed onto his mattress I had no energy for anything but rest. I can't remember a time since hooking up with him where we had slept together without *sleeping* together. Yeah, admittedly, I was still kind of miffed. Part of my anger was really embarrassment for having revealed my big secret, but the other part of it was anger at myself for failing to divulge the full truth.

For now, everything was on track for the exchange. I must settle for that. Tarek would trade Alessandra for the Screaming Mummy. I was counting on it.

The following morning, as I packed the few overnight things I had brought, I activated the large screen TV in Norman's sitting room. The news showed a horde of demonstrators blocking the entrance to the museum.

"What's going on?" Norman asked as he exited the steaming bathroom from having a shower. His massive torso muscles rippled above the towel he had wrapped around his trim hips.

I dragged my eyes away from admiring his physique, and dropped the white silk nightgown I was folding to point at the TV. "Demonstrators. They're protesting against Ramy Basseem."

"Good," Norman said.

But it *wasn't* good. They were throwing stink bombs at the heritage entrance, accusing the Egyptian archaeologist of conspiring with Islamic extremists.

"It's because of that incident last year accusing him of helping those terrorists to steal Egyptian artifacts," he said. "They don't want him near their museum."

But the man had been acquitted of the charges. The case never even went to trial.

I glanced over. "Do you believe he's a smuggler and a thief?"

The answer I received was disdainful. "I don't know him well enough to judge."

Neither did I. But he definitely wasn't a jihadist. Not unless some ideological holocaust had wiped out his brain in the last decade.

A sharp series of rapid taps came at the bedroom door. Luke shoved it open and poked his head in through the gap. "Trouble at the museum," he announced.

"We know." I pointed at the TV screen where two thick lines of protestors permitted only a narrow path for museum employees to enter the building. They pumped signs and wore t-shirts that shouted:

Terrorist
Go Home!

One person hurled a classic Basseem bush hat on the pavement, and lit it on fire with a Zippo lighter. Others joined in, tossing Basseem shirts and khakis to fuel the blaze. Flames exploded, and I cringed. Where was the police? Much as I hated the megalomaniac Chas had become I doubted he colluded with terrorists. I shut off the TV, glanced over at Luke. The sudden silence made my voice ring oddly. "That doesn't affect our plans though does it? We're still going to Egypt?"

The billionaire archaeologist had bad news. I knew him well enough to read most of his expressions. This particular face meant he had something to say that impacted on me.

He was delaying, and I knew it because he relieved me of the remote. He switched the TV back on and as I went to snatch it back, the altercation happening live drew my attention.

The guest curator had arrived at the museum. He was alone. He was elbowing his way through the press of demonstrators and media, heading for the steps. He skirted the miniature bonfire with scorn. Someone yanked his bush hat off his head. They lobbed it into the inferno and he swung about in a rage. When he saw his hat in flames on the pavement he cursed and raised a fist.

Seconds later, the police appeared on the scene. A young man spat at the curator and was hauled away. Two women with a carton of eggs between them threw five at his face and chest before the authorities wrestled them under control.

"*La vache,*" Norman said. "This is not good."

And for Norman to say that about someone he was not particularly fond of was serious. I'm pretty sure he had clued in to what Luke was about to reveal next. Arianna had called

Luke just before his appearance in Norman's room. One of her assistants had been harassed as he was coming in to work. That heads-up had given her reason to summon the police, but Chas arrived first.

"The boss wants you, Depardieu," Luke said. "She needs you to be Basseem's personal bodyguard for the duration of his stay."

"NO," Norman protested. "I am going to Cairo with Lucy."

"I know you detest the bastard. He's low on my like list too. But Arianna has a point. As long as Ramy Basseem is a guest of the Royal Ontario Museum we have no choice. We *must* protect him."

"That's a job for the men in blue. Or one of the museum's security guards."

"They beg to differ. And the guards work for the province. As you can see—" Luke waved a hand and we all returned our attention to the TV.

A uniformed security guard waited just inside the entrance to receive the curator once he made it to the door. He was being shielded by a police officer and together they hunched over, running up the limestone steps. Someone from the crowd flung an object. It landed on the stairs, shards of glass flying, and burst into flame. That was no stink bomb; that was a Molotov cocktail. The breath was sucked out of me as I watched. Oh geez, the demonstration had degenerated into violence. The two just missed turning into human torches.

The cop shoved Basseem inside one of the revolving doors into the waiting arms of the security guard. Then he spun about to arrest the perpetrator.

"This is *not* good," Norman repeated.

Fortunately only police were on the steps at the time. They had been keeping the mob at bay armed with Tasers and nightsticks. They were trying their damnedest not to use them but the mob's blatant lack of respect was coming to a head.

"That's why Arianna needs you to protect him," Luke insisted.

I noticed a look pass between them. Or was it my imagination? It made me think of yesterday when I saw Arianna and Chas conspiring with that military looking Arab woman in the ROM's café.

"It'll only be for a few days. He'll be here until the opening; that's it. After that, he's gone. And not our problem any more." Luke exhaled but before Norman could object further he added, "You can follow us after you see him safely on the plane. You can take my private Lear jet, and follow with the mummy." The original plan was for Norman and I to go ahead, and for Luke to make arrangements to bring the Screaming Mummy. "Don't worry, big guy. *I'll* go to meet Sayid with Lucy."

"Still no," he answered.

Luke frowned. "There is no one else she trusts."

"Since when does she trust *me?*" That look again.

"Since always."

My man shook his head. "Basseem would be no safer with me. It's more likely *I'd* be the one to murder him."

Luke's puzzled expression grew deeper, an indication of something more complex than was apparent. He mused over Norman's last comment. "Hmm. I can see why *I'm* not one of his cheerleaders; he's an obvious enemy in *my* world. You though—I can't quite see your issue…" His eyes suddenly dilated.

Oh no. He didn't think *that*, did he? C'mon. Luke *couldn't* be serious. There was no way he could possibly know that Basseem was Chas. His eyes left Norman's and landed on mine.

I gave him what I hoped was a perplexed scowl. Not him. Not now. Not *ever*. The speculation was absurd, and I realized I had better stop staring at the man like he was someone that mattered to me.

Norman touched my arm. "It's okay, sweetheart. Nothing can keep me from going to Cairo with you."

Nothing? I returned my gaze to Luke.

Norman felt the tension in my body through my forearm. I knew this decision was a trial for him. It was a trial for me. But he respected my choices. And even when I erred he never flagged in his support. He understood why I had to go to Egypt. He understood why Arianna needed him to stay in Toronto.

I turned to him. "You have to stay. Arianna needs you."

His expression said NO.

Mine implored. *Please.*

"Fine." His tone was rough, reluctant but firm. He turned his gaze on Luke. "All right. I'll do it. I'll play bodyguard to the conceited turd. But don't you let Lucy out of your sight, Trevanian. Or I will personally deal with you. And you won't like it."

All three of us laughed. Norman would never do anything to harm his best friend. The two were bonded like brothers.

CHAPTER 14

Luke had been consulting with his pilot and now we were preparing for takeoff from the Pearson International Airport in Toronto. He came to sit in the luxurious leather seat beside me. I gave him a distracted smile.

How much had I told him about Chas? I wished I had kept my romantic past a secret. What good would it do for him to know that his professional rival Ramy Basseem was my first?

Before yesterday I had never discussed any of my exes. Why would I? My dating history was irrelevant. Besides, Norman never talked about *his*—except for one. Gillian. He had been compelled to tell me about her. Ultimately, sharing his past with me had affected *our* relationship. Her actions had changed his life and his friendship with Luke. And Gillian's sudden reappearance (before her unexpected death) had made an earth-shattering effect on mine.

Was this the same thing? Was Norman feeling the same way I had when I first learned of her?

I swallowed several times to pop my ears. Luke leaned back into his seat and cocked his head, and the corners of his mouth turned up. "Penny for your thoughts?" he said.

"Make that a hundred."

"A hundred pennies or a hundred dollars?"

"Dollars." I grinned.

"That important, huh?"

No. That embarrassing. My memories of Chas were cloudy, milky. Our relationship couldn't have amounted to a whole lot more than a few tongue-probing kisses, handholding, make-out sessions and lots and lots of puppy dog adoration on my part. I had exaggerated the whole thing, and then the big kerfuffle happened. I lost my virginity to him, and when he found out that he was my first—*that* was when everything tanked.

I rolled my eyes away to stare at the sky outside. We had risen above the clouds and were approaching cruising altitude.

"What's on your mind, Lucy?"

"Why did you force Norman to stay behind? You know you could have convinced one of your other bodyguards to do the job."

"I needed someone I trusted to keep an eye on Basseem."

"You mean *Arianna* needed someone you trusted to keep an eye on him. Why? How is he a threat?"

"I am not at liberty to say. Besides, *your* words not mine. I never said he was a danger to her."

I swatted his arm. "There was a time when you told me everything." This was true. I knew everything about his privileged background including his wealthy and philandering father, his difficult years growing up as a billionaire's son, and his ignominious stint as a smuggler's teenaged goon. I even knew about Aras, his heretofore secret, half brother.

"You were the one that wanted to join ISORE," he accused. "The rest of us just came along to keep you out of trouble."

I could tell by the suppressed smirk that he was joking. But it was true. As a member of ISORE I was included only on a need-to-know basis.

He took my hand and entwined my arm with his before lacing our fingers together. He shoved the armrest up so that it no longer sat between us, and snuggled our tangled arms between our hips as we slumped side-by-side. I propped my head against his shoulder comfortably. It was nice that we still felt at ease with each other even though we no longer slept together. Sure, Luke loved me in his own way but he could never love me the way Norman loved me, the way I needed to be loved. There was a reason for that and I was perfectly okay with it. I just wished Luke realized it.

I tilted my eyes up to see if he was sleeping. He had gone unusually quiet. His thick-lashed eyes were closed, covering those probing green irises that made most women melt. His breathing was even, but somehow I suspected he was awake.

My vision travelled up to the ceiling of the aircraft and then roved down the walls. The white, grey and blue color palette took its inspiration from nature by resembling clouds floating over a white sand beach. LED pot lights sparkled like a starry sky above the long curvy lines of the furniture, and modern wood and leather décor. Beyond this section were bedrooms with personal skylights and en suite bathrooms, a kitchen and dining area, even a conference room. And let's not forget the bar.

I sighed. Wow. Luke was so rich and he owned the most beautiful things. I mean this airplane for example: it was a fantasy come true. I could have had all of this had I stayed with him. But something never felt quite right. That something had a name and I wished he would own it. Not that it would have made any difference to me whatsoever. Even if *she* was not in the picture, there was only one man for me. He was the one who was willing to shove aside his own interests and make sacrifices for mine.

My hand was gently squeezed and I glanced over.

"Are you hungry, Lucy?"

"I will be."

"I'll put in an order with the chef. I feel like a steak and fries. How about you?"

I agreed to the same. We ate a lot of fancy food while on the road, and once in a while we preferred something simple, and maybe not all that healthy. But oh well…. After Luke had requested the food he lay down beside me again.

"Comfy?" he inquired.

"Oh, *so* comfy."

He smiled. A moment later I felt a nudge against my arm. "Hey, Lucy," he said. "Why do you think it didn't work between you and me? We had some good times together, didn't we?"

I nodded. Really good, really fantastic times.

But he wasn't Norman, and I wasn't Arianna. He must know that.

I shifted to look at him. The leather gave a quiet squeak. "Why don't you tell her that you love her, Luke? You two belong together. You shouldn't be living apart. And BTW everyone knows that neither of you signed the divorce papers."

A flush of color touched Luke's Hollywood suntanned complexion.

So, I had nailed it. It was always her—even when he was with me.

He went unusually silent.

At least he wasn't denying it.

Eventually he said, "I don't think she feels the same way."

"Bullshit."

He jerked at my remark and laughed. I seldom used the B word or the S word or the F word, but this time it was the only word that fit.

"Well—she hasn't given me any indication that she wants things to change," he insisted.

I harrumphed and said, "She didn't sign the divorce papers. She hosted a major museum event at your house—like it was *her* house. When was the last time she lived there?"

"I don't remember. At least two years. Maybe longer."

"If you ask me, I'd say those were clear signals that she wants you back."

"Her life is all about the museum and ISORE. She has no time for me."

"But she loves you."

"You think so?"

"I do."

Luke sighed. "Love complicates things."

I yanked myself up into an upright position and glared at him. "Damn right it does."

He snickered. "Yeah, look at who I'm giving advice to."

I sat up so that I could see him boldly. "Arianna is the kind of woman who needs a man that's tougher than she is."

"No shit, tell me about it. That's a tall order to fill. Where is she going to find a guy like that?"

"I mean *you*, dummy." I slugged him in the shoulder.

He grinned. Of course, he had known that I was talking about him. Then he turned serious. "I don't know about that. Seems like it's that very toughness that has us at loggerheads all the time. We can't be in the same room for more than fifteen minutes before we're at each other's throats. I admire and respect what she does, who she is. But we are both way too strong-willed."

"Then be *stronger* willed. Show her how much she matters to you. Do the Rhett Butler thing. Sweep her off her feet and carry her up the winding staircase and dump her on your bed."

"She'd have me arrested."

I giggled. "Or maybe not."

CHAPTER 15

Art and artifacts are stolen on a daily basis from not only war zones like Syria but also during peacetime in poor and questionably stable countries like Egypt. Theft has fueled a black market worth billions of dollars. It's an interesting thing, because when you think about it, these objects have no intrinsic value. Like paper money or digital currency, the value is only in what we have decided it is worth. So unless an object is made of gold or diamonds why do collectors pay so much for them?

These ideas tumbled about in my mind as Luke's private jet maintained cruising altitude. How had Chas become implicated in this terrorist plot? I knew Islamic extremists stole art for some of the same reasons Hitler stole art. Hitler hated other cultures and he hated their art and any cultural objects that defied his own beliefs. But Chas AKA Ramy Basseem was Egyptian. He was someone I knew intimately. How and when had he turned so extreme? Or was his ruined reputation the result of a media fabrication? Was that why he didn't want to admit to knowing me? He was embarrassed? Well, guess what. I was equally embarrassed. Humiliated even. Oh why-oh why-oh why were my musings having this effect on me? I could feel the heat of an impending blush and was helpless to stop it.

"Is it too warm in here?" Luke asked. "I could have the AC cranked up."

No, no. I shook my head because I didn't trust my voice. And my hands in fact were icy cold.

"You can annihilate an entire generation," Luke said after I forced my wits to re-gather and posited my thoughts to him. "You can set fire to their houses, and yet somehow they will find a way to return. Look at what Aras' Syrian family managed to do. No civil war could keep them down for long."

Amen to that. And there was more to Aras' current activities than even Luke was aware of. The shot of panic had passed and I relaxed.

"But if you erase a people's history," he continued. "You wipe out their achievements. And then it is like they never even existed. Art. Antiquities. Religious symbols. Are about power, Lucy. That's why they are worth so much money."

"But why would Ramy Basseem have anything to do with that? You told me that his mother was a white American and that his dad was black and native to Cairo. He's an archaeologist. His job is to study culture. Why would he want to erase anybody's culture? Or history. And besides, he was acquitted of the charges."

Luke shrugged. There was no answer to that. And it was all speculation anyways. No one really knew why Ramy Basseem's name was tied to the artifact heist. Coincidence? Maybe. But that was as far as it went. And really, what was the point in continuing this conversation? It could only lead to more confusion. Time to let the topic slide….

With more than ten hours to kill you would think I would be filled with irrepressible tension and anxiety. Irrationally, now that I had buried all thoughts of Chas, I felt the opposite. The flight proved to be a pleasant journey. Travelling in any of Luke's modes of transport was always luxurious and beyond comfortable. It made the time pass absurdly quickly, and, despite the gravity of our impending mission, eased my mind of worrisome thoughts. Being miles and miles and miles away from Chas, allowed me to drop the whole Ramy Basseem thing from my mind. I breathed an exhilarating sigh of relief.

***

Above my head the skylight allowed the first rays of the sun to shine in as I awoke refreshed from sleeping in my own private inflight bedroom.

I rubbed the sleep from my eyes and rose from the luxury memory foam to use the elegant lavatory. Then I joined Luke for breakfast in the dining room.

The food, a lobster omelet and French toast with real maple syrup, prepared by his private chef, was superb. I declined the proffered Mimosas and had black coffee with honey instead. Orange juice mixed with champagne was deadly. Certainly for me that was true. I could drink the stuff like soda pop, but boy would I pay for it when the buzz wore off. It simply was not worth it.

I glanced out the window to my right. Below me, to the north, was the rich, fertile Nile delta, flanked by golden desert, where the famous river drained into the blue-green Mediterranean Sea. The city of Cairo itself sprawled across both sides of the river and sat at the head of the fanning delta. Titled the "City of a Thousand Minarets," it was easy to see why. Even from this height the Islamic influence was obvious.

Cairo is a modern city as well as an ancient one. It purportedly boasts the largest film and music industries in the Middle East. It is an international media and commercial headquarters and the home of the Arab League. Despite heavy pollution and crazy traffic its population continues to grow and even now is well over nine million, with millions more comprising the suburbs and making it easily the largest metropolis in Egypt. A modern religious and political mecca, Cairo has an enthralling culture and its history is even more fascinating.

As I stared transfixed through the waterless blue sky, yellow-pink limestone peaks bloomed into view. Contemporary glass and chrome skyscrapers mingled with medieval Islamic architecture, bordered by even more archaic monuments from the past. These were the Great Pyramids of ancient Egypt.

The enormity of the city and the awesomeness of the surrounding landscape overpowered my imagination. Desert and city colors spotted with green oases of planted trees and flowers created a breath-gasping sort of splendor that was almost surreal. Even the yellow haze—the consequence of urban pollution—made for a strange kind of beauty.

Completely mesmerized by the view, it occurred to me that something was wrong.

Curiously, we had stopped descending. I glanced at Luke. He had noticed also. He shrugged when I attempted to ask. He was always connected to his people one way or the other, and spoke through Bluetooth to his pilot. His expression changed as he listened, and a frown creased his handsome features. "Right," he said. Then turned to me. "We've been rerouted to Alexandria. To the Borg El Arab Airport."

"What—? Why?"

"A Syrian delegation is expected to arrive at Cairo's International Airport today. The private jet terminal has been closed to all flights for security reasons. Protesters are being rounded up even as we speak."

"There's political tension between Syria and Egypt?"

"Apparently."

"Dammit," I said.

Luke gave me a look of mock amusement. It was true I hardly ever used swear words. But damn this was a delay I could not afford. Johnny would be in Cairo by now. I had texted him before takeoff and had received no response. It would have been nice to have him meet us at the airport with a helicopter. What was the point in having a pilot on your team if he couldn't be put to good use?

That particular plan would have cut the travel time by a third. As it was we would be three to four hours by bus or train to catch up to him. Then I realized who I was travelling with. Luke never used public transportation. He would hire a limo. Even so, it would still take hours by car.

"Don't worry, Lucy," he said. "We'll get to the bottom of this." He spoke remotely again, and although it appeared as though he were talking to himself, I knew he was making arrangements for a car and chauffer via Bluetooth.

We landed outside Alexandria and debarked at the private jet terminal. Luke's influence was strong even here. In some situations, money talked. There was always some official with itchy palms.

We waited no longer than ten minutes before we were fast-tracked through customs and were in a private air-conditioned Mercedes with a gap-toothed driver.

There was something oddly familiar about this driver. I had been in the Middle East long enough to know that Muslim men—despite their proclivity to sport beards and mustaches—did not *all* look alike. I could see only the back of his head, as I was seated behind him with Luke to my right. However, when he lifted his chin to check the rear view mirror, his eyes briefly touched mine. A troubling sensation of desperate cold gripped my insides. This was absurd. Why did he make me feel this way?

I sought my phone, typed a message and tapped send. My text was on its way to Johnny to inform him of our forthcoming arrival. I briefly thought about texting Aras but with Luke seated next to me I decided against it. He would ask me why I was texting Aras. And Aras had requested that I stay mum on our correspondence. I still had no idea what the man was up to or even where he was. But he had maintained radio silence for twenty-two hours.

When I received no immediate response from Johnny I returned my phone to my handbag.

"*Désolée*," the driver said. "I must make detour into the city to refuel. I do not have enough petrol to make it to

Cairo."

The driver spoke broken French. I guess he thought that neither of us knew Arabic. He was correct as far as I was concerned, but Luke was a different matter. The billionaire, gracious as ever, responded in French.

Another delay. I struggled to contain my frustration. Who didn't gas up before picking up a fare? I glanced at Luke who obviously thought it best not to quibble. If the vehicle needed gas, it needed gas.

I grit my teeth in frustration. No point in complaining. The driver was making good time, and at the speed we were going it would take less than twenty minutes to reach the city limits.

He made it in fifteen. I released a sigh of relief. And then everything came to a bottleneck. We were stuck in traffic.

Great. What next?

It took everything I had to stay in my seat because every muscle in my body tensed. Where the hell was the gas station?

I was lousy at the waiting game. Why hadn't I paid more attention to my yoga classes? The idea was to put into practice those exercises specific to quieting the mind and body when under stress. My first inclination was fight or flight. In this situation I could do neither. So when put in those terms, this was about as stressful as it got.

Calm down, girl. Relax. There is nothing you can do to speed things up.

If only this were a routine business trip or a casual holiday. Then I could relax, but as it was…. I shrugged, massaged my stiff neck. I attempted to meditate, to think of something pleasant and to focus only on that. I selected an image of the blue Mediterranean and its glorious beaches.

Thirty seconds was all I got before my brain started buzzing about everything else. Oh how I wished I were on a romantic vacation rather than on a dangerous mission. I would have loved to visit this place as a tourist with my man. It was famous for many things, but particularly its stunning corniche. The architecture lining this seaside road of Alexandria's downtown waterfront evoked the decadence and opulence of the 19th and early 20th centuries. Novelists had set their stories here!

Sadly, any romantic interlude for me and Norman would have to wait.

How ironic that we were forced to land in Alexandria. I was here to save my friend Alessandra, and in the process I would once again have to face my nemesis Nizar Tarek. I was not looking forward to that.

Inside the car I could get no sense of the grandeur of this magnificent city, founded by Alexander the Great, and beloved by Cleopatra. All I knew was that it was situated on the curving coastline of the Med at the confluence of the Nile River and the sea, and even that was hidden behind dense skyscrapers.

Did I not say my mind was all over the place?

And then queasiness unsettled my stomach, and I got the creepiest feeling I was being observed. There was only one person who could be doing that—because it wasn't Luke, whose head was down reading messages on his phone.

My sight flitted to the rearview mirror, and the driver's gaze darted away. The man was watching me. I know he was. Despite his dark complexion the whites of his eyes looked yellow. They had a pink veining in them like he'd had little or no sleep. Why should he be sleep deprived? It was we who had flown halfway around the world.

The gaze was on me again. And then gone.

He had moved his face away so that only his lower right cheek and part of his mouth showed. The corner was curled in a small tight smile.

A disturbingly *familiar* smile….

Oh my god. Those lips. That thick-lipped smile. I recognized it. It belonged to that driver, who worked for Norman's criminal father (now dead), who was in cahoots with that murderous guerilla Nizar Tarek.

Was the whole redirection of our plane a ruse?

Was the plot to isolate us and take us to Tarek?

The terrorist had demanded I come alone. Did he know that I hadn't?

My hand metaphorically went to my forehead. Yes, I was mentally slapping myself. It was obvious—because, of course, he knew.

I slowly bent to retrieve my cellphone from my handbag. Luke was still engrossed, reading something on his phone when I texted him the message:

The driver is one of Tarek's men!

CHAPTER 16

Luke's eyes twitched towards mine, startled that I should have sent him a text. He read the message, and next to me I felt him flinch. His head involuntarily jerked at the driver. I made a concerted effort to remain in position.

My vision never left my phone; the driver must not suspect we were communicating about him in private. My thumbs flew over the keypad:

We have to get out of this car.

I caught Luke's slight nod. He was thinking the same thing. But how, how were we going to get out of this car?

My attention shot towards the window. We were still in the city; we were just passing the street leading to the train station. I recognized the international sign of locomotive and track with an arrow pointing south.

All of our firearms were packed in our luggage. We had been forbidden to go through customs carrying them on our bodies. We had not thought to retrieve a handgun after claiming our bags. Anything we owned to protect ourselves with was now locked in the trunk of this car.

Luke had returned his attention to his phone. Without

moving head or neck his green irises landed on the flimsy scarf around my neck. It was thin but it was long, and I understood what he was suggesting. Yes. This would work.

I slowly unwound it as though I were too warm for comfort—after all this was a stiflingly hot country. I fanned myself with the scarf before dropping it to my lap. And Luke's hand slid over and twined it into both of his.

The driver spoke. "You wish that I should turn the air conditioning up higher, Monsieur?"

Clearly, he had noticed my removal of the scarf. I glimpsed the upward flicker of the driver's eyelids. The question had been thrown over his shoulder and asked in broken French.

"*Mouais,*" Luke said. "But not too much."

The windows to the car were darkly tinted, and from the outside nothing could be seen of the interior. Whatever happened in here would remain in here as long as the windows were sealed tight. And they were.

When the driver's eyes dipped down to find the button to adjust the AC, Luke made his move. The scarf looped around the man's throat. The car jerked. The man flailed and his foot left the accelerator. The car was already creeping at a snail's pace but now it lurched to a stop.

"Get out of here, Lucy!" Luke shouted at me. "Run!"

Instinct triggered my muscles and I opened the car door.

"Don't wait for me!" he yelled.

That demand sent shivers throughout my body freezing me into a mental and physical paralysis. Not too long ago Norman had ordered me to do just that—and I had almost lost him.

Luke kicked me with his foot and I half tumbled, half clawed my way out the rear passenger door.

I landed on the pavement in a semi crouch and turned to squint inside the car. An abundance of activity coming from the front seat was distracting me from making good my escape. Luke was having trouble keeping the driver from thrashing. Rest assured Luke would never kill him. He was just waiting for me to get to a safe distance before he released him and escaped himself.

One final urgent gasp came from the driver before I slammed the door and ran.

I dodged between the honking cars and dashed across the street. Vendors called out their offerings. Mothers with strollers, old men with canes, businessmen in suits and traditional dress, and clots of young people coming and going. Out-of-town visitors with cameras and cellphones looking exuberant and some completely lost. There was so much activity on the road that no one paid attention to a stalled car and a young tourist inexpertly skirting traffic. That was how I imagined my flight from the Mercedes must appear to the random observer. With me playing the role of tourist.

Once on the sidewalk I dared to look back. I knew Luke was trying to give me a long head start, and if I had a smidgeon of concern for the driver's life I had better seriously run—lickety-split.

I sprinted down the street towards what I hoped was the train station. Luke had once impressed on me that if we ever got separated to lose myself in a crowd and he would find me. I gripped my cross-body handbag to my side tourist style, confident in the knowledge that he would text or call when things were safe. That was the purpose of cellphones.

My head was spinning. What street was I on? I had no idea. I forced myself to calm down and focus. Traffic shot past at a dizzying pace and the pedestrian walkways streamed thick with humanity. I was standing winded on a loud, constantly moving intersection, and I had to get off.

I stared wildly left and right. A big sign over a recently renovated glass and brick building read:

Sidi Gaber Railway Station

Admittedly it was in Arabic but a quick search on my phone gave me its English name. It was one of the main city terminals where I could purchase a ticket to Cairo. I plunged through one of the glass doors and found myself in the busiest human thoroughfare I have ever had the misfortune to visit. I glanced behind me hoping to find Luke at my heels. And then I returned to the door for a better look, but saw no trace of him. Knowing the crafty billionaire, he would have taken a different getaway route to divert any pursuer from tailing me. I had zero minutes to lose. I negotiated my way past travellers, young and old, women with children, some pregnant, many wearing headscarves. The odd man wore a turban and some sported beards. I stood in line to buy a ticket, my heart still hammering against my ribs, my breathing difficult to control, like a vacuum.

It seemed to take forever to get a ticket, the person in front of me kept gabbing away like there was no tomorrow. Well—there *would* be no a tomorrow—not for me—if I failed to get my tush onto a train ASAP.

Finally, ticket in hand, I wove through the terminal. It was a big place, three floors I believe, bustling with restaurants and escalators leading to the upper levels where there was obviously a farmers market. Many of the people riding the down escalators hugged cloth or retractable plastic string bags to their sides. These were bulging with oranges, potatoes, lettuces with their roots still clotted with dirt, tomatoes on the vine, bunches of dusty purple grapes, and brown paper clutches of figs and dates.

The station had four tracks. I checked the train schedule on the digital screen over my head—seven minutes before departure. The train for Cairo left from Track 3.

At security my body and handbag were scanned with a metal detector. Seven minutes can seem like you only have seven seconds when you're in a hurry. Those few moments it took to pass security seemed like forever, but once through, people yelled and shoved, trying to reach the train.

I burst past the barrier with a handful of other bodies and fought a path to the platform.

The smell that greeted me was unpleasant. Mostly sweat

because it was hot. Garbage because there was not enough trash cans. And the ubiquitous tobacco smoke. Nearly half of the male population in Egypt smoked. There was also dirt, dust and litter trapped in every nook and cranny that wasn't covered by some waiting passenger's feet.

I had visited enough Muslim countries to know how overcrowded they were. In order to get on and off a train you had to be ready to bully your way through.

Much as I hated to be rude or pushy, taking an aggressive tack was the only method to ensure you arrived at your destination on time.

The dusty locomotive grated to a halt and the doors to the trailing cars ground open. The most fit of the passengers poured out first. I saw pregnant women and old men being shouldered aside as the urgent travellers unloaded. At the same time those of us waiting on the platform had to muscle our way aboard because any minute the train doors would close. The railway kept to a tight schedule. Trains in Egypt always arrived and departed on time, passengers be damned.

I was jammed between a young man in yellow dreadlocks and high-end training shoes (an obvious tourist) and an elderly woman carrying bags of potatoes and oranges and eating a fistful of figs (an apparent local), when the doors started to squeeze close on all three of us. I popped inside and they popped outside to the cacophony of screams demanding the conductor to wait, but it was too late for some.

Those left standing on the dock would have to catch the next train, and those who had failed to exit would have to debark at an alternate station. The trick was to position yourself right at the doors.

I moved down the aisle of the car I had entered. Nowhere to sit. I walked to the next car. It was the same, royal blue seats, and pinky-purple strip lighting along the tops of the windows. It was clean too, which surprised me. The interior of this train must have been recently refurbished. But again, nowhere to sit.

The next car was less full. It was ironic since the platform was so crowded with waiting passengers, but as I mentioned earlier, the conductors did not wait for the train to be full before they gave the signal for the train to leave the station. Keeping to schedule was all that mattered, and aggression was what got you aboard.

I found a seat near the front and dropped wearily onto the thin upholstery, allowing my handbag to rest on my lap. The engines were rolling into full gear, and the *clickety-clack, clickety-clack* sounds began to calm me down. As a bonus, no one was seated beside me.

The city scenes faded from view, and the dusty buildings and grimy tracks showed cleaner stones between the railway ties. I know. Why was I staring at the railway ties? I had to stare somewhere. I was afraid if I looked up—and back—a raving terrorist's thug would attack me, AKA the thick-lipped Arab driver. Worse, Luke wouldn't be there.

When I did glance up it was into the face of the conductor.

"Ticket please," he said in broken English.

That request sent a smirk to my lips as it recalled to my mind that scene in *Indiana Jones and the Last Crusade* where Harrison Ford threw a Nazi over the side of a Zeppelin spouting that he had "no ticket". My sarcastic wit soon went south however when I went to show the ticket to him. Little did I know—at the sudden realization that it was not in my hand—that I could be living this scene for real. Where had I put it? In my bag? I riffled through my purse but the ticket was gone. I searched my pockets. No luck there either.

"I bought a fare," I insisted. "Look here, I have the receipt." Oddly, I did have the receipt. So where was my ticket? In that crush on the train dock had I lost it? Or was I the victim of a pickpocket? *Please, please don't throw me off the train!*

"Ticket, please," he repeated.

I flashed the receipt in his face.

"No. I need ticket."

"It seems I've lost it. But this is proof that I paid for it."

He shook his head. "No. That no good. You get off train next station."

"*Si vous plaît*," I said. Surely, this man had some compassion. I was a lost and frightened tourist, or so I hoped he believed.

"I can pay you," I pleaded, continuing in French because my Arabic stunk. "I must stay on this train. I must get to Cairo."

He took pity on me as everyone was watching this pathetic foreigner (*moi*) begging for lenience in a language that was clearly not her mother tongue. Whether he understood me or not was questionable, but the French seemed to work.

He muttered something in Arabic, and then nodded. "*D'accord*. Fifty Egyptian Pounds." The latter was spoken in French.

I dug in my purse to come up with the coinage. I fished out my cellphone, then a compact, then a comb, laying everything on the empty seat beside me. My fingers trembled over my passport and my keys. It would not be smart to leave those where someone could steal them. Argh! Where was my wallet? There! I had it.

I filed through the few bills I possessed, searching for the right denomination, not noticing the passing shadow that hovered for an instant. I paid the man in cash and he smiled laconically. He punched a couple of small holes in a ticket to verify its authenticity and handed it to me with a suave "*Merci*."

Well, if that was all it took, why all the fuss?

I watched him leave, and kept one eye on his back as he punched tickets from the last couple of passengers before disappearing behind the sliding doors of the adjoining car.

Phew! Close one. I mopped my brow with the back of my hand, then gathered my things and replaced them into my purse. I zipped up my bag, secure in the knowledge that the precious contents were returned, before I slumped into my seat with all my worldly possessions clutched to my chest. This time I had carefully tucked the ticket inside a snug compartment next to my wallet. I looked out the window before shooting a glance at the front and rear doors. No Luke. And no terrorist's thug.

It occurred to me then that I should contact Luke. Surely, he had escaped? I exhaled, waited a few seconds until my breathing felt more or less stable, and then unzipped my bag and maneuvered my fingers inside it. I fumbled around a few seconds before locating the hard plastic casing of my iPhone. Wait a minute. Something felt wrong. Where was the protective silicone case? The back was cold metal. Tremulously, I yanked out my hand and glared at the contraption enclosed in my fist.

This was not mine! Where was mine? It wasn't even the same operating system. It was an Android. With a brand name I'd never even heard of labeled on the back. What was a Lava? I double glared at it. Flipped it over. Not the prohibitively pricey, state-of-the-art, latest generation iPhone that Luke had equipped all ISORE members with.

I dumped the contents of the purse on my lap. Everything else was there.

Except my phone!

My head shot up. Passengers were sleeping, staring out the window or reading their phones. My eyes darted rapidly around the train car.

The bastard. That French-spouting, dastardly conductor had switched devices on me. Who else could it have been? I had no gun. Still, I had a mind to get up and comb through every compartment of this train until I found him. But what good would that do? He could be anywhere or nowhere. Terrorists were like that. That's what I got for having a weak spot for French. Ugh. Distracted again. So easily—like a puppy with a squeaky toy. Norman was French. And he had charmed me with the language's musical cadence and sexy rolling R's. I was a sucker for a French accent and that conductor had played me with the characteristic French charm.

Now what was I going to do? All of my contacts were on that phone. I was effectively cut off. I knew none of my contact information by heart. For security reasons we changed phone numbers after each new mission. And although I was regretting it this moment—seriously, who memorized phone numbers anymore? Damn, if I only knew Luke or Norman's numbers. The loss of my phone made me realize how dependent I was on technology, and how little I used my brain. What would it have taken for me to memorize Luke and Norman's latest cellphone numbers?

I flipped the device I held in my hand nervously from front to back.

Could I even use this thing? Did it have a passcode? I clicked it on. Apparently it had no passcode and I could use it if I wanted to. But I didn't have a single contact memorized that I could call. Did they use 911 in Egypt?

Or what about the Internet? If I had access to the World Wide Web I could at least get through to the ROM and get Luke's number from the museum.

Before I could experiment, a text appeared on the screen.

I told you to come ALONE.

CHAPTER 17

My eyes flitted to all corners of the car. Oh my god. Was he on this train? If he was, I was trapped.

"When you arrive in Cairo stay at the Ramses Station. Await my instructions."

There was nothing to tell me who the texter was—only a telephone number. The dialing code was 20-2. That meant it was local. The Country Code for Egypt was 20. That much I knew. And the Area Code for Cairo was 2. The texter could only be one person. Nizar Tarek.

I was terrified to respond to the text. Would he tell me the truth if I asked about Alessandra? Unlikely. But I had to say something.

"Who are you?"

"You know who I am."

That reply sent a creepy chill up my spine.

"Are you on my train?"

"No. But I have eyes on you. Do as I say and your friend will not be harmed."

"What guarantee do I have that she is alive?"

"None. But do you want to take that chance?"

Did I have a choice? If Alessandra was alive she would stay that way—provided I complied. If I did not—I didn't even want to go there.

Before I could respond another message appeared on the screen.

"Do not try to contact your friends. The phone is monitored."

Of course it was.

There was nothing more to do until the train stopped at my destination.

***

I should have been more frightened than I was. But surviving a terrorist camp had toughened me. It had also familiarized me with the type of men who led these organizations. These men were narcissists. They were also single-minded. If they had a defined purpose they stuck with it until it was accomplished. Nizar Tarek had had several opportunities to kill me. He had not. Even after I had shot him, the next time I encountered him he still let me live. So this time was no different. He needed me to verify the identity of the mummy. Why?

As long as I still served a purpose my life was safe.

Had I known it was going to take more than four hours to get to Cairo from Alexandria by train I would have hopped onto another taxi. I belatedly learned that the trip by car was only a two and a half hour drive. Except how could I trust the taxis knowing that Nizar Tarek had thugs working for him everywhere?

Finally, I arrived at the Ramses Station. I shouldered my way along with the debarking crowd, and found myself in the middle of an ancient but recently renovated terminal. The interior was refitted to resemble an ostentatious glass and chrome Dubai shopping mall, which clashed with the original Islamic style that was visible here and there in fresco detailing. All of the trappings of a Dubai shopping experience were available to me if I had the time to explore. Alas, no. Window-shopping would have to wait for a more opportune occasion.

I was hot, sweaty and tired. I wanted to head to a hotel to have a shower and some food. I had, however, promised to wait at the Ramses Station, so here I must stay until I received further instructions.

But he had neglected to say whether I should wait inside or outside. I fished out the cellphone and checked for messages. Nothing. The constant movement, voices, and smells of humanity had gotten to me. My nerves were jangling. The doubt and suspicion that I had successfully squashed long enough to get me here was threatening to resurface.

The original plan was for Luke and I to join up with Johnny. After that, whatever orders Tarek delivered would be in the loop of ISORE intelligence. The men would keep out of sight but they would have my back. I would not be alone.

Now all had changed. I was alone.

Everything about this situation was making me sweat. There was no direction to go without getting jostled or shoved by somebody. And although the AC made it bearable because it was coolish inside the station, for the life of me I needed the fresh air, despite the outdoor heat.

Out I went.

Before I got two feet across the burning pavement I heard a voice speak from behind me. “Do not turn around.”

My hands flew to my chest. My heart practically leaped out of my throat. The voice was familiar.

I turned. The man standing there scowled but did not touch me. He indicated with his eyes that I walk into a dark corner in the shade.

“I told you not to turn around. Are you deaf?”

I cannot tell you how surprised I was. I nearly dropped into a dead faint.

He was dressed in his trademark safari jacket and khaki’s, and wore a new bush hat on his head. What was he doing here? How had he arrived so fast? And where was Norman? My thoughts leaped from one to the other nonsensically. I desperately wanted to call Norman but that was impossible without my real phone. Not only did I not have his new number memorized, but also the phone Tarek had switched for mine was bugged. But Chas—what the hell was he doing here?

It never occurred to me, even now, that he didn't remember me. My mouth just formed the words:

"Chas! Why aren't you at the ROM. You're supposed to officiate the grand opening of the Mummy exhibit in a few days!"

"We can't chat here. Racine, your life is in danger. You should never have come. Wait in the shadows until I can see if the coast is clear."

Racine? Then he *did* know me. He was faking in Toronto. Why—why—why—*why?*

I burst out into the sunshine to follow him. Then I stepped back. Until I had more information it would be prudent to obey. What the hell was going on? Why was he acting like a spy? What did he know about my mission to save Alessandra? And why would he care?

He came back to me after a moment of combing the landscape. I could see nothing suspicious, the traffic was typically insane and crowds of people thronged the streets.

"I have a car," he urged, and reached for my hand.

"No," I said. I shook his hand off. What the heck was he trying to prove by holding my hand? "I—I'm waiting for someone."

"Yes. I know."

Huh? I stared at him. "What do you mean? How do you know?"

"Your boyfriend, Depardieu, filled me in on your situation. When he couldn't get in touch with you he panicked."

Hold on. Norman never panicked.

To my vapid look of utter incomprehension he implored, "Look, I'll tell you everything when we get to my hotel. But we have to go—*now*."

"But I was told to wait here."

By this time I realized that Ramy Basseem knew more about my business than I would have liked. He knew about Tarek. After all, he was at the museum when we identified the mummy, even though Arianna had not allowed him to read the letter.

"I—I was sent to escort you," he said.

Whaat? I yanked my arm away. So he *was* acquainted with him!

"If he sent you, then why are you acting so secretive?" Then a worse notion struck me. "Are you a terrorist?"

"Seriously, Racine. You know better than that."

"Then how do you know him?"

"Not here."

I put on the brakes. "Why did you pretend you didn't recognize me in Toronto?"

"Oh, please, Racine. Do you really want to go into it right now?"

This was Chas. He might be known as Ramy Basseem today, but he was still Chas. I had to trust him. I had to trust somebody. He couldn't possibly be working with the terrorists. There was something else going on, and if I wanted to know what it was then I would have to raise the stakes.

I trailed along behind him to his vehicle. He had a driver. Did no one drive on their own anymore?

It was not a Mercedes. It was a comfortable town car he had hired to blend in. We settled in the back seat and he handed me a sealed bottle of water.

When I hesitated, he retrieved it and twisted off the top.

My suspicions were far from being put to rest. He had answered none of my questions. Was there a risk of being drugged and taken captive to some underground tomb where I would be lost for eternity? My paranoia was taking flight again. It was well known that the Pyramids of Egypt, those under excavation by archaeologists, had tunnels that would baffle the most experienced of spelunkers. In fact, I had heard it straight from the horse's mouth. Ramy Basseem was filming a documentary inside the Stepped Pyramid of Djoser when he had agreed to replace Yasmine Lim as the curator of the Mummy exhibit at the ROM.

Chas took a long thirst-quenching slug, rubbed the lip with his sleeve and re-offered it to me. I refused to accept the bottle and drink from it—not until I knew which side he served.

I waited eight seconds.

No dramatic gagging and turning purple in the face. No slumping into a drugged stupor.

I took the bottle and drank. The water in the bottle sloshed back to a level position.

"Where's Norman?" I demanded, wiping my knuckles across my lips.

"So, this is the guy, is it? Mr. Right?"

"None of your business. Where is he? And why are you here?"

Chas threw a quick glance at the driver who was preoccupied with the road. I got the troubled feeling that there were things he was keeping from me. Or maybe he was just being cautious because of the driver. He answered innocently, "The watchdog had to stay behind another day to help your boss."

What a jerk. I almost slapped him across the face for his insolence. Gibes like that were typical Chas. But who was I to criticize? There was a time I had called Norman things like that myself, except they were said with affection.

"What happened?" I asked.

His look was calculating. "I don't know how much you're aware of. Did you watch the news on TV or read about it online? The morning after the reception at the Trevanian mansion the museum was inundated with demonstrators. It was pretty vile. The mob was totally out of control. The protest turned into a riot and there were a few arrests."

Hesitation made him pause. He was leaving something out.

"The police feared for my life. *I* feared for my life. They told Dr. Chase that for the safety of the museum and its visitors I should leave the country. I agreed. But Depardieu was needed by Security to help keep things under control after the police presence departed. The city could ill afford to have them patrol the building for the next four or five days. And they worried something worse was planned for opening day—unless I did an instant vanishing act."

One would think it was hard to detect a blush in darker complexioned people. That was just wrong. We all have the ability to blush to the eyeballs. So yes, I could tell there was something more he was scared to tell me. His face had taken on a hint of deeper color. I asked pertly, "How did you manage to create so many enemies, Dr. Basseem?"

He gave me that trademark grin that had once so utterly disarmed me. "I made a mistake."

He *was* hiding something. A dart of adrenalin chilled my veins. Well *obviously* he was hiding something or he wouldn't have acted like a stranger. Mistake? What mistake? Exactly what did he mean by that? Had he hopped into bed with the terrorists, and now wanted out?

I must ignore it—for now. I wanted information on the bodyguard's arrival, and insisted he provide it. After all, Norman was supposed to accompany the mummy. What would we use to appease Tarek if the mummy failed to arrive? We were already pushing it with our original plan when Luke was supposed to bring it a day later. Now, it looked like it would be several days late. How would we stall Tarek? Or should I say: how would *I* stall Tarek?

"When is Norman arriving?" I demanded.

"Probably tonight. Depardieu promised your boss he would help her convince the demonstrators that I was gone. I flew out a couple of hours after you did. He said he would follow as soon as he was able."

Whew. That meant the mummy would be on its way and the plan was back on track. Then another thought drove home.

And yet you managed to land in Cairo around the same

time as me? The man was full of surprises.

I caught his look. Were my suspicions that obvious? Still sharp as a whip because he answered smartly, “Trevanian isn’t the *only* one who flies on a private jet.”

Wow. How Chas had changed. He was rich? Oh my god. Not Luke Trevanian rich, but still. He could afford to charter a private plane? This dark, handsome stranger was no longer my Chas. He was Ramy Basseem. And for future reference I had better remember that.

CHAPTER 18

"You owe me an explanation, Chas," I said after a few minutes had passed. The bumps and rumble of the rough highway made my voice vibrate in my throat. I turned my head from the passing scenery to observe his expression. It took everything I had not to allow my feelings for him to erupt. Yes, I had feelings. Mixed and volatile feelings.

"Well?" I nudged. "Make it quick. You owe me an explanation."

"I know."

"Well? Why didn't you want my friends to know we were already acquainted?"

"It's not your friends I was worried about."

"What then?"

His eyes drifted to the driver then back to me. He leaned in and I felt his breath on my cheek. "I'm being watched."

I jerked my head away from his nearness, rolled my eyes at him. He was being a drama queen.

He looked at me in earnest. "Until that note appeared inside that poor mummified girl's mouth back at the ROM's lab I thought you were safe."

None of this was making sense. Why would he care about my safety? And who did he think I was in danger from? Tarek? If so, what exactly was his connection with him?

"What do you know about Ines?" I asked, annoyed.

"Is that her name? Weird that you can talk about it so easily. The Lucy Racine I knew—"

"I am not the Lucy Racine you knew. Now tell me. How are you connected with that terrorist and how did you know about Ines' death?"

"I'm not and I know nothing. Not directly anyway. That is not the mummy I'm interested in. The mummy that interests me is the same one that Tarek is after."

Basseem was searching for Cleopatra's body. Did he think I was such a fool that I would believe that Tarek was after the same thing? What did a terrorist care about Cleopatra? This line of questioning was going nowhere. I changed tactics. "You still haven't answered my first question. Why did you pretend not to know me back at the museum?"

"Why didn't you insist that we *did* know each other?"

I shrugged. Okay, here was why: I refused to further elaborate on my relationship with Chas to Norman (it was nobody's business), and I saw no harm in telling him so. But Chas? His behavior was incomprehensible.

He nodded. "So, you don't trust the boyfriend, eh?"

I felt my face flood with heat. "Of course, I trust him."

"You and I," he said. I felt his nearness again as he leaned in towards my side of the car, and I fervently denied to myself that he caused the heat. "We were something back in the day. I've missed you, Racine."

I had no idea what I was supposed to feel. *You chased me out of your place with a tennis racket!*

He shook his head nonchalantly. "Guess I had my chance and I blew it."

I said nothing out loud. I was triply confused. What was he saying? That he *did* have feelings for me? That he had, even back then?

"My career was just starting, sweetness. I couldn't afford

to let a girl get in my way."

I glared at him. Could I realistically believe this garbage?

He took my hand and this time I was too stunned to draw it away. "Listen, Racine." The seductive familiar tone set my nerves a-trembling. "Are you really serious about the French guy?"

I clawed my hand back, jerked myself back to my senses. "I love him. And what's more, he loves me. So, I'll thank you to keep your paws to yourself."

He stared at me for a split moment, and then laughed. "Sorry. I was being impulsive. You used to have a thing for me, and hey—how can I know if I don't ask?"

"Well, now you know."

He shrugged, backed off but his eyes gleamed with a spark of mischief.

"So—to answer your question. I didn't acknowledge that I knew you because I needed to get a lay of the land, I wanted to know how you felt about me first."

"You could have just asked."

"I could have, but what would you have said? After over a decade, Lucy Racine, what *would* you have said? I didn't want people to be suspicious," he explained, "that I had any ulterior motives with regard to you."

"What ulterior motives could possibly involve me?"

His eyebrows arced as though I had said some unfathomable thing. "Oh, you'd be surprised."

For the remainder of the trip we were silent. I was stymied as how to respond—so I stayed mute. There were innumerable unanswered questions I wished to carpet-bomb him with, but thought better of it. He was too composed. What was he hiding? Oh, how I would love to know.

***

The scenery blew by. Distracted, I was unable to appreciate my surroundings. It wasn't because we were driving particularly fast that I failed to note any landmarks. It was just that Chas' unexpected appearance had thrown me, and shaken me to my core.

Both buried in our thoughts, I deemed it best for us to remain so. My stomach growled but I ignored it.

A while later, we arrived at the Nile-Ritz-Carlton which Chas informed me was the former Nile Hilton before its refresh. I noticed that one side of it overlooked Tahrir Square and the Egyptian Museum. Was that planned? The Egyptian Museum brought home a whole boatload of memories.

Not all of the rooms had balconies, but those without had broad, square windows some of which hovered over the river, offering spectacular views. When we entered the modern lobby I was hit with a blast of cold air, the gift of modern air-conditioning. As the glass doors swung behind us I glimpsed a terrace restaurant with live music in full sight of the museum. The smell of food coming from the restaurant again reminded me of my empty stomach.

The lobby itself was ornamented in sumptuous red and muted gold. I was beginning to realize how that color combo was a favorite of the Egyptians.

The furnishings and décor were modern, simple elegance, and the fixtures brass and crystal. Textured tile covered the walls. From the ceiling strategically positioned recessed lighting sent an elegant sparkle.

We took the elevator up.

Chas' room was on the top floor, a sky-blue carpeted executive suite with a wide balcony overlooking the magnificent Nile. The living room had a full sofa, two arm chairs, a coffee table, a sideboard for serving food and storing belongings, and a gorgeous, round, solid rosewood table for in-room dining. On the window side I caught sight of a nicely furnished patio for outdoor entertaining.

Who, I wondered, was paying for all this luxury, Ramy Basseem or his terrorist overlord?

Through a spacious connecting entranceway a king-sized bed in elegant white, mossy green and steel grey colors that slid between two built-in, polished wood, glass-topped bed stands was visible. At the sight of the bed I quickly doused the unwanted emotions and extracted my attention to our current space. Unfortunately, not quickly enough. Chas' gaze trapped mine.

Why was he doing this?

I refused to play his game. The room we stood in was large enough to hold a curved, textured sofa and a two-tiered coffee table also of rosewood. I scoured my brain for something to say to distract me from the sumptuous bedroom. Nothing but frivolities came to mind.

I did come up with a nice accusation. "So you just left Arianna in the lurch?"

"I had no choice," he replied.

"You always have a choice."

He scowled. "Not this time."

His phone suddenly rang. He stared at me, then shrugged and answered it. Of course he answered it. Whatever was happening in Dr. Ramy Basseem's social sphere was of far greater importance than *my* measly life and death struggles.

"Yes. I'll be there as soon as possible. Set up for the mural scenes in the central tomb. And Abraxas, I don't want you to audition for a substitute narrator. *I* am the voice of the series. So, don't you dare do that!"

Ah. Dr. Basseem was talking to his director? I had heard the name of Leon Abraxas before. The conversation concerned his upcoming documentary: *In Search of Cleopatra's Tomb*.

"Anxious to get back to filming your blockbuster?" I asked snidely.

Chas gave me a glare of grossly arrogant pity as he disconnected the call.

No. I am not jealous of your fame.

"So—you know about that?" he asked.

I was grateful for the new topic to occupy my thoughts. He was the king when it came to creating exciting historical narratives (that brought in hundreds of thousands—maybe even millions—in revenue). And maybe getting people excited about history wasn't all bad—even if it was done with commercial intent.

"I heard you were on the verge of discovering Cleopatra's tomb," I replied. "Or you know where her mummy is—or something of that nature."

"Did Trevanian give you the scoop? If so, he probably got it wrong."

"How so?"

"I don't believe the history books are accurate," he explained. "I don't believe that Cleopatra and Mark Antony committed suicide in Alexandria."

"Then—what?" The generally accepted story was that Cleopatra allowed herself to be bitten by a venomous snake and that her lover fell on his own sword after learning of the fatal event.

"I think after a period of hiding she either died or she was captured—and assassinated. And then, humiliated by their defeat, Mark Antony committed suicide."

It was true that no one really knew what happened to the two lovers. But most agreed that they killed themselves when the armies of the Roman emperor Octavian overran Egypt. So this really was what his documentary was about? Chasing down the resting place of Cleopatra?

"Well, think about it, Racine," he said. "Egypt is so much desert and tombs. There are not only pyramids out there, but also vast networks of tunnels connecting all of the lesser tombs and crypts—a perfect place to hide. The Roman army would never find her in the Saqqara necropolis. They wouldn't even think to look for her there. Those monuments are more than two thousand years before her time. To her they would already have been ruins, a great place to lose yourself."

That was insane. "What would be the point in hiding among all the dead bodies?" I remarked. "Besides, she would have starved to death."

"Well, maybe *that's* how she died. If it is I am going to find out. But I don't think so." He paused dramatically.

"Starvation is too passive. Cleopatra would never have allowed herself to succumb to something so common. No—I believe Octavian found her and murdered her."

Chas had a knack for melodrama, but this was—well—what was his proof?

It seemed he wasn't in the mood for giving me a sneak preview. I suspected that the great reveal would all be in the documentary. And he wasn't about to release any spoilers.

"I'm guessing you want a hot bath and some food?" he asked. His hand rose to his left indicating the direction of the bathroom.

Much as I wanted to know more about the Basseem documentary, I was more invested in his role in my current misadventure. What was the real reason he had returned to Egypt? And how did he know where to find me? Unfortunately, I was losing the energy to listen. And even though Ramy Basseem's actions seemed suspect (it wasn't like he was a total stranger), I was pretty certain I had little choice but to trust him. My main concern at the moment was Luke. Where was he?

I felt a strange thrill of terror and excitement. I had gone solo before. I had even willingly walked into a terrorist camp once, but I had never really been alone. I had no idea where Luke was. And if Chas was to be believed Norman was still in Toronto. Johnny was somewhere in Cairo, but he had no idea that I was too.

And Alessandra. Where was Tarek keeping Alessandra? Without the Screaming Mummy I had nothing to bargain with except my own life.

For the first time since I had joined the perilous organization of ISORE I felt abandoned. Unlike my sojourn into the terrorist camp in Afrin, *no* one had my back.

As I was thinking these thoughts, I stripped down in Chas' hotel bathroom, lowered the toilet lid and piled my clothes on top of it.

Goosebumps rose on my naked flesh and I realized these had nothing to do with cold. It was very warm in here.

They had nothing to do with the danger of my mission either.

They had everything to do with Chas.

I was in the shower when I saw through the dripping, frosted shower glass door, a shadow coming towards me.

CHAPTER 19

I stiffened. I needed to get access to a towel. I turned off the tap, wrung the excess water from my hair and reached for the mobile showerhead. This ultra-modern luxury bathroom had three showerheads, and I seized the lowest one and removed it from its chrome holder, now dripping wet.

An image, a blast from the past flooded my brain. The last time either one of us had found it necessary to fend the other one off it was he who was on the offensive. I realized now how deeply I was affected by this memory.

But what self-respecting person wouldn't be scarred after doing what I had done?

In my mind's eye I saw the image of his raised right fist as he threatened me with the ordinarily innocuous piece of sports equipment. In hindsight, it was hilarious that he had reacted in that manner, but at the time I had failed to see the humor. I had gone to his home to declare my love for him and that was his response.

Granted I had been dead drunk. Yasmine, Chas and I had gone out earlier for drinks because it was our last day at the Egyptian Museum. We had drunk too much. In any event, *I* had. After Yas had gone to her room I had made my way over to Chas'. After all he had 'deflowered' me.

Chas was quite adamant that he didn't love me, and didn't want to marry me. He had been quite decent about it as I recall. But you know how it is when the alcohol takes over. You really don't know exactly what you said or did. All I remember is that I had refused to leave, and he had had to chase me off with the tennis racket.

Will I ever be able to laugh about it? Unlikely. Even now I felt an unwanted shudder of shame. No matter what he claimed, on that infamous day he was dead serious about getting rid of me, and I had been struck by a momentary craziness by visiting him uninvited to change his mind.

Me, impulsive? Ha!

The craziness had long since passed. That was youth and high spirits, alcohol and desperation, born of unrequited love. Now that I knew what real love felt like, I could fairly say that what I had imagined I'd experienced back then wasn't even love. It was a crush.

Why were crushes so bitter and so real? And why did they make you feel so stupid when they were over?

A footstep sounded. Dammit Chas. Why are you doing this? The past was the past. Was this some sort of revenge? *Once and for all—No means NO.*

I squeezed the handle of the mobile showerhead. Was I seriously going to hit him with this? Yes, if he forced himself on me. Because why else would he enter the bathroom when he knew I was having a shower?

Jeezus. Why had I left the door unlocked?

Don't say it. Do not even imply it. I did *not* have mixed feelings.

The reason I had left the door open was because I never locked the door. Yes. That was why. This sounds bizarre, but since childhood I have harbored the fear of locked bathroom doors. I worried it would get jammed and I'd be trapped. And just how embarrassing was that—having to be rescued from a bathroom?

Okay, that did happen to me—once—when I was young. My mom had had to call the fire department to save me.

But I digress. Oh boy, was I digressing. With the showerhead in one hand and the handle of the sliding glass door in the other, I slowly eased the panel aside.

"Lucy!"

I swallowed a startled shriek. I recognized that voice. *Mercy.* I had almost whacked Luke on the head.

He dragged a towel off the chrome bar and thrust it at me. "Honest to god, Lucy. Were you going to wallop me with that?"

Oh my god. Was I? As the steam parted, Luke's face materialized. I hugged the towel to my chest gladly, and replaced the showerhead in its crook before wrapping the fluffy terry around me. "What were you doing sneaking into the bathroom?" I derided him.

"I wanted to make sure you were okay."

"I *was* okay until you decided to scare the bejeezus out of me. Where's Cha—I mean, Ramy—Basseem?"

"He's in the living room waiting for room service. I told him to order enough for three." Luke's hand went to the wall switch and I heard a click. I had forgotten to turn on the fan to vent out the steam.

As the comforting hum began, I started to pat myself dry. I had almost called Basseem Chas. Had he noticed my slip?

Luke and I were intimately familiar with each other, being recent exes and all, and I never felt uncomfortable around him but...

"You were going to beat Basseem to a pulp with that?" The expression on Luke's face was half incredulous, half amused, as he indicated the dripping showerhead behind the glass. Because who else would I have been expecting?

"No," I said. "I—I didn't know who it was. You could have been that terrorist."

Luke laughed. "You mean the driver? I don't think he's going to be sneaking into anybody's bathroom any time soon."

I tugged the corners of the towel under my armpits.

"You didn't kill him, did you?"

"No. But he did pass out from lack of oxygen. Guess he didn't care too much for your shade of peach in a scarf."

I chuckled while Luke continued: "I made sure there was still a pulse before I disarmed him and tied him up."

Using the same scarf I expect.

"And then I stole the car. I was not familiar with the route so it took me about three hours to get here. That's why I don't drive myself unless I have to. Get to skip the getting lost part. Saves on time… So—since then, I've been calling and calling you—"

I took this as a hint to relate to him the whole story of what had happened to me on the train with the lost ticket and the phone switch after I'd left him.

"Bastard. He's got goons everywhere."

"So how did you know where to find me?"

"I knew you would have caught the train to Cairo. So I drove to the Ramses Train Station and inconveniently got caught in a bunch of traffic. Just as I pulled into the terminal I saw Basseem pick you up."

Luke shot a glance at the door.

I paused from toweling down my hair. I assumed he was worried about Chas. I had my own doubts as to whether he was being completely truthful. His behavior and his answers were contradictory and erratic. And why would Tarek need me to authenticate the Screaming Mummy if he had Egypt's Indiana Jones?

Well, that question was probably easy to answer. Tarek didn't really need me to authenticate it. He just wanted me here so that he could wreak his revenge. The mummy was simply another item to sell on the black market, though truth be told, it wasn't worth as much as some other ancient treasures. So, the question remained: why the son of Ramses III, a murderer and betrayer of his own father?

None of this meant that Chas was our enemy. He had conveyed me here to safety.

I asked, "Why would Basseem be working for the

terrorists? He let you into his room. He *must* be okay."

Except for one thing. Chas had implied that Tarek had sent him to meet me at the station. And then, afterwards he had denied it.

"If Chas is working for Tarek—"

A knock came at the door.

Chas' voice boomed: "Hey guys. Hope I'm not disturbing anything. Don't know how you people do things in *your* country, but we don't customarily walk in on people in the shower."

There was a pause before the voice continued: "Food's here. If you're hungry."

I was starving. Luke and I exchanged glances.

Had Chas overheard our conversation from the other side of the door? Had we said anything he shouldn't hear? That depended on whose side he was working for.

Luke opened the bathroom door and the last of the steam escaped. Chas stepped back, caught red-handed.

"I was waiting for your answer," he said apologetically, face coloring.

"Like you weren't listening in on our conversation?" Luke demanded.

"I am not a pervert." He mumbled something else that sounded like 'unlike *some* people.'

He was probably referring to the fact that I was naked, clutching a towel to cover myself while Luke was having a casual conversation with me. Chas shook his head in exasperated bewilderment. "I don't care what you two are gossiping about. I just thought Racine might be hungry."

Abruptly, Chas turned and left.

My luggage stood just outside the threshold against the wall. Luke dragged the large powder blue suitcase onto the wet marble floor of the bathroom. He closed the door for privacy and turned back to me.

How thoughtful of him to bring up my things. Here we were in possession of our baggage once more, and that meant we had access to our guns.

A question suddenly crossed my mind. What had he done with the driver?

Luke was about to leave to allow me to dress in peace when I raised my eyebrows with the intention of asking. He smiled because he was ready with the answer. "I told the would-be assassin to go back to his boss and inform him that his attempt at getting rid of me had failed." He spoke in a tone so low it was barely audible. "Then I untied him."

The whispering was just a precaution as Chas could have returned to listen outside the bathroom door. Admittedly, Luke's suspicions were beginning to rub off on me.

Here was what we knew about Ramy Basseem:

He had been asked to replace Yasmine Lim as the curator of the Mummy exhibit at the ROM.

His presence at the museum and the high profile news coverage of him had caused protests resulting in an all out riot at the museum.

Threats to his life forced him to leave at once. Now there was no curator for opening night.

He immediately returned via private jet to Cairo.

He met me at the Ramses train station.

He brought me to this hotel.

He let Luke into his room.

Did any of this mean he was complicit in Nizar Tarek's schemes? The truth was, we did not know yet what to make of Ramy Basseem. Had he really been sent by Tarek to collect me? And if so why had he brought me to this hotel? And why had he let Luke into his room to speak with me?

I whispered in turn. "Do you think Tarek hired that driver to get rid of you?"

He shrugged. "He warned you to come alone. Now he knows you are not."

"I'm sorry, Luke. I didn't mean to endanger you."

Muffled amusement glistened in his eyes. "Like *I* have never endangered you." A pause, then: "Basseem filled you in on why he left Toronto?"

I nodded.

He toed the suitcase. “Get dressed.”

Luke left the bathroom. As quickly as possible I did as requested. I heard no altercation outside the door and so assumed that Chas had not returned to snoop. *Good. Points for him.*

I fluffed out my hair and applied a small amount of makeup.

It was nice to put on clean clothes. I stepped out of the steamy bathroom in an ankle length white, turquoise and black floral wrap skirt and sparkling white, silk tank top. I readjusted my bra so that nothing inappropriate was showing. The last thing I did before entering the living room was to dig out the substitute cellphone from my purse.

Through the opened door of the patio the smell of delicious food drifted in.

Except for hints of garlic, I couldn’t identify what the dishes were. From where I stood my mouth started to water.

My legs parted the folds of the skirt as I strode barefoot and damp-haired into the living area and met with a strange scene.

Luke was standing over Chas with a gun.

CHAPTER 20

"I told you I am not working for Tarek," Chas said.

"Then why did you tell Lucy that Tarek sent you to meet her at the train terminal?"

"I never explicitly *said* that. I only allowed her to think that to get her to come with me. Did you think I was actually going to let her hang around to hook up with a terrorist? Don't you get it? Racine and I were once an item. I still care what happens to her."

That comment set my face aflame. What I remembered of our entanglement was a totally different set of circumstances.

Luke stared. "You—and *Lucy?*"

I gulped. All right there was no point in denying or delaying the inevitable. I waved a hand cavalierly and hoped my discomfort was well masked. "Luke, meet Chas."

Luke's widened eyes lowered. For two seconds he said nothing, and then he turned my way. "Of course. It all makes sense now. Does Norman know?"

"He does," Chas cut in. "I didn't even have to tell him. He guessed."

Naturally he did. Nothing slipped past the bodyguard. A flood of warmth for him overwhelmed me. When had he first guessed? Was it in Luke's spa room or sometime after that? Or was it *before* that, when we initially saw him in the lab?

Oh, hell. What did it matter? He had known all along and he had not made a point of sticking it in my face. I don't think I could have loved him any more than I loved him right now.

"The French guy asked me to watch out for her."

"And why would he do that?" Luke gesticulated with the gun. "He isn't exactly your biggest fan."

Since when did Chas care about me? Seriously, when did he *ever* care about me? Since when were we an item? Until his recent confession his behavior back then had certainly fooled me.

Chas rose from the armchair where he was seated, and moved toward the sofa with hands raised, indicating that he only meant to retrieve his cellphone. He plucked the device from one of the sofa's end tables and beckoned Luke over to show him a video. And although I was still rather distracted, I swiftly crossed the room and had a peek too.

On the screen, Chas was at work on the Mummy installation at the museum. He was alone except for a couple of technicians. They were helping him arrange some ancient grave goods in a display case. Everyone else was on coffee break.

Somehow a protestor had slipped past security and held Chas at gunpoint. The fanatic was accusing him of genocide and all sorts of crazy things. Chas defended himself insisting that he wasn't a terrorist and that all of the accusations against him were false. The man refused to listen. He pulled the trigger just as Norman's body went flying across the screen and knocked the revolver out of the gunman's hand. At the same time the gunman crashed to the floor, a bullet went soaring and hit the wall. There was a split second of stunned disbelief on Chas' face. He had been within an inch of losing his life. A moment later Norman rose to his feet, his hands dragging the gunman up, arms twisted behind his back.

Luke and I exchanged startled looks. A technician had

captured the entire thing with his phone.

Showing us this video had taken courage, and to be honest it made Chas look bad. Indiana Jones should not need to be rescued by anybody.

However, I understood why Chas had requested the owner of the video send it to him. He needed it as proof that his life was in danger. It was the only way he could renege on his obligation to the ROM with his dignity intact, and return to making the documentary in Saqqara.

"I owed the Frenchman one," he said, flatly. "And now would you mind putting that thing away? I think having two guns pointed at my head in twenty-four hours is enough for anyone."

I gestured to Luke to lower the gun. If Chas meant me harm wouldn't he have done it when he had me alone? I was pretty certain he was safe. Further explanations could wait.

My stomach was complaining. I hadn't had the chance to eat since breakfast. I had no clue what time it was except that by the angle of the sun it must be close to the dinner hour. The balcony door was wide open and the food that had been set out on the table was getting cold.

CHAPTER 21

A scarlet umbrella on a moveable stand shaded a round cast-aluminum patio table set for three. At the sideboard behind the table was an uncorked bottle of red wine. A trio of filled glasses had been left alongside it to breathe. There was no way around it, and no nice way to say it. Egyptian wines left something to be desired, and this one would *need* to breathe.

A few wasps buzzed close by and Chas slapped them away. “Nasty critters.”

“If you swat at them, they’ll only get more aggressive,” I warned.

“Don’t want them in the food.” Was Chas allergic to wasp stings? Otherwise he was overreacting.

“They’re more likely to go after the wine,” Luke said.

“I should call the desk. Get someone to deal with this.”

“Don’t be ridiculous, Chas. We don’t want anybody spraying poison while we’re eating.” And I intended to eat, wasps or no wasps.

I wished the two to stop bickering. It was clear they had little use for one another and were using any excuse to be combative. Furthermore they were forcing me to play referee.

“Hey. Have either of you heard about that new species

recently discovered in the U.S.? The way it parasitically reproduces is so gruesome that scientists named it after Egypt's evil desert god. I believe the deity's name is Set; he killed his own brother and chopped the body into countless pieces—but of course you both already know that. Anyway, this new species lays its eggs inside the Gall wasp. The larvae then eat its way inside the wasp's body before emerging through its head. Is that creepy or what?"

They both stared at me, and Luke laughed. "Yeah, that *is* pretty gruesome."

"Can we just eat," Chas said.

He indicated that we sit. Then he lifted the silver lids to several plates. This—the garlic, onions and olive oil—was what I had smelled earlier.

My cast aluminum chair scraped across the patio's concrete floor as I positioned myself at the table. Luke sat on my right with Chas on my left and I did my best not to elbow either of them as I reached for the small dishes called *mezze*. The plate nearest me held *baba ghanoush*, a smoky eggplant dip that I scooped up with a torn piece of soft, fresh *eish fino*, a bread roll, something like a French baguette but with a more tender crust. There was also *duqqa* a spicy nut and herb mixture. I eagerly dunked my bread into that as well.

We tucked into *kushari* made from pasta, lentils, rice and tomato sauce, topped with chickpeas and fried onions. Two of the dishes I recognized was *hawawshi*, a traditional serving of folded pita stuffed with garlicky minced lamb and vegetables, notably peppers, zucchini and tomato, and the soft white buffalo's milk cheese decorated with fresh batons of cucumber and lemon wedges.

It was generous of Chas to order wine with the meal. He turned to collect a glass from the sideboard and set it on the table in front of me. Château des Rêves Cabernet Sauvignon was an Egyptian vintage made with grapes from Lebanon. I glimpsed Luke's smirk at the label. After all, this was Egyptian wine, and the country was hardly celebrated for their winemaking abilities.

I understood why Chas had ordered it. He supported local. And that was something that had not changed about him.

Would the billionaire drink out of politeness? Even though it was obvious that he and the Egyptian archaeologist were archrivals Luke was raised properly. He was charming and charismatic. Those qualities had led him a long way. Was he about to give them up because of mediocre wine?

The vintage was light garnet in color with a nose of oak, earth, leather and dried cherries. A slightly peculiar, unidentifiable smell reached me as I sniffed. While Chas' back was turned Luke whispered that he knew this particular label from a trip in his youth. It delivered an unfortunate hint of cough syrup. Maybe that was what I detected.

There were also some dusty tannins, which might have been okay except that a slightly hot finish abruptly drowned them.

My back was to the wine bottle. Luke was facing it. That was how he had recognized the label. He had a clear view of it. Chas' chair was more or less beside the sideboard about two feet away, and now he turned and handed Luke a glass, while raising his own in the opposite hand.

"*Santé*," Chas said. He had used the acceptable French form.

"*Fi sihtik*," Luke said.

"Cheers." I raised my arm. Was Luke being deliberately petty by toasting in Arabic? I was about to put the wine to my lips when Luke abruptly knocked it out of my hand.

What the—? The wineglass shattered on the concrete floor missing my feet by inches. A small pool of red-gold liquid spread to within a hand-span of my toes.

I get it. You hate Basseem. And yes maybe the jerk was mocking Norman by toasting in French. But a lot of people used French in the Middle East.

Oddly, Luke's gaze was averted from the incident. Instead, he stared at the sideboard before peering at his own glass. Something alien floated inside it.

Insects drawn to fruity drinks, and even wine, typically drowned when sampling the goods. I told him so as I lifted my bare toes to wipe them down with my napkin, and to avoid stepping on the broken glass. I cannot tell you how many times I have had to fish a fly out of my wine while indulging myself on outdoor patios.

I tucked my heels under my chair and returned the napkin to my lap. I passed Luke a spoon. The dead wasp was drifting around like a fish belly-up in a red-gold sea. "Dig it out."

I paused and dropped another glance at the shattered glass. "Did I have one in *my* wine too? If so, it was hardly necessary to be so dramatic. You could have just told me instead of knocking it to the floor. I assure you I have no penchant for bug meat."

"You didn't have a wasp in yours," Luke said. Then he noticed my bare feet. He barked at Chas, "Go get her some shoes."

"You expect me to go foraging around in a lady's luggage? What do you think I am—one of your servants?"

"Just do it, Basseem," Luke said. "Or I will make you drink this wine."

At this instant I truly believed that someone was going to slug somebody, and then Chas' gaze fell to the mess on the concrete floor where I was still holding my knees bent so that my toes were tucked under the chair and off the floor.

"Watch those shards, Racine. I'll go get you your shoes. Where are they?"

"My Sketchers are in a white shoe bag inside my suitcase."

He nodded and gave me a gracious smile, and I remembered again why I had once fallen for this guy. When he chose he could be a gentleman. In contrast, at this moment, it was Luke who came across as crass.

When he was gone I turned on Luke. "What was that all about? You ordered him to fetch my shoes? Why didn't you demand he fetch a broom while he was at it? And furthermore, why not go get them yourself? You're usually the chivalrous one."

Luke sighed and pointed. "I wanted him out of hearing range. Look—"

I turned towards the wine bottle.

"What about it? I know you hate the vintage, but it was kind of rude to smash it out of my hand like that. You could have broken more than the glass."

His chair screeched against the concrete floor as he seized me by the forearm, and turned my face with his other hand. "Look at the surface of that sideboard."

I gasped. I had wondered briefly why we were no long pestered by wasps, but instead of seeking an answer I had merely been grateful that they were gone.

Gone? Yes, they were gone.

They were *dead*.

I grabbed Luke's wrist and stared into his green eyes. "The wine was poisoned?"

There were over two-dozen dead wasps lying on the surface of the sideboard.

"Why else would there be so many dead?" He scooped up the floating insect with the spoon, and placed it on the table. It lay immobile.

Crazy thoughts went galloping through my brain. "You think he tried to kill us? Why would he do that?"

"I guess we will just have to ask him, won't we?"

As if on cue, Chas returned to the patio with the laces of my turquoise Sketchers swinging from his fingertips. In his other hand was a paper bag to clean up the mess.

His gaze went to where we had been staring just seconds before, and he deliberately leaned in to confirm that his eyes weren't playing tricks on him.

"No," he said swinging back and fixing his attention on us. The bag dropped from his grip and fluttered away. "You seriously don't think *that*, do you?"

Luke rose, grabbed the running shoes and passed them to me. "You have a better explanation?"

"I did not poison the wine!"

"Then drink it." Luke plucked his glass from his own place setting, and thrust it in the Egyptian's face. "Prove to me it isn't poisoned."

Chas hesitated. He put it to his nose. Sniffed. "I'm not drinking that. I think it's gone off. It doesn't smell right."

"No kidding, it doesn't. Why are you trying to kill us?"

"I am not trying to kill you. I am not trying to kill anybody."

My cellphone suddenly dinged. Or should I say Tarek's substitute phone suddenly dinged. I had placed it on the table beside me while we were having our meal.

Chills chased up my spine. I stared at Chas. I seriously questioned whether I should believe him. The men were staring at the phone.

"It's him," I said. "He's sent me a text… Chas, what have you done? I was supposed to wait for instructions at the train station." I turned to Luke, fear in my eyes. "What if he kills Alessandra?"

Luke patted my arm for reassurance. "What's it say?"

I picked up the phone and read the message. This was a horrible time for catastrophic thinking. I showed it to Luke, my heart pounding.

"Where are you, Lucy Racine? My messenger went to meet you. You were not at the station."

"Tell him you are at a hotel."

I did as Luke suggested.

A few seconds later, I received an answering text.

"Where is the mummy?"

My eyes sought Luke's again.

"Tell him it's arriving on a later flight."

"What if he doesn't believe me? What if Norman can't get his hands on it?"

"He will. I made arrangements before we left. And if he's caught stealing it, I will force Arianna to release it into his custody."

"Oh, Luke, I don't think that's possible. The mummy

doesn't belong to us. It belongs to the Egyptian Museum."

"I—can get it released," Chas interrupted. "I have some influence with the authorities. It's the Screaming Mummy you're talking about? You need it to trade for the life of your friend, this woman you mentioned, Alessandra Piero. Am I correct?"

Luke frowned. He realized that we had forgotten all about our host when the text arrived.

Chas came to me. I had put my shoes on and now he pulled me to my feet. His hands sought mine. "What kind of trouble are you in? Tell me and I might be able to help."

"What did Norman tell you?" I asked him.

"Only that the terrorist who killed and mummified that girl wants you to deliver the Screaming Mummy to him in exchange for Alessandra Piero's life."

Luke yanked me away from Chas and I stumbled into his arms. I gazed desperately into Luke's face. Did *he* believe him? But why would Chas know all of this if Norman hadn't told him? Unless—unless he was working for Tarek. Then Tarek would have told him.

"Luke, give me your phone."

"Why?" he asked releasing me.

"I need to call Norman."

There had been no time to contact him earlier. And if I knew Luke as well as I was certain I did, he would have avoided contacting his best friend until he was convinced that his best friend's woman was safe. He had promised that nothing would happen to me. He had promised he would never let me out of his sight. In less than twenty-four hours he had already broken that promise.

Luke withdrew his phone from his shirt pocket and located the number. What time was it in Toronto? What did it matter? I knew Norman would talk to me even if it were three o'clock in the morning.

No answer.

"He's probably on the jet already," Luke reassured me. "Hopefully he had no problem getting the mummy."

"And if he didn't get it?" I asked feverishly.

"Then we *pretend* that we have it. You had better answer that text."

I messaged that I was at a hotel, and that the Screaming Mummy was expected to arrive tomorrow. I promised that I would go to meet it at the airport and make arrangements to have it delivered to the museum by late afternoon. Oh, the irony of it all. Prince Pentawere had taken that lengthy journey overseas only to make a U-turn and come back to where he started. Tarek should have escaped with the mummy while it was still at the Cairo Museum. That made more sense. Of course, it *would* have been in processing for months before its trip to Canada. Security would have been stepped up. It would never have been left alone.

But I knew the real reason the terrorist thief had left it until now. He needed a reason to coerce me to Egypt. He knew Alessandra's rescue was imminent, and he wanted control over me. He wanted to monitor my every move. And this was the way to do it.

He texted me back.

If you are lying, your friend is dead.

CHAPTER 22

I shot a worried look at Luke. My phone dinged again, only this time it wasn't *my* phone. It was his.

"I'm at the airport," the text said. It was from Norman!

Thank goodness.

"You have the mummy?" Luke responded.

"Affirmative."

"Stay put. We're coming to meet you."

"Lucy's with you?"

"Yes."

"Why isn't she answering her phone?"

"Will bring you up to speed when we see you."

I grabbed Luke's phone from him and texted: *"I love you. Can't wait to wrap my legs around you."*

The return message read: "*Hope that was you, Lucy, and not Trevanian.*" He included a laughing emoji.

Luke looked at Chas. "Sorry to eat and run, Basseem. But we have a date with a mummy."

"Wait—You will need me if you wish to get that mummy through customs quickly."

That was true. But Luke's suspicious mind prevailed. "How do we know you were telling us the truth?"

Chas pointed to the phone that Luke cradled. "Call the

Frenchman. Ask him if what I told you was a lie."

Luke nodded. He instructed me to wait while he went inside to make the call.

I stood on the patio with Chas and directed my attention to the spilled wine.

"I did not poison the wine, Racine. Why would I do that?"

I desperately wanted to believe him. "Tell me the truth, Chas. *Are* you working for Tarek?"

"Why would I work for a terrorist?"

"Because you got fired from your high-profile job at the Ministry. You miss being in the spotlight."

"I have no desire to help the terrorists. They kill people." He stopped speaking and appraised me with genuine warmth. "Honestly, Racine. You know me. I am not that much of an opportunist. Those accusations against me were false. All I've ever wanted to do was bring history to life for the people. History tells us who we are, and what we can be. And tourism brings revenue to the country. *My* country. You have no idea what it's like because you live in a rich and prosperous nation. You don't know what it's like to have your economy tank because tourists are afraid to visit due to the threat of terrorism. When I was on top, when the people loved me, before this stupid incident with the theft of Egyptian antiquities by terrorists, I had raised my country to the top of Fodors' must-visit vacation spots."

At that moment I truly believed Chas thought he was descended from the pharaohs. But was he an accessory to any sort of crime?

He had been falsely accused once before. He was treated badly by the demonstrators at my museum. That was a stain on us. No one should be treated like that even if they were proven guilty. We were better than that.

"I believe you."

"Thank you, Lucy."

This was the first time he had ever called me Lucy.

A moment later Luke rejoined us. He shot a brief glance

Chas' way before he addressed his comments to me. "His story checks out. Norman sent him on ahead. Informed him of your situation, asked him to contact you. Everything happened exactly the way he told it. And exactly as we saw it on the video." He turned to Chas. "You're off the hook. Depardieu is having trouble at customs. We need your help."

Chas grabbed his hat from the table and went indoors to get his wallet and key fob while we followed. "I'm driving," he said. "I don't think we can trust anyone at this point."

I rolled my eyes at him. We were supposed to trust *him?*

"Which airport?" I asked Luke as we got into the car.

"Cairo International."

Apparently, the Syrian delegation—the cause of our flight's rerouting to Alexandria—had left the airport and entered the city. Cairo's private jet terminal had reopened for business.

It took us almost an hour to arrive because of traffic. We didn't need 'Ramy Basseem' after all. When the authorities heard the name Luke Trevanian they gave us special permission to head right onto the tarmac. Strange that it was so easy. Although Luke was a billionaire he was also a foreigner, and money could only buy privileges if you knew the right people. Nonetheless no one stopped us. And then I understood why. When we got there chaos met our eyes.

Norman was in handcuffs, the mummy had been confiscated, and Luke's plane had been impounded.

"What is the meaning of this?" the billionaire demanded. "*That* is my aircraft and *that* is my employee."

The customs officer and the security accompanying him paused from what they were doing. "Then *you* must be Dr. Trevanian. The man we are seeking. This mummy was reported stolen from the Royal Ontario Museum in Toronto where it was on loan from Cairo for a special exhibition."

Arianna wasn't kidding when she had forbidden us to go to Egypt on a rescue mission.

"I'll straighten this out," Luke said. He dug for his phone.

An authoritative hand clapped over his. "No phone calls until you have been processed. You must come with us."

"What about Norman? Monsieur Depardieu. You can't arrest *him!*" The outburst came from me.

"He was found in possession of the stolen item and will be held for questioning."

"NO!" I shrieked.

Norman wrestled out of the officer's grip. "Just one moment," he said to the Security that was ready to disable him with nightsticks. "I'll come with you. I just have to calm down my wife."

Wife? I nearly swooned. He gave me his 'play along' look. I knew he had called me his wife so that the officers would allow him to speak to me. They did, but warned that we only had three minutes.

"Uncuff me. Please. I am not going anywhere, I promise."

The officers glared skeptically at him, but he was acting so sincere and so passive that they gave in. Besides, the place was swarming with cops and security guards. There was nowhere to run.

I threw my arms around Norman's neck. I knew he could knock all four of those officials down with one blow if he wished, but that would only get him into deeper trouble. So he refrained.

"Lucy. I have to go with these men until we get things straightened out. Don't worry. Once Arianna knows why we did it, she'll come around. I don't think she wants half her team rotting in a jail cell in Egypt. Promise me you won't do anything impulsive while I'm gone."

I clung to him like a small child. I refused to let them take him away.

"Jesus, I wish I'd known the mummy was going to be a problem. I would have told Luke to keep you close and stay where you were. I cannot believe this is happening. Five minutes after I hung up with Luke they swarmed me. It's all right, honey. I won't be detained for long. Unfortunately, it looks like Luke is going to have to come with me. But they've got nothing on you so you are free to go. Do not do anything to make them change their minds. Do you hear me?"

Two policemen were making moves to take him away. Luke was already in their custody.

"My phone," he whispered, and his French accent thickened. *Fais moi juste un câlin.* "Give me a big hug, then swipe it out of my pocket—but discreetly. That way we will be in touch. Luke apprised me of what had happened *avec votre*— When I get hold of that craven terrorist bastard I will shove his phone down his throat. Meanwhile you can call Luke's phone with mine. I do not think they'll take his phone from him. My passcode is your surname spelled backwards."

I did as he bid, giving him an enormous, caressing hug until my hand covered the rectangle of his cellphone.

He gave the white silk tank top a tug at my back and ran his hand to my butt for good measure. Just to make it look good.

He kissed me hard on the lips. "Baby, do you ever look hot, in this thing." We put on an ace performance for any spectators, and the police dragged him away.

"Whatever you do, don't trust Cha—Ramy Basseem. I just got a text from Aras. Your friend Yasmine Lim, the curator that was supposed to open the exhibit…." The rest of what he wanted to tell me whimpered off into the wind.

I stood in the middle of the tarmac, flustered. What had Aras texted him that had changed his mind? He had reassured Luke just before we left the hotel that Chas was trustworthy. What had happened in the last three quarters of an hour? Why were the two even in touch?

Aras hadn't been able to get through to me and had contacted Norman.

It must be something important, something regarding Yasmine. How would Aras even know her?

I started after him but a security guard approached and advised me to leave.

I spun around to look for Chas. Where the dickens was he? When I got my hands on him I would wring his neck! Had he lied to me?

I scanned the airstrip for Luke but they had already brought him inside.

Now I stood on the tarmac alone.

In the near distance, by the grounded plane, Security was tagging the fuselage with yellow tape, and on the outer edge of one wing a familiar figure in a hoody briefly appeared, his dark glasses reflecting the glare of the sun.

I felt a dart of *déjà vu*. Aras? Was I seeing things? No, it couldn't be him. What would he be doing in Egypt?

When I blinked he was gone.

I almost ran in the direction where I had seen him last but that was among the plane's equipage. Already several security men noticed my fixation with the aircraft and showed signs of approaching. I made a split second decision and discreetly turned away. I had thrust Norman's phone into my bra so I had better get out of here before any of them noticed I had one unusually angular breast.

Private aircraft docked at Terminal 1. The gate led to Hall 4. I passed through the glass observation deck and looked down to see security and police officers around Luke's personal jet.

The boys had been taken inside to a detention center. I looked around me at the chrome elevators and balconied restaurants and bars. There were boutiques and potted palm trees, and recessed lighting in the ceiling. Everything glittered. A border of artificial turf surrounded an enormous fountain where visitors could toss coins. As I looked up I saw the familiar golden arches of McDonald's and a Burger King.

I know. Why was I admiring my surroundings? I wasn't. I was trying to calm down. And this was how I did it. I had to focus in order to get my heart to stop pounding. I had to find a way to pull my thoughts together instead of letting them fly every which way. My eyes landed on a unique jewelry stand. It was shaped like an Egyptian felucca with the figurehead of a woman that appeared to be a caricature of Cleopatra. It even had a mast and sails. The wooden bulwark supported a glass countertop. Behind the glass were gold and silver necklaces embedded with lapis lazuli, turquoise earrings, filigree bracelets, and all sorts of other colorful gemstones.

Funny, no matter how poor a nation was their airports always appeared rich.

Oh, what to do! I could wait and see if the boys were released (that could take hours or even days). Or I could go after Chas. But where would he have gone? Probably home to his ritzy hotel room. I had no clue where his real home was. Did he have a house? Did he live in Cairo or elsewhere? My best bet was to return to his hotel. If I was smart I would go back to collect my luggage. There was a gun in one of my bags. I was aching to feel the grip in my hand, to satisfy the urge to shoot something.

I get it. That doesn't sound like me, little Lucy Racine from the suburbs of Toronto. But over the past few months I had changed. I still believed that killing was wrong. But that didn't mean I couldn't blast off a round or two in a shooting range to break the tension. And if someone had a gun pointed at me—or someone I loved—I wasn't just going to stand still and do nothing.

I found a restaurant that was relatively empty. That was unusual for Egypt. This, however, *wasn't* Egypt. It was an airport. All airports around the world were like No Man's Lands.

I sat down and removed Norman's phone from my bra. I almost kissed it—I was so relieved to have this link to him. I listened to the ring at the other end, but then my call redirected to voicemail. The authorities must still be interrogating them.

I left the airport terminal, and followed the signs to Ground Transportation. Instead of hailing a taxi, I crossed over to the bus terminus to catch a shuttle into town. The queue where I waited was getting longer by the minute, and I tried the phone again. Still no answer from Luke. Or Johnny.

The authorities had probably denied Luke the use of his phone. As for Johnny—I had been waiting for a response to my text hours ago. Where was he? Why wasn't he replying?

My first stop would be Chas' hotel room. He owed me some answers.

Wait a minute. Now that I thought about it, maybe Chas had gone somewhere else. Maybe he had gone to Saqqara. He was filming his documentary at the Step Pyramid of Djoser. That was in Saqqara, was it not?

A quick search on Norman's phone showed that Saqqara was indeed the site of the Step Pyramid. And here was a link to Ramy Basseem's newest 'Astonishing Adventure'. He was searching for Cleopatra's tomb or at least her mummy (in Saqqara of all places!). From what I understood of her history, when the emperor Octavian conquered Egypt he chased Cleopatra and her lover Mark Antony out of the capital, and when they realized all was lost, they committed suicide. Her body was never found. Many archaeologists have attempted to solve the mystery. However, it was Ramy Basseem whose hope it was to enthrall the public with his latest documentary. He meant to put Egypt back on the map of top tourist destinations.

Just because a few historical figures hinted at Cleopatra's suicide, did it mean it was true? If she had committed suicide, where was the body? Who had discovered it? Shouldn't that also be in Plutarch's histories?

I shook my head, perplexed. Chas was always one for the books. He took the most sensationalistic theory and tried to manipulate it into the truth.

Furthermore, he speculated that Cleopatra was not the great beauty Hollywood made her out to be. Yes, she was brilliant, charismatic and a great stateswoman. But Elizabeth Taylor she was not. She might even have been a seductress—she certainly had all the qualities of a woman—but pretty? No.

I was wasting time. The romantic in me liked to envision her with goddess-like loveliness. But seriously, what did I care if Cleopatra was a great beauty or not? I needed a plan. I must make my next move, not stand here idly debating the physical assets of a dead queen.

Annoyed at how easily thoughts of Chas could distract me, I shoved Norman's phone into my pocket. Easy access was important should it ring. I must also keep it separate from Tarek's device.

Feet aching from remaining in one spot for so long, I shook off my thoughts and stepped out of the queue returning to Cairo.

As I strolled to the bus line headed for Saqqara, I shifted my long-strapped handbag from one shoulder to the other. With all the contraptions inside it, the bag was getting cumbersome.

Then, something struck me. Why was it *this* heavy? I suppose I had failed to notice earlier because I was too distraught. But now I was focused, and suddenly I realized that my purse was *unusually* heavy. A bulge in the side of the leather made me trace its outline suspiciously.

Aha!

While I had been appropriating Norman's phone, he in turn had slipped me his gun. I imagine it would be fishy for him to be found in possession of a firearm. It was safer to sneak it to me.

My hand searched inside the bag to confirm my guess. The pistol was there, and I allowed it to remain there. Egypt was not America. It was not the kind of place where a woman could display a firearm without being arrested.

The sun was hot. Where could I find shade without abandoning my spot in the queue? I might lose my seat on this bus, so I decided to lump it and suffer. The sun was broiling. I was near blinded by glare despite my sunglasses, which kept sliding down my nose. Sweat rolled along my cheeks, not from worry or anxiety but from heat. I was past the anxiety having much effect on my body. Every response now was a physical reaction to the discomfort of being exposed to the sun. Thank God I had thought to use sunscreen, but if I kept sweating like this the protection would be short-lived.

Was this what it was like to suffer from heatstroke? Or was I hallucinating? That man in black hoody and dark shades, near the taxi rank. Was he the same man I had spotted by Luke's plane?

I swear I would recognize those reflective lenses anywhere.

I was on the verge of joining him when a thought occurred to me.

This was really paranoid of me, but how could I take any chances? Tarek had spies everywhere. How could I be certain that the man was Aras?

Maybe I should just make that terrorist's phone disappear. I fetched it out of my purse. That at least would lighten the load somewhat. A garbage bin stood off to the side by the curb. My hand hovered over it indecisively. Would the dark-glassed, hooded peeping Tom react if I tossed the thing into the trash? Now I was scared. But that would tell me conclusively if he were the enemy.

"I wouldn't do that if I were you," a voice said from beside me.

My heart jumped. I clutched the phone as though dropping it would detonate a bomb.

CHAPTER 23

"Are you trying to give me the slip, Ms. Racine?"

I was petrified into silence. The man facing me was not Aras.

That didn't mean that he was a stranger. Oh, I knew him. I knew him all right. Broad shoulders and neck below the bearded chin. His familiar dark eyes and dense brows within a rough complexion were unforgettable. He wore army green, and it was easy to mistake him for one of the Egyptian guards.

He was the last person I hoped to see.

He had a gun aimed at me under his jacket. What I understood from this and all of our previous interactions was that he would spare my life until he had the mummy in his hands. That didn't make me feel a whole lot safer but at least he had no plan to kill me. Yet.

There was something about that mummy, something so important that he needed me alive.

"You are a slippery one, Mademoiselle. I cannot trust anyone to keep an eye on you. So, I decided to come myself." He glanced up at the bus stop sign. The words were in Arabic and English, and the letters spelled out the bus destination as Saqqara. "Going on a trip were you? Without my permission?"

A cellphone suddenly rang. Not his, nor the one being strangled in my clenched fist. No. The device making all the racket was the cellphone in my pocket. Norman's phone.

He squeezed my wrist until I dropped the old phone.

"Answer it," he ordered. He reminded me that he had a weapon, and that it was pointed at my chest.

I observed the tip of gunmetal glinting out from beneath his jacket, and despite uncontrollable trembling obeyed. I dug into my pocket and located Norman's phone. My voice as I spoke into it echoed the shaking of my hand. I hoped the caller was Luke or Norman. The sound of either of their voices would give me courage, and maybe I would be able to signal somehow that I was in trouble.

The caller was neither. It was Johnny, our long lost helicopter pilot, at last.

"Lucy?" The deep, calm voice of Johnny Sayid warbled in my ear.

I was not surprised when he spoke my name. Who else would have answered Norman's cellphone if not himself?

With all the excitement that had happened today, I had only sporadically thought of Johnny, if at all.

I paused before I acknowledged that it was me. Had he rented a helicopter to get around? There must be a way I could signal to him that I needed a spontaneous rescue.

During my pause, I was dragged into a quiet section of the bus station where a clump of planted palms cast shade.

With one hand gripping my free wrist, he guided me to where he wished me to stand, out of sight of the main hub. When I resisted, he raised the gun pushing it through the opening of his jacket into full view. As was typical in crowded places, no one noticed. Most people had their ear buds in and their faces down staring at their phone screens. We were well away from the row of painted lanes where the buses arrived to unload and receive new passengers, and although travellers frequently passed nearby, no one paid attention.

Behave as though everything is normal he warned with his eyes. With the index finger of his other hand he tapped the icon for the Speaker Phone.

Releasing my wrist, he tilted the nose of his weapon, a gesture that I talk.

What else could I do? I opened my mouth, gagged at how dry my tongue had become, and then said, "Johnny? You got my text?"

"Are you in Cairo? I waited for you at the airport in Toronto, but when you were a no-show—" He hesitated. "Lucy, are you okay? You sound funny."

I gave a rundown on our flight and our trip into town, carefully skipping the details. I tried to act normal. I swallowed the lump in my throat and wiped the sweat from my damp left palm on my skirt.

My abductor would shoot me if I screamed for help. By this time his gun was in full view. He no longer bothered to hide it inside his jacket. And I sized it up in three seconds flat. I was an old hand at recognizing the make of firearms by now. It was clear that the thing aimed at me was a revolver, and that it was fitted with a silencer. Ironically, I was equally certain that even if he shot me in this very public place, no one would notice. Ear buds in, heads down. Phones on. No—nobody would notice.

"Anyway," Johnny said. "Trevanian didn't answer when I called so I left a message with his voicemail. I decided to call Depardieu too. How is it that you have his phone? And what happened to yours? You were the first person I tried to contact."

He sounded light-hearted, very uncharacteristic of him. Had he found a lead on Alessandra's whereabouts? If he had he *must*, absolutely *must,* keep silent about it. If Tarek knew that Sayid had located his hostage he would move her before there was a chance to free her.

I wanted to ask where he was, but in my present predicament that would put him in danger.

"I found something, Lucy," Johnny went on, before

falling silent. Was he puzzled by my lack of response? "I am not going to waste time explaining. This is something you and the team need to see in person. I can't even begin to describe it. It is so incredible. It will blow all the current theories sky-high… "

What could this thing possibly be? The terrorist was alert, ears open. I hoped to high heaven that Johnny would keep from blurting it out.

His voice broke into my thoughts. "I can't do this over the phone. There is more, oh, so much more to tell you. I swear, Lucy, you will have to see it to believe it." He paused to sample my reaction. When my response was only silence he said, "*And*—I am almost one hundred percent certain that Tarek is neck deep in it."

My eyes involuntarily shot upward. The gaze of the terrorist pierced mine. Although it was impossible to judge his thoughts I only prayed that mine were equally opaque.

You mean Tarek is stealing Egyptian antiquities? What did he want with Egyptian antiquities? My eyes flitted away. I was desperate to avoid his gaze because he could hear everything we said, and it was imperative that he not read my face. In the past, terrorists had trafficked Syrian artifacts to raise funds to support the government takedown in Damascus. That however had failed. So what was the newest plot?

"Lucy? Are you there?"

"Yes. I'm sorry. I was thinking."

Did he have any idea why Tarek wanted Egyptian relics? If he did, I begged fervently that he would stay mum.

"Tell me what happened to you, Lucy. Where are the guys and why are you not answering your own phone?"

Tarek caught my eyes when I said nothing. He mouthed at me to stick to the truth. I spoke nervously about the Arab driver and my misadventure on the train resulting in the loss of my phone. And then I recounted the monitoring of my every move through a substitute device. I made a concerted effort to control my trembling while an evil smile spread across my captor's face. He wanted me to divulge all the horrors I had experienced since I landed in Cairo.

"Oh my god, Lucy. I was right to dissuade you from coming with me."

"Well, it's too late now. I'm here." My greatest desire was to explain what had happened with the Screaming Mummy, and our trouble with the airport authorities. But every word we spoke was overheard.

"Get rid of that jihadist's phone immediately," Johnny said. "He has nothing on you now." A pause, a long pause as he wondered why I waited to speak.

And then he relayed the wonderful and totally unexpected news.

"Piero is safe."

Alessa was safe! But how? My stomach did a triple flip. When had she escaped? I turned my lowered lashes upward and saw my abductor smirk.

Alessandra had escaped and I was in the clutches of the evilest man on earth.

I gulped, and my heart leaped with horror, and at the moment nothing else Johnny said could possibly register in my brain. Thank God Alessa was free, but what was going to happen to *moi?*

"Can I talk to her?" I whispered.

I hadn't meant to whisper but my heart was racing so fast I could no longer speak without sounding breathless.

"Now is not a good time. I just wanted to touch base with you in case we lose the signal. She just went through a deep tunnel and is expecting me to follow. Lucy, are you sure you're all right. Your voice… Oh the devil take it—my phone is dying, Lucy… Any minute I could lose the signal. I am going to have to talk fast. But don't worry about Piero. She's fine."

It was typical of Alessandra Piero to follow her lead rather than concern herself with personal affairs. She must have been aware that we were worried sick about her. She however was a professional and she acted like a professional.

The job came first. And our feelings came last. Then it struck me. Where were they? What tunnel was he referring to?

"We will figure out what's going on here. With Piero free we don't need to put you in jeopardy. Tarek still has it in for you. I have a feeling he won't quit until you are dead. I don't want to put you in danger. Norman will never forgive me. Go home, Lucy. Please."

Too late, I wanted to say.

Tarek gave me a deadpan face, and made a threatening gesture with the gun. He would kill me if I revealed his presence to Johnny. Desperately, I wished to explain that I had seen Norman, here—at the airport. But I dared not expose the fact that Norman was in Cairo.

"Remove yourself, Lucy. Catch the next flight out. Don't even bother to pack."

Whatever he had found, it sounded important. Explosive. With the boys detained by the Egyptian authorities, and Johnny and Alessandra elsewhere, I was alone—alone with Nizar Tarek.

"Lucy, get out of Cairo. Go home. I can't talk anymore; the signal is practically gone…" The last bit of what he had to say cut off.

"Hello? Johnny? Johnny are you there?"

CHAPTER 24

My last link to safety was gone.

Tarek took the phone from me, pried the protective cover off and dropped it to the ground. He smashed the precious piece of technology onto the concrete pavement, and watched my face dissolve into despair. The broken pieces rattled and rolled. I had a sudden urge to burst into tears. Somehow I managed to keep control. For theatrical effect he squashed the toe of a combat-booted foot on the pitiful remains before locking eyes with me.

"You disobeyed instructions. You brought your friends with you."

"What does it matter," I grumbled, glancing down at the cellphone carnage. I irrationally wanted to retrieve the handset to see if it still functioned. "You were always going to kill me."

He scattered the fragments with a well-placed boot. "Yes. But I still want the mummy. Where is it?"

Despite my pulsing heart I scowled. "It's been detained by airport authorities."

"Why?"

"Because we had to steal it out of the Royal Ontario Museum's exhibit." Like he had to ask. I almost openly scoffed at him. And would have—had I been less scared.

"It is here?" He pointed in the direction of the airplane hangars.

He knew way too much. He no longer needed me. He could get a gang of thugs to raid the airport for the confiscated item tonight.

He pulled me deeper into the shadows and I thrust my hand into my purse. He was faster than me, and he knew my intent.

He grabbed my arm and twisted it up behind my back. "You have a gun in your purse, do you?"

I shook my head, croaked, "No."

"Tsk—tsk—tsk. *Bitch.*" His Arab accent had devolved into crude American invectives. "Motherfucking little bitch. And after we had such a nice dinner together in Aleppo. I treated you well, did I not? But instead of paying the ransom your people broke into my camp, rescued you and thwarted my plans." He stopped to breathe. "And then you had the balls to shoot me."

You tried to kill Norman! I had the sense to keep this outburst contained.

"I did not wish it to end like this, my dear. I had big plans for you after I received the mummy. Do you wish to hear what they were? I want you to suffer the way you made me suffer. Only worse. I had plans to mummify you alive, the same way I mummified your young friend. What was her name?"

"Ines," I whispered.

"Yes, Ines. You should have heard her scream. She must have screamed for hours before she died. How I would have thrilled to see the same for you. But I have no time. I need that mummy, and can waste no more time on a worthless American woman."

I am not American I wanted to holler. But what difference would it make. A westerner was a westerner to him.

"Your services are no longer required." I doubled over

as he shoved his revolver deep into my ribs.

"You need me to authenticate it," I squeaked.

"I am beginning to think—no—I *know*—you are too much trouble. It is time to say goodbye."

We were in a bustling, outdoor bus terminus. Did he mean to shoot me here?

A denser, shorter clump of palms grew off to the side and he towed me into their shade. "*Adieu*, Ms. Racine," he said. "I have not enjoyed knowing you—at all."

I squeezed my eyes shut when I realized there was nothing I could do but scream.

A thud came loud and hard, and the vile jihadist lost his balance and possession of the gun. I dived for it. Whatever or whoever had hit him struck again but this time he was ready. He ducked out of reach, did a quick forward roll, and ran like an antelope into the parking lot, minus his weapon.

In my fury I paid no attention to my rescuer. My only thought was revenge. That man—no, *beast*—had caused me so much suffering. I yanked myself up from where I had fallen scrambling for the renegade firearm. I was furious. I had allowed myself to be caught. Now nothing but payback would do. My sole focus landed on the fleeing terrorist that I now sought through skewed sunglasses.

One well-placed shot, and I could bring him down forever.

Where were his thugs? I glanced wildly from side to side. They could have finished the job by now. But he had none. He had genuinely come after me alone.

I nudged my lopsided shades into position with a knuckle. Tarek had wasted no time locating his vehicle. He slithered like a frightened lizard into a black SUV. Before the car door slammed shut, the vehicle raced off the parking lot.

At the time I thought nothing of the fact that he had dived into the backseat. One of his brutes must be driving the getaway car. But somewhere in the back of my mind the profile of the driver's grim face sparked a memory. Uncertainty hovered, while instinct told me decidedly that it was a woman. A woman I knew.

If they meant to return and run me down, they had another think coming. I leaned forward with the revolver doubled-fisted in my hands. It was too big for me and felt awkward in my grip. Nonetheless I was ready to riddle their tires full of holes.

I jumped as blunt fingernails reached around and clawed my arm. I spun in holy terror and aimed.

"Aras!" I croaked.

I could have punched him! It was Aras of the mysterious texts, and the one who had knocked the revolver out of Tarek's grip. He had been keeping watch over me all along. I was never in danger. I threw my arms, gun and all, around his neck and squeezed, hooking the hoody from his head.

"Ow," he said. The exclamation was followed by a chuckle. Then I saw who it really was.

I stood stupefied as my brain sorted out my mistake.

How had he escaped the authorities and where was Luke? The hoody no longer covered his hair or any part of his face; it had dropped to his broad shoulders. Now that I saw him up close, I would have recognized those reflective lenses anywhere. They *did* belong to Aras, but it wasn't *he* who was wearing them.

"Goddammit, Norman," I said. "I nearly shot you." I slammed my arms around him again and this time my body melted into his." I was so relieved that my heart clenched and my breath labored. He engulfed me in a powerful embrace and kissed me on the lips.

In those long hours we'd been apart I had forgotten how strong he was.

"Let me go, Norman," I gasped. "Before you break something." A few seconds passed while I caught my breath. Then I bombarded him with questions. "What are you doing here? How did you know where to find me? What happened with Luke?"

Norman's back was to any spectators so it was unlikely they had witnessed anything improper. Perhaps now is not the best time to reiterate, but Egypt like all Middle Eastern countries require modesty for women. Kissing and hugging in public between men and women is a no-no. But as mentioned earlier, the addictiveness of the cellphone had most people pretty much oblivious of their surroundings. Even in an unpredictable country like Egypt the populace felt secure enough to keep their ear buds in and their faces glued to their screens.

Maybe one or two people from a nearby bus queue had glanced up at the scuffle. But even had they the interest, nothing of what we discussed would have been audible. Public displays of affection, however, that was another matter. Best to leave the hanky-panky for the privacy of a hotel room.

"A thank-you would be nice," Norman said. He wrested the terrorist's revolver from me, shoved it under the hoody into the waistband of his pants, and smirked. "Maybe I should keep this?"

Fine with me.

Regardless of his casual attitude something was on his mind. The French inflection was obvious in his voice, and he was also in a bit of a hurry. I was still stunned by how much he resembled the Syrian freedom fighter in that hoody and those sunglasses. He took my hand and urged me to follow.

An open jeep sat in the parking lot. I assumed it belonged to Aras. We crossed the hot pavement, where tall weeds were growing through the cracks, and I swung open the passenger door. His gaze glanced off my legs where the fabric of my turquoise, white and black floral skirt had split at the side, exposing my thighs as I tentatively lowered myself onto the sun-scorched seat. He inhaled hard. "What were you doing wearing *that* at Basseem's hotel?"

He had a point. Why *was* I dressed like this?

As his eyes rolled up to stare at me for a long few seconds I scrambled for an answer, then he clasped his broad palms on both sides of my face and kissed me. When released I choked for breath. Again.

"Top up or top down." He was referring to the jeep, not my tank top.

Not that it mattered, although top up was preferable. I had had enough of the sun, and felt really and truly fried. Typical Norman to always consider my comfort and wellbeing, no matter the circumstances.

However, that did nothing for the guilt that suddenly swamped me.

"I was on my way back to see—uh—Basseem—" I stopped. He knew the two were one and the same; there was no point in pretending. I corrected myself by saying calmly, "I was returning to find *Chas* when I was ambushed."

"No doubt." He turned from where he had placed his hands on the steering wheel and glanced my way.

The guilt suddenly felt overwhelming. I glared at him. *No doubt?* He knew I was on my way to see Chas?

"How did you get away?"

He shot a downward look at the clothes he was wearing, unfazed by my diversion. "Apparently you recognized the getup." He patted his chest.

"I *did* think you were Aras." I pointed to the reflective sunglasses. "Those are definitely his."

He shoved them up over his forehead to see me better before saying, "He made an appearance at the airport shortly after Luke and I were detained."

So I *wasn't* hallucinating. That *was* Aras I saw hiding by Luke's plane.

"They put us in a detention cell. Aras managed to sneak in posing as one of the engineers assigned to scour the jet for further contraband. After Security left us alone, he managed to get access to us and switched clothes with me. I had no problem getting out."

I am not going to question why engineers dress like hoods in Egypt. I suppose they only put on their work duds after they arrive at the airport.

The two were almost the same height and build. Norman was just a bit more bulked up but the hoody was stretchy.

"Aras did *that?* For *you?*"

"I always told you he was a decent guy. But he had other reasons. I won't get into it at present. Right now we need to hook up with the team."

"But when the authorities return to question you, won't they notice the miraculous change in your appearance?"

"That's *their* problem. Aras made the suggestion. And I wasn't about to argue. We all agreed that your safety took precedence."

I plastered him feverishly with kisses. I loved this man so much I think my heart would break if he didn't return my affections right here, right now. I locked my arms around the back of his neck and pressed my chest to his. Why-oh-why-oh-why didn't he ask me to marry him? I would—in an instant.

He nipped at my ear. "Much as I'd love to do the nasty with you, sweetheart, this jeep is not the best place. We are in the middle of a very public locale."

People loaded down with luggage were coming and going from their cars. I giggled into his throat, gave him one last squeeze and dropped back.

We disentangled our clasped hands—much to my regret. I knew my man, and things were on his mind. He was prioritizing and compartmentalizing, and he hoped I was oblivious to his cerebral machinations.

"What about Luke?" I asked slumping into my seat. "What will happen with him and Aras?"

Norman adjusted his own seat to avoid replying. I wanted answers, I insisted on answers, and addressed his silence by responding to my questions myself. "He'll be out as soon as Arianna drops the charges. And she *will*—once she understands that Luke authorized the loan of the mummy."

I *had* to believe that Arianna would drop the charges. I *had* to believe that she would step up and do the right thing, explain the misunderstanding to the Egyptian authorities and free her ex and his half-brother.

Norman shook his head. He dropped the sunglasses over his eyes, pressed the ignition and placed his hands on the steering wheel. He shot a look out the rear window and backed out of the parking space. "That woman has no power to drop the charges."

A thrill of fear impaled me. How could that be? They *had* to get out. "I can't believe she would allow Luke and Aras to rot in a foreign jail." And when I say Aras I really mean Norman. The authorities were under the delusion that they had the billionaire's bodyguard in custody, and would have reported their names to our boss.

"What choice does she have?" Norman replied. "She has no jurisdiction over that artifact. In hindsight I would say that sneaking the mummy back here was a dumb move on our part. Especially without the boss's permission."

"How did you manage that by yourself?"

"Money speaks. Luke opened up his bank account. All sorts of rats crawl out of the woodwork if the price is right."

He pulled out of the parking lot and turned onto the main drag. I had no idea where he planned to take us. At the moment I hardly cared. As long as I was with my man—and far away from the terrorists and their nefarious plans to torture me—I was in paradise.

But what about Piero and Sayid?

"Do you think Alessandra is safe?" I asked. It did not occur to me at the moment that Norman might be unaware of her escape. I only knew how vengeful Tarek was. I wouldn't put it past him to hunt her down just to punish me.

"*She* is irrelevant to the extremist cause. They want *you*."

I frowned at him, unhappy with his answer.

Norman cut me off as I opened my mouth to argue. "Piero was a foolproof way of luring you to Cairo," he argued. "We never should have taken the bait."

"He could have just nabbed me at the airport when we arrived. He didn't."

"You came accompanied. But he did try to get rid of

your 'chaperone,' didn't he?"

Norman turned his eyes back to the road. Although his emotions were in turmoil he was masking them well.

I decided to change the subject. "What is Aras' part in this diabolical scheme? How did he come to be here? Surely he must have told you something about his plan?"

Then it occurred to me that while hiding, Aras must have seen the whole shebang go down. He must have witnessed the confiscation of the Screaming Mummy, the impounding of his brother's jet, *and* the arrests.

Norman removed his hand from the steering wheel and gave my arm a reassuring caress. The deep rumble of his voice was as soothing as his touch. "Don't worry, honey. Our guys are far from being idiots. They'll figure something out."

It was true. They would. I knew they would. Now that Alessandra was out of danger, my personal mission was to determine who else was implicated in the terrorist plot.

What *was* the plot? As I examined Norman's profile it dawned on me that if anyone had figured it out, Aras had. And maybe, just maybe he had shared his findings.

The top was up on the jeep, but the windows were wide open; the sun was still grill temperature and the wind was cooling me. He was driving fast. We were outside the city limits heading towards the desert.

I clutched at my hair as it whipped across my eyes. "Where are we going?"

"To Abusir."

"Why?"

"Isn't that where you were headed when I found you in that awkward situation by the buses?" The dark, reflective lenses of the borrowed sunglasses shifted from the highway to my face, and I knew Norman was laughing at me. It was just like him to make light of a grave situation in order to ease my anxieties.

"Well, that just happens to be where I am headed as well. I have a reservation at the Sakkara Inn."

"Oh, going on vacation, are you?" I teased. His sexy

French accent was seducing me into a light banter. Now that I was safe and in the company of the love of my life I could relax. "Just when did you make this reservation, and why wasn't I included? Or do you have a mistress on the side?"

He flashed me a grin, then returned his attention to the road. The traffic leaving and entering the airport had dissipated, and the route to the desert empty. The absence of traffic had to do with the time of day. It was approaching sundown. Norman demanded a burst of speed from the engine as he slapped down his right foot. He pretended to ignore my remark regarding the mistress, and said brightly, "We are meeting Sayid and Piero there—although they don't yet know it. Aras was supposed to rendezvous with them prior to our switching identities. I am taking his place."

He scratched his head energetically, releasing a sprinkle of sand from his hair. Affectionately, I dusted his shoulder with a lingering hand. He must have collected that earth sample during the recent brawl.

"Besides, I hate staying in Cairo. Too much riffraff." Was he referring to Tarek—or maybe to Chas? "I much prefer it in the village."

A notion occurred to me as I let my hand fall away. When had he become aware of Alessandra's escape? Had *I* mentioned it? My puzzled expression must have triggered his next comment.

"I just learned about Piero an hour ago—from Aras. Honestly, Lucy. I can read you like a map. You seriously think I would have allowed you to come to Egypt had I known she was free?"

"How did she escape?" I demanded. Something more urgent popped into my mind. "Wait a minute. How is *Aras* involved in all of this?"

"Oh, so much drama, baby. It's really pretty simple. Alessandra Piero is a former Interpol agent. She is also a current member of ISORE. If you really want to know how she escaped—" A scowl suddenly collapsed his brow. "—Ask the boss."

At first his insinuation infuriated me. Our boss knew all along that Alessandra would escape? That was why she had forbidden us to rescue her? What was going on? Why had she kept her plans secret?

"Norman."

"Ask the *boss*," he pressured.

"But you're keeping something from me. Tell me. *Is* Aras working for her?"

He guffawed and we almost spun off the highway. He righted the wheel and said, "Stop making jokes. Aras—working for ISORE? Don't make me laugh. Or next time I might not be quick enough to steer us back onto the road."

He glanced at my baffled expression. "Really, Lucy. Of all people, you should know better than that."

All joking aside, the next time he spoke his voice was serious. "The only concern that that soldier has is the restoration of his country."

He floored the gas to punctuate his statement and the highway flashed by.

I, however, was far from finished with the subject. Okay. Maybe Aras wasn't working for Arianna, but he knew a lot more about the inner workings of ISORE than he should. Me, I could understand being left out of the loop, but Luke? Never. And what Luke knew Norman knew. Unfortunately, Aras wasn't here to verify.

"And how is Syria concerned with an ancient Egyptian mummy?"

His answer was decisive muteness.

Why was he being so close-mouthed? What was Arianna up to, and why not trust her own team? My next words were swept away with the wind. Talking at this point was futile. But that didn't stop my mind from going a mile a minute. The only one of us the boss trusted was Alessandra Piero—and maybe the Syrian freedom fighter, Aras. *Why Aras?*

My brain was wearying, my thoughts convoluted. Surely the mystery had to be much simpler than it appeared?

It all began with the text in Toronto.

Do not scream when you see the mummy.

How did Aras know about the death and mummification of Ines? And why so interested in the problems of the Screaming Mummy? Like I said before, Prince Pentawere's dried up corpse had only modest value as a historical relic. But as a political instrument: was *that* its value?

After all we had been through together we should not be second-guessing each other. I glanced involuntarily at my bare left-hand ring finger. It occurred to me then that I was keeping just as many secrets from Norman as he was keeping from me. Was that why he hadn't asked me yet?

Love required a leap of faith, he had said.

Was I not able to make that leap of faith?

CHAPTER 25

For most tourists to Egypt a visit to the pyramids means ogling Giza's famous monuments, namely the Sphinx and the Great Pyramid of Giza (one of the Seven Wonders of the Ancient World), but thirty kilometers north of Cairo sits the vast necropolis of Saqqara the birthplace of pyramid building. Constructed nearly 5,000 years before our time, the Step Pyramid is the landscape's most prominent feature and a magnificent reminder of the early architecture of the pharaohs, and one of the Old Kingdom's special landmarks.

This pyramid is the tomb of third dynasty ruler Djoser and was built by the architect Imhotep. For its time, the Step Pyramid was a revolutionary advancement in architecture, and became the prototype that the great pyramid builders of the future emulated. Not surprisingly, it is the oldest pyramid in Egypt.

My first impression was that it was massive and indeed built to resemble stairs leading to heaven. It had six tiers and stood sixty meters high. It was constructed from quarried sedimentary rock, and at the present time, one third of it was covered in scaffolding. From where we stood the scaffolding was only visible from one side. I assumed all of this was part of Chas' efforts to stabilize the monument.

But let me backtrack for a moment because we were supposed to meet Sayid and Piero at the hotel.

Our teammates were not at the Sakkara Inn when we arrived. I had used the public phone in the lobby to contact Johnny's cellphone, but was sent straight to voicemail. I was surprised that Abusir even had cellphone service. The village was close to the necropolis, which was in the middle of the desert. The nearest city was Cairo and yet it was still over an hour drive by car. The nearby village of Abusir was a new tourist haunt, but it was unlikely there would be a signal tower there; or maybe I was wrong, and there were towers all over the desert. The world had changed; everyone was dependent on cellphones.

The proprietor had informed us that our friends were probably visiting the sights, the nearest of which was the Step Pyramid of Djoser, so here we were. Of the helicopter pilot and the ex Interpol agent however there was no sign.

Norman pulled up on the packed sand just short of a cluster of fallen sandstone blocks and we exited the jeep. He lit up a cigarette as we gazed at the amazing scene glowing in the sunset. I frowned at him and he gave me an impish smile. He had promised to quit.

The sun was low. Thin wisps of pink cloud swept across the deep blue sky. The air was still very warm and dry, but the breeze was welcoming. We had less than an hour before dusk.

The site, like all archaeological sites, was amazing, and looked exactly like any of the Internet photos I had ever seen of it. When I was a young intern at the Egyptian Museum in Cairo, I had missed the opportunity to visit.

The pyramid sits at the center of a thirty-seven acre complex surrounded by a recessed limestone wall containing thirteen fake doorways. The original entrance is on the southeast side. Where we currently stood, a second, wider entrance, leading through the Mortuary Temple and a multiple-pillared colonnade, gave access on the north face.

Off to one side there was evidence of an on-going

excavation. Chas's handiwork I presumed. Two rows of mummies had been partially unearthed, each containing at least twelve individuals with their heads exposed. Why hadn't he bothered to unearth their bodies? At first glimpse the ghoulish sight sent chills down my spine. Maybe he figured they were irrelevant to his search for Cleopatra. They had been dried in the sun until they looked like human-shaped pieces of leather with desiccated faces, and from their homogenous arrangement and lack of grave goods it was obvious that none were of royal lineage. Oddly, the heads were all turned in the same direction facing north, sending my attention to the peak of the pyramid.

"Interesting. They all seem to be looking up," I remarked.

Just to be clear, Djoser's pyramid was unlike later pyramids, and was constructed in layers of stone blocks. Each level was solid and according to archaeologists, the pyramid had been built and rebuilt several times before it took on its current configuration. The tombs and tunnels were underground, and the solid pyramid sat on top.

As we lingered outside, admiring the colonnade and temple, Norman cautioned me to be careful. Much of the structure was crumbling, and not only did scaffolding cover the exterior, but also parts of the interior walls were shored up with giant inflated air bags.

Despite precautions the monument was still in danger of collapsing. The complex was unstable. Tourists were no longer permitted inside. That meant the moment we stepped over the threshold we were trespassing.

Norman discarded the half-smoked cigarette on the sand at the entrance, in front of the yellow caution tape, and buried it with his boot.

He was dressed in borrowed army fatigues beneath the black hoody. He removed the top outer garment, revealing a gorgeously fit upper torso in tight olive drab t-shirt, and shoved the sunglasses into his pocket. He passed the hoody to me, bringing the smell of tobacco with it.

"You may want to put that on. You're not exactly dressed for spelunking."

He was correct. And it wasn't out of respect for the dead that he suggested I wear the hoody. Aside from the fact that bare arms and cleavage were a no-no in sacred places, it was dirty and rough in here, and I had little to protect my exposed skin. I stupidly still sported the white silk tank top and black, white and turquoise floral, ankle-length skirt. It was a wonder they had not arrested me at the airport. Ordinarily, I would have covered up but distraction had overwhelmed my good sense, causing me to forget. They had taken me for a tourist, and all ignorant female tourists dressed something like this.

Norman patted my hip and smiled. Inappropriately, I felt a surge of desire. This man smelled of smoke and sand and diesel oil and I was still turned on.

"What's with the long face?" he asked.

"You stink of cigarettes. And it annoys me that the way you smell makes me want to dry hump you."

He laughed. But he knew beneath the sarcastic humor I was seriously concerned.

"I want to quit, Lucy. For *you*. But this isn't the best time to go cold turkey." He stepped over the yellow caution tape.

"I know. I'm sorry."

As Norman gestured for me to follow, I glanced down at my running-shoed feet. Fortunately, after the 'poisoned wine' incident I'd had the sense to request my Sketchers. That was when Chas went to fetch my shoes. The thought of him brought a sharp pang of suspicion—could he really have tried to poison me?

I rolled up the sleeves to free my hands, and paused for a moment from zipping up the oversized hoody. Then I ducked under the yellow caution tape in Norman's wake.

A long flight of steps led from the courtyard of the Mortuary Temple to the beginning of a passageway ten meters below the ground. It then continued more or less straight. The vast, gloomy shaft was filled with scaffolding, and, as I had been warned, at the far end two giant air bags supported the ceiling. It was true then; any minute the roof could cave in over our heads.

Chas was documenting his search for Cleopatra, featuring himself as the star of the show; and as far as he was concerned, the more danger the better. They didn't call his series '*The Astonishing Adventures of Ramy Basseem* for nothing.

"Watch your step," Norman cautioned as he raised the flashlight's beam from floor to ceiling. "There hasn't been any maintenance in here for decades."

Signs of humanity materialized as we followed the path where bare light bulbs connected to a generator hung from the scaffolding. The lights were off, but Norman flicked a switch and they blinked on. The bulbs were spaced quite far apart and sent just enough light to see by. He doused his flashlight to conserve the battery.

On the ground the odd article of clothing and empty water bottles littered the floor. Was this evidence of the film crew? And yet there was no sign of film equipment, and no voices.

I grabbed Norman by the sleeve of his t-shirt to detain him. "Before we go a step further you need to answer some questions."

Stubbornly, I swung to position my body in front of the shaft he meant to explore.

"When Aras showed up at the airport he must have told you why he was in Egypt. I can only piece together one reason why he is here. He is also after the Screaming Mummy. Why, Norman? Why is he so interested in the Screaming Mummy?"

"I thought you wanted to join up with Sayid and Piero."

He was trying to sidetrack me, and that was annoying.

"I do. But I don't think they're here."

"Oh?"

"Come off it. Stop beating around the bush. Give me some answers. *Is* he working with the team?"

He hesitated. Then answered, "All right. I believe so."

"But Johnny said nothing to me—"

"That is because—when he discovered what was going on only a couple of hours ago—he decided he wanted you out of it. *I* want you out of it." His voice sounded tight. He was fighting the emotion. "*Zut*, Lucy. You're in danger."

I reached out a hand to reassure him. And turned on my cocky persona. Now was not the time to get soft or he would drag me kicking and screaming onto the first flight back to Toronto.

"Tarek wants me dead. So what else is new?" I said lightly. "But before that, he originally needed to get me to do something. I just don't know what it is. It had something to do with the mummified prince."

In the ensuing silence I imagined Norman's brain cells whirling like a centrifuge. "He's skeptical whether the mummified prince is actually the prince. It's been stolen before, and replicated, *and* recovered, and at this point the authorities should be questioning its authenticity yet they sent it off to the ROM's exhibition anyway."

"You are telling me things I am already aware of," I complained.

"Yeah?" He sounded slightly miffed. Was Norman not as informed as I thought he was? He shrugged. "Well, it was news to me."

"Why is Aras in Egypt? The truth."

I knew he was aware of the reason that had brought Aras to Egypt—he had to be. Aras must have given him some excuse when he rescued him from airport jail.

With all the cryptic texting I had gotten the impression that *I* was Aras' confidant, not Norman. What had happened to change things?

He sighed. Did I not say he could read my thoughts? "*You* happened, Lucy. Aras should never have mixed you up in this."

"Mixed me up in what? And why are you suddenly best buds with him?"

"Us, best buds? Hardly. But when he saw how his actions had tangled you up in events that you had no business being in—and how he had endangered your life—he contacted me. Call it guilt, call it whatever. I was pissed at him and let him know it."

"That's why you let him switch places with you."

"That's why I *insisted* on it."

I fell silent for a moment. The heroism of this man never failed to amaze me. No wonder I was head-over-heels in love with him. I glanced over. "So, why *is* he in Egypt?"

"You wouldn't believe me if I told you."

This time I grabbed his bare arm. "It's *me*, Norman. I *always* believe you."

He smiled. "Okay. Maybe Aras *is* here for a purpose. And so is Piero. Did you not think it was strange that the boss made no plans to have her rescued?"

I had always thought that strange. Arianna had not confided in any of us. Or had she? Maybe it was only me that had been cut out of her confidence—me and perhaps Johnny?

"And how is it you are suddenly privy to executive decisions?" I asked.

"Did I say that? What I meant was—I know something big is going down. And so does she. Unfortunately, it is going down in the next twenty-four hours so we don't have much time."

"Stop talking like a spy. What is it? What exactly is going down?"

He went quiet. My curiosity spiked. Unless he was some kind of clairvoyant I had the feeling he had been inside this tomb before. When? *When* was he here before?

It seemed he had no intention of explaining anything yet. He nudged me with the palm of his hand. Indicated for me to step aside. He leaned into the shaft that I had been blocking, and listened. I followed his example. Only a hollow echo, like the sounds of our own breathing, came from deep inside the tomb's numerous passageways. Some of these were looter's tunnels, and created a confusing maze.

He started forward and I re-rolled the hoody's long sleeves which were slowly unraveling themselves before I hurried behind him.

It was only after we were in the tunnel that I realized he had successfully diverted me again.

His back was to me and he wouldn't hear me talk unless I shouted. Frustrated but resigned I dragged myself on.

We navigated a lengthy, twisting passageway. Parts of it were very narrow, especially where it turned. As we progressed further I kept getting tripped up by the bulk of the hoody as it snagged against the rough walls.

We continued to descend.

Finally, we reached the subterranean floor.

CHAPTER 26

I straightened from my hunched position, and watched the dust rise with me. The air had the smell of dried mud and antiquated dust. I stretched my spine, then my knees, and flexed my toes, as I rubbed my hamstrings and stood at my full height before arching the kinks out of my neck. Negotiating a tunnel stooped over was backbreaking work.

A vacuous dome made almost entirely of solid granite surrounded us.

On the floor was a tumble of limestone blocks with five pointed stars shallowly carved onto their surfaces. Above us irregular cavities appeared broken in the stone. These were inlays, and at some point in the past they had worked themselves loose, and had fallen from the ceiling.

School history lessons reemerged in my mind. In almost all cultures, the king was associated with the eternal North Stars.

"Are the film crew still here?" I whispered.

"I doubt it. No jeeps outside. No equipment inside. No one is allowed in the interior of this pyramid due to its precarious condition. But I believe Sayid and Piero are somewhere around here."

Clearly, the 'No Visitors Allowed' rule was not

enforced. *We* were here. And the film crew had recently left the location.

What I knew of the scale of Djoser's tomb alone meant that finding our friends without cellphone service was going to be a humungous task. The pyramid was part of a mortuary complex designed to inspire awe. With the main structures combined—the Step Pyramid, the House of the North, the House of the South, the Serdab, the Heb Sed Courtyard, the South Tomb, Temple T, and the Northern Mortuary Temple—the site was the size of an ancient Egyptian city.

The task was near impossible, not knowing exactly where to search, but Norman was preoccupied by something other than locating our teammates.

The thing he meant to show me—what was it? Because naturally I assumed that that was what this trek was all about. I looked about curiously and stopped to listen. If ever Johnny and Alessandra were here, they had made themselves scarce.

"I don't hear anyone," I said.

He shone his flashlight on a broken granite sarcophagus.

Now I realized our location. We had reached the inside chambers of the tomb where the king's body was laid to rest. All of those underground corridors with rooms branching off had been filled with thousands of stone vessels inscribed with the names of earlier kings. They were meant to protect the body and the grave goods of the pharaoh. Those efforts, however, had been wasted. Over the centuries grave robbers had done their worst, and when I looked inside the damaged sarcophagus even the royal body was missing.

Was this what Norman had wanted me to see? No. This was Djoser's tomb. Naturally, his sarcophagus would be here. It was made of solid rock, impossible to move.

A random thought occurred to me. Why was Chas searching for Cleopatra's burial site here? It was only a fleeting thought but it set my mind on a different track.

"Chas must be crazy," I muttered absently.

Norman paused. My abrupt change in subject had thrown him off. "What do you mean?"

Something had altered in Norman's manner. Admittedly, I had been testing him, otherwise why would I have said that out loud. I had called the Egyptian archaeologist Chas. I was fully aware that Norman had learned the man's true identity, but so far he had made no overt admission to me.

He tried to cover up his emotion by acting casual. "What about him?"

The day's frustrations suddenly overwhelmed me and I snapped. "Why are you so jealous of Chas?"

"Whoa," he said. "What brought that on?"

Yes. What? I floundered. Then sputtered out the truth. "Stop playing the innocent. I know that he told you who he was."

His hesitation was fractional. He nodded. "I pretty much guessed it."

"If you know that Ramy Basseem is Chas, then why are you acting so strange?"

"I don't know what you mean."

"Yes, you do. You're acting weird, Norman. Just weird. After all we've been through together and after everything I've confided to you, why don't you trust me?" My hands flew into the air in exaggerated despair. "What is going on with you?"

He reached out to steady me. "Nothing is going on with me, Lucy. I swear."

"I don't believe you. You're acting weird. What happened at the airport? What did Aras tell you?" I suddenly had a totally irrational thought. Did Norman really think I had rekindled a romance with Chas?

All right, on occasion, ever since my ex reappeared in my life, I had wondered what would have happened had he and I become a couple. But I wasn't serious. That was a stupid fantasy that I did *not* wish to happen. Why was it that men utterly failed to understand that? A fantasy was not a desire. A fantasy was a 'What if?' Fantasies were, in fact, dangerous things that you never, *ever* wanted to occur in real life!

He hung his head. This huge six foot plus giant was hanging his head.

Oh no. It was true. So we *were* on the same train of thought.

"Norman," I accused. "How can you think that?"

"You went to his hotel room."

"Because I had nowhere else to go. And I was afraid of Tarek."

"As well you should be."

He gathered me into his arms. "I am just so grateful that I got to you in time."

I collapsed against his chest and sobbed. Exhaustion was beginning to take its toll on me. He kissed my tears. And my wet lips and ran his hands up my spine. "I love you so much, sweetheart. You have no idea how hard it was for me to let you come here with Luke. And when that terrorist bastard got hold of you—" He grabbed me and kissed me with a feverish intensity. He glowered into my eyes and said quite plainly, "I hate Chas."

That statement caught me up short. The emotion in his voice was fierce. He hated Chas as much as I hated Nizar Tarek. That was definitely an overreaction. Chas was a saint next to Tarek.

I pulled up Norman's t-shirt. I shoved my hands up against the rippling muscles taut against his ribs. Chas was nothing to me and I had to prove it to him.

Chas could go to hell.

I ran my hands over his bare skin and dragged the t-shirt over his head. "I can't tell you how long I've been waiting to do this."

"It's not the most comfortable place, Lucy."

I hauled the massive hoody up and over my head and dropped it to the floor. "Park it right here, buster."

A soft rumbly chuckle came from his throat. He lowered me to the fluid fabric and slid my skirt up to my thighs.

I know this was a most inappropriate time to be thinking about sex. But my sister was about to give birth to my niece.

It made me realize how much I wanted to have a baby with this man. How much I wanted to be his wife. I have never said those words out loud or even to myself. I just knew it. Luke knew it. Even Alessandra and Arianna knew it.

Why was it that Norman was the only person who didn't know it?

So, as he lowered his pants and slid my red panties down to my ankles I felt aroused in a way I had never felt before. I had never thought about sex as a means to an end. I had never thought of it as anything but pleasure. Having a baby would be a game changer. But the consequences of procreating never seriously entered my mind.

And what about him? What were *his* thoughts on the subject? And that made having sex in this tomb the most erotic place I had ever done it—with the sexiest man I had ever done it with—in my life.

***

Norman tucked his shirt into his pants. It was hard to see with just the single flashlight and the odd light bulb burning in the gloom. He regained the flashlight from me and let the beam bounce off the walls.

Certainly the lumpy floor of a pharaoh's tomb wasn't the most comfortable bed we could have chosen to display our feelings for one another, but how could I wait? How could I let him believe I had even a smidgeon of romantic interest in Chas? The idea was revolting. Was I in denial? Absolutely not! If ever it came to it, Norman was my baby daddy. Hopefully, he thought so too.

I was fully dressed and still tingling from the afterglow of his love. My thoughts I kept to myself. This was not the time for planning our future. Although I had to admit it was tough trying to redirect my mind to the reason why we were here.

"What is Chas' interest in this pyramid, Lucy?"

We had somehow returned to the topic of my ex.

I set my expression in order and stopped thinking my

silly thoughts, and gave him a serious questioning look. "Weren't you the one who told me his harebrained theory about the dead body of Cleopatra? Weren't you the one who said that *she* is what his film is about? He thinks her mummified remains are somewhere in the Saqqara necropolis. Or even here inside the Step Pyramid."

Norman lifted the hoody from the floor and handed it to me.

Why wasn't he laughing—or at least smirking? Didn't he hear what I had said? Chas thought the tomb—or the body—of Cleopatra was somewhere in this vast burial ground. And he was making a documentary about it.

"Really," he muttered. He turned away; the chamber walls absorbed the rest of his speech.

In the gloom, an opening appeared near the floor large enough for a man to pass through. Before Norman indicated I follow he informed me that we were about to enter a low tunnel, part of a network of five miles of passageways burrowed beneath the pyramid. The trip would require us to hunch down once more.

As I struggled back into the hoody and rolled the sleeves up, I came to the solid conclusion that ancient Egyptians were short in stature.

"The dead king was obligated to pass through these tunnels to fight wild creatures before he became Osiris, the god of the Underworld," Norman explained.

Fine for the dead king if he wanted to become a supernatural being, but what about me? That was the last thing I wished.

I tucked the hem of the hoody into the waistband of my skirt. Then crawled behind Norman. The tunnel widened and expanded in height, enough for us to stand up. I was blind in the dark because only he had a flashlight. Every now and then I gasped with pleasure as his light struck a part of the walls and I could see that the ceiling was now well beyond our reach. The subterranean passages were adorned with fine reliefs. Blue faience tiles resembling the matted curtains of the royal residence covered the great shaft leading out of the burial chamber. The shimmering glaze of the cobalt and emerald mosaic gave the impression of being inside a gigantic ceramic vase.

By the time we emerged I realized we had entered another large vault encased in granite. It was filled with more of the inscribed stone vessels. These were sculpted from limestone, alabaster and slate. Anything of contemporary monetary value had long been removed.

I assumed Chas knew about this place. Was he really going to send his film crew in here? And yet as narrow and as inaccessible as the route to it was, I gathered he would if he could.

The place was magnificent and I blinked at the incredible sight. Something about the scene was surreal and immobilized me where I stood. Normally, I would have been wandering about exploring everything in sight but there was a sacred feeling about this place that instilled respect and awe.

There had to be several thousand stone urns. Those made of white alabaster glowed with an ethereal beauty as the light from Norman's flashlight struck their luminous surfaces. It was postulated that Djoser's resting place was surrounded by a maze of tunnels and vaults—filled with these urns—to foil grave robbers from plundering the tomb of the king.

But Norman wasn't interested in the grave vessels, and again I got the sense that he had been here before but when? I also felt that I was privileged to a sighting that no one other than he—and Chas—had witnessed.

"What is it, Norman?" I whispered.

He was in a corner of the chamber where he had emptied one of the stone urns. This one was a tall, slim, elegant specimen of exquisite, pale translucent alabaster, carved with what looked like an alternating rope design. A tumble of silver had poured out, and lay in a gleaming scatter on the floor. He rose to his feet, eyes lowered. His posture suggested he held something precious in the palm of his hand. All misgivings thrust aside I was infinitely curious now, and crossed over to join him.

He glanced up and said, “Have a gander at this.”

This was what he had wanted to show me? “What is it?” I asked.

He flipped the object from front to back to front again. “An Egyptian coin.”

One of many.

I turned the thing over in my fingers. The image engraved on it was that of a woman. At least I suspected it was a woman. I could only guess at the gender because of the hairstyle. Part of her hair was drawn up in a bun; the rest of it fell in ringlets around her shoulders, but the face…? On second thought, the features were too masculine. Was it Pharaoh Djoser, perhaps? Did they have this type of coin in his time or that kind of hairstyle for men?

Norman broke into my thoughts. “Cleopatra,” he said.

My jaw dropped open. “No. Couldn’t be.” My imagination immediately made comparisons with the Royal Ontario Museum’s granite sculpture. It bore no resemblance to this. “She—she looks like a man.”

“Isn’t that Basseem’s theory? That she was ugly?”

“Well, I wouldn’t call her ugly—but man-ish, definitely man-ish. How do you know it’s her?”

“Look at the inscription.”

I had seen this pattern of symbols before on numerous replicas in museum gift shops. The inscription read **‘Cleopatra, Queen of Egypt’**.

I flipped it over. On the other side was another engraved profile. This one was most certainly a man, hooked nose and all. **‘Mark Antony’**

He nodded. “This is why Basseem believes Cleopatra died in these tunnels.”

CHAPTER 27

Okay. So one question was answered. Chas had discovered evidence that Cleopatra might have been in these tunnels. A horde of silver coins embossed with her and her lover's image. Maybe it was enough for him to keep searching for her mummy. But how did the coins have anything to do with Aras? The final resting place of an ancient queen—famous though she may be—was irrelevant to his mission.

Norman had hinted that the sudden appearance of both men in Egypt was linked, but how? I came to the conclusion that my man was trying to distract me so that I would stop pestering him with questions. Clearly, he was still focused on the Egyptian archaeologist's self-aggrandizing agenda.

No way he was diverting me that simply.

"You still haven't told me," I enunciated. "Or shown me. Why is Aras in Egypt? His fight is with the restoration of his homeland. *Syria.* What has this coin got to do with Syria?"

"Maybe everything," he said.

Then he proceeded to fill me in on the details. Egypt and Syria were on the brink of war. Foreign relations between the two nations had never been good. But recently they had formed an alliance. Now, that was all shot to hell. The terrorists had planted rumors accusing Syria of stealing and selling Egyptian artifacts to rebuild their war torn country. Nizar Tarek and his cousin the infamous extremist leader, Cham Nassar, were behind it. Aras was trying to stop the plot.

"Those terrorists that stole that cartouche, among other relics? That was with the aid of your friendly neighborhood Indiana Jones—Ramy Basseem."

I quickly came to Chas' defense. "There wasn't enough evidence. He was acquitted of the charges."

"Sure he was."

Norman was joking, of course. He had to be. Why on earth would Chas want a war between Egypt and Syria? For revenge? The Egyptian government was responsible for his blacklisting, but igniting war between Syria and Egypt for firing him from his dream job? Surely that was a stretch.

"What are you implying, Norman? That Chas is a terrorist? That he's in league with the Islamic extremists and he intends a major takedown of the Middle East?"

I snorted.

"I am not insinuating anything. I am just relating the facts as I understand them."

"And what's that got to do with his search for Cleopatra's body?"

"Don't you get it, Lucy? That find would be worth a fortune. It would be on the scale of the discovery of King Tut's tomb. Whoever discovered it would get a lot of attention."

I paused to ruminate over all he had told me. It brought to mind something Johnny had mentioned. He and Alessa had found something important. Was it this? No. I seized our only source of light from Norman—his flashlight—and quickly scoured the granite chamber with a broad sweep of my eyes. Indeed thousands of alabaster, limestone and slate urns covered the floor, but these urns were not enough to elicit the reaction he had displayed. It was something bigger, something unbelievable—the coins maybe?

Where *was* the dynamic duo anyway?

I searched for my phone—Norman's phone—but before I had any other ideas I realized it was gone. Tarek had smashed the brand new iPhone to smithereens.

"Oh geez, I lost your cellphone, Norman."

"I saw," he said.

"How will we call Johnny?"

He removed another device from a pocket in his pants, unlocked it and handed it to me. "Aras lent his to me. Don't think you'll get a signal though. We're too far inside the passageways."

"When I talked to Johnny earlier—when Tarek had me hostage—he mentioned that they were going into a tunnel. You believe it's one of these, in Saqqara?"

"Likely," he said. "But there are miles upon miles of passageways in this monumental graveyard. They could be anywhere. And you look done in, honey. It'll be dusk by now. Maybe they've returned to the inn. If not, when we arrive I want you to stay in our room and wait for word from Luke or Aras. If Sayid and Piero aren't there when we return, I'll come back and find them."

"But I won't have a phone."

"You can keep this one—" He tapped the phone that was in my fist and it glowed to life.

"But what if you need it?"

"I won't need it. I have the drone, Luke's drone. That is probably the fastest way of finding them."

"Johnny gave you the drone?" I thrust the flashlight at him, and began to scroll through Aras' contacts.

He laughed. "Not exactly."

"How? When did you see him?"

Norman turned from me for a second as though he were embarrassed and then said: "You know when you went to use the Ladies Room at the inn when we first arrived?"

"Yes?"

"I checked in to Sayid's room and borrowed the drone."

By 'checking in' he meant he had discreetly passed

through a locked door while no one was looking. In other words he had picked the lock, broken in and taken what he desired. The man worked fast.

I glanced down, found the number I was seeking and tapped it. "Where is it?" I asked, sliding my eyes up briefly.

"The drone? It's in the jeep."

I couldn't help but chuckle. Poor Luke. Did he have any idea what was going on with his drone?

The phone was silent. Norman was right, and there was no service inside the tunnel. We were surrounded by earth, sand and rock, material far too dense to allow for a signal. I listened a few seconds more, and then handed him back the device.

***

By the time we returned through the stone corridors past the vast, multiple urn chambers and found our way outside, it was nightfall. The desert was cast in eerie shadows, and the Step Pyramid and its surrounding structures loomed hard and black against the twilit glow. Soon the only illumination would come from the stars and the moon. There was no night lighting here. The Saqqara necropolis was not afforded the same attention by officials or tourists as the Pyramids of Giza, and had an isolated, dead feel about it. Exactly like a burial ground.

Norman drove us back to the Sakkara Inn with the headlights on high beam. By now it was solid nightfall. We parked in the near empty parking lot and went up to Reception to inquire about our friends.

"No. I am sorry," the proprietor said, indicating the purple, white and yellow lobby with a flourish. No one was seated in the modest, gauchely decorated, dimly lit waiting area. "The *monsieur* and *madame* have not returned. Perhaps they went out into the village for an authentic Egyptian meal. It is very popular for the tourists to do that if they do not wish everyday to eat in my establishment. But I have very good food. Would you like to book a table?"

"A table for two," Norman said. "In about an hour. Is that enough time for you to get rested and cleaned up, Lucy?"

You would think he was asking me out on a date. I sniggered. It was more than enough time for me to splash some cold water on my face and neck, and wash my hands.

Norman offered me the cellphone while the proprietor watched (was he questioning my fashion sense? I wore the oversized hoody over my skirt once more) before he recalled that the device was locked. He retrieved the phone from me, removed the passcode and returned it. We had already lost more than one cellphone on this mission. You can see how often they needed replacement. No wonder none of us bothered to memorize our contacts' numbers anymore.

"You can contact the drone and it will relay all messages to me." Norman showed me the remote that he withdrew from a back pocket. It was also a mini computer and phone. He texted me the number.

"Very cool," I said. "You and Johnny are going to be in a heck of a lot of trouble when Luke discovers you stole it."

"I am just borrowing it," Norman scoffed. "Sayid stole it."

Norman accompanied me to our room and then went downstairs to see if he couldn't find some bottled water. We were both parched. I closed the door in the darkened room with the borrowed cellphone in my hand and tried again to call Johnny. Starlight poured in through the open windows as I waited for him to answer. Nothing. I drew the curtains and turned on the bedside lamps and then scrolled though the address book. Alessandra's phone number was not among the contacts, but Arianna's was.

Now this was peculiar. And before I had spent even a nanosecond pondering why Aras should have the chief of ISORE's phone number, I noticed something strange at my feet. My eyes rose from the base of a large powder-blue suitcase to its solid handle. Oh my god! It was my luggage. How had it arrived? Who knew I was here?

I should have gone instantly for the gun, but I stupidly

forgot about Norman's pistol in my handbag because my first response was to run.

I made for the door. Was a terrorist waiting for me behind the curtains?

Then my rational brain returned. How could it be Tarek?

As I stood paralyzed by indecision, the balcony door swung inward and a man stepped inside. A warm breeze followed and then I recognized him. Relief and annoyance simultaneously assailed me. His sudden forceful appearance and masculine smell unsettled me.

"Honestly." I swallowed, clutched my chest and made a rapid attempt to recover my composure. Clearly, it was *he* who had brought me my luggage. "I swear I could kill you. What are you doing hiding on the balcony, and how did you know I was here? Do you realize you nearly gave me a heart attack?"

He put his fingers to his lips. Then he indicated the dimly lit parking lot with a tilt of his fashionably stubbled chin, and asked, "Who was that I saw you get out of the jeep with?"

My god, he was being melodramatic! I echoed his melodrama by interpreting the question to mean 'Friend or Foe?'

"Friend," I said.

"Are you sure he's a friend?"

"Of course, I'm sure. That was Norman. How could you not recognize him? What I'm not sure about is *you*. Why did you abandon us at the airport?"

"I had no choice, Racine. I can't afford to get mixed up in anything illegal. And FYI? I thought the bodyguard was arrested with the billionaire."

I decided to ignore Chas' comment. I was also glad that I had not started to undress yet. I tugged the two sides of my skirt together where the wind from the balcony had swept it aside. "There is nothing illegal going on. That mummy was simply being returned to the Egyptian Museum."

"A likely story." He paused. "What? Do you think I'm

stupid? I know what you were doing. You were going to trade that mummy. *My* mummy for your Interpol pal, Alessandra Piero."

"Ex Interpol pal," I corrected. "And how do you know about her?"

In the orange light of the bedside lamp his face looked ruddier than usual. High emotion was hidden behind a veneer of sophisticated cool. I mean *really*, what had him so steamed up?

"How do you know about *her?*" I repeated.

"Your boyfriend let it slip. I already told you. Don't you ever listen? Still the same scatter-brained, Racine."

I let that one go. On reflection, I suppose he *had* told me.

"Do you have any idea how valuable that mummy is?" he asked. "I can't let it out of my sight."

Was that why he had accompanied the exhibit to Toronto in the first place? If so, why hadn't he intercepted it? He could have stopped it from being transported back to Egypt. I sighed. His role in the mystery was getting messier and messier. It also struck me once more that Norman had warned me about Chas. With so many distractions, however, he had neglected to explain why.

Completely flabbergasted and more than a little exasperated, I replied, "I am beginning to realize that I honestly have no idea why the mummy is so valuable. Do me a favor, Chas, and tell me. Why *are* so many people interested in this mummy?"

A slight hesitation stopped his words before he spoke. "Lucy, there is something you need to see."

So—it was Lucy now, was it? What happened to Racine?

"But we need to lose the bodyguard."

Chas was only ribbing me, and I was in no mood for jokes. Norman was my bodyguard, my lover, and my best friend. Chas was none of those things. Well, maybe a friend? But what would his reaction be to that? Who was he anyway? He was Ramy Basseem. He was no longer just Chas. Our acquaintanceship was past history. Why should I trust him?

"I am not going anywhere with you," I said. "I want to get cleaned up. And then I need something to eat. Norman will be back any minute. We have reservations on the rooftop patio in"—I did a quick mental calculation—"forty-five minutes."

"Make some excuse, Lucy." His tone was urgent. "Ditch the bodyguard. You need to see this."

I could hardly do that. He was Norman. *My* Norman.

"Go away, Chas," I said. I went to the door and opened it. My hand indicated the vacant hallway, an unambiguous invitation for him to relieve me of his company.

He studied my determined posture. Then turned, and with a forceful sigh made a theatrical exit.

I watched his broad back as he strutted down the narrow, mustard-colored corridor. From this angle he could easily pass for a young Harrison Ford. He went past a few potted palms that appeared plastic rather than real, and disappeared down the stairs. I returned to my room and slammed the door. Locked it.

CHAPTER 28

The balcony door, which happened to be made of wood, stood partly open. I bolted it, before tugging on the curtains to make certain they were securely drawn.

I stripped down and threw my skirt and top onto the red and mustard bedspread, did a double take when I realized that the design on the cover was an Egyptian queen (Cleopatra?) with the characteristic royal headdress.

The bathroom was small with a white pedestal sink and salmon-colored marbled tiles that reminded me of square slices of processed ham. There was a shallow standing shower with a chrome towel bar on the adjacent wall, holding two yellow and white-striped towels.

A glance at my bare skin in the vanity mirror informed me that a quick splashing on hands and face would only smear the dirt around. I was that filthy. What must the innkeeper have thought? But then he was probably used to grubby tourists. After a day scrambling over the dusty ruins in the hot sun we all ended up looking and smelling pretty much the same.

I would need at least thirty minutes to shower, do my hair and makeup, and change clothes. What was taking Norman so long to get the bottled water? I was almost tempted to drink from the tap, but that might result in a bad case of Montezuma's Revenge.

The shower stall was narrow, and I stepped in and turned on the faucet. I arched my neck to the showerhead to revel in the sensation of heated water pouring off my face and down my torso. There was something about hot running water that was so civilized, even when you were trapped in the middle of the desert. I cupped the small, complimentary bath bar and lathered up, breathing in the steam.

The foamy soapsuds slithered off my skin. It felt great to scrub the grit off my body. I decided to wash my hair when I realized just how grimy I was. The water rushing down the drain frothing with soap appeared slightly brown. Deciding against the strange-smelling complimentary shampoo, I used my own. Verbena and Lavender.

When I was done I drew back the white plastic shower curtain and ducked wet-footed onto the tile floor. My skin was hot and flushed, moist and glistening. I dried myself off with the two small towels provided, one for my body and the smaller one for my hair. After applying a bit of makeup to hide the shadows under my eyes, I was afraid to plug in my hair dryer. The electrical outlet looked unfamiliar so I opted against risking electrocution and combed it damp.

Norman still wasn't back. Was he filtering the water himself? *Just kidding.*

I knelt on the floor, feeling warm and clean, skimpily wrapped in the yellow striped towel and opened my suitcase to dig out something to wear. As I accidentally bumped the bed in my search, I noticed that the phone I had left on the bedspread was displaying a text. I reached over, lifted it, and saw that the message was from Norman.

"Gone to pick up Luke and Aras from airport jail. Will be back soon."

My initial reaction was disappointment because I would have liked to be present at the reunion. But when the reality of their freedom sank in, a thrill of relief replaced the resentment.

"Why didn't you wait for me?" I quickly tapped.

"You were in the shower. Stay put. Have a nap. Will be back."

"They've been released?"

"Yes. Can't talk. Gotta drive."

Crap, I thought. If Chas hadn't kept me those fifteen minutes I could have been out of the shower when Norman returned with the water. I could see the bottles now on the little table against the wall. I took one and quenched my thirst.

Well, at least I could call Luke now. Then it dawned on me that I was in possession of Aras' phone. Norman was using the drone to text me. I laughed.

First, I needed to get dressed. Afterwards I would go to the rooftop restaurant and order a drink. Boy, did I ever need a drink. Then I would call Luke. Norman, I knew, would have told him where I was and that I was safe.

I had a white Marilyn Monroe style, knee-length halter dress with a matching shawl to cover my back and shoulders while in public. I put this on and added a pair of strappy white sandals. I wanted to look nice when the boys returned, and at the same time it was not my intention to offend the locals, hence the shawl.

I could hardly wait. The trip there and back shouldn't take more than two hours. And already an hour had passed since Norman had left the hotel. They would arrive soon. There was no traffic on the desert road this time of night.

The hotel was a mere three stories, and was small as hotels went but cozy. The entire thing was painted sand yellow with white trim on the windows and stair rails. On the rooftop, lit lanterns lined the balustrade giving off a warm, even light.

I was shown to a very nice nook with a splendid view. The seat cushions were covered in some cheap material resembling crushed red velvet; and the table was of wood with a decorative clay urn and tea lights in glass jars on top. The dining set sat on a carpet of red, black and white. The sun was gone and the awning of natural fibers overtop for shade was rolled back to reveal the stars.

"You are expecting the monsieur?" the waiter asked. Everyone was aware of everyone else in this tiny inn.

I nodded. "But he will be a little late." I glanced around and saw that there were very few patrons at the restaurant. "He has gone to pick up two more of our friends so there will be four of us."

"Of course," he said. He hovered around me, not wanting to depart until I had made a request from the bar. As far as the locals were concerned, foreigners were heavy into partying while on vacation. "You would like something to drink while you wait?"

"Please."

I decided against getting plastered before Norman returned, and ordered the non-alcoholic beverage *limoon*, which was simply cold water and lemon juice blended with sugar and fresh mint—a kind of lemonade. As the waiter made his exit to fill my order I turned to the view, a marvelous vista of the Saqqara pyramids, now merely silhouettes in the night sky.

A dart of adrenalin raced through me as a voice broke my solitude.

"Eating all alone, are we?"

I tore my eyes from the dusky scene. Chas stood over my table with a short cocktail glass in his hand; the amber liquid surrounding a single ice cube appeared to be Scotch.

"Mind if I sit?" He removed his bush hat and dropped it on the table without waiting for my consent.

He was dressed in his own brand: Basseem khakis, t-shirt, and lightweight safari jacket just as he had been earlier in the evening. His planting himself opposite me before I could object was a blatant message that he was in charge. "You look very nice in that dress."

He was persistent. I had to give him that. I graciously ignored the compliment however because it could mean only one thing.

"I told you to go away," I said.

He leaned on his elbows over the tabletop. "Just hear me out."

When I slapped my palms down and only scowled at his hat, his fingers crawled towards mine.

"I need your help. Please, Racine. For old time's sake."

For old times sake? I cannot say how much that offended me. Exactly how did he remember the old times? For me the memories were dagger wounds and I had an irrational desire to rip up his hat.

He leaned further forward and took both of my hands to force my attention away from his headgear. It worked. My eyes slid up to seek his face. His expression was earnest, very sincere, and heart wrenching. His warm brown eyes penetrated my gaze; his lips moved. "You loved me once."

Oh my god. He was playing that card? This strategy was indefensible. Look how he had treated me. He had chased me out of his apartment with a tennis racket. I could hardly keep the shame and anger separated. Did he really think reminding me of my youthful stupidity was going to ingratiate him? Thank God I was drinking lemonade and not a martini. Thank God I had decided to skirt that path. We all know what happens to me when I get just that little too tipsy.

"You—need—*my*—help?" I drew my hands away quickly.

He nodded. "I must get hold of the Screaming Mummy."

"Why?"

"I need to put it through some tests. But first I want you to look at it and verify to me that it is indeed the original."

Something about this comment rang bells in my head. Tests. Yes tests. It was something about running some tests.

On this mummy.

"Why does everyone want this mummy authenticated?" I asked. "What makes you think it's a fake?"

"I don't think it's a fake."

"Then what?"

"A case of mistaken identity."

Huh? What did he mean? That the Screaming Mummy wasn't Prince Pentawere, Ramses III's son? I scowled. "If that isn't who it is, then who is it?

"Haven't you guessed by now? I would have thought the clues were enough to guide you to the logical conclusion."

He waited, and when I appeared inexplicably incapacitated and totally unable to respond he said, "Haven't you been listening to my theory?"

Sure, I had been listening. And yeah, even a middle school kid could have guessed what he was implying. But the idea was completely out to lunch. Did he seriously believe that the Screaming Mummy was not the corpse of Prince Pentawere but the desiccated body of Cleopatra?

My eyes sought his for confirmation.

"I can prove it to you," he insisted. The expression on his face informed me that I had arrived at the correct deduction.

I stammered, "Y—you mean the body of Cleopatra was in the possession of the Egyptian Museum all along—and nobody knew it? H—how could that be? Where was the mummy found in the first place?"

"That's the thing. Nobody knows the true origin. Over the ages it, like a lot of royals, were dumped into mass graves after their tombs were looted. This mummy was always assumed to be Prince Pentawere because of the screaming face and the associated story. But ever since all of the thefts and recoveries no one has ever scientifically authenticated it."

"I don't believe it. From what I can remember it was fully documented. I made detailed illustrations of this mummy over a decade ago, when we—" Here I stopped. I had no desire to revive dead memories.

It was true that you could not tell the sex of a severely desiccated mummy through visual examination alone. Anything gender-specific was shriveled to nothing, dried flat, and unrecognizable. A mummy that had never been embalmed had absolutely no fluid left in it so it was impossible to identify as male or female—not without DNA testing. And no DNA tests had been conducted on this particular specimen, at least not since its last disappearance. When tourism sank to almost nothing due to a decade-long spate of sporadic terrorism, the money vanished from Egypt's coffers and there were no funds to do any kind of testing.

However—if Chas' theory was true? Most historical documentation cited the Egyptian queen's death as suicide. She had allowed a snake to bite her or she had administered the poison herself. He on the other hand postulated that Cleopatra had perished trying to escape Emperor Octavian. What horrid thing had she experienced to cause her to die screaming?

I was getting ahead of myself. Far, far, too *far* ahead. My imagination was in overdrive.

His head was bobbing up and down fast. "Had I known then, what I know now—" he began.

"Stop being so cryptic," I complained, and frowned. "What do you know?"

A second of dramatic silence followed and then he replied, "I found her sarcophagus."

You found—her—Sarcophagus? Where? How?

He had my full attention now.

When I just sat there in total silence Chas resumed. "Every sarcophagus is carved to fit a certain body. It must fit exactly, like a piece in a jigsaw puzzle. In Cleopatra's time coffins and sarcophagi were carved to look like the person inside it, and fit the exact curves of the mummy's shape."

I knew that.

"I can guess what you're going to ask next. Why didn't I just take the mummy while it was still in Egypt? I didn't suspect that she was *that* mummy until she was already in transport to Canada. That's why I made sure—"

My frown deepened. "That's why you made sure of what?"

He hesitated. "That's why I made sure *I* was the one

selected to open the ROM's Mummy exhibit when Yasmine fell ill."

I should have been suspicious at this moment but I wasn't.

"Where is it?"

"Where is what?"

"Where is Cleopatra's sarcophagus?"

"Why should I tell you that? You don't even believe me. Besides, that would be a spoiler for my documentary. The big reveal happens on camera. But I need that mummy."

Ah. I finally understood. If Chas had truly discovered Cleopatra's sarcophagus then he needed her body for the climax to his show. Ramy Basseem would be the hero of the archaeological world. It was exactly as Norman had claimed. The find would be earthshattering, like the 1922 discovery of King Tut's tomb. Cleopatra's burial place might well be the breakthrough of the 21st century, and the disgraced archaeologist would finally get restitution. They would elevate him to super celebrity status.

My brain was dancing with questions. If his theory held true, then…who the heck carved Cleopatra's sarcophagus? Was there also a crypt? Was it filled with jewels and gold and riches untold? Oh, what an imagination I had.

And now my mind was doing somersaults spinning back a day or so. How did Arianna figure into the plan and who was that Arab woman with her at the ROM's café?

"Why do you want me to see the mummy?" I demanded.

"Because you are one of the few people who knows what the original looked like."

"And you want me to come with you?"

A series of rapid nods made me want to grab his skull to stop the bouncing. "I want you to come with me—*this minute*."

My head shook from side to side just as rapidly in undisguised mockery. "I am waiting for Luke and Norman. They'll be arriving in half an hour." Yes, that was how long we had been talking.

His next words stopped me cold.

"Trevanian and Depardieu have been lying to you."

His hand shot across the table and seized my wrist as I recoiled from his words. My pulse began to race. Those two men were my life's blood; they would *never* betray me. Why would he say that?

Unless—whatever Arianna was neck deep in, the boys were too?

I forced my emotions down. "About what? What exactly have they been lying about?"

"About the *real* reason they're in Egypt."

For the first time since we debarked on this mission, a shiver of doubt entered my thoughts. As if my nerves weren't rattled enough. No. I must not allow myself even a shadow of a doubt. They would never lie to me. Never!

Or would they? How long had I known them? Really. My mouth was dry, my heart drumming. My breath was labored. I was stymied. How dare Chas make me feel this way! I scowled, glared. Sent him stare for stare. He was just trying to play me. Unbalance me. Make me give him what he wanted—my help. But this implied game of double espionage was proving tiresome.

There was no motivation for the boys to lie. Sure, Luke was a rival of the esteemed Ramy Basseem (and by using the word 'esteemed', I was being snide), but Luke was hardly an Egyptologist. He would not steal his opponent's thunder. And Norman? How was a bodyguard a threat to his career?

And yet there was still a connection between the Egyptian archaeologist and the director of the Royal Ontario Museum.

"The mummy is in the possession of the Egyptian authorities," he said. "I need to get access to it before they send it back to the ROM."

Why was Chas so nervous and so desperate? Wasn't he associated with the Egyptian Museum? Wouldn't they just *give* him access to the mummy?

As I turned my puzzled face towards him, he got my

drift before I even asked.

"Don't you get it, Racine? I no longer work for the government. I have no clout with them or with anyone else. In fact, that whole terrorist thing destroyed my career. The negative publicity was devastating. My only hope is to make this blockbuster documentary and restore my reputation. I need you to help me get hold of the mummy."

So his whole story was faked?

At the moment what I felt for him was pity. He knew it, and played it for all it was worth, and then to cap it all off he gave me the clincher—the sad cow eyes.

To my detriment I caved. "How—how can I help you if you don't want me to tell anyone?"

"I need your help—to steal it."

My mouth opened to object.

"I know about ISORE. I know about your connection with them. I know you rescue endangered antiquities."

CHAPTER 29

It was at this moment that the waiter returned with my iced lemon drink. Talk about slow service. I had totally forgotten about the drink. I thanked the waiter and he smiled, bowed politely, and left the glass on the table on a paper cocktail napkin. I took a sip of the refreshing citrusy beverage and waited until he was out of earshot before I resumed my conversation with Chas.

"Yesterday, in Toronto—" Or was it the day before? I had lost all sense of time. "—I saw you at the Royal Ontario Museum's café with Arianna Chase and an Arab woman. She was dressed very conservatively, like some kind of government official."

Chas nodded. "She works for the Syrian Ministry of Foreign Affairs. Her name is Colonel Rima Abadi. She is part of the Syrian delegation that arrived this morning to deliberate with the Egyptian Ministry of Antiquities. She came to meet with your boss and myself. Dr. Chase was in possession of something she desired, and I could provide the necessary documentation. She made a detour to Canada when she learned that I was to open the exhibit at the Royal Ontario Museum."

"That was *quite* the detour," I remarked acerbically.

"Damascus to Toronto—to Cairo—in twenty-four hours?"

Chas smirked. I had failed to see the irony. Both of us had made the trip from Toronto to Cairo.

Fine. I could understand how the Syrian minister benefitted from the collaboration, but what about him? What was *he* getting out of the arrangement? I shot him this question.

"Abadi promised to use her influence to reinstate me in my former position of Egyptian Supreme Inspector of Antiquities."

Her influence? What kind of influence did she have?

That couldn't be all there was to it. She was a foreign minister and would hardly have much say in local employment policy. He was hiding something but what? When he refused to elaborate I asked, "Why? Why would she do that?"

I racked my brains to recall the tiny bit of conversation I had overheard at the ROM. They were talking about tests and proofs…

And then I had it. What else could it be about?

My tone was accusatory as I spat out my question. "Why is Abadi so interested in the Screaming Mummy?"

My insight into the Syrian official's ambitions had him stymied and he only answered after a brief pause. "How did you know that she was?"

"Let's just say a little birdie told me."

"You are full of surprises, aren't you, Racine?" His tone sounded derisive and skeptical at the same time.

"So, I'm right. Abadi also wants the mummy. That was the 'something' that Arianna had that she wanted. But why?"

Chas toyed with his drink. Then he leaned forward clasping his hands together on the tabletop. "She accepts my theory of Cleopatra's death. I know—well—I *think* I know where the sarcophagus is." A pause. "At any rate, I *know* where the body is. I just have to put the two together and verify that they fit."

I mused this over silently. Why would the Syrian

government want Cleopatra's mummy? *That—I just don't get.*

His next comment informed me that he had read my expression accurately without any intention of enlightening me. "I need to get custody of it before the Syrian's do."

Countless conflicting ideas were tumbling in my head. Did Luke know about this? Chas was busy drumming his fingernails on the tabletop. Beside him the ice cube in his drink dipped up and down.

What could *I* do about it? I shrugged my shoulders. The sarcophagus was merely a rumor as far as I was concerned. Because, really, why would the mummy and the sarcophagus be separated?

"How is Arianna involved in this scheme?" I demanded.

"She was supposed to keep the mummy safe until tests could be run on it. Toronto has the facilities; Cairo doesn't. Everything was on track to prove I was right about the mummy when those stupid riots upset everything and forced me to leave. I intended to return secretly under a different name. Then your boyfriend took off with the goods."

He stopped fidgeting and stretched out his hand. "I have no doubt your boss will follow it to Cairo."

"You still haven't answered my question," I reprimanded. "Why does Rima Abadi want the Screaming Mummy?"

"*Her* answer? Or the *real* answer?"

What was he insinuating? That the Syrian government's claim to improve foreign relations with Egypt was a lie? That in fact their intent was the opposite?

"Ostensibly," he said. "Colonel Abadi and Dr. Chase are preparing to stop a major revolt by pacifying the Egyptians. The Egyptian people have gotten wind of this sarcophagus, and according to Abadi it is the terrorists that are spreading rumors that Syria is stealing Egyptian artifacts in order to scorch relations between the two countries by causing a populace revolt.

"Now, if it's the truth you want, I believe it is a whole

other game. The Syrians are actually robbing Egypt blind. And blaming terrorists."

Was that the lead Alessandra was following when Johnny called me? He had mentioned underground passageways, and a find that was so incredible that it had to be seen to be believed.

I mulled this over for less than a minute. What else could it be? They had found the sarcophagus—among other treasures. *That has to be it.* And so… was the discovery of the sarcophagus the reason why they couldn't wait for the rest of the team to turn up in Saqqara?

I got the feeling that Arianna had been in touch with Alessandra all along. And Aras? Was he in on it, too? Norman had implied that he was. Did the whole team know? Had Johnny been faking his ignorance all along? Impossible. He alone wanted me to accompany him to Egypt… But wait a minute. Then, he had changed his mind. I was so confused I wanted to scream. There was only one thing I was sure of. Everyone had lied to me. I pulled my hand away from the brown encroaching fingers of the handsome Egyptian archaeologist and switched drinks with him.

Why had I let my hand sit there so long when I knew he wanted to seduce me? Why was feeling his touch even tempting? Alas, my brain and my body seemed weirdly disconnected.

I swallowed half of his whiskey in one gulp. The burning liquor warmed my body even as it heated my throat. I needed to feel safe; I needed to trust someone. I had not felt this undecided about the ISORE team since I learned of their existence.

"What evidence do you have?" I demanded.

"The Syrian delegation, headed by Colonel Rima Abadi, is here for peace talks. The Syrian government denies the rumors that they have anything to do with the theft of Egyptian antiquities that are ending up in Syria or that are being sold on the Black Market to subsidize the nation's restoration projects. You must have heard the rumors that the

Syrians have secret sources of money to pad their military. The civil war has destroyed the urban infrastructure in Syria. In order to rebuild their towns and cities, they need to squash any rebel cells that resurface, and *that* requires cash."

He stared me boldly in the eye.

"Your boss is in it up to here, Racine." Chas placed a flattened hand under his chin to indicate the depth of her involvement. "Syria can't be restored without piles of money. Stolen antiquities bring in millions."

No. *No*, how could I believe such a radical story? Arianna was not involved in this wholesale theft. She was the opposite. She rescued endangered objects and restored them to their countries of origin. Why would she steal Egyptian antiquities to help Syria rebuild itself? So what if she was a friend of the nation's First Lady. No matter how corrupt their government, the head of ISORE—the director of the ROM—could *not* possibly be in league with them.

Chas interrupted my thoughts. "Think, Racine. Just think about what will happen if the public gets wind that some Syrian government agents, posing as terrorists, are working underground in Egypt. And that they are in possession of Cleopatra's body and will soon be in possession of her sarcophagus. This is the rumor the terrorists are propagating in revenge for being used as their scapegoat. Egypt will have to retaliate. There will be outright war."

I took a thoughtful sip of the Scotch as Chas watched.

"I need to get the Screaming Mummy away from all of them. I need to prove my innocence and my theory—and make it public. If it's in my custody and under my protection, and Egypt reinstates me as Supreme Inspector of Antiquities I can protect it from the schemes of these foreign masterminds."

Was he including my boss Arianna Chase in that accusation? Another thought walloped me. Norman had told me to 'ask the boss' when I wanted to know how Alessandra had escaped. He also suspected that she was involved in some sort of intrigue. A disturbing sense of uneasiness settled in the pit of my stomach. Could Chas possibly be right about her?

"So, will you help me?" he implored. "Will you help me to retrieve the mummy?"

My silence should have spoken volumes. Except that it didn't. I kept flipping back and forth. I fisted the whiskey glass and downed the remainder of the spirit.

Could I do this? *Should* I do this? Oh, who to believe?

If helping him was the only way I could get to the truth then I would do it.

I turned back.

"We can't do this alone. But I *will* help you. On one condition."

"What's that?"

"We bring Norman in on it."

CHAPTER 30

The sound of multiple footsteps came marching up the main staircase to the rooftop patio. I gestured for Chas to leave. I shoved his empty glass at him and grabbed my lemon drink. I promised to meet him at the Saqqara necropolis at midnight—inside the colonnade. How could I risk my man seeing me with him before I'd had an opportunity to explain? How could I take the chance that he might interpret this tête-à-tête as a romantic tryst rather than a plan to save an historic object and prevent a war? No. I had to get him on board first.

Chas grabbed my hand, squeezed it hard, and then kissed me hard on the lips before he scrambled down a side stairwell, meant for the hotel staff—leaving me in a state of utter shock.

I forcibly collected my thoughts, trembling in confusion, changed gears, took a large swallow of the *Limoon* to wash away the taste of the Scotch—and his lips—and turned to greet my friends.

My heart was racing, but all interpretations of what had just happened must be driven to the rear of the bus. It was show time and I had to put on my game face.

The three attractive men were a sight for sore eyes. All were tall, muscular and well built, and appealing in different ways. Norman's eyes twinkled when he saw me. I leaped to my feet and rushed over, perhaps just a tad overzealously. The covert discussion I had been conducting with Chas must be hidden. His hard and fast attempt to claim my affections must be buried. No one must suspect a thing.

I threw my arms around Norman's neck and he scooped me up in his arms. He kissed the side of my throat then set me down. I hugged Luke who rubbed my back affectionately and gave me a peck on the cheek. Then I delivered Aras a heartfelt squeeze. Our eyes met briefly but other than that we gave no hint that we had been in touch with each other before this moment.

"Thank God, you're safe," Luke said. "Come, let's go sit down. I could eat a camel."

"Great to see you in one piece," Aras said with his typical mocking smile.

I tried to mask the wonder on my face. Or maybe bewilderment is the better word. To be honest I could barely breathe. Too much had happened in the last few minutes to make sense of it all. For the moment I must push it all aside and focus on the present.

Aras had asked me not to inform the boys of my correspondence with him, and now he was acting like they shared his secrets.

My quizzical look got no response, and I supposed I would have to remain in suspense a little while longer.

We went back to my table and ordered a round of drinks. Or should I say Luke did the ordering. He convinced the proprietor to bring up his special stash. It was going to cost. But apparently this was a moment to celebrate. I was torn. I truly was happy to see my pal and once lover the billionaire, but his loyalty—despite his marital troubles—was always with Arianna.

Unfortunately, Chas' face and his stupid words found their way into my head once more. *Trevanian and Depardieu have been lying to you.*

The latter I trusted without a doubt. If Arianna wasn't

somehow involved I would have felt just as confident about Luke. And his brother? Aras had been playing a cat and mouse game with me from the beginning. The only one of the team who had been upfront with me was Johnny. He was the only one who had instinctively defied orders and had gone to rescue our kidnapped teammate regardless. The others had hesitated.

I studied the three men who sat at the table. Luke was directly across from me, seated next to his half-brother. My man was beside me on the outside, pinning me against the balustrade. I leaned my head over the balustrade and looked down across the near empty parking lot, inadvertently searching for my mysterious ex—the Egyptian archaeologist who had vanished into the darkness. I cupped my hand over my mouth and exhaled. Lemon and whiskey. *Oh please, I do not reek of Scotch.*

When I redirected my attention to the table Luke smiled at me. It was an odd smile, full of guilt. Not a smile I was comfortable with.

If you think I suspect him of something illicit you are wrong. When it comes to legalities I trust him implicitly. He had risked his life for me more than once. But what was it he was keeping secret? And why?

The waiter arrived with two expensive bottles of French wine. Chateau Brane Cantenac Margaux. I was surprised the hotel had this vintage in their tiny cellar, for the cellar must be miniscule since the hotel itself was smaller than average. By a billionaire's standards this wine was cheap because with the markup it cost around six hundred dollars a bottle. By *my* standards however it was way over pricy, and seemed to be an attempt at distracting me.

And another thing. Luke kept peeking at his watch. Why? What difference did it make what time it was? What was he waiting for—a call from his ex-wife?

I needed to get control over this situation. I wanted to be the one to ask the questions. Just as Luke snuck a quick glimpse of his watch once more, I asked the first thing that came to my mind. My eyes flickered from the billionaire to his brother. "How did you guys get out of airport jail?"

The two men exchanged furtive glances. I really was beginning to feel betrayed.

Luke's eyes had gone from mine to the main entrance of the patio. He semi-rose then addressed me. "We need to introduce you to someone, Lucy."

I looked up as Luke got to his feet and everyone else turned at the arrival of a tall, dark Arab woman. She was dressed in a charcoal grey suit with a white blouse. Holy cow, did I ever feel self-conscious decked out like a Marilyn Monroe impersonator!

I sucked in a ragged breath. I recognized her. She was the Arab official that had been having coffee with Arianna and Chas in the café at the Royal Ontario Museum back in Toronto. No time to muse it over. It was just a feeling. On sighting her I had the uncanny sense that I had seen her even since that time.

She came to our table and the waiter brought over a chair. Apparently my overtly feminine apparel had skipped her notice. Norman's gaze washed over me but he suppressed any obvious reaction. My plan had been for us to be alone, not have an audience.

She was all business. As she sat down, one question drove me mad. You mean Luke knew her? She had just been lurking in the background waiting for him to give her a cue to make her entrance?

Her name of course was Colonel Rima Abadi and I already knew she worked for the Syrian Ministry of Foreign Affairs. I was in no mood for niceties. Luke made the introductions and I pretended that I had never seen her before. Truth was, I was pretty convinced that I had seen her at least twice. If only I could remember when the second occasion had taken place.

Like Norman who never drank alcohol, she chose sparkling water instead of wine.

The cellphone in my handbag suddenly rang. *Saved by*

the bell. I fished the phone out of my handbag and gave it a swift glance. No number I recognized. And why should I recognize it? This was Aras' phone. He gave me a look, which I interpreted correctly. He wanted his cellphone back.

I excused myself on the pretense of answering the call, and to everyone's utter consternation, I rose, made my way across the patio restaurant, and walked (well maybe staggered a little as Chas' Scotch caught up with me) down one flight of stairs to the next floor. I opened the door and found myself in a quiet, empty hallway.

My reason for escaping the impending interview with Abadi was twofold. One, I wanted to get Aras alone so that I could interrogate him as to his mysterious texts. Two, the interlude would afford me a few moments to compose myself before talking to the Syrian official.

As I suspected he would, Aras followed me a few minutes later. After all it was *his* phone that was ringing.

The phone had gone silent after failing to be answered.

Aras extended a hand as he approached without speaking a word. The corridor where I waited was exactly like the one outside my room. It was painted a dirty mustard color with white trim on the doors and, here and there, stood potted plastic palms.

I passed him the phone, and he glanced at the number and the name that had gone to voicemail.

"What's going on Aras?" I asked. "Why all the cloak-and-dagger stuff. And now you're complicit with your brother? I want some answers. And I want them *pronto*."

He stuffed his phone into his pocket. "I'm sorry, Lucy. I should never have brought you into it."

Heard that one before.

"But you did," I objected. "Now tell me what's going on.

He hesitated as he opened his mouth to answer as though he anticipated an awkward reaction from me. "Your friend, Ramy Basseem, poisoned the curator Yasmine Lim. And he tried to poison you, too."

So Luke had familiarized him with the story of the dead

wasps. There had been no time to verify Luke's suspicions by having the wine tested, so to me that whole incident was still speculation. "If your only reason for thinking that is because of those dead wasps in the wine at Basseem's hotel, then that's no proof. Do you even *have* any? Proof that is?"

"It was verified by the lab. She was poisoned."

"It doesn't mean that Chas did it."

He frowned. "*Who?*"

I was unable to stop my hand from cupping my mouth at my slipup. "Basseem. Ramy Chas Basseem," I said modestly, hoping he wouldn't notice.

Aras shrugged. "I was only trying to protect you."

"Not your job," I snapped. I was tired of the team hiding secrets from me to keep me safe. When would I ever be a full-fledged member of ISORE if they continued to treat me with kid gloves? Then I remembered that he was not part of the team.

"Why are you here?" I demanded.

"To keep an avalanche from starting."

"So—it's political?"

"With me it is *always* political."

"Why do you want to protect a terrorist from the Toronto police?" I demanded.

"Because the more people who are after him, the more likely he will go underground. It's time to put that bird to sleep."

"He killed Ines," I whispered.

"I know. I'm sorry. There was nothing I could do about it. She was dead before I could get to her."

But he *did* try?

The question was rhetorical. Of course, he did. He was Aras.

"So the guys know why you're here?"

He nodded. "At first I didn't want to involve them. But then I saw that they were already involved."

What did he mean by that?

When nothing was forthcoming I requested an

explanation from him.

"Ask your boss," he said.

Norman had spoken those exact same words.

Aras glanced sideways, outside, toward the staircase that led to the rooftop patio. It was dark over the courtyard and the parking lot, and the dim lighting inside only turned the door's windowpane into a mirror, exposing our slightly distorted reflections.

"Time to head back before they suspect some sort of conspiracy between us."

"*Are* we conspiring?" I inquired.

The corners of his lips curled ever so slightly before Aras turned to exit the corridor. He climbed up the outdoor flight of stairs. I watched his back as he moved ever further away. Clearly, that was all the explanation I was going to get. I had no choice but to follow.

On our return to the patio everyone at the table glanced up. If they were surprised to see Aras escorting me they made no reference to it.

"Sorry about that," I said. "Important call." I had no idea whether the phone call was important or not. Aras had snatched the cellphone out of my hand before I could make any sort of judgment. The only thing I knew for certain was that the caller was unfamiliar.

Norman rose and allowed me to slip into the seat across from Luke before he took the spot beside me, and Aras sat down next to his half-brother.

The Arab woman looked angry. That's all I can say. I imagine no one had ever left her company—in the middle of a conversation—to answer a personal phone call in her entire professional life. No Sirree. She was too important.

I apologized again. "It was my sister in Toronto. She's pregnant. I thought perhaps she had gone into labor."

The lie went down exactly as I expected it would. It shamed her. Unfortunately, that only aggrieved her more. To her credit she was a good actor. But nothing got by me. I knew the taut politeness was merely exceptional acting.

Lucky for me the boys did not give me away. They were quite aware that the cellphone belonged to Aras. And no one—except for them—would be calling me on his phone.

"We were discussing the Egyptian archaeologist," Abadi said. "Thank goodness you did not go with him. That rogue Ramy Basseem, he has deceived us."

The only person I felt had been deceived was me.

From this moment on I was going to be very careful of what I said, and to whom. I sent Norman a sidelong frown. His face darkened enigmatically. I could see in his expression that Colonel Rima Abadi was probably a stranger to him. But Luke?

He was in her confidence. There was no doubt they were acquainted. Had Arianna introduced them while they were in Toronto? His whole manner was relaxed. But then he and his bodyguard were opposite sides of the same coin. It could mean something or it could mean nothing.

What about his brother? Did *he* know her too? It seemed not, but his face was unreadable. That was typical of Aras to show a deadpan expression. I needed to piece this narrative together. Aras' motives were ambiguous but his heart was not. He was loyal to a fault. He would never do anything to harm me anymore than Luke or Norman would. I had to hang on to that—especially since our covert meeting in the hallway downstairs.

Colonel Abadi bent forward and shook my hand (it was cold, hard), gazed assuredly at me.

"Miss Racine," she said. "I wish to speak to you about Dr. Basseem. There is reason to suspect he may have terrorist ties."

I felt like I should be the one asking the questions. But she had the bigger personality and the more important position, so I answered. "I'm afraid I know almost nothing about him. Dr. Basseem and I were colleagues when we were student interns at the Egyptian Museum in Cairo over a decade ago. And he certainly showed no signs of having terrorist ties then."

She exchanged a meaningful look with Luke. Not until they told me the truth was I going to reveal a thing.

"Lucy," Luke said. "Colonel Abadi is part of the Syrian delegation that came to meet with the Egyptian Ministry of Antiquities."

"So?" The Scotch was having an effect. My reply sounded rude but it was too late to retract. Besides Chas had given me a heads-up. I already knew who she was.

"She got us released from airport security. Arianna dropped the charges—as long as we cooperate with the minister here." His hand briefly indicated the female Syrian representative.

My eyes flitted from Luke to Aras. I really wanted to trust them. I loved these men. But I was sorely at a loss at what to say or who to believe.

"Ms. Racine," Abadi said, resting her elbows solidly on the table. "We know about Dr. Basseem's theory."

Yes, I am aware of that. I still said nothing. After downing the Scotch so fast I probably shouldn't be switching to wine. Nonetheless, I raised my glass to my lips and sipped. It was the only thing I could think to do to control my nerves.

"We know about Cleopatra's sarcophagus."

And you know about her mummy.

"We need to get custody of it before the Syrian extremists do."

So terrorists *were* involved. Thus far her account jived with Chas' story.

I let my wineglass settle on the tabletop. "And you think Dr. Basseem is working with them? What do you want *me* to do about it?"

"You are friends with Dr. Ramy Basseem," she said.

My reply was blunt. "We are acquainted."

"Then you can help us."

I pretended to listen.

"The Egyptian authorities are in possession of the mummy. We need the sarcophagus to be sure. If the body fits the coffin we will know definitively that she is Cleopatra.

Then we can return the sarcophagus to Egypt in a show of good will, and clear up any misunderstandings between the two nations. We are not thieves." There came a sharp silence as she waited for my reply. "You can help us locate the sarcophagus… We cannot allow the terrorists to get hold of this national treasure. Basseem will show you where it is. Lucy—you don't mind if I call you Lucy—?"

I *did* mind, and did my utmost to refrain from objecting. Instead I asked, "What makes you think Dr. Basseem will take me into his confidence?"

"He trusts you."

Oh? And how would she know that—unless she had put a tail on me?

That was a creepy thought.

"Well? Do we have your cooperation? Your director at the Royal Ontario Museum assured me that we would."

Violent emotion, like pressure, piled up against my inner skull, and I glanced edgewise at Norman but he was no help. Across from me Luke's facial features showed encouragement. He wanted me to capitulate.

"Please, Miss Racine. This is a matter of National Security."

A spike of adrenalin woke me up like a ghost returning to life.

I felt a sensation of déjà vu as my eyes went to Aras. Wasn't it he who had made that exact statement—in a rather cryptic text—just a short while ago? He offered no reaction, and I redirected my focus on the Syrian minister.

"We know of your history with Ramy Basseem," she explained.

A hot flush began to creep into my cheeks. How dare Luke expose my secrets! Or was it Norman? I had trusted them both when I revealed my brief romantic entanglement with Chas. Norman knew the intimate details; Luke had only guessed at the relationship. Either way I felt betrayed. I gave each a fierce scowl of disapproval. Nay disappointment.

I am no more in bed with him than you *are,*

metaphorically speaking. I compelled the acidic remark to remain unspoken even as I envisioned the recent tête-à-tête I had witnessed between Colonel Abadi, Chas, and Arianna in Toronto.

Rima Abadi fixed her cold gaze on me. "You would be helping to prevent a war."

What. By revealing the location of Cleopatra's sarcophagus so that you can steal it? Ha!

As far as I was concerned there was very little to mull over, and my gut instinct told me to steer clear of Colonel Abadi and her plans. Nevertheless I said, "I'll think about it."

She handed me a card with her contact information on it and got to her feet. "You *do* that."

Something about this woman rubbed me the wrong way. My intuition urged me to be cautious. How could Arianna have anything to do with this unpleasant woman? Chas had accused the two of conspiracy. According to him, Abadi's government was stealing antiquities from Egypt and blaming it on the terrorists. Not that I had any sympathy for terrorists but the corruption was appalling. And yet it was the perfect ploy. It would be too obvious what the Syrian government was up to if they sold their own artifacts. Besides, Egyptian artifacts had notoriety like no other. Chas was dead on. If that mummy were indeed the body of Cleopatra it would be worth a cool fortune on the Black Market.

It was a wonder how many rich people were willing to buy artifacts, no questions asked.

Light bulbs were firing like lightning bolts in my brain. Chas wasn't simply paranoid. His greatest fear was that Abadi would sell him out. He already had an indelible stain on his reputation. No matter that he was acquitted of all charges of antiquities theft. He was branded. If all went south Ramy Basseem was her scapegoat. He had to get hold of Cleopatra before she did.

CHAPTER 31

"Yasmine Lim was *poisoned*," Norman said. "The cardiac arrest was a direct effect of the toxin. All of the tests have been done. They are conclusive."

He reached out to take me into his arms but I swirled away. I sat down on the edge of the bed, spreading my skirt out nervously. "Chas did not poison her," I argued. "Why would he do that?"

"To get access to the mummy." His hands swung slack to his sides and he strolled over to the other side of the bed.

"I'm sorry, Norman. I just don't buy it."

We were inside our room after we had eaten and drunk, and the Syrian official had departed. I had acquainted Norman of my plan to help Chas. Not unexpectedly, he was dead set against it. Being an enlightened and somewhat considerate man he had tabled his true feelings and agreed to discuss it. Just as he had with his brother, Luke had related the poisoned wine incident to his bodyguard, and Norman had added two and two together. I disagreed with his verdict. And made no bones about it.

He however was adamant. "The Syrian minister as much as said that Ramy Basseem poisoned the original curator to make it look like a heart attack to get her out of the way. He needed to replace her at the exhibit opening so that he could manipulate the Screaming Mummy without anyone questioning his actions."

I made a bitter face. "I don't trust that female suit. Just what do you know about her?"

"It's okay, *Chérie*," he said, his voice softening. He was trying very hard to control his anger. He thought that my ex was charming me, using me to bring about his desired ends. I hated what he was implying. He was using French to pacify me. I wasn't falling for Chas' charms but I *was* falling for his.

He came around to my side of the bed. I struggled with my need to be enveloped in his arms. I had a thing for arms—big, powerful, muscular arms.

I slipped off the mattress and went to the balcony door and opened it.

A rush of warm air brushed my face and shoulders. I had left the shawl on the bed when I arose. My skin tingled.

I moved to the railing and looked out over the blackness. The courtyard was dimly lit and empty. The scanty palms decoratively planted between the cobblestones swayed and rustled. Beyond the small courtyard the few cars in the parking lot were motionless and dark. No figures moved in either place. The Syrian minister must be gone.

The steps of Djoser's pyramid rose towards the heavens like a crown. The smaller tombs and temple structures were stark against the glowing night sky.

My dispute with Norman had become slightly heated and I needed to cool down before I could focus, and return to the debate. I scooped a handful of my long hair from my shoulders. The soft breeze tickled my neck and throat and before I knew it, Norman's lips and breath had replaced the wind.

He stood slightly behind and beside me, his hands sloping down the underside of my armpits to my bare back. I was far from finishing my argument against Colonel Rima Abadi. But somehow my brain had gone blank.

The movement of his lips along my throat was annoyingly distracting and equally tantalizing. I wore three-inch high stilettoes with my white Marilyn Monroe halter dress. The wind swept skyward from below and lifted my skirt up from behind.

I let it.

Norman caught a fold of cloth with one hand and slipped the other between my bare legs. He unsnapped the pearl fasteners that held each side of my panties to my hips and let them fall free. He had told me once that all ladies undergarments should have snaps for convenience. That had made me laugh because in my experience such things did not exist. Apparently, I was wrong. Not only *did* they exist and cost a fortune, they were also made from silk, with pearls and silver snaps.

The wind caught my skirt again and tickled my naked behind. His hands approached my nape. The hasp holding the halter was the only thing between his fingers and my breasts. It unhooked, and the two triangles of white fabric fluttered down to my waist. He cupped my breasts and buried his face in my back.

His erection pressed between my cheeks and I felt his fingers test for readiness. I did not disappoint him. He flattened his palm in the wetness and before I could murmur assent I felt him spread my legs with his own and then his fullness filled me.

I was standing in my stilettoes, my skirt half up my back and my breasts hanging over the railing. God help us if anyone saw what we were doing.

***

Eight minutes later we were back inside. I still hadn't told him what Chas had divulged to me. If I wanted his help he needed to know.

I was re-clasping my halter and he had pulled up his pants. Why, if we were only going to go to bed his eyes questioned? But I had unfinished business to attend, business that he could help me with—or not—as he chose. I quickly glanced at the complimentary (albeit old-fashioned) radio clock on the nightstand. It was barely ten o'clock.

We had returned to our original discussion. He still wasn't sold. He was trying to rekindle our amorous mood and waited to put on his shirt.

My eyebrows puckered. "You know I can't have a serious discussion with you when your washboard abs are staring me in the face," I complained.

I grabbed the shirt out of his hands and yanked it down over his face.

"And *I* can't have a serious debate with you when you look like Marilyn Monroe's baby sister," he replied.

I suppressed a smile. When it appeared I was not game for round two of his sexual exploits he finished tugging his shirt down over his chest and said, "Chas has changed. Sure he's charismatic. It's part of the act. But he's not the same man you knew as an intern. He is now the notorious TV charmer Ramy Basseem. He's a celebrity, Lucy. And you know what snakes they are."

"Stop with the double talk," I interrupted. "Say what you mean."

"I am not double-talking. I am saying *exactly* what I mean. The man is a snake. Ramy Basseem is an opportunist and a possible thief, and a double-dealer. He will go where he benefits most. Right now that is the opposite direction from helping the Syrians avoid a war with Egypt. Right now he wants to be famous for proving a piece of history."

I let loose a hiss of exasperation. I was fed up with the Chas-bashing. There was only one enemy here, and *he* was a *she*. "I don't want to discuss him anymore. I want to know what you know about Rima Abadi."

"That was what I was trying to explain to you before you went off on a rant about Basseem. Luke explained the whole thing to me on the drive back."

My hackles were up. "What did he explain?"

A knock came at the door and I looked up from where

we faced one another on opposite sides of the small double bed.

"Hey, you two." It was Luke's voice. "Are you decent? Can we come in?"

We? That meant Aras was with him. They had gone to escort the Syrian minister down to her car while Norman and I had returned to our room.

"Just a minute," I called out in the direction of the closed door before Norman could speak. I unzipped my dress, unfastened the hooks to the halter, and he stared at me incomprehensibly. I slipped out of the dress and gestured for him to go to my suitcase and fetch me my robe. I refused to admit Luke until I knew which side Norman supported. I was standing in front of him stark naked; he had no choice but to do as I asked.

I tied the sash of my sateen robe around my waist. I went to him and used my eyes to seek his confidence. I desperately needed him on my side.

I placed two fingers against his lips and mouthed in quiet tones what I had seen in the café at the ROM in Toronto. I informed him of all that Chas had related concerning his suspicions of Colonel Rima Abadi. "I don't know what Arianna's relationship is with that Syrian official, but I wouldn't want to be on a sinking ship with her. I am not even sure I trust Luke."

I told him in savage whispers what Chas had divulged to me. That Syria was selling stolen Egyptian artifacts—artifacts that the *government* had stolen—to help fund their rebuilding program and pad their military. It wasn't just rumors. It was fact.

"*Merde*, Lucy. You actually believe him? Luke would never be part of a corrupt scheme like that."

"Well, someone is funding it. And *you* are just as suspicious of her as *I* am."

His eyes went as round as coins.

I nodded vigorously, and he disputed my claim. "I don't suspect her of anything like *that*," he whispered harshly.

I gestured for him to lower his voice. "Then what *do* you suspect her of?"

He shrugged. "I'm not sure. I just didn't like the way she handled the whole Piero situation."

The 'she' we were discussing was Arianna. And I didn't even have to mention her name for him to comprehend exactly to whom I referred. So he *did* have his suspicions.

I went to the bed and messed it up.

"But Alessandra really is safe?" I whispered, looking up.

"As far as I know."

I mimed that he should pull off his shirt and he did. I picked my white dress off the suitcase and threw it onto the floor.

"Okay?" he mouthed, and opened the door for Luke and Aras to enter.

Luke crossed the threshold first. It never ceased to amaze me what a strong presence the billionaire managed to bring into a room. He was a master of the 'power pose.' He needn't speak a word and everyone's attention was fixed on him. "Coast is clear. She's gone."

Huh? My eyebrows arched in wonder.

Aras followed him. He was wearing Norman's clothes.

"You can stop the pretense, Lucy," Luke said, reading my mood perfectly, and the faked situation. The sateen robe hadn't fooled him in the least. "We aren't the ones you should be afraid of."

"I don't know what you're talking about," I said.

Luke perched on the edge of the tousled bed staring at the white dress lying on the floor.

His eyelids lifted. "What did Basseem tell you about Rima Abadi?"

How to say this without sounding contemptuous? It was difficult—if not impossible—to bring myself to believe that our boss was conspiring with the Syrian minister. And yet I saw what I saw. If the explanation Chas had offered was true, the two women were definitely in cahoots. I had seen it with my own eyes.

"Arianna is not helping Rima Abadi to steal artifacts for her country," Luke said.

I gave him an earnest sigh. "Maybe she doesn't know what Abadi is doing?"

"Oh, she knows all right. That's why Piero was planted here. The person we are not sure of—" He paused to study my reaction "—is Ramy Basseem."

I objected. "He's not a crook. And he didn't try to poison us."

"How do you know?"

"Because he is no more a fan of Colonel Rima Abadi than I am. And I know that she is not on the up and up."

I was still annoyed that Luke and Arianna had kept me in the dark. Even after all I had gone through for the team, it seemed to me that Aras knew more than I did. I felt betrayed and wished to reveal nothing more.

"What do you mean, Lucy?" Luke demanded.

My next words held everyone's rapt attention. "I *mean*—Rima Abadi is working with the terrorists. She's a traitor."

Everyone stared at me in disbelief.

"What evidence do you have?" This time it was Aras that asked the question. His voice was stiff with suppressed excitement like he was waiting for me to confirm a long-held hunch.

My memory spun back several clicks. "I saw her with Tarek. She was the getaway driver when that scum of a terrorist tried to murder me at the ground transport terminus. I saw her behind the wheel." It had taken a while but my memory had finally made the connection. "Why else would she rescue him? Norman was ready to kill him. And if he hadn't made the attempt, *I* would have."

Silence descended like thunder. Not the meek, mild, Lucy Racine they were familiar with? Oh my. When would they get it? I had once shot Tarek (granted he did not die). I had been a captive in a terrorist camp, and I had entered voluntarily. And when no one else would help me I had gone alone to rescue my man. What was wrong with these people?

Why couldn't they see how I had grown?

Maybe they didn't want to. Maybe they liked the girl in the stiletto heels and the Marilyn Monroe dress.

Then Norman's eyes landed on me. Lit up. He had seen her too. "Lucy's right," he corroborated. "That was *Abadi* who drove the escape car for Tarek at the bus depot. Otherwise I would have killed him, except that my gun was MIA."

I had it. He had slipped it into my handbag previously.

"Lucy is a genius. It didn't register until now, but can't you see? Colonel Abadi is in bed with Nizar Tarek," Norman pressed.

"All the more reason we can trust Chas—I mean Basseem," I added. No one noticed my slip or my awkward recovery. More likely everyone knew that my long ago ex-boyfriend, Chas, was no more no less the infamous Ramy Basseem.

Luke mulled the news over. Abadi's jihadist connections had come as a surprise to all of them.

"What we need is proof," Aras decided. "Without proof that she is working with the terrorists we can't stop her. And if we don't stop her, she could start a war between Egypt and Syria, and bring down the Syrian government."

"Isn't that what you want?" Norman asked. "To get rid of the current regime?"

"Not this way," Aras said. "Too many innocents would die."

Norman had always said that Aras was a decent man, and at this very moment he was proving it.

Luke turned to me. "You trust Basseem?"

"At the moment, I trust him more than I trust Arianna," I said uneasily.

Luke muddled over my answer, before exchanging glances with his buddies. They nodded simultaneously and he reached out a hand to me, and stood up. "Sit down, Lucy. I think we have some sharing to do."

Cautiously, I took a seat on the edge of the bed.

As Luke began his narrative I was glad I'd had as much to drink tonight as I had. The alcohol, while enhancing my emotions, had put a freeze on my motility. My body felt like jelly so I just sat and listened.

The story unfolded pretty much as I had guessed. Everyone was in the loop except for me. I struggled to control my mounting anger. Call it frustration, call it disappointment, call it whatever, but in reality it felt like rage. I wanted to blast them all for keeping secrets from me. And yet somewhere in the back of my rational mind I understood why they had done what they had done.

Here is what happened.

Alessandra Piero's appearance in Egypt was a plant. I never had to worry about her safety because ISORE's plan had always been double-edged—to kill two birds with one stone. She saved my sister by pretending to be *her* when Tarek abducted her. And she infiltrated Tarek's organization on Arianna's behalf, and fed back information on the extremists' plot, which was to destroy relations between Egypt and Syria with the intention of usurping the Syrian government.

Piero had let Arianna know that Colonel Abadi and Ramy Basseem (aka Chas) were connected. Chas' mistake was in trusting Rima Abadi. He was in dire straights when she approached him and offered to subsidize his activities. It was she who had paid for his private jet that flew him to Toronto and returned him to Cairo. She had told him that she needed his help to verify the identity of the Screaming Mummy. She had followed his search for Cleopatra, and when he revealed his theory, *that* was when the Syrian minister really got interested. She seduced him into cooperating by enticing him with fame and fortune, and the return of his reputation. It worked.

Now she had to get Arianna on board by appealing to her sense of duty and her love of the ancient world. The preservation of antiquities was Arianna's reason for living, and the idea of terrorists blaming a legitimate government for theft and possibly triggering a war had her incensed. Abadi had heard about the influential director of the ROM from the Syrian First Lady who sang her praises.

"But Arianna wasn't fooled," Luke said. "She grew suspicious. She didn't want to risk losing sight of Abadi's activities so she deliberately played along. She wasn't at all certain about your friend Basseem, but he was irrelevant as far as she was concerned—just a minion. Until she learned from Aras that Yasmine was poisoned. Then she thought perhaps he was a bigger player."

Here I interrupted him. My next words were hard to spit out considering my recent interaction with Chas. "So, you thought I couldn't be trusted because of my past relationship with him?"

No one could look me in the eye. Not even Norman.

I could have gone off half-cocked and just left their company. I could have exploded with rage from the insult. I did not. It made sense. At one time I was bonkers over Chas. I guess when I revealed to Norman the true state of our former relationship he got nervous. After all I was so crazy about Chas back then that I had tried to get him to marry me. What an idiot I was. It was all I could do not to blush.

And for the record, this time *he* kissed me. I did *not* kiss him.

I realized now that I had been twisting the sash of my robe around my index finger. None of the men noted my discomfort. There was no teasing. They didn't exactly have stellar pasts either, and for that reason there was no judgment. It was just that they were never quite sure whether I sided with Chas.

"So everyone knows about us?" I asked helplessly, unraveling the sash from my finger.

I avoided eye contact with Norman. This was something I found hard to swallow. Chas was right. Both Luke and Norman *had* lied to me. Or if they hadn't outright lied, they had withheld the truth. Otherwise, I should have been in on the plan from the start.

At this very instant I seriously wondered: if Norman asked me to marry him would I say Yes? Trust was fundamental to a marriage. It was fundamental to any relationship.

Norman caught the drift of my thoughts and said, "I didn't tell them, Lucy."

It was still difficult to look his way. Instead I studied my feet. I was precariously perched on the corner of the mattress with Luke pacing in front of me. Norman had sat down beside me and was now trying to take my hand. And Aras? I don't know what Aras was doing. I was too busy looking at my feet.

"Arianna asked me to do a profile check on him," Aras said. His voice came from my left by the door. "It was common knowledge that you, Ramy Basseem and Yasmine Lim did internships at the Egyptian Museum in Cairo when you three were students. I went to visit Yasmine at the hospital and she told me about your history with Basseem. I spoke to her doctors. They confirmed that she had been poisoned. I reported all of the information to Arianna. And when she told me the guys here had been detained at the airport, I went to see them. I was worried about *you*."

"Thank you, Aras, but you don't have to worry about me. I can take care of myself."

"Sure you can."

I turned back to Luke who had stopped pacing. "What about Johnny?" I inquired as calmly as my elevated emotions would allow. "Was he in on it, too?"

"Not at first. Arianna didn't want Johnny on this mission."

"Because of his feelings for Alessandra?" I prompted.

He nodded. "Same reason she didn't want you and the big guy involved." He shot a swift glance at us. "Love makes everything complicated."

Yes, he had said that once before—or something to that effect—when making a reference to his ex-wife. Love made everything complicated. But it didn't have to.

By this time I had managed to control any residual anger. I allowed Norman to take my hand. My confidence remained intact having sensed how bad he felt. Yes, my idiocy at age nineteen was common knowledge. But *everyone is an idiot at nineteen. You know what Luke and I did...* Norman's exact words. When you think about the repercussions of their behavior at that age, I would agree that those two had messed up worse than me.

So, let bygones be bygones. That was then; this was today. But for some reason I was stymied. I knew there was a reason Chas wanted to ditch Norman, and I had to figure out exactly what that was.

"So, do you trust me now?" I asked. I was looking at Luke but my question was really directed elsewhere.

Norman squeezed my hand. That was a firm Yes. Luke grinned at me. "We adore you, Lucy. And you make it impossible for us to question your motives."

I rose from where I sat and grabbed Luke's wrist. His watch read 11:05 pm. I had promised to meet Chas at Saqqara by midnight. We could still make it if we left immediately, and drove like a bat out of hell.

But change of plans. The members of ISORE still suspected him.

They brought up the incident of him aiding terrorists to steal an Egyptian cartouche. Luke reminded me that Ramy Basseem was personally acquainted with Nizar Tarek.

"Stay away from him, Lucy," he warned.

"But I thought you wanted me to help Abadi."

"I want you to fake it. Tell her that you'll do it. But never be alone with *him*. I'll bet you anything he helped to steal that cartouche."

For the first time since this whole debacle began I wondered about the cartouche. How was it involved?

Only Chas could answer this question.

Tomorrow the boys intended to return to Cairo to monitor events and tie up some official business. Abadi would remain under surveillance.

It was late, and there was no more we could do tonight. The unexpected events of the day had made everyone tired and they soon returned to their rooms.

The team slept soundly that night, everyone except me.

CHAPTER 32

In the morning we drove back to Cairo. Luke, Norman and Aras were due in court to clear their names officially, to sign statements and other formalities to satisfy the Egyptian authorities, and to get Luke's private plane released. I was on my own for a couple of hours. I spent the first twenty minutes on the new phone that Luke had purchased for me, searching for information about Rima Abadi. There was the usual stuff concerning her career in politics and how she had come to her job at the ministry. One obscure link caught my eye. Apparently, she had completed a PhD in Egyptian archaeology before she entered politics. She was a skilled epigrapher and could read hieroglyphics. Her specialty had been Egyptian cartouches.

There it was again. The *cartouche.* Did it have something to do with Rima Abadi?

Where did she live now? I wondered. I did a search. Apparently she resided in a modest condo in Damascus.

And then an old news story caught my eye.

The civil war in Syria had made it dangerous for the privileged to live there. So many, including government officials, had purchased homes in foreign countries.

Call it instinct, call it whatever, but I wanted to know if

she was one of those people.

A further search revealed where the rich and famous resided in Egypt. Some new subdivisions had risen along the Nile River just past Luxor. Wouldn't mind seeing those. Luxor was known by the ancient Greeks as Thebes, and was famous for the Temple of Karnak and the Valley of the Kings.

I texted Norman to notify him of my intentions. I was already at the riverfront and contemplating how best to get to Luxor.

"Wait for us, Lucy," Norman texted back. *"Luke is going to make arrangements for a private cruise. It will get us there fast. And in style."*

"Won't a plane or helicopter be faster?"

"That will look suspicious. And the authorities will be monitoring our movements. Especially since we just got charges dropped."

"Ok, how long will you be?"

"No more than a couple of hours."

A couple of hours? That was going to be some wait. But I agreed.

"And keep your eyes peeled for suspicious-looking people. Tarek isn't done with you yet. Stay visible and wait for us in a public place. The riverfront is swarming with tourists. Go there."

I walked toward the marina where the private yachts moored. Further on I could see commercial riverboats, cruisers and the white sails of feluccas.

I was wearing sunglasses and the sun was shining directly into my eyes, but I could see someone leaning against the guardrail overlooking the pier where the smaller cruise ships docked. His outline was black with no identifying features clear, but the shape was definitely that of a man. His face was hidden, yet I knew instantly who he was. The confident stance, and the broad-brimmed bush hat gave him away.

A strong moment of self-consciousness in the form of

adrenalin shot through my veins. I glanced down at the vintage T-shirt I wore. Recklessly, in a moment of nostalgia I had bought a Basseem label from the ROM's gift shop. The Capri pants however were Calvin Klein, as were the rope-soled, wedgy espadrilles. Why had I worn this particular top today?

After he kissed me last night it was the last thing I should be wearing…

Oh hell. He saw me. No point in pretending that I hadn't made eye contact. He'd only follow me if I tried to make a getaway.

I approached quickly and he straightened to meet me.

"Racine," he said.

"Chas."

"I gather things got complicated last night? I saw Rima Abadi's car as I left through the service stairwell. I waited for you at the Step Pyramid. I figured it was because of *her* that you were a no show."

I nodded, shifting my sunglasses overtop my freshly shampooed hair. Could he smell the verbena/lavender scent?

"What did she want?" he asked.

"She wants me to work with her. She wants me to hook up with you. She thinks you will reveal to me the location of Cleopatra's sarcophagus. And then I can stab you in the back by bringing *her* the information."

A weird smile crossed his features. He shook his head, snickering to himself. It was that same partly attractive, partly scary, predatory smile that I always associated with him. This time however it seemed the victim wasn't me.

"What's so funny?" I demanded.

"I *want* to tell you," he replied. "But I think you will have to experience this for yourself. Are you in?"

"In on what? I'm waiting for Norman and the boys. They'll be here pretty soon."

"All the more reason we should skedaddle."

He took my hand; I tugged it away. "Stop flirting with me. Stop kissing me. Stop trying to hold my hand. I am *not* your girlfriend, Chas." So much for playing it cool. I was flustered and he knew it. The fragrant shampoo, wearing his label—was a test of his will. *And* mine.

His eyes took in the windswept flow of my hair to the vintage T tucked into my tight Capris. The incriminating logo sat just over my left breast. Amusement curled his lip. "That could change though, couldn't it?" His voice was very soft.

The gall of him! I regretted using so much shampoo. How could he help but smell it. Worse, why had I ever bought this dumb T-shirt?

This time the hungry smile was clearly meant for me. He wiggled his fingers once more. A reflex action almost made me take them and before I could chastise myself *or* him, he asked: "Do you want to know the whereabouts of Cleopatra's sarcophagus or not?"

I slapped his hand away. "I do. But I think we should wait for the rest of the team."

"We can't. I don't trust them. And they have no reason to trust *me*. They'll only hold us up and screw up my plans."

He reached for my hand again. No kidding they had no reason to trust him! This time I karate-chopped him at the wrist. "I told you once and I'm telling you again. I am not going *anywhere* with you. And *stop* touching me—"

I delivered a glare to drop a wolf mid-lunge, and then said quite plainly: "You agreed to let Norman help. You want the mummy, don't you?"

His arm swung to his side. He shrugged. Apparently he was quite unfazed by my rejection. "New plan. The mummy is safe where it is. I can return for it later. Right now, locating the sarcophagus and the crypt is more important than retrieving the mummy."

"You—you think there's a crypt?"

"Not one hundred percent sure. But I know how to find out. Are you in or are you out?"

"Out."

"Racine. Lucy. *Please.*"

He doubled down on the big cow's eyes stare. At one

time I would have moved heaven and earth for that look.

No more. He was a smooth operator, but so was I.

"I need your help," he begged.

I inhaled deeply, then answered coldly: "I thought you found the sarcophagus. Did you lie to me again?"

"No. I am not lying. I may not have its exact location, but I know how to find it. And that's the same thing as having it in my hands. No one else knows where it is, and they don't know how to locate it. I do. Please, Racine. I've heard stories about ISORE. You people have a reputation for passing through locked doors."

This was true.

He added, "I can't do it alone."

I tried to control my scowl. His attempts at seducing and manipulating me annoyed me no end, and that was partly my fault (T-shirt, hair). I had to make it clear. I had no romantic interest in him at all. And, *and* I absolutely—*absolutely*—refused to work with a criminal, a backstabber or a liar. "Tell me first," I said. "And don't spin me any yarns. Are you working with the terrorists?"

There was a split second of hesitation before he replied. "No."

I started to object but then decided to turn away. Norman and Luke might have a point. Ramy Basseem could be dangerous. The very fact that he possessed a manipulative charm was dangerous, not to mention the assorted feelings that went along with it. Fortunately, we were in a public place. There was nothing he could do to harm me here. I had a gun in my purse.

"Lucy, wait," he said. "Look. I'm sorry I kissed you." He hung his head, very effectively. "I mean. You're an exciting woman. You've grown into an amazingly exciting woman. So how can I not find you attractive? But I am deeply apologetic for having offended you by displaying my feelings. It was impulsive. I should have kept it in check. Now that I know my feelings are not reciprocated I will cease and desist. You have my word. Now—are we good?"

His expression appeared sincere, but I knew Chas. He was a charmer and the charmer gave the charmee exactly what she wanted.

"This has nothing to do with the kiss," I said. "But promise me you will never try that crap on me again."

"I promise."

"And no more lies."

He nodded.

I glared suspiciously at him. He was being too glib.

"All right. No more lies." He paused to inhale and then released the long-held breath. "You want the truth? Here's the truth—"

He began a story that had me gaping open-mouthed.

"Well over a year back I stupidly got involved in a theft with the rare, black onyx cartouche… Take that horrified look off your face, Racine. And hear me out. I had no idea it was a theft. I thought Tarek—yes Tarek was one of the thieves involved—was simply a Syrian curator who wanted to test a theory. He had all the right credentials and was accredited by the Syrian government. How was I to know the depth of corruption in that regime? Anyway, he wanted to borrow the cartouche. I signed the papers for the loan. I was clueless that he never intended to return it. So, *no*, I am not working with the terrorists. I was duped by them. Can't you see how humiliating that was and why I wanted to keep the truth hush-hush?"

"And Abadi?"

"I learned much *much* later—after I was released from jail—that it was she who commissioned the theft of the cartouche." She was the dirty government official who had vouched for Tarek. Stupidly, she had trusted a terrorist. Terrorists never kept their word, and Tarek was no different. He double-crossed her—lied—and told her he was forced by his leader to sell the cartouche.

"Wait just one second." I raised a hand to halt his speech. "I saw Tarek with Abadi. If he double-crossed her why would they still be working together?"

He shrugged. "Beats me. But as far as my part goes I did not knowingly help them to steal it. It wasn't until I was arrested that the story about terrorist involvement came out. Believe me, Racine, had I known they were terrorists, do you really think I would have signed out the artifact?"

I fell silent and Chas continued.

No one suspected Abadi's role in the heist. Lucky for him the investigators eventually believed him when he swore his innocence. It just took awhile, and he still had to spend time in jail. "Can you imagine how humiliating that was?" he asked. "It was all over the news media. Didn't you see the headlines? *Egyptian Indiana Jones cavorting with terrorists!* The banks froze my assets during the investigation. It was so unfair. It was Abadi that bailed me out. She did some damage control to divert the spotlight from me. So later, when she asked, I agreed to help her recover the goods."

"But if you knew she was dirty why did you help her?"

"I *didn't* know it—not then. She told me her government wanted the artifact so that they could return it to Egypt in a show of good faith."

I was beginning to catch on. That would exonerate them from accusations of collusion with the terrorists. Tarek as I well knew was Syrian.

"You see, I never thought much about this artifact. It was just one cartouche out of hundreds that the museum owned. Okay sure it was made from black onyx, but unless it came from something huge like an obelisk the stone itself is not that valuable. What I was totally oblivious of at the time was that it wasn't just any old cartouche. Rima Abadi wanted *this* cartouche. And remember, she posted my bail. That's why I agreed to work with her. As time went on I became suspicious. Why this particular cartouche? What could possibly be engraved on it that was so important?

"So, do you understand now, Lucy, why you are the only one who can help me? She doesn't know I am aware of her unusual interest in the cartouche. She contacted me and that was the first thing she asked me: where was the cartouche?

Well, I didn't know. But *now* I do."

"Where is it?" I demanded. "Who did Tarek sell it to? How much did he get for it?"

"He never sold it. He hid it. In the one place Abadi would never think to look."

"And where is that?"

"On her Egyptian property."

My jaw almost dropped. She did have another home outside of Syria. Of that, I had guessed correctly.

"What makes you think Tarek hid it in her house?"

"Because he told me when I tried to get it back from him that it was in the last place Abadi would ever search."

"That could be anywhere, Chas."

"But it isn't."

I shrugged. Fine if he wanted to believe that, but why was this cartouche in such demand?

I asked him.

"Its monetary worth is minimal," he replied. "That's not what makes it so highly prized. Even though it was carved in black onyx rather than the more typical red granite. No. Tarek is ignorant of its true value. The only reason he stole the cartouche is because he realized it is worth more than what the black market will pay. Abadi knew this, long before he did. That's why she wants it so badly. The difference between her and Tarek, however, is that she realizes what it *really* is and he doesn't. From what you've told me, it's clear she thinks I will reveal to you its whereabouts, and then *you* will tell *her*." A subtle pause occurred, just long enough for me to guess his next question. "*Will* you tell her, Racine?"

Not on your life. I trusted that woman as much as I trusted a scorpion.

I vigorously shook my head. "So the hieroglyphs on it are some sort of directions?"

"Yes. Or a map."

A map to the location of Cleopatra's tomb?

He nodded. He had read my thoughts.

There was one thing that still puzzled me. How had the

mummy and the sarcophagus become separated? Someone, somewhere down the line, in the past, must have recovered the Screaming Mummy. How long had it been in the possession of the Egyptian Museum and how could they not know?

Granted, that mummy had been stolen and recovered several times. Somewhere along the way there might have been a mix up. Things got lost in the past; documents got shuffled around, forgotten or destroyed. And memories faded with time. Or maybe it had happened in the ancient past. After all, Cleopatra had lived over 2,000 years ago. Tombs were looted regularly. Almost from the moment the dead were interred someone attempted to raid the gravesites. Pharaoh Djoser's body had been stolen from the Step Pyramid. Wherever Cleopatra's body had been originally laid to rest, it was stolen also. And then over the centuries it got lost, misidentified, and finally ended up at the Egyptian Museum in Cairo where it had been mislabeled as Prince Pentawere, Ramses III's royal son.

I was breathless just thinking all of this. There would be ample opportunity to research it later. Right now, we had to locate the cartouche and learn if it truly was the key to discovering the location of Cleopatra's tomb.

"Okay." I nodded. "I believe you. Do you know the address of Abadi's Egyptian house?"

Chas nodded in turn. "Come on. I rented a boat."

"Shouldn't we fly? That would get us there more quickly."

"Abadi has the airport under surveillance, and all of the official heliports as well. If we leave from there she will have us followed. Same thing with a car, the bus and the train; she will have thought of all of that. A river cruise, however? Slow and casual. What reason would she have for following a gently cruising felucca? We can pick up the pace when we're safely out of range. And even if she does have a tail on us, we won't appear to be in a hurry. It will put them off guard and allow plenty of time for us to lose her people in the ruins of Luxor."

CHAPTER 33

The felucca Chas had rented was a junk heap, hardly the luxury vessel I was expecting. Sure, I understood he was no billionaire like Luke Trevanian, but still…

My feelings must have shown on my face because Chas grunted. "I'm off the payroll until further notice, Racine. Make the best of it."

How could I complain? The boat was large, although—shall we say—rustic, and it had a cabin in which we could sleep. Oh God, sleep. That was going to be an issue, but I supposed Chas would have to be piloting the boat so maybe it wasn't. I shook the stupid thoughts out of my head. Of course it *wasn't* an issue. When it came to my heart, I had made myself diamond clear. *Focus, girl.* I looked around. Chas had encouraged me to take a tour while he tinkered with the engine.

Inside the cabin were food, water, blankets and extra clothing, and other necessities. Chas had thought of everything. I spent only a few minutes scouting out the arrangements below before I returned to the deck. The boat was equipped with a motor so we wouldn't have to rely on wind power. In fact the sails were furled.

"Where's the skipper?" I demanded, approaching like an

experienced hand. Spending time on Luke's yacht had taught me a thing or two about boatmanship.

"Ahoy, mate," Chas sniggered. He doffed his bush hat as though it were a captain's cap, and started up the engine. It choked before rising to a crescendo, then dropping to a putter.

Suddenly I heard a yell. It came from somewhere onshore and was in Arabic so I had to guess at the meaning of the exclamation. But this much was apparent; it had something to do with us.

Several dark, hooded men were pounding the pavement, pointing and shouting in our direction, and racing towards the wooden dock. Who were they and what did they want? I had no wish to find out.

"Let's get out of here!" I shouted to Chas.

Chas spun the boat into the open water. He made to open full throttle but the old engine choked before responding. My hand slammed down on top of his, seeking control of the lever—as though anything I could do would speed up the process.

That temporary stall of the motor was just long enough for the nearest of our pursuers to leap from the wharf. He was moving too fast so his face was a blur to me, but he reminded me of the thick-lipped driver Luke had ditched en route to Cairo.

He landed with most of his body inside the boat but nearly capsized us with the effort. I threw myself to starboard (at least I think it was starboard) to counterbalance his weight.

The man was strong, and heaved himself up and hurled himself straight at me. He dived across the deck, caught my ankle and dragged me towards him and that's when I fell, ducking the bullet just as Chas drew a pistol from nowhere and shot the man in cold blood. I felt the hand gripping my ankle release. Whatever part of him that was hit was vital, and he rolled with the rock of the boat, sliding along the wet boards to the side and splashed into the Nile. The boat would have capsized had Chas not thrown himself crosswise against the opposite rail.

I rose to see where the attacker was. I don't know if the man was dead, but a few seconds later, bubbles emerged and he dragged himself to the surface sputtering, a plume of red blossoming around him in the blue water. Chas refrained from firing a second shot, and thrust the gun into his belt while rapidly making his way to the stern to ramp up the motor.

"Get down," he instructed, stopping by my side, just long enough to snake a sweaty arm around me to force my compliance. I swear the hard muscles of his biceps flexed in a deliberate hug as his hand cupped my elbow, his arm pressed across my breasts and his lips moved against my hair.

"Don't let them see you." And he shoved me out of the way and took control of the boat.

We lurched forward leaving the injured man floundering in our wake while a crowd started to build along the shoreline, positioning their cellphones.

"Basseem! You're a dead man," someone barked from the dock. The threat was in Arabic but this was Chas' translation, and after what he had done to save my life I could only assume he was telling the truth.

I was still reeling from the shock of being attacked, and then ordered about by Chas, and, unexpectedly, my hackles rose. My blood boiled. I had experienced more desperate situations than this. How dare he manhandle me!

We were far down the river now and it would take a while before they could make chase. The feluccas at the wharf were all sailing vessels, and except for ours, none of those available were equipped with motors. If our pursuers managed to get hold of a helicopter however, they could track us like they were hunting a duck.

I crawled aft to squat down in front of Chas, determined to shut down his amorous attempts once and for all. But then I decided to shelve the lecture when I saw that his hands were full trying to make good our escape.

"Why were they after you?" I demanded shouting into the wind.

Chas turned from where he hunched at the throttle, cranking up our speed and searching for pursuers. "What makes you think they were after *me?*"

Yes. What made me think they were after *him?* It was me the terrorists were chasing. Because I dodged the bullet (literally) Tarek would continue his pursuit of me until I was dead. And now they would be hunting Chas as well, and it was entirely my fault.

"Damn, I wish they hadn't seen us," Chas cursed under his breath. He glanced up at the sky. "Any chance we could bum a helicopter ride from somewhere?"

His hint was loaded with meaning. He knew about Sayid and Piero, and that Johnny was a pilot.

That got me to thinking. Those two had found something. What? And why hadn't I heard from them? I knew now the discovery couldn't possibly be the crypt of Cleopatra because they had no cartouche to tell them where it was. But holy crow, could they have stumbled across the tomb by accident? If so, they would need help because not only were the Syrians searching for it, but the terrorists were, too.

"A helicopter? Yeah. Good idea," I said. Although, where one could possibly land around here was impossible to know. I glanced around searching for my handbag that held my phone. Last time I had tried to contact Johnny I had received no answer. It wouldn't hurt to make another attempt.

My purse was on the deck and I must have forgotten to zip it shut after I replaced my phone inside it upon encountering Chas at the pier. The contents were scattered every which way over the dirty, wet floorboards.

I rummaged through what effects remained in my bag, scowling. Everything was here except my phone. Oh no. Not again! Had it fallen overboard when that thug tried to sink us? All I remembered was that I had been in the process of removing the bag from my shoulder when all hell broke lose.

"What's wrong, Racine?"

"My phone. It's gone. Must have dropped into the river when the boat was tipped.

"Never mind. Use mine." He dug it out of one of his numerous pockets, unlocked the passcode and passed it over. "You're going to contact your fly boy buddy?"

I nodded. How *did* he know of Johnny's aptitude for flying? But then I remembered the two had met in the ROM's prep lab over the gruesome discovery of Ines' murder.

Crap. I had no memory of Johnny's new contact info.

I decided to call Norman instead; I desperately needed to hear his voice. He also had a new phone and I had learned my lesson well enough to have at least memorized *his* latest number.

He answered almost immediately. "Oh, thank God, Lucy. It's you. I couldn't figure out whose number was displaying on the caller ID. What happened to your new phone?"

"One guess," I said.

"Seriously? You lost it already?"

"Tell Luke I am so sorry."

"Forget it. What happened?"

I told him who I was with and where we were bound and how I happened to lose my phone—again. He was disappointed to learn that I had joined up with Chas, and told me he and the boys were on my tail. They would meet us at Abadi's house as soon as they could get hold of some kind of transport and GPS the location.

In my peripheral vision I saw Chas getting nervous when he realized I was speaking to Norman and not Johnny.

"Tell them not to fly," he interrupted. The look on his face was veiled, but not so much that he could hide that he preferred to keep Norman out of the picture. "I've had second thoughts regarding the helicopter. We can't have so many targets, else they will spot us."

"Did you hear that?" I asked Norman.

"Affirmative. If we come by boat we'll be a day behind you. We're still stuck here filling out forms and making statements. Maybe the delay is just as well. We don't want Tarek's men tracking us to you. And Lucy," Norman said before he hung up. I could tell he was controlling the emotion in his voice. His words: *I hate Chas* were not forgotten. "Be careful. Basseem is not to be trusted. Do you still have my gun?"

It was sitting among my belongings beside my handbag on the deck. Funny, how it had not tumbled overboard with my phone.

"Yes. See you soon." We hung up.

I stared across the open expanse of river.

"You should have told them not to come," Chas said, cutting into my thoughts. "The more people involved, the more likely we'll get noticed. And the more likely we are noticed the more likely we will get caught."

I launched myself upright from where I was resting against the bulwark and turned to Chas. "If we are going to find Cleopatra's tomb then we need to cooperate with each other. And when I say 'we,' I mean you and team ISORE." I planted a hard gaze on him. "You need *us* to steal the cartouche. And we need *you* to find it. If it really is a map to Cleopatra's tomb then we have to return it to the Egyptian people and stop this looming war."

I stopped lecturing to judge his response. Chas' muscles slackened as he sucked in his rebuff.

"Wars have been started for stupider reasons than this," I said. "We can stop this one if we work together.

***

Rain rarely falls on this section of the Nile Valley, so without the river, Egypt as a nation, would perish. Deprived of the annual flooding to wash the nutrient-rich silt onto the land the desert would take hold, and with no fertile valley to grow food and raise livestock people and animals would die. Ancient Egyptians recognized this ecological, symbiotic relationship when they likened the landscape to a lotus. The delta was the flower, the oasis of Al Fayoum the bud, and the river and its valley was the stem supporting the whole.

The Nile was truly the lifeblood of Egypt.

As the sky turned red-gold I went below to search for something to eat. No matter how dire life got, if there was one thing you could not fight that was hunger. Biology would always win out over any mystery your brain was trying to solve. I caved to my body's urge to nourish itself.

There was flatbread, still soft and fresh in plastic wrappers, Styrofoam containers of goat cheese, green and black olives, and tiny fried fish swimming in oil, plus a tub of tahini salad. Grapes, figs and dates cupped in folds of waxed paper completed the smorgasbord.

I was starving. There were no utensils, so I tore a piece of pita bread in half and used it to scoop up the soft goat cheese. The gentle hum of the engine lulled me into a false sense of security. It would soon be dark and Chas cut the engine until it was merely a quiet purr. We were travelling more slowly now, but still at a steady pace.

Just as I shoved the makeshift sandwich into my mouth the thud of footsteps overhead sent my eyes to the hatch. Chas dropped down through the square opening, athletically bypassing the few steps, and joined me.

"Who's driving the boat?" I asked. Truly. I was worried.

He was no one's fool, and smiled, catching the mild sarcasm and delivering an honest comeback. "Nobody. It's okay. It'll be fine for a few minutes. The course is straight for at least another kilometer and not a soul is on the river right now. It's getting too dark."

I glanced at the portholes and saw that this was true.

Chas crouched beside me bringing with him the fragrance of Old Spice, and reached into a compartment to draw out a bottle of Egyptian wine.

"Oh, no thanks," I said. "Water's all I need."

He removed two bottles of Aquafina from the same compartment and handed one to me.

The bottle felt warmish and was probably unpalatable to the taste buds, but let's face it, tepid water was better than no water at all.

I had stopped eating on his arrival, and he suggested we bring the picnic supper topside. "Can't leave the old girl for long without a skipper." He was referring to the felucca.

He grabbed a carryall that seemed already to have something inside it and stuffed the unopened bottles in. He also fetched a kerosene lamp. Then he ordered me to help him collect the food and bring it on deck.

Once outside again, I appreciated the breeze and the cooling temperatures. It was warm and dank below. Above us the sky broke wide with luminous stars. We had left the lights of the city far behind, allowing the darkness of the natural river-scape to become a stage for nature's celestial dance.

We spread the meager feast out in front of us on top of a locally woven blanket, made of un-dyed goat hair, laid over the wooden planks at the stern of the boat. I sat down opposite him. Chas checked the throttle to ensure that it maintained its steady thrum. He shot a look past me, through the rigging to the bow to affirm we were still on course and that there would be no obstacles needing our attention, hence interrupting our repast. The river was silent. On the banks tall rushes grew. We had cruised past the most populated areas and were deep into the Egyptian countryside. Here, only locals lived: fisherman, small-scale farmers, and village laborers and craftsmen. I could see every now and then a sporadic light from their tiny homes.

When satisfied that all was safe Chas set a Zippo lighter to the kerosene lamp. The wick caught and a single, bright flame illuminated our meal. Then he turned to the food.

He was as ravenous as I. That was obvious. His manners were rustic and he eagerly served himself first. He dipped his fingers into the carton of oily fish and spread several of them onto a piece of flatbread. Then he scooped some of the tahini salad, still using his fingers, and placed it on top of the little fish. Then he folded the pita into a half-moon shape and took a large bite. Anyone else serving himself this way would have appeared disgusting, but there was something so cowboyish about Chas that it would have seemed strange had he used a knife or spoon.

"Why are you so nervous, Racine?" he asked, chewing neatly. The gold eyebrow stud on his left side twitched slightly.

I swear he had not gotten any of that mess on his face. Of course, I couldn't say definitively, as it was quite black on the river and the starlight barely illuminated his face. The kerosene lamp sat in the middle of the food and its light scarcely reached us.

"I am not nervous," I said.

"Then why aren't you eating?" He fetched a corkscrew from the canvas carryall and opened the wine bottle and drank straight from the lip. "Sorry, no glasses." The remark was in response to my raised eyebrows. "This isn't exactly the Princess Cruise line."

I had to laugh at the obvious wisecrack.

"That's better," he said. "You have nothing to be afraid of from me."

He wiped the lip of the bottle with his sleeve and handed it over. Vaguely, and not entirely irrelevantly, I wondered where that sleeve had been. "It'll make the night pass faster. Give you sweet dreams."

"I'm not sure I want sweet dreams," I said.

His gaze absorbed mine intently. "What *do* you want?"

Not you, I thought.

"It's been a long time, hasn't it? So many things have changed since those days at the Egyptian Museum."

Miscellaneous memories were beginning to crowd my mind. I decided one slug of the red ambrosia wouldn't hurt and took a gulp. "I don't even remember those days. Except spending all that time sketching the mummy."

"Ah, the mummy." He could see that I was trying to divert the conversation. He looked up and smiled. "Those were the days. Fun days. Days with little responsibility."

"Oh sure, *you* seemed to be pretty irresponsible, all right." Against my will I was beginning to relive my time with Chas. I was young. He was my first. He should have been more sensitive after he found out.

"I had no idea, Racine. Why didn't you tell me—? And I mean *before* we reached the point-of-no-return."

"All bridge under the water," I said. Or was that water under the bridge. *Oh who cares?* I took another sip of the wine and lifted my head to see Chas' eyes on me.

"Hey, I *am* sorry. If I had known I would have held back."

He took my hand and gently fondled my knuckles. I whipped them back and almost slugged him. He smiled. "Okay. I get it. Still No… For now."

"For *ever*," I said.

He shrugged. He took a few bites from the olive carton, a couple of green and a larger number of black. He spat the pits out over the side and wiped his hands on his khaki pants before he pulled three dusty books out of the canvas carryall. These he plopped onto his lap where he sat next to the motor. He checked the throttle, then took the wine bottle from me and took a slug, clunked it down on the wooden boards of the deck, and flipped a few pages.

The books had hard covers with hand-stitched bindings and fabric jackets. I was at once astonished and disgusted with his behavior. These were sources written by the Greek essayist Plutarch, the Roman historian Cassius Dio and the physician philosopher Galen of Pergamon. Translations they may be, but they were still around a hundred years old, and some of the earliest. They should be in a museum library, not in his backpack.

He had to lean on the book he was studying to keep the pages open towards the kerosene lamp. I almost chided him for treating the ancient volume so carelessly. Of all people he should know better. He was an archaeologist. His mandate was to preserve all physical as well as intellectual aspects of history.

I moved to his side, reached over and cranked up the wick on the lamp to enlarge the flame. Gently, I removed his elbow from squashing the spine. "What are you reading?" I asked.

He reversed the book and shoved the aged tome at me. The pages were yellowed and brittle, and glowed in the fiery light.

> *Cleopatra sent to Caesar a letter, which she had written and sealed; and, putting everybody out of the monument but her two women, she shut the doors. Caesar, opening her letter, and finding pathetic prayers and entreaties that she might be buried in the same tomb with Antony, soon guessed what she was doing. At first he was going himself in all haste, but, changing his mind, he sent others to see. The thing had been quickly done. The messengers came at full speed, and found the guards apprehensive of nothing; but on opening the doors, they saw her stone dead, lying upon a bed of gold, set out in all her royal ornaments...*

It was a turn-of-the-twentieth-century English translation of the death of Cleopatra, written by the Greek essayist Plutarch. The Caesar to whom she referred was Octavius (or Octavian depending on who was translating), later known as Augustus.

"So there *was* a crypt, a tomb!" It was near impossible to keep the excitement out of my voice. "They mention a monument with doors that shut."

I scoured the page to see if there was any description of a location.

"I've read every source backwards and forwards. There is no clue to the whereabouts of her burial site," Chas assured me.

"Too bad. That would have saved us having to search Abadi's house for the cartouche." I honestly dreaded the idea of breaking and entering the Syrian official's home.

Chas nodded. "None of the historical documents have ever recorded a location for her tomb. But here's something else to help us identify her." He pressed a finger to the page. "She had two women buried with her. Her maidservants."

I paused from reading the text where his dirty fingernail underscored the relevant line. I glanced up. "*And* a bed of gold."

Chas was admiring my insight with that familiar, stupidly attractive, hungry look on his face.

I grabbed the bottle of wine and poured a mouthful down my throat.

His eyes shone with excitement in the starlight.

I did everything in my power to ignore them. His persistence was admirable and even flattering, considering our abysmal history. But there was no turning back. All I cared about now was finding Cleopatra's burial place.

I returned my attention to the book. Something caught my attention. Could this mean anything? But it was only another theory of how Cleopatra might have died. Most historians preferred the anecdote of her committing suicide by submitting to the bite of an asp, a viper or a cobra. This passage made mention of a long-toothed comb whose ivory tines might be mistaken for the fangs of a snake. Was poison involved? Almost certainly.

None of the people searching for her body, however, really cared how she died. What they sought was her golden deathbed. Her sarcophagus. Where could it be?

I read on:

> *Octavian was concerned that they both (Cleopatra and Antony) might destroy their wealth, which he (Octavian) kept hearing was of vast extent; for Cleopatra had collected it all in her tomb which she was constructing in the royal grounds, and she threatened to burn it all up*

with her in case she should fail of even the slightest of her demands. Without this treasure Octavian's soldiers could not be paid. Privately, therefore he intimated to Cleopatra of pardon and even of love, so that by this means at least she would make away with Antony and keep herself and her money unharmed.

Here again was mention of a tomb. Being built on the royal grounds. Where might that be? To which royal grounds was the writer referring?

I jerked my head up to see Chas still observing me, his shadow flickering in the lamplight across the deck.

Unfortunately, these writings were only helpful if we actually found a tomb. Then we could do a comparison with the descriptions. Without the cartouche however we had little chance of guessing the exact location of Cleopatra's crypt.

CHAPTER 34

It was still fairly early in the morning and the soft apricot light illuminated the lush greenery of the vegetation, especially the date palms that grew along the river's banks. A flock of egrets flew overhead on some sort of annual migration, and out on the water itself were fisherman in traditional wooden rowboats casting their nets.

Over night we had plotted our strategy once we reached the neighborhood of Luxor. For the record, Chas kept his word when he said I had nothing to fear from him. After we had finalized our plan, I turned in. He slept on deck while I slept below in the cabin under the scratchy, wool goat blanket. In order to be inconspicuous we had decided to avoid staying in any of the numerous ritzy hotels. If Abadi sent people searching for us we intended to remain under their radar.

The closer we got to Luxor the slower we decided to travel, and by the time we set eyes on the orange sandstone shoreline we had cut the engine and journeyed into the small village of Habu under sail. No one followed.

Chas had not come unprepared. The location of the property was easy travel distance to some of the historic sites, namely the Valley of the Kings and the Valley of the

Queens. He had a map of the various residential areas in the vicinity, and knew the exact location of Abadi's Egyptian home.

Before we left the boat I borrowed one of his ancient tomes, and secretly stuffed it into my cross-body handbag.

The trek from riverbank to village core took twelve minutes. Another ten minutes brought us to Abadi's abode.

We crossed a lovely irrigated garden through a charming wrought iron gate. There were tamarisk trees and date palms. The flagstone path wound around a stone fountain in the shape of a seated lion, and led to a solid white door with black hardware.

This side of the house faced a grand temple in the quiet Habu village on the West Bank. As we stood at the threshold, we realized the home had been newly renovated because one peek inside one of the front windows showed gleaming brand new stone and woodwork. It was a large impressive structure, some would describe as a villa, newly refurbished in the interior and with a traditional mosque-like appearance on the outside.

Briefly it occurred to me to wonder: how did a government official afford all of this?

As far as we knew, Rima Abadi was still in Cairo, so we should be safe for a short while. I expertly unlocked the door using nothing more sophisticated than a couple of pins. Apparently locks the world over employed the same technology. And even if she'd had a state-of-the-art security system, I could probably disable the system. I had seen Norman perform the act numerous times, and he had taught me a thing or two. Which was why Chas should be thanking me for having the bodyguard in my life.

On entering the house a blast of cold air greeted us. So, she had central air-conditioning, a luxury affordable only by the elite and the rich. Curious though. Why was it on if she wasn't home?

The sight that met us caught me off-guard, as I had not expected to see replications of tacky Egyptian motifs on the walls. With a second look however, I realized these were not tacky reproductions at all, ergo the air conditioning to protect the paintings from heat and humidity.

Up close, they appeared disturbingly authentic. If these were real, it would be wise to install an alarm system to protect them. Then it occurred to me that no one in this village would break into her home. Why would they? And why would they think any of these pieces of art were real?

"What's the plan?" I asked Chas. "Where do you think Tarek would hide the cartouche, providing that your theory is correct?"

We were standing in the living room, which had sparkling white walls with Persian rugs on the floor and expensive furnishings. Her taste in colors left something to be desired but I could tell that nothing in here was cheap. Red and gold appeared to be the dominant colors for the upholstery. There was a black sofa with orange and yellow pillows. On the main wall a section of a tomb painting, which again I had mistaken for a reproduction caught my eye. This had a classic Egyptian figure standing, dressed in colorful robes in turquoise and orange. I gave it further scrutiny, examined it with a semi-practiced eye. No doubt about it. I was no expert, but the thing appeared genuine.

I glanced at Chas. He nodded. "They're real all right."

I took a step closer to inspect a painting on the opposite wall. "She's been smuggling art from Egyptian ruins and hiding them here?"

"Yup. Pretty clever huh? I bet you dozens of people have walked into her home and never suspected it."

"Nothing we can do about that right now," I said. "It's the cartouche we're after."

"That thing is priceless. Tarek would not want Abadi to accidentally stumble across it, although I doubt she spends much time here. Another reason why this would be a great hiding place," said Chas.

Where would I hide a priceless artifact if I were a terrorist? I mused the question over. Problem was, I was not a terrorist so how would I know?

This house was huge but not enormous, nothing like Luke's mansion. However, it did have a spacious living and dining room, another sitting area and a massive modern granite kitchen complete with white subway tiles and white cupboards. It was very incongruous with the traditional architecture if you asked me. Most of the rooms had arches shaped like onion domes and curved insets.

Why? I wondered. Why did she have such a beautiful, spacious kitchen when I doubted she even knew what a skillet or a wooden spoon was? Colonel Rima Abadi exhibited nothing of the domestic in her outward appearance.

We began by searching the kitchen cabinetry but then I realized how inefficient that was. Besides, why would Tarek hide the treasure inside a pot or a utensil drawer? Wouldn't those be the first places where she would see it?

No, we had to be more creative than that.

Were there any secret rooms or cabinets in the walls?

We decided we could cover more ground if we split up. I left Chas and climbed the stairs to the second floor, while he continued on the main floor. Here were three full bathrooms each installed with sumptuous tile. One of the quest bedrooms reminded me of the inside of a stone monastery, complete with ecclesiastical flourishes and screens on the triangular windows. Many of the rooms, in fact, had this architectural feature of archway with the furniture set in and beneath them. I ran my hands over and under suspicious spots on walls and floors. Nothing gave. And as I turned to leave the last of the five bedrooms I noted that even the doorway to the balcony exiting the master bedroom was shaped in the form of an onion dome.

I stepped outside to the stone balcony to clear my head and take in the view. Something was bothering me. I kept hearing a strange sound, a muffled noise—an irregular but quiet thumping. Was it a problem with the air conditioning? *No. I don't believe so.* It was barely audible, and when I had asked Chas earlier if he had heard it, he paused to listen, and the soft thuds, although practically inaudible, had stopped, so he never even heard them.

At first I thought they were coming from outside which was the main reason I stood on the balcony now. But they were undetectable out here. All I could hear was the wind, the swishing of palm fronds and birds. There was also the odd traffic noise. And across the way, where I spotted the Habu Temple, the chatter of tourists was clear. Part of the temple had scaffolding on it and workmen were restoring sections of the masonry. Was it that *chink, chink, chink,* I was hearing? No. What was irking my senses was not tinny in timbre but more like repetitive dull thumps.

When I returned indoors, I detected the sound again. Was it coming from above or below? *What* was directly above this room?

Chas was elsewhere searching the villa. I decided to head to the rooftop where I had glimpsed a patio, and after climbing the stairs I opened a door that led to a roomy outdoor sitting area. I stared in amazement. There was almost enough space to land a helicopter here!

The patio covered the entire rooftop. It had a large red canvas cabana with seating for dozens of guests. In the open area were more chairs with coffee tables and several paired chaises longue by the balustrade. The only thing unusual about this patio was its size. Who needed an outdoor entertainment area this big? What—did Abadi rub shoulders with the entire Egyptian government here?

Well, apparently this would not make a good hiding place for a stolen artifact.

I almost turned away after admiring the view of the Nile, which I could just make out overtop the ruins, when something near the door caught my eye. These amounted to a few leftover pieces of marble tile and the mortar for sealing it—and a sledgehammer.

Where had I seen this tile? In one of the numerous bathrooms? No. It was downstairs in the dining room. There was a lovely violet marble alcove where teak shelves had been inlaid. On these shelves were various glass and crystal stemware. I hurried past the bedrooms downstairs to the main floor. As I walked into the dining room I was seriously disturbed. I could hear the muffled thumping again. This time I was certain where it came from.

I clawed the glass vases and crystal candlesticks from the shelf inside the shallow marble alcove and set them haphazardly on the dining room table. Then I tackled the wine and cocktail glasses on the lower shelf. The shelves were set on brass brackets screwed into the marble, which made them easy to remove. I was just about to lift the top one when I was startled out of the act.

"Racine, what are you doing?" Chas' voice accosted me. "You're making a mess. We can't afford to disturb this place too much in case we have to make a run for it."

He started to force the shelf out of my hands but I shouted, "Wait!"

This time the thumping started in earnest. It was barely audible. I gestured for Chas to place his ears against the marble.

"Listen!"

We exchanged puzzled glances. There was someone behind this wall.

"Run upstairs to the rooftop patio," I ordered Chas. "There's a sledgehammer by the door on the outside. Fetch it. We are going to smash this wall down."

"Are you out of your mind, Racine? That's willful destruction. We could go to jail for that."

"Like we won't go to jail for breaking into this house? Get your ass moving, Chas. There is someone suffocating behind this wall!"

"Fine," he said and raced out the door and up the stairs.

He returned in less than four minutes. By that time I had unscrewed the brackets with a knife I had found in the silverware drawer, and removed the wooden shelves. Chas gestured for me to back away and he swung the sledgehammer at the marble wall. It cracked and splintered, showering down onto the brand new floor. He swung again and this time the mortar gave, breaking into large pieces still glued to the drywall beneath. When the dust cleared, Chas poked his head inside the pillow-sized hole. I popped up under his arm and looked too.

The dust was settling. We both coughed and waved away the cloud. A woman was bound to a chair with duct tape. Her mouth was duct taped too. The dust was starting to make her wheeze.

She had been bouncing up and down on the chair trying to make as much noise as possible when she heard our voices inside the house.

My heart darted into ruinous palpitations when I suddenly realized who she was. The rest of my body went inert.

"Go to the kitchen, find a sharp knife or scissors!" Chas ordered.

The butter knife I had used as a screwdriver would not serve at all.

The air was stuffy behind the wall but not dead. There were cracks in the exterior wall that had allowed for oxygen. Thank God. Otherwise Alessandra would have suffocated.

"Racine!"

I shot up off my knees, scattering bits of drywall and tile, and raced to find the required implement.

When I returned Chas had managed to widen the hole enough for him to duck through and enter sideways, creating even more dust and debris. I followed him, gingerly stepping over the broken marble and mortar.

We approached the chair, removed the duct tape so that she could speak.

"Lucy!" She choked out my name. Her long, dark hair fluttered as she shook herself alert. Although there was air seeping in from small cracks in the outside wall, the oxygen level was thin and I was certain she felt somewhat doped from the lack of fresh air. She sucked in a huge breath. "Get me out of here; Sayid is in trouble. They think he knows where the cartouche is."

I placed a hand on her shoulder to steady her. Then I went to work on releasing her taped hands and feet. She was also bound at the waist and chest to forcibly restrain her in the wooden chair.

"How could he possibly know where the cartouche is?" I demanded. And how did *she* even know about it? But no time for questions; she was right we had no time to lose.

I fumbled with the stubborn tape. It refused to rip and I was ready to give up when I scored the blade of the scissors against her wrists. The tape split and I peeled it away.

"Then it's not here," Chas said from the back of the chair, tearing at the tape with his fingers. I passed him the pair of scissors, and he sliced through the tape before he handed them back to me.

"No. It's not here." She attempted to twist to get a better look at the speaker. "And who the hell are you?"

Chas sidestepped so that he was in her view, fisting a ball of tape. He patted his chest where a tiny logo was stitched. For the first time, I actually paid attention and examined the logo. It was a gold pyramid with a large capital B in red, superimposed over top of it—the same logo that decorated my vintage T-shirt. "My name is Ramy Basseem," he answered, and paused. "You're wearing my label."

Her eyes dropped briefly to her olive drab tank top underneath a matching shirt that also sported the famous label. "You—*You're* Ramy Basseem?"

He bowed. "None other."

I stripped the last of the duct tape off her ankles with the help of the scissors and she gasped. I helped her to stand up.

After allowing me a brief hug, she shook me off. Alessandra Piero was not big on PDA, and I forced myself to rein in my urge to publicly display my affections. It had been weeks since her abduction; I mean what did she expect?

I hugged her again.

The only witness to our emotional reunion was Ramy Basseem, but it seemed Ramy Basseem was one person too many, and she gently nudged me away. Even so, I wanted her to know how much I appreciated what she had done by impersonating my sister. Because of her my sister Colleen was safe in Toronto awaiting the birth of her first child.

"Are you okay? How long have you been here?" I asked, squeezing her arm.

"Could have been *too* long. But it wasn't—thanks to you."

Alessandra stretched to her full, elegant height, thick hair, somewhat tangled from her ordeal, cascading down her back. She was almost as tall as Chas, leaving me feeling dwarfed. Yeah, Piero could have been a supermodel but she chose this life instead.

"Who did this to you, Alessa?" I asked.

"Some thick-lipped, gap-toothed Arab and his cronies, who couldn't speak a word of English. I think the name I caught was Jaffar. Serendipitously, he had no idea that I could understand every word he uttered. We were ambushed. Sayid was taken away by some men."

"Tarek's men?" If they were, it made no sense.

"Abadi's," she corrected, and shoved a hand into one of her pockets and drew out an elastic band with which she promptly began to fasten her hair into a low ponytail. "That woman is dirty. And she's dead set on starting a war between Egypt and Syria. And for no other reason than she is a greedy bitch—a *self-serving* avaricious, goddamned bitch of a terrorist, who will end up being rich and living on whichever side happens to win. That makes her worse than Tarek."

As far as I was concerned, no one was worse than Nizar Tarek.

I knew that Alessandra was merely venting. She wasn't accustomed to being victimized and, in fact, would deny that that had happened, explaining away her captivity as part of the plan. I, however, knew better. Otherwise she would not be using invectives so freely. Normally she was the cool-headed one. But it wasn't every day you were sealed up behind a wall.

She kicked away some chunks of drywall (or was it plaster?) and debris from the broken wall, and flinched. “No more time for chitchat,” she said between gritted teeth. “Let’s go.”

She was in pain but was ignoring it through sheer will. The way she had had to correct her balance after that action of kicking the rubble made me look down. I stooped and gently pulled at the cuff of her right pant leg. She flinched and elbowed me away in annoyance. I rose, exclaimed, “Oh, geez. Your ankle, it’s swollen.”

“Just a sprain. I kicked one of those sons of bitches hard, missed his soft parts and hit the marble wall when he dodged. That was my mistake. I let myself get too angry. I’m fine.” She turned to include Chas in her next question. “Who’s driving?”

“We came by boat,” he said.

“Boat?” That, clearly, was an unsatisfactory answer. “That’s too slow. We need a jeep.”

When I reflected over the miles of river we had covered to get here from Cairo and the time it took, I arrived at a different conclusion.

“A jeep my eye. We need a helicopter.”

CHAPTER 35

The unexpected *whup whup whup* of spinning rotors resounded in the air. The three of us stared incredulously at each other. Our prayers had been answered or our dreams had come true. One look at Alessandra's face said it all. She was hardly one to pray or believe in dreams. She was a hardcore realist.

I went to one of the picture windows to look out. The others followed. Was I seeing things? Indeed, a helicopter, jet-black against the cerulean sky, sharp as a cutout, hovered over the rooftop patio.

"Be careful, this could be a trap," Piero warned as she hobbled back from the window.

I knew her ankle was hurting her more than she let on. I could at least wrap it up with some torn fabric to take the pressure off. Or run to the refrigerator to see if the freezer contained any ice. But I knew that it was useless to ask her to let me dress it. Although I could try.

"You two stay here," Chas instructed. "I'll go and look. If it's Tarek, he'll be here for *you* two. So stay put."

Alessandra scowled but she knew he was right as far as her kidnapper was concerned, and she had other plans, so I tabled the freezer expedition because Chas' request wasn't going to stop her from following ten seconds after his departure.

When we reached the rooftop patio I spied a huge, moving shadow shading the outdoor entertainment area. It looked like a giant insect with a quad of spinning wings. Hidden from view by the wall, Chas was staring up at the pilot. He appeared puzzled—or disappointed? Piero noticed too but made no comment, and I noted that she had dragged the sledgehammer with her.

The pilot stuck his head out the window and I could see a familiar outline. It was Johnny! But how could I be sure?

I glanced at Alessandra who *was* sure. "Sayid!" she shouted, plunging under the rotors backwash. "What the hell took you so long?"

His answer was lost in the chopping of the rotor blades, but his hands were in motion as he mimed for us to move the furniture out of the way. He was going to attempt a landing. Oh crap, I thought. Seriously? He couldn't land on the ground? But when I looked down at the surrounding garden there were too many features in the way, including the large fountain and the wrought iron gate, *and* a grove of tamarisk trees.

Between the three of us we made short work of the patio furnishings, stacking and shoving them off to the side; and when there still appeared to be too little space, we tore down the canvas cabana, smashing the poles of the metal frame with the sledgehammer to flatten it to the ground, and heaved the stacks and bundles over the guardrails. We had already smashed in the dining room wall; what was a little broken chaises longue and an oversized tent?

In no time flat, we were inside the chopper. A few minutes after it landed we were back in the air.

I sat up front with Johnny while Alessandra reclined in the rear, favoring her swollen ankle, and Chas sat between her and us.

I wanted to throw my arms around the pilot and hug him just as I had hugged Piero. But he was in the driver's seat so that would have been certifiably dangerous. I put a headset on so that I could talk to him while muffling out the roar of the engines and the rotors.

Apparently, he had escaped from Abadi's men who thought they could get the location of the cartouche out of him by sealing Alessandra up in the wall. He had pretended that he knew where the coveted artifact was—after all he was a Syrian rebel, so Abadi assumed he was in cahoots with Tarek. But Johnny Sayid was trained like all members of ISORE in deception and martial arts, and he somehow got away and returned to fetch Piero. Concerned over the extra pair of ears (my pal Chas), he left out most of the details.

"I was surprised to find you and Basseem there," he said, indicating Abadi's rapidly shrinking abode with a dip of his chin.

Outside the bubble screen, I watched the village of Habu fade away in the deepening day. Abadi's exotic villa vanished as the river came into full aerial view, and snaked away into the hazy distance. I could almost make out the spot among the reeds where we had abandoned the felucca.

Johnny accelerated our ascent before turning his sun-glassed eyes from the view of the clear sky ahead of us to my face.

I met his gaze with sincerity before I spoke. "Basseem thought the onyx cartouche was hidden in Abadi's house."

"It's not," Johnny said.

"You know where it is?"

"No. But I know something else. And that's why we're headed back to Saqqara. We have some unfinished business. But first I want to ditch the Egyptian cowboy."

His eyes twitched back to the rear of the helicopter. I turned to see Chas meet my gaze. He was clearly not happy with this turn of events and was plotting something—but what?

My loyalties were to ISORE and the team. If Sayid felt we had to rid ourselves of Chas, then it was incumbent that we did. But the news could wait until we landed.

Should we leave Alessandra at a hospital? One glance at her told me no. She would bolt and follow us the moment we left her, and yet I wondered how much more her injured ankle could take before giving out.

She gave me a cold look, like she knew my thoughts.

I turned back to question Johnny further. He had been hinting about an incredible discovery since our last conversation, which now seemed eons ago, but was only a day or so past. He said nothing more to my verbal fishing, but concentrated on getting us to Saqqara as quickly as possible, and I had the good sense not to nag him needlessly. Prudently, he had no wish to discuss something that Chas might overhear. Although I doubted Chas could comprehend a thing above the noise of the engine and the rotors.

Johnny had his reasons, and mine was not to question why…

It was almost a three-hour flight before we arrived in the desert just outside the ruins. From the air the massive site was a maze of mortuary structures contained within recessed limestone walls. The pyramid rose from the center of the complex. A number of buildings including chapels and pavilions served for ritual purposes. To the south was a great court with an altar, and the roofed colonnade, resembling tree trunks, led to this court.

From our aerial vantage we could even see the towering peak of the Great Pyramid of Giza and the iconic Sphinx across the desert to our right.

The sun was low in the sky and hot, and no tourists bespeckled the landscape as we began our descent.

A temple lies on the north side of the pyramid along with a statue of the king. We landed just outside the *serdab*, a stone structure surrounding the statue. Because of the poor shape of the main attraction (one side was entirely covered with scaffolding), visitors could view the famous monument from the outside alone.

No one was allowed inside Djoser's tomb, and visitors could only gain access to the interior of the Step Pyramid with special passes. Chas had one of these special passes because he was filming a documentary. Team ISORE had not applied for permits, and there was no one to check anyways. It was 5:00 pm and the site was closed until 8:00 am the following morning. So Chas was superfluous to our gaining entry. We had already learned from previous forays into the Step Pyramid that no night guards were on hand to stop trespassers.

"What did you find, Sayid?" Chas demanded. His voice came cold and deliberate from behind us.

"Say nothing," Alessandra cautioned.

The helicopter was on the ground, the rotors gently winding down. The engine shut off. We waited until the whirring had ceased before unfastening our seatbelts.

"This is where we part ways, Dr. Basseem," Sayid said, turning around. "Trevanian and Depardieu are on their way to join us. I've rerouted them from their trip to Luxor via helicopter radio. They should be here within the hour, and when they arrive I'm sure we'll have consensus that you should return to the city."

"You can't just abandon me out here!" Chas objected wildly. The gold eyebrow stud on his left side was twitching up and down.

Sayid shrugged. "You had no qualms about abandoning *Lucy* at the airport."

My eyes jerked up. How did he know? Then I realized the boys must have updated him on my escapades when he contacted them.

"They were arresting people. I couldn't afford to be incarcerated again," Chas whined.

"And *we* can't afford to have you nosing around, given your track record." Alessandra bit off his words.

"First aid is under your seat, Piero," Johnny said. He looked at her like he wanted to do something more and was doing his utmost to contain himself.

Alessandra dug out the few bits of equipment that Sayid had stashed in the specified location. There was a flashlight, a couple of bottles of water, gun cartridges, a bottle of some generic aspirin, and a box of zip ties and thick, white gauze. There was also one roll of stretchy fabric bandage. I plucked this out from among the other options.

Ignoring her objection, I climbed over the seat and tightly wrapped Piero's ankle with the stretchy bandage, then I used two plastic zip ties to hold them in place in case the tuck decided to work itself loose. This would apply compression to the injury and prevent further fluid buildup.

"It's inhuman to just dump me here with no provisions," Chas argued. "I have no means of transport."

Alessa leaned forward from where she sat near him at the rear of the helicopter with me at her feet. "Debark. *Now.* You can walk back to the village and hire a taxi."

Chas scowled, half stood and waved his hands theatrically. "You have no right to give me orders. This is government property. I forbid you to enter these ruins."

"You can't forbid anyone anything," Johnny said. He left the pilot's seat and came around to collect the equipment. He stabbed a thumb in the direction of the window. Nearby were the crumbling, yellow structures of the Saqqara necropolis. "You are no longer responsible for the protection of these monuments. You have no legal status. No jurisdiction. No job."

I felt a twinge of sympathy for Chas. All of it was true. He had told me so himself. The man didn't have a friend in the world.

I gave my colleagues an imploring smile. What would it hurt for him to come with us?

Then I realized that they still did not trust him.

I got up from dressing Piero's leg and moved to the other seat beside her so that I was out of the way.

"You can't make me leave," Chas insisted, fully standing now.

"We should have left you at that demon lady's house," Alessandra countered. She studied the clutter of objects at her feet. Her thoughts were already fast-forwarding to the next task in her organized mind. "All right, then stay. But you are remaining inside the chopper."

She pulled the box of plastic zip ties toward her and when Chas saw what she intended to do, he kicked out, aiming for her injured foot. The thud it made caused me to wince and dive out of my seat to help her as she doubled over.

Sayid wrestled him down as Alessandra rose, white-faced from searing agony, and seized his wrists. The strength that woman had never ceased to amaze me. She locked his wrists together until they were bruised blue, while Johnny ferociously bound his feet until the plastic cut into the flesh. Ordinarily Sayid would have tackled the situation more calmly but he had failed to predict Chas' malicious act, and that was Chas' worst mistake. There was no changing Johnny's mind now. Or Piero's. Together they shoved him into a seat at the far rear of the aircraft, and belted him into place with the seatbelt.

With his hands and feet bound with zip ties and the seatbelt over his arms, holding his hands secure, he was as mobile as a mummy, freshly wrapped.

"You can stay here until we get back," Johnny growled. He stuffed the flashlight and the gun cartridges into his pockets. The aspirin and one of the water bottles he tossed to Piero. "If you try to move this bird, you will probably crash it and kill yourself. So think twice before you make any stupid attempts."

My mouth was partially open as all of this unfolded. It was so unlike Sayid and Piero to be so harsh. "Guys," I said. "Is this really necessary?"

"I'm sorry, Lucy," Alessandra answered. "I trust this weasel as much as I trust a desert cat."

She dumped three white tablets into the palm of her hand and snapped the cap back onto the plastic medicine bottle. She poured the pills down her throat followed by a long gulp of water.

"She's right," Johnny rejoined, tossing me the other

water bottle. "We don't really know which side he's on. Look how quickly he turned on Piero."

"I'm on *your* side," Chas wailed. "I helped to save you, Agent Piero. Why would I do that if I was working for the terrorists?"

"Yeah? And look at what you just did to my injured ankle. But I can let bygones be bygones if it turns out you just did that out of cowardice or malicious desperation. Don't worry. I'll return the favor—when I've learned irrefutably that you are clean—with interest."

Piero flung that last remark over her shoulder.

Hunched over, she stepped over Chas' feet and he was powerless to do anything about it.

"Let's hit the road, Lucy," she said. Then she turned back to the captive. "Just be grateful we don't gag you as well."

"How's the ankle?" Johnny asked as he stuck out an arm to help Alessandra off the helicopter.

She waved his hand away, grabbing the safety rail instead, and answered, "I'll live."

CHAPTER 36

We approached from the rear of the great monument, and I noticed for the first time a small, modern, temporary shed erected behind it. What was in it? It had an old-fashioned padlock attached and possibly belonged to the archaeologists or the film crew to store their equipment.

Single file, we entered through the main entrance on the north side where the Mortuary Temple stood beneath the colonnade. This time I paid no attention to the mummies lined up along the pathway. Whoever they were—servants or slaves, or ordinary denizens—none of them were the queen.

Then we took the stone steps to the main shaft where the scaffolding and airbags propped up the ceiling. Sayid left the generator's lights off. Instead, we used a single flashlight, and followed the same passageway Norman and I had used earlier until we came to several looter's tunnels. Here we diverged from the beaten path. The going was rough and erratic. The looter that had tunneled through, searching for a shortcut to the pharaoh's riches, had had no idea of which direction to go and had created a narrow, ragged tube that joined those of other robbers to form an incoherent labyrinth. Johnny, however, having taken this path earlier knew exactly where it led.

To me, the route was unfamiliar and I searched for any signs of trespassers or even of scaffolding and protective airbags. It seemed to me, if any part of the tomb complex needed that kind of safety measure it was here. But none were obvious. Most of the caverns were shallow and the passageways too narrow.

Bits of the walls trembled and fell to join the chaos on the floor as we brushed by.

Our progress was slowed only slightly by Piero's injury, and when Sayid suggested she wait for us in one of the galleries we bypassed, she balked. "So, who gets to keep the flashlight," she snapped.

We had only one. True. We could hardly leave her alone in the pitch dark for a couple of hours. But it was either that or we stride off into the blackness with no light. Or she came with us.

She insisted on accompanying us and Johnny stopped making combative suggestions. From what I knew of Alessandra Piero, it would take a lot more than a sprained ankle to keep her down.

The current tunnels were rougher, dustier, much less used and almost certainly forbidden zones (though that was irrelevant to us), and had our team at many points down on hands and knees. Despite the fact that the shafts occasionally opened out to chambers filled with alabaster, limestone and slate urns, these galleries were considerably smaller and more numerous than those that Norman and I had experienced.

After several twists and turns our only source of illumination, a single steel-handled flashlight, eventually illuminated a small granite crypt. This crypt, it seemed, had recently been opened. Thick dust and rubble appeared all around, and huge chunks of fresh rock crowded the floor. We climbed over the raw debris until we could stand upright on mostly flat ground.

One item caught the eyes as you entered. It was a stone sarcophagus, undecorated, and definitely not worthy of a queen. The historical transcripts describing her tomb said she lay on a bed of gold. Still, if Cleopatra had been a refugee why would Octavian have buried her in a grand tomb of her own making? He wanted the riches for himself and would have looted it down to its last piece of gold, so it made perfect sense that he would have laid her in a plain coffin.

Alas, this was *not* the tomb of Cleopatra. Next to the sarcophagus were a shield and sword—a *Roman* shield and sword. Johnny's flashlight raked the wall where the weapons leaned. The metal from which the armaments were fashioned was dull with age but the identifying features remained, glinting in the artificial light. The shield was oval and flat with heraldic figures embossed on the surface. At one time it was painted in solid colors but now the colors, red, burgundy and gold were muted and worn in places. The sword was a long, thick blade with a gilded hilt, and the grip had recently been handled as fingerprints appeared in the white dust. Both were fine specimens of 1st century Roman metal craft.

Unfortunately, most museums had an overabundance of this type of find, so these particular specimens were only worth as much as whoever was inside that coffin.

Did Tarek know of this discovery? Did Rima Abadi?

"Did either of you touch that sword?" I asked turning my face at Piero and Sayid.

"*I* did," Johnny confessed. "It was lying on top of the sarcophagus along with the shield. I removed them so that we could read the inscription."

"Did you open this—this vault?" My gaze had drifted toward the newly destroyed entranceway and all of the fresh wreckage piled up just inside the threshold. "Certainly, you two didn't have time to make this mess?"

They shook their heads in unison, smiling ironically. That meant either Tarek or Abadi were aware of this tomb. Or both.

I returned my attention to the sarcophagus. It was plain, of solid red granite, at one point in history highly polished. Time had dulled the surface but it was still a lovely specimen. Again, however, rather common. One question stirred on my tongue. Why was the sarcophagus buried here below the pyramid of an ancient pharaoh?

"See for yourself," Alessandra said, after I voiced my thoughts aloud.

Johnny passed her our only flashlight as she was nearest, and she splashed the top surface with its light. "This was what was hidden underneath the shield and sword."

The inscription was in Latin and was easily transcribed even with my rudimentary knowledge of the language.

MARK ANTONY

Johnny leaned forward and blew away the lingering dust. "I told you it was incredible. I told you it would smash all the current theories of how the two famous lovers died."

My first reaction was to shriek with excitement but then I paused to organize my thoughts, and nibbled at a hangnail. "If that is Mark Antony's tomb, Cleopatra's must be nearby."

"Piero and I were hoping it was. But we failed to find any evidence of it. It was while we were on our way out after searching for her tomb that Abadi's men ambushed us. We should have been more careful but we weren't expecting visitors. They caught us off guard. Thankfully, we were nowhere near the passageways leading down here. They spotted us leaving Djoser's pyramid. But they weren't taking any chances, although they never mentioned this find. Abadi told them to take us to her home. And no, she wasn't with them. They contacted her by phone… *That*, by the way"—his head jerked toward the exit—"is *their* helicopter. They transported us from here to there by air."

"There were four of them and only two of us," Alessandra amended.

I listened raptly. I had been dying to ask for particulars of Johnny's escape but was unable to do so. Sayid was reluctant to speak in Chas' presence. Now that Chas was no longer an issue I encouraged them both to enlarge on the details.

Johnny resumed the story. "They made the mistake of ignoring us after they knocked us out. I only pretended unconsciousness. I got hold of one of their radio headsets while in the rear of the chopper and heard every word spoken. They mentioned the cartouche after we had landed on the helipad outside the village of Habu. I thought little of it until we reached the house. That's when I got the genius idea to pretend I knew the location of the cartouche. That way I could lure them away from Piero.

"If I hadn't mentioned the cartouche to them I would have shared the same fate as her. Stupidly, they believed they needed me to show them where it was. After they had duct taped Piero and sealed her behind the wall and took me away with them, I made my escape.

"Those idiots left the chopper running with the pilot inside. I managed to give my three captors the slip and shoved the pilot out the door, and took off before they could get up off their faces."

Johnny Sayid was one of ISORE's most valuable players. No doubt he had done exactly as he had described.

His eyes shifted from the sarcophagus to mine, then back. Before I could ask for more information about the cartouche he said, "They let it slip that the cartouche was really a map."

Light bulbs were flashing like tumbling dominoes in my head. My next words came out like an epitaph. Flat and to the point.

"So now, *everyone* wants that cartouche."

He nodded. "Mark Antony's tomb is nothing without Cleopatra's."

I mused over all that Sayid and Piero had revealed. They had scoured every inch of the area containing Mark Antony's tomb. And no sign of Cleopatra's had turned up.

What about the book I had borrowed from Chas' felucca? Might it mention Cleopatra's burial place? I fumbled inside my cross-body handbag for the slim volume.

Perhaps it had something useful in it. It was an old English translation of Dio Cassius' historical account of Cleopatra's affair with Mark Antony. Did it mention her tomb? Chas was fairly thorough in his research, but could he have missed something?

I flipped silently through the pages as my colleagues watched. A passage was marked in yellow highlighter.

> *On August 1, 30 BC, Antony confronted Octavian, but his fleet and cavalry surrendered without a fight, and the infantry was defeated. Cleopatra fled to her mausoleum and sealed herself and her treasure inside, accompanied only by her maidservants... A message then was sent to Antony that she had committed suicide, perhaps to prompt him to do the same... This he did, but the wound was not immediately fatal and, hearing that Cleopatra still was alive, he was taken to her, being hoisted through an upper story window and dying there in her chamber...*

Here was another mention of Cleopatra having a crypt or mausoleum within which she had sealed her treasure, her maidservants and herself. But this account claimed that Antony accompanied her. While interesting and corroborative with Plutarch's writings it was useless without a hint of the crypt's whereabouts. Inconveniently, Chas' plan was still the best one.

"Do you suppose the cartouche is hidden *inside* the sarcophagus?" I asked.

I gestured at the culprit.

"I doubt it," Alessandra answered. "And if it is. It's quite safe in there." She tapped the surface of the stone lid with the heel of the flashlight. "We'd need a couple of crowbars to lift that. And I don't see any tools of the sort stashed here."

CHAPTER
37

Johnny was about to correct her when the three of us turned. I swore I had heard footsteps. I quickly closed the book and stuffed it back into my handbag at the same time Johnny put a finger to his lips and switched out the flashlight.

Voices murmured. Deep voices. None of us had cellphones, one way or another we had been relieved of any communication with the outside world. If only we had thought to 'borrow' Chas' device then I could have called or texted to see if those voices belonged to our team.

Johnny had gone to one side of the door, Alessandra to the other. I was squatting down beside the sarcophagus with Mark Antony's sword in my hand. Flustered though I was I was more curious than scared because whoever entered through that doorway would change the course of our actions.

The invasive beam of a flashlight pierced the darkness, slamming into the rough-hewn wall and just missing me where I crouched.

Johnny was about to do a two-handed slam with the heels of his hands on the first interloper, when I recognized the silhouette. "It's Norman!" I shouted.

Piero's gun sharply withdrew into the dark, while Sayid

flashed his light on and it hit Norman in the eyes. "*Merde*," he said dragging a crowbar in his right hand. "It's just us."

The sound of his French accent sent relief throughout my body. I rose and my grip on the sword loosened.

Luke's athletic form emerged next from the doorway, and he stepped over the rubble into the vault, sending a shallow cloud of dust stirring at his feet. "I thought you were expecting us. What's with all the Kung Fu crap?"

"Can never be too sure," Sayid said, and laughed. He was equally fit and his dark, muscular body eased out of the shadows.

The billionaire archaeologist glanced around the small gallery. The ceiling was domed, just holding the five of us comfortably, and for that reason I describe the space as a vault rather than a chamber. "Had a hell of a time tracking you until we picked up your trail," he said. "Thanks by the way."

Johnny sent him a perplexed look, and when Luke failed to catch on and explain, Sayid gestured for him to follow to the sarcophagus. "Man, am I ever glad to see you. Have a look at this, Trevanian." He sent an edgewise glance at the tool in Norman's hand, and said as an aside, "Oh, good, you brought it."

Luke nodded at Norman and the crowbar, and left to accompany Johnny at Mark Antony's tomb. I rose from where I was hiding, and Norman leaned the crowbar against the wall. He was the most muscular of them all and his cutout against the dim lighting was accentuated and made me almost fall to my knees. But was that why I loved him? Secretly, I shook my head. Most certainly not.

He came to me, his smile quick with humor. "Taken up fencing, have you?"

I dragged my eyes away from his buff physique, and no, that tight T-shirt was not helping. On occasion, I can be somewhat shallow. Norman, though, was not your run-of-the-mill fit freak. He really was beautiful and almost no one, no matter the circumstances, could fail to notice. Not even me—who should be so, *so* used to his looks by now.

He was always oblivious to his gorgeousness, and I agree now is an odd time to appraise his physical attributes. But after that edgy felucca trip downriver with Chas, I could only appreciate my man more. *And I don't care that we are inside a hollowed out subterranean cave underneath God knows how many tons of solid rock.*

He stared at the sword and chuckled, jolting me out of my reverie. The polished metal, where it was free from tarnish, gleamed in the low light. He took the grip from me and examined it superficially. "Wow. It's the real thing? Mark Antony's blade?" When I happily nodded, he examined it more thoroughly, and then propped it against the wall behind us. "Better leave it somewhere safe."

Was that a jab at my impulsiveness?

There were only two flashlights in this space, Luke and Johnny's, but the vault was small so it was enough, although poorly lit. Norman appeared huge in the shadowy cavern and I looked up at him shyly. Why was it, when we were forced to be apart for a while, it was as though we were starting our relationship from the beginning all over again?

And yet, had it been that long? No more than a day or so had passed—or so I thought. I was losing all track of time.

"*Hé*," he said.

"Hey," I replied, only in English. I loved it when he spoke to me in French. For my part I pretended ignorance but he knew I understood almost everything he uttered. The language had been one of my best electives in school. Nevertheless we continued to play the tantalizing game.

"You okay?"

"Better than okay. Now that *you're* here."

"You have no idea how glad I am to hear you say that. So—" He paused. Then completely switched to English. "What—happened with Chas?"

I suddenly felt self-conscious about the T-shirt I was wearing and wished I could turn it inside out so that the label was hidden. More, I wished I had never bought the damned thing in the first place.

When I failed to respond immediately, he repeated his query—this time in French.

Did he think that asking the question in French was going to make it easier for me to answer? Exactly what did he mean by that question? Was he asking: 'what happened *between* Chas and me?' or was he asking: '*where* was he?'

I decided to be evasive. "Don't worry, he won't be a problem. Johnny and Alessa took care of that."

He shot a backwards glance at the team. Sayid, Piero, and Luke were discussing the find, and if he noticed the Basseem label at all, he ignored it. His eyes glimmered with amusement when I stood flustered and inert. Guilt was immobilizing me and the memory of the river boat-trip had my brain in a seizure. We had done nothing wrong. In fact it was on that journey that I came to the concrete conclusion that I had no romantic feelings for Chas—and probably never had.

It would have been nice if I had avoided revealing my relationship with Chas. It made things awkward and one of us had to break the stalemate.

It was him. He lifted his arms and, unselfconsciously, I fell into them. Any guilty feelings concerning Chas vanished.

The heat of our bodies intensified as I realized that I was beginning to feel cold. Not that it was particularly chilly underground, but after the warmness outside, the contrast could lower body temperature fast. I gratefully allowed his warmth to encompass me. I sighed. And he stole a kiss before Luke's voice abruptly hurled us back into the real world.

"Good job, Sayid," Luke was saying. "This is an important find. And you, Piero. Your contribution was above and beyond. I don't know how you managed to survive those weeks with Tarek. When did he discover your identity?"

"When he wanted to bring in a baby doctor to find out when I was due. I'm sorry, Lucy." She twisted to search for me.

She found me slipping conspicuously out of Norman's arms. She made a point of ignoring her interruption of our intimate reunion and said, "He wanted to use your sister for a sex slave and raise your niece as his own. I decided I had better cut my losses and make a quick exit. We had enough Intel to know what Abadi planned. It is getting the proof that's the hard part. I don't know how deep into the regime this goes. Or how far up. I made my exodus as soon as I was able, and Sayid found me with the drone."

Luke's eyebrows lifted. "*My* drone?"

"Sorry, Trevanian," Johnny said. "The *Firefly* was my best bet."

"Never mind." Luke turned back to Alessandra. "You deserve a medal. But ISORE doesn't give out medals, so you'll have to make do with a very heartfelt thank-you."

"Unnecessary," Piero responded.

I rushed forward to give her that heartfelt hug she had so thoroughly earned. She resisted but just barely.

"No time for the mushy stuff," Luke said, and waved Norman over with a flick of his wrist. "Depardieu, get some photos of this stuff. Especially this sarcophagus and its engraving." He returned his attention to the rest of us, and exhaled. "Time to get everyone up to speed."

The five of us hovered around the stone sarcophagus as though it were a boardroom table, while Luke began the briefing. He sought each one of us out and established eye contact before making his speech. Whatever he was about to say was part apology, part gratitude. I could tell just by his earnest expression. Meanwhile Norman took a few quick photographs with his phone.

"Arianna finally told me what was up with the Screaming Mummy," the billionaire explained. "That it was in Toronto for tests and not just as the star attraction of the ROM's Mummy exhibit. And the reason for the tests was because Basseem thought it was Cleopatra's mummy and not that of Prince Pentawere, Ramses III's son. Colonel Abadi was waiting for the results. She wanted to verify that this was indeed Cleopatra before she moved on to the next stage of her plan."

Silence descended. For some of the team members, this was the first time they had heard of Ramy Basseem's theory. For them the identity of the mummy was still in dispute.

But no longer. Personally, I needed no scientific analysis to confirm my suspicions. I had already guessed the results contained in those lab reports.

"It is *not* Cleopatra." The confidence of my assertion cracked the deathly quiet. My certainty had nothing to do with my intimate sketches of the mummy. That experience had been too far in the past, and I hadn't examined it in the same way since. What made me so positive of its identity was because of the curious events that had transpired up to this point. Call it a hunch; call it intuition. Call it magic. *I don't care.* But I knew in my heart the mummy was *not* Cleopatra. "It is definitely a man," I asserted. "And very likely Prince Pentawere."

It was my turn to be singled out with all eyes focused on me.

Luke was the first to turn away. "That's true," he corroborated. He declined to expand on my declaration, and simply fiddled with his phone until he found what he was searching for—a digital copy of the lab findings.

"Arianna emailed this to me. The DNA tests prove conclusively that the Screaming Mummy is male." His focus shifted back in my direction. "Did Basseem know all along, Lucy? Was he just spinning you a yarn so that you would go along with him? Was that why it was so easy for him to abandon the mummy?"

I pondered the question seriously. "No," I decided. "I believe he honestly thought the Screaming Mummy was Cleopatra. He just realized it was safer where it was—in the custody of the airport authorities. I can say with one hundred percent certainty that he did *not* know."

There was a deafening moment of silence before a voice came from the entrance.

"But now that I *do* know, that mummy is even more valuable than ever."

In the doorway, I caught a flash of a safari jacket and a bush hat before they vanished. A whiff of Old Spice followed. The initial shock stunned me into paralysis, but lasted less than thirty seconds. I dived into action with a shout.

"Chas!" But he was gone.

"That was Basseem! Catch the spineless bastard," Sayid yelled.

Luke was slightly taken aback by the intensity of Johnny's feelings. And so was Norman who had even more reason to throw acid at the man. Norman was about to take a further picture of the inscription but was so shaken off guard when Chas made his appearance that he dropped his phone on the lid of the sarcophagus to pull out a gun, and ran after Sayid.

Unfortunately, Chas knew these tunnels far better than the men pursuing him. We heard their footsteps vanish into the distance. But the delay in catching up to the cunning Egyptian had just as much to do with the labyrinthine configuration of the passageways, as it had to do with the speed of the runner and his familiarity with the terrain.

How had he removed the zip ties binding his wrists and ankles? I had to start giving Chas more credit for ingenuity. There was a reason the public nicknamed him Egypt's Indiana Jones.

As long as he didn't make off with the helicopter. Surely, flying wasn't one of his notable skills?

Again. Must *stop* underestimating him.

"Gone," Norman said, when he and Sayid returned. "Son-of-a-bitch." That last part he had voiced in French.

Luke was inspecting the sarcophagus for any other inscriptions that might lead us to Cleopatra's tomb. None were evident.

"Let him go," Luke said, glancing up from his task. He was calm rather than disturbed. "What harm can he do?"

"We zip-tied him and strapped him into his seat inside my bird," Johnny explained. "If he managed to get out of that on his own, he's a man that needs watching."

"I agree," Piero said. "That weasel knows something. What did he mean when he said: now that he knew the Screaming Mummy was male that it was even more valuable than ever? What does Prince Pentawere have to do with Cleopatra?"

Tongue-tied, we muddled over the riddle.

Nothing ingenious came immediately to mind. How could the mummy have even more significance if we crossed it off as Cleopatra? If the mummy proved conclusively to be Prince Pentawere, why might that be important? The two royals lived in widely divergent eras. Prince Pentawere was born circa 1173 BCE. Cleopatra was born in 69 BCE. First century versus twelfth century. That was a difference of eleven *hundred* years!

I had no answer. None of us did. And I understood exactly why my team members thought that *I* should come up with some rational explanation. Of all of us I was the closest to Basseem. Of all of us I understood best how his mind worked. I had the greatest chance of figuring out his plan of action, but alas I was stumped.

My vision drifted down to the granite lid of Mark Antony's sarcophagus; I desperately needed to know what it contained.

Norman read my mind first. He agreed that we should open it and when we made the suggestion verbal, everyone came to consensus.

Norman went to retrieve the crowbar that Johnny had requested they bring with them. Sayid had wanted to know the coffin's contents all along, and clearly Luke had concurred or he wouldn't have brought an appropriate tool with which to open it.

Piero and I held the flashlights as we watched the hook of the solid, carbon steel prong wedge under the heavy stone. There was one thing that men were just better at than women.

And that was brute strength. Their height and breadth and notable upper body strength left us pleading no contest. Especially when it came to the men of ISORE.

Norman levered all of his weight onto it. I could almost measure the spike in testosterone. His muscles swelled into thick rippling cords of power, and the dense slab lifted. The other two men, almost as powerful, shoved the lid off, halfway to the other side.

A cloud of dust rose from the interior. The smell was of stone dust, not bone dust.

We stepped back to allow the suffocating particles to settle before leaning forward.

As the haze cleared we looked down.

The sarcophagus was empty.

No body.

And no cartouche either.

The disappointment in finding the sarcophagus empty was heart sinking. We all felt it. But my feelings were mixed. Had the others truly believed Mark Antony's body would have been left intact? For me, the empty stone box was exactly what I had expected.

Why would Chas abandon the sarcophagus (assuming he knew of it) if it contained a single clue to Cleopatra's mausoleum?

And then I saw it. Tucked into one corner, a small ivory comb encrusted with lapis lazuli and emeralds—no larger than a child's hand. The gemstones were tiny and so, were worth little in themselves, but if this was what I thought it was—

"What's that doing in there?" Luke demanded.

We leaned in. Norman was about to pluck it out of the dust, bare-fingered, when I stopped him. An eerie sensation had rippled up my spine. I don't know why. But I felt a premonition, almost a physical warning that if he touched it something horrible would result.

"Yes, leave it," Alessandra said. Gems meant nothing to the ex Interpol agent, and she turned and addressed her next remark to Luke. "You have no jurisdiction over any of these finds."

Luke nodded and Norman withdrew his hand, and I felt strangely relieved. Alessandra gave me a puzzled look that said, 'it is only an old artifact'.

"Wait a minute." Luke leaned over to examine the bejeweled object without touching it. It was lovely in its simplicity and the gemstones sparkled in the flashlight's glow. That however was not what had caused him to reconsider the situation. "We might be able to get a DNA sample from it."

I knew what he was thinking. I had already made that leap. Could this be Cleopatra's? If so it was a clue not only to her body's whereabouts but also to her mode of death, and if my hunch was right, multiple tests were the only way to verify it.

The museum was not in possession of Cleopatra's DNA, but they did have her half-sister's. Arsinoe's skeleton was discovered in the ruins of Ephesus in Turkey. If twenty-five percent of the DNA sampled from the bones and the hair ornament were a match, this was a strong indicator that the comb belonged to a relative. Half siblings shared twenty-five percent of their genes. That relative would most likely be Cleopatra. After all, Mark Antony and Cleopatra were lovers, and the comb was found inside Mark Antony's sarcophagus.

And as far as the poison went, that was even easier to identify. My only worry was whether the poison was still deadly. If the poison remained potent, it was crucial no one touch the comb.

While Alessandra and Johnny were concerned over cultural ownership, Luke's priorities overrode any ethics regarding international rules. If testing this comb gave Luke the answers he needed, he would face the penalties of breaking the rules later. Money spoke, and if the consequences of inaction meant risking a civil war, he chose to pay the price.

I concurred.

I dug in my handbag and drew out a small plastic makeup bag. I immediately dumped all of its contents back into the purse, and when the makeup bag was empty I turned it inside out and maneuvered it like a glove to pick up the comb without allowing it contact with my skin.

"Keep that safe," Luke advised as I zipped up the makeup bag and returned it to my cross-body handbag. He waved us in the direction of the doorway. "Let's blow this joint."

There was no point in feeling upset over this setback. Since no corpse had been found, we had no reason to remain.

"What's the plan?" Johnny asked.

"I'd rather discuss our options in the open air. My brain is beginning to feel fuzzy. The oxygen levels inside these shafts are thin. There's a reason these underground passageways are forbidden to tourists."

My head bobbed up and down enthusiastically. The sooner we got out of here, the safer I would feel. Every now and then powder and rubble fell from the walls, seemingly with nothing to cause it except for the vibrations of our movements and our voices.

With five of us we were a little more careful negotiating the network of tunnels. At times we were practically crawling on the ground. Johnny had the most experience with the subterranean maze so we followed him single file. He took the route he was most familiar with.

He and Piero had stumbled upon Mark Antony's vault accidentally, and Luke and Norman had only found it because, like Hansel and Gretel, we had left a trail of breadcrumbs—only ours was made of white plastic zip ties. I could see them still at every turn or so. The idea was mine.

On our return trip I plucked up each one to obliterate the trail, in case anyone else decided to come this way.

By the time we reached the front shaft where the generator was and which would take us outside, I was exhausted. The sight of the giant airbags and scaffolding was welcome. I sat down beneath one of the imposing airbags to wait for the others to join me before making the effort to climb the steep stone steps to the surface.

Alessandra appeared, and then Luke, with Norman taking up the rear.

"She has to rest before we go on," I said, pointing to the base of the stone steps. I had thought to bring the pain pills and handed Alessandra the bottle. She took three and washed them down with water from a bottle of Aquafina, then she passed me the water and I drank.

"I'm fine," she said.

I glanced at her ankle. If she was fine, then I was a monkey's uncle.

"Don't look at it," she ordered.

I turned away.

It still bothered me that Chas had left without sharing his epiphany. I had the uncanny sense that he was aware of Mark Antony's sarcophagus. And that it was empty. It was this and his persistence on insisting that the infamous Egyptian queen could be found somewhere in the vast necropolis of Saqqara that had me interested. And then there was his parting remark.

What made the Screaming Mummy more valuable than ever if it wasn't the body of Cleopatra?

Granted, I couldn't blame Chas for being pissed off. After all, we had bound him hand and foot, and deserted him inside the helicopter even after he had facilitated Piero's rescue. But ISORE had their reasons for mistrusting him. And it wasn't merely because of the malice he had exposed by attacking Alessandra's injured leg when he failed to get his way. There was no question he was conniving, clever and even a mastermind. So, what had he come up with?

My brain tumbled over all of the information that I possessed. For some reason the image of Ines' mummified body intruded into my thoughts. There had been a tube of paper with a handwritten message inside her mouth. What did the one thing have to do with the other? I shook my head in confusion. What was the connection between Prince

Pentawere and Cleopatra, and what could possibly make the Screaming Mummy so important?

Then I had it. It wasn't the identity of the mummy that mattered. It was the mummy itself. The terrorist, Nizar Tarek, didn't want the mummy because of *who* it was. He wanted it for *what* was hidden inside it.

He never wanted me to identify the mummy. He just wanted revenge on me for tricking him into kidnapping a highly skilled ex-Interpol agent and ISORE team member rather than my pregnant sister, whom he had planned to use to torment me.

So far I had foiled that plan.

Now everything made sense. The importance of the mummy, and why everyone—from the Syrian government representative Colonel Rima Abadi to the terrorist Nizar Tarek to Ramy Basseem aka Chas—wanted it so badly. Chas, that scheming, duplicitous, backstabbing man of genius, had figured it out.

The cartouche.

It was hidden inside the mummy's body.

Just as I was about to make my grand announcement an explosion came from outside the pyramid sending blocks of stone crashing down, smashing into shards of rubble, burying the stairs and raising clouds of choking dust.

The only thing that saved us from being squashed into infinity was the airbags and scaffolding over our heads.

CHAPTER 38

If not for them we would be dead, and as the dust settled I realized we might as well *be* dead. Our exit was sealed.

Luke had been about to call Aras when the explosion startled him into dropping the phone on the stone floor. Norman was holding the flashlight for him when the lights went out. We sat in dense blackness. "Everyone okay?" Luke called out.

We answered one by one.

Gradually, our eyes adjusted. It wasn't complete blackness in here. Over our heads, to the right of me, at the top of what used to be the staircase a ragged gap of grey light, about one foot long and half that wide, illuminated our situation. The rest of the stairs was blocked with stone.

Norman made his way over to me. "Thank God, you're okay."

He brushed a stray lock of hair from my face and checked me for injuries.

The others fumbled for the flashlights we had lost. Johnny's flashlight was still working but the second one was damaged on impact. The lamp beam landed on Alessandra and she told him to shut it off. He didn't. Instead he turned it on each of us to ensure we had escaped the avalanche of stone unscathed.

"Has anyone seen my phone?" Luke asked.

Johnny turned the dancing light onto the ground and spotted the device.

The glass was cracked as he picked it up and a few fragments sprinkled to the floor. If the interior mechanism—the chips, processor or battery—was damaged we were in big trouble because most of us had lost our phones. Sayid and Piero had been relieved of theirs when Abadi's men captured them; mine had gone overboard in that attack on Chas' felucca. I turned to Norman who was groping for his, and then I remembered that he had left it on the sarcophagus when he dashed off after Chas.

Now Luke's cellphone was our only lifeline to rescue.

But the phone refused to work. No matter how many icons he tapped none of them responded.

No one panicked. We had been in worse situations than this. The question was: had the collapse of the entryway been an accident or was it deliberate?

Who knew we were here—other than Chas?

It could be anybody.

Tarek. Abadi. Yes—even Chas. But my inner voice told me no. My heart refused to believe that Chas could do anything as unconscionable as this.

At present, it really didn't matter. We still had to get out.

The men were already at the base of where the steps should have been, and large chunks of limestone buried the entire stairway, intermingled with loose rubble.

The crumbling walls of the shaft we were in, and the high ceiling, currently held only because of some shaky pieces of metal and a couple of precarious airbags. The metal beams of the scaffolding could give out any minute, and the airbags if they had any weak spots could burst. In fact there was so much rubble and broken chunks of stone around us that if not for that ragged air hole I couldn't be certain where the exit was.

Everyone was using their hands to test the stone at the

base of the steps. Some were scooping up handfuls of rubble and reallocating it to the side, but that only sent more of it sliding down. If only we could open that overhead gap wide enough to let us out. But one false loosening of the rock and the whole thing could come avalanching over us.

I was paralyzed by shock and was waiting for my body to respond to my brain. *Get up. Go and help the others!* But my body remained motionless, as though it were glued to the floor. I did manage to roll my eyes upward and focus on the pale crack, high above my head.

There was no way we could climb up there without risking sending more rock and rubble crashing down, sealing us off from freedom once and for all. The only saving grace was that, despite the stuffiness and the difficulty in breathing, we would survive rather than suffocate. Fresh air was allowed through that gap.

But starving to death or dying from thirst would be no more pleasant than asphyxiation.

Now that I had stopped shaking I could see how some of the debris around us was broken off from the walls. We were safe from a total structural collapse—at least for the time being. Mostly the ceiling was intact, but for how long?

Alessandra crawled over to me. "Lucy, all you all right?"

"Yes," I said.

"Then help us think. Five brains are better than four. We need your brilliant insight to get us out of here."

Alessa's hands were dark with dirt. Even with her injured ankle she had not hesitated to join in the physical work.

I knew it was futile, but I obeyed. I think we all knew it was futile. There had to be twenty feet of stone between the outside and us.

Luke stepped back from the rock fall and started to fiddle with his phone again. If he could just get it working he could call someone to help us.

"Any luck?" Norman inquired.

Luke shook his head.

"Well, we can't just stand here and do nothing."

"We could try yelling," Johnny suggested. "If we all shout for help at the same time we could make quite a bit of noise."

"Only if there is someone out there to hear," Alessandra said. "And if there is, we had better hope it is not Abadi's men or Tarek's terrorists. If they caused this, we do not want them to know we are still alive." We all stopped talking for a few seconds as the truth of this sank in. "What is more likely to happen is the vibration of our voices will bring more of that rock down on us and seal off our breathing tube."

"I agree," I said. "I think shouting is a bad idea. A better choice might be to have one of us climb up there to scout out the situation and test the stability of that rock fall."

"An excellent suggestion," Alessandra chimed in. "I volunteer."

"You're injured," argued Johnny. "You're staying down here."

"Who then? You, Depardieu and Trevanian are too heavy, and we don't know if that pile of broken masonry will hold your weight without starting a major rockslide."

"One way to find out," Norman said, starting for the slope of stone and rubble.

"Not you," Luke objected. "You're the biggest of us. You have the best chance of creating a disaster."

We all looked from Luke to Johnny. Neither of them were much smaller than Norman. The odds of failure were the same for them.

"I'll go," I volunteered.

No one wanted me to go because, although I was a cheerleader back in the day, that was ages past, and currently I was the least athletic of them all.

"Wait. Isn't there an alternate entrance?" Luke suggested. "I believe it was in the southeast corner."

"That would mean going back through the tunnels and we don't really know its exact location. We have no map. We would be guessing. And what if—after traversing blind through all these tunnels—we get lost. Or worse, what if we find the entrance and it's blocked?" Piero objected.

What's more, it was impossible for her to drag a sprained ankle through those miles of tunnels without eventually collapsing. Tough as she was, even Alessandra Piero was made of flesh, nerves and bone.

Johnny went to her but she nudged him away.

"We're wasting time dickering," I said. "Let me try. I'm the lightest."

At the base of the slope of broken limestone masonry I began my climb. So far, so good. The rocks were rough and solid, giving me traction, and most were stable. Here and there, a block trembled and I quickly lifted my foot and planted it on another stone.

I made progress at a snail's pace.

As I crawled vertically up the shaky incline I felt the tension in my muscles. One false step and I could loosen the whole thing, and send it crashing. Slow, cautious, movements were what it would take. I paused for breath. The acoustics in this shaft were sharp and I could hear the voices of Johnny Sayid and Alessandra Piero even though they were using soft tones. Once I realized one could hear better up here than down there, I struggled with the urge to eavesdrop. Their conversation was getting personal. Piero was still insisting it should be her up here, not me.

"You're in no shape to make that climb," Sayid said.

"Stop babying me." Her tone was laced with annoyance.

Johnny fell silent, and his shoulders went slack. It was obvious there was plenty on his mind.

How exactly did Alessandra feel about Johnny? She was one of those people whose emotions were closed off from the outer world. I realized too that, although I considered her a special friend, I hardly knew a thing about her, and if anyone had a clue to the details of her personal life it would be Johnny Sayid. But did he talk? Not much.

While these thoughts were percolating in my mind Johnny's voice broke through. "You've done enough for the team. Let someone else do it… After everything you've been through, being the prisoner of that despicable terrorist, being sealed up in that wall—" His breathing was getting harsh. As I glanced down I could see that Luke and Norman were trying hard (but without success) to avoid listening. "G—goddammit, Piero," he stammered. "If I lose you now because of a stupid sprained ankle—"

There was utter silence below, and then a strange low-level humming came from above. I had a tough choice to make: look up or continue playing Peeping Tom. Either way I was distracted from my task. Good sense told me I should have been concentrating on climbing, but you know what they say about curiosity. It killed the cat. I had to know for certain, and kept my eyes focused down.

Holy crashing pyramids. Johnny Sayid was kissing Alessandra Piero!

"What's the matter, Lucy?" Norman called up. His and Luke's attention was fixed on me.

He shone the light into my eyes and yeah, the cat metaphorically died.

I lost my footing. I was only about nine feet up so the fall could have been so much worse, but thank God the broken masonry at the bottom was stable and Norman rushed up to catch me—dropping the flashlight to the floor—before I hit the rocks.

"Oh my god, Norman. Are you okay?" I asked, twisting around. A shower of rubble followed, but fortunately it was just small stuff and the larger chunks of stone remained unmoved.

I had landed in his arms, but the impact of my fall must have jolted him hard.

"Never mind about me. How are you?"

"I'm fine. You cushioned my fall. I am so sorry. That was stupid of me."

Everyone else had rushed over at the sound of my shriek.

"I told you I should have gone instead," Alessandra admonished.

"I lost my footing. I got distracted."

"By what?"

I struggled to avoid looking at her. She would be humiliated if she knew I saw her kissing Johnny Sayid. *I* also would be humiliated—because what a stupid thing to cause my fall. None of that was my business.

My eyes rolled up. My slip had disturbed the rocks above. The crack looked smaller!

Luke, noticing the target of my concentration, voiced my worries out loud. "That gap is definitely blocked further. It was hard enough as it was to breathe down here. Arianna will kill me if I don't get home with that mummy safe and sound. *I'll* go up. Maybe I can move some of those rocks when I get topside. It looked pretty stable while you were up there, Lucy."

Norman spoke next, morphing into bodyguard mode. "Arianna will have my head if I let a rock fall on your skull, Trevanian. Stay here. Try to get that phone working and if you do, call your ex and let her know how you feel. I am getting sick of you pouting like a sick sheep because you won't tell her you still have the hots for her."

The billionaire looked like he was going to upbraid his bodyguard big-time or just club him over the head with his phone. "*You* should talk. How long have you been carrying that piece of ice with you? Yeah, don't look so surprised. I know about it… I've known about it for ages. Just *ask* her you, idiot, before it's too late."

The slip of tongue, I was certain, had been unintentional and caused an awkward silence over us all. Did everyone understand what he meant or was it just me? I could feel the heat of embarrassment flushing up to my eyeballs.

Why was Norman just standing there? Why didn't he say anything?

Luke glanced up at the gap of light in the dark ceiling and a strange humming came to my ear again. Was I hearing things? We were all behaving like crazy people. The weak oxygen was making us barmy. If we did not stop talking all at once and so fast we would get even more lightheaded.

Then Johnny came to my rescue. He grabbed Luke's arm. "Hell. The logical person to go is me."

When Norman started to object, Johnny decided to divert him by pushing home Luke's point. "Look, Depardieu. We—none of us—know how long it is going to take to get out of here. I don't know if we will *ever* get out of here. Do you want to die without letting that excellent woman know how you feel about her? Trevanian is dead on. Just ask her. Before it's too late."

My mistake. Johnny wasn't saving me after all.

It was up to me to save myself.

But how? It was so unfair for Luke to put the pressure on his best friend like that. And Johnny, what did he think he was doing? But I suppose Norman had started it. He had made the initial provocation by suggesting that Luke confess his feelings to his estranged wife.

Argh. *How is this conversation happening around me? What is with this stupid monologue that is circulating inside my head.* Yes, the air was thin because the gap in the ceiling was small and the air was dusty, and five of us were trying to breathe it at once. But we were all experiencing an unusual touchy feely moment. And it wasn't just me. It would embarrass the guys and Piero no end when we finally escaped this hellhole.

If we escaped this hellhole. And believe me, if we did not escape soon…

I mentally shook myself. *Of course*, we would get out of here. Like someone had insisted earlier, we had been through worse situations. Hey, maybe that someone was me? I really was feeling seriously giddy.

I have to admit I *was* curious as to why Norman hadn't popped the question yet.

But this was an inopportune time. We were sitting beneath six layers—several hundred (or thousand?) tons—of solid stone. The silence was unbearable.

We are not going to die. So nobody is going to ask

anybody anything.

We were not ourselves. I was used to this kind of touchy feely stuff because of my sister Colleen. She was the queen of touching and feeling and gossiping. But *she* wasn't here and *I* was, and I had to put a stop to this even though I knew the surreal situation was merely a result of oxygen deprivation. I pulled myself together. Someone had to break the awkwardness. Failure was not an option. I just had to reach the top and see how stable the pile of rocks was, and how hard it would be to move some of that blockage out of the gap.

A strong hand reached out and spun me around. Norman's hand. I was standing on solid ground where he had set my feet after rescuing me from my fall. He lowered himself to one knee. He had something clenched in his left fist. It was a small white box and I recognized it. Seriously? He had been carrying that thing around with him all this time?

I knew what it held. I had seen it before. Once upon a time—in Aleppo—when I thought he was dead because an explosion had collapsed a tunnel onto his head. Only it hadn't. And he was safe. And here he was. Again. In a similar situation. Only this time we were all together. The team was *all*—together. And they were watching with rapt attention.

Wow. Was he really doing this?

Here?

I couldn't believe he was doing this.

He couldn't believe he was doing this.

His accent came into prominence when he was nervous, and believe me he was nervous because he sounded like a classic Frenchman. He mumbled some words: "*Je pense—*" then reverted to English. "—I think you know how I feel…" He glanced over at the dirty faces of our dear friends, but all I noticed was the deep sexy rumble of his French infused words. "I think you bowled me over the very first moment I saw you. I have never stopped thinking about you since."

He opened the box and the beautiful diamond glimmered in the dark light.

His eyes took on a deep emotional depth. It was too dark to describe his expression in any other manner; I could feel the emotion more than see it.

He dipped his head, voice soft, low. "I'm ready to take that leap of faith, Lucy." He raised his chin and our eyes locked. "Are you?"

I suddenly understood what he meant by taking a leap of faith.

Like a zombie or someone under the influence of drugs, I dropped to my knees, took the ring out of its modest box before he could, and slipped it onto my finger. Even in this lack of proper lighting it glittered as all diamonds did.

"If that's not a definitive 'Yes,'" Luke said. "Then I don't know what is."

We rose to our feet together. Norman's hand cupped my cheek, and his head came down to mine. His lips found their mark. It was a long sweet kiss, no tongue, just a soft, gentle pressure before it became hard and demanding.

I heard a voice interrupt. Oh yeah, there was the humming again and then: "Wonderful. Everybody loves everybody. So—do you want to get out of here now?"

I jerked myself out of my daze of joy. We all looked up to see Luke's high-tech drone, buzzing overhead. It had retracted its propellers and angled itself through the narrow gap before extending its wings again, all while we were emotionally preoccupied below. And then he had set it to voice mode.

"Dammit, Aras," Alessandra said. "How long have you been spying on us? Did your camera record all of that?"

"You bet," the voice said. Aras' normally serious demeanor took on an uncharacteristic playfulness. "For posterity. So you might as well kiss your sweetie in public because after this is over, the whole world is gonna know about Johnny Sayid and Alessandra Piero."

"I am going to kill you," Alessandra threatened. She

tried to snatch at the drone but it dived out of her path. Johnny grabbed her hand and kissed it and Piero resisted, but then with sudden semi-amused resignation she allowed him to do so.

The drone hovered over our heads, just out of reach. "By the way. Congrats, Lucy. And you, Depardieu. Could not have got yourself a finer woman. She's worth a million. But you already know that."

"Enough with the chitchat," Luke cut in. He reached for the drone but it shot out of his range. "Are you going to get us out of this hole or not?"

CHAPTER 39

"Do you have help, Aras?" Johnny asked.

"That is a firm negative, Sayid. It's just me. Didn't dare lead anyone else to the treasure."

So Aras had known about the sarcophagus of Mark Antony as well.

The drone buzzed around and I could see that he was aiming one of the cameras on the steep slope of fallen rock. Nobody thought it strange that we were conversing with a very small, talking, flying robot. I could see now why Luke had nicknamed it *Firefly*. When it tucked in its quad propellers it spun in the air like a June bug, a spot of pale light in the darkness.

"Are the stairs completely blocked?" Aras inquired.

"Pretty much," Luke said. "Except for that gap where the drone came through." The *Firefly* spun around to investigate the damage to the rest of the shaft. It stopped by a wall of dented scaffolding and a still inflated giant airbag.

"Do you have any tools?" Norman asked, directing his question to the ceiling.

"Negatory," Aras replied via the drone. "I wasn't expecting to have to dig you guys out of here. There's a really big slab blocking most of the entrance." A brief pause took place, as I imagine he was assessing our prospects. "Who the hell did you piss off this time, big brother?"

"Dumb story," Luke muttered. He was obviously ill at ease. All of our misfortune was due to extenuating circumstances. None of it was his fault, and yet he felt responsible. He raised his voice slightly. "Can you start moving some of the smaller stuff from the outside? We'll work from in here once we figure a way to shore up the walls around the rockslide. Then deal with the slab when we can make our way safely up."

"Why not use the airbag and the scaffolding?" I proposed.

"Perfect," Alessandra said. "That will prevent a further rockslide while we remove some of this masonry and debris."

"Still have the crowbar," Norman cut in. "It will help to lever some of the bigger pieces out of the way."

"Send that up to me." That suggestion was from Aras by way of the drone.

I was about to volunteer to make the treacherous climb with the crowbar when Luke shot out a hand to stop me. I stepped back to allow him to speak.

"The drone's got a magnetic base if you switch it on," he instructed Aras. "Lower my *Firefly* and I'll attach the crowbar to her. Now you'll just have to use some deft maneuvers to angle her out of here."

It was all done within five minutes. Aras like Norman, Luke, and Johnny were very physical men. Need I say more?

We were free within the hour.

***

Outside, we stood beneath the partially collapsed pyramid gulping in fresh air. A section of the colonnade was also victim to what now was visibly a bombing. The row of mummies gazing toward the pyramid's peak lay unharmed and no longer had the chilling effect on me that they had possessed when I first laid eyes on their desiccated expressions. The earth around them was disturbed but that was from the excavation, not the bombing.

I stepped past the mummies, and as I inhaled to appease my oxygen-starved lungs I detected a powerful odor of motor oil. In my limited experience of war zones, that chemical smell signified the deployment of explosives.

The sun was down and no people were anywhere. Which was good for us, as we could ill afford the bad publicity.

Only starlight illuminated the ruins. Beyond the temple and other structures I glimpsed the top of one jeep in the silvery light. The helicopter was out of sight as we had landed on the other side of the pyramid. Norman waved the single flashlight we retained in our possession. The narrow beam swung back and forth like a searchlight. It struck the direction of the vehicle. My gaze returned to the empty desert. We weren't mistaken. There should have been two cars but there was only one.

"The bastard stole our ride," Norman informed Luke.

"That means he left the chopper, and Aras' jeep is still here."

Aras nodded. "That's my jeep all right. I parked it there. Where did you park yours?"

"Over yonder." Norman swung the flashlight beam to his left.

"Do you believe that fucking ass of a conniving weasel detonated a bomb?" Luke asked. He sniffed the air.

This time I found no way to defend Chas, and I interpreted the rough language as gut reaction. The boys were angry and how could I blame them. It was hard for me to fathom that Chas was capable of such callousness. Did I even know him at all? And to what extent would he go to achieve his ambitions?

I stared at the devastation around us. What kind of an archaeologist would do this? Wasn't their mandate to preserve historical monuments, not destroy them? This was the reason why I found it hard to accept that Chas was responsible for the damage to the pyramid. But perhaps I no longer knew him. He had changed. He might even be a criminal. Because if it was he who had planted and detonated the explosives—and by now Johnny and Aras had confirmed that plastic C-4 explosives were responsible for the collapse of the pyramid's entrance—then he was nothing more than a fugitive from the law.

So, *was* this his handiwork? And if it was, I needed no more convincing. The act was willful and blatant destruction of a priceless heritage site, not to mention attempted murder—*mass murder.*

"Give me the drone," Luke ordered. "I'll upload a photo of Basseem from the Internet and send it after him. He knows where the cartouche is and we are going to foil his plan."

"No need for the drone. I know where he's going," I said.

Four faces, pale in the starlight, turned to seek me out.

"Where?" Alessandra demanded.

"To the airplane hangar where they impounded Luke's plane." I searched for Luke in the eerie darkness, located him holding the drone that Aras had returned, and asked, "Did they confiscate the mummy?"

"As far as I know the Screaming Mummy is still in the hangar alongside my jet. Arianna and Abadi promised to sign over its custody to me. They released it when they released the plane but it hadn't been authorized or loaded yet. I figured since the hangar was locked it was safe inside its crate. That thing is damned heavy. You can't exactly pick it up in your arms and walk away with it."

I nodded, grabbed Luke by the arm. "Then, that is where he's gone." Still, no one seemed ready to leave. There were a few minor details to clarify but I thought they could wait. Every fiber of my being wished to get moving. "Luke. Norman. What are we waiting for? The airport. Your airplane hangar." I agitated Luke's arm. "That's where Chas has gone."

"Just a minute." Aras turned his attention to me. "I've missed something here. That is where *who* has gone?"

I answered impatiently. "Chas. You know him as Ramy

Basseem." *Please, my tone didn't sound irritated but we were wasting time.* We could get Aras up to speed on the way.

"The cartouche is inside the mummy. It has to be," I added.

Aras gave me a perplexed look. He had no idea as to what I was referring. I quickly turned to the others who *did* know. "That's the reason why he said now that he knew the Screaming Mummy was not Cleopatra, it was more valuable than ever."

"Of course." Luke bowed in agreement. The wind was picking up and the sand was lifting around us. He was handling the drone like the sensitive instrument it was. And that made me wonder how such a contraption could even do its job in this harsh environment. Wouldn't its complicated parts get jammed up with dust and sand? Ah, the miracle of modern technology.

We had made our way to the jeep by now. It was closer than the helicopter. We stood around waiting for any last minute suggestions or insights from each other. None came. Still, no one made a move. I knew what the issue was. I glanced at Alessandra.

"What is the hold up?" she complained. "Let's go."

"*You* are going nowhere," Johnny argued. He shot a look at the helicopter rotors that were in sight just beyond the ruins. "You have a rendezvous at the nearest hospital."

I glanced down at Alessandra's ankle. It was swollen to the size of a grapefruit. There was no question Johnny's diagnosis was the only possible one. We—all of us—had arrived at that same conclusion.

Luke advised, "Get that injury seen to, Piero, before it gets worse. Sayid, you take her with the chopper. The rest of us will ride with Aras."

Alessandra grimaced. Clearly, the pain was affecting her, although she was not giving in without a fight. "But it will take you an *hour* by jeep."

Her complaint was in vain.

"Don't care," Luke said. "You are more important. Get going."

Alessa stopped arguing. She and Johnny went to the helicopter, she favoring her hurt leg.

Norman and Luke, Aras and I settled in the jeep.

***

By the time we got to the airplane hangar the mummy was gone. We were informed by airport security that Colonel Abadi and her men had taken custody of it.

If I had retained any lingering doubts of the Syrian official's innocence they vanished instantly.

"Where did they go?" Luke queried. He was making an extreme effort to be polite because if he ticked this guy off we would get nowhere.

The security officer shrugged as it was no longer any business of his. Apparently no crime had been committed.

"How could they just allow those crooks to take the mummy?" I demanded as we left the building.

Luke's shoulders lifted slightly. "Abadi has influence."

I paused to think. We could still beat her. Something I had read in that history book by Cassius Dio triggered an idea. We were halfway across the parking lot when I suddenly came to a stop and dug it out. Aras who was following behind me almost walked into me. I did a half-pirouette, apologized, and spun back to flip through the pages until I found the passage.

The words were barely legible by the light of the lampposts.

> *Octavian now confronted a dilemma. Although said to have wanted to parade Cleopatra in his triumph, he may have remembered that the appearance of her younger half-sister Arsinoe... in chains... had 'aroused very great pity'. Too, such a display might not reflect well on Caesar, himself... But she could not be allowed to live or Octavian be seen as responsible for her death. Some*

> *dissembling, therefore, must have taken place on both sides: Octavian inviting Cleopatra to return to Rome and Cleopatra pretending that she would go. Instead, she may have been given an opportunity simply to die by her own hand.*

Something about the last sentence struck me. Then I experienced the greatest 'Aha' moment of my life.

Die by her own hand! Chas had nailed it—*and* missed it. Cleopatra had not escaped into the labyrinthine Saqqara necropolis to cower and die. Octavian *had* killed her. At the very least he had provided her the mode by which to conduct the deed.

How did I know?

We would have to backtrack to Chas' floating library of historical sources and the discovery of a lover's grave.

Although at the time we were unaware, we had in fact discovered the murder weapon. It hid inside the tunnels beneath the Step Pyramid, in the cold, stone depths of Mark Antony's sarcophagus—in the form of several long-pronged, poisonous teeth.

At this very moment I had the offender inside my cross-body handbag, snug in my makeup bag.

How did I know the comb was at the heart of the mystery? Call it a hunch, a guess, a premonition or just an eerie feeling. But I would bet my life on it. Octavian wished to hide his treachery by making it appear as though Cleopatra had taken her own life.

After a thorough, technical, laboratory examination I would wager my entire life savings that the jewel encrusted, ivory comb was hollow. More, it was filled with poison. And if you haven't guessed it by now, the teeth of the comb were sharp (one of the first things I noticed about it) and could leave puncture marks, easily mistaken for a viper's bite.

I had no doubt it was a gift from mighty Caesar himself.

I awkwardly thumbed through Chas' book, shifting my body impatiently to avoid casting an obscuring shadow.

Somewhere between those pages was verification of my hunch. I just knew it. I balanced the spine in one hand and it kept slipping, while I frantically fumbled pages with the other. The men stared at me as though I had lost my mind.

"Help me, Norman," I pleaded. I positioned him under the lamppost with a hand trembling with excitement, directing his broad, long shadow away from my view. Then I dropped the book into his cupped palms to use as a lectern while I continued to search for the text. The night breeze was no help. It caught the pages and flapped them like a fan. Norman's thumbs planted themselves on the offending pages to hold them in place. Supportive to a fault, he asked no questions.

A few moments of disappointment and I realized I was searching the wrong book. The author of the current one was Cassius Dio. The tome I *needed* was Plutarch's and it was still on Chas' abandoned felucca, anchored among the reeds on the bank of the Nile River, three hundred miles away, near Luxor.

A passage in Plutarch's writings had described this exact comb. The description was in the first volume—the one where he described two pricks on Cleopatra's arm that may have been caused by a sharp, long-toothed hair comb made of ivory, and loaded with poison.

That was why I had stopped Norman from touching it. At the time it was a reflex action with no explanation. Instinct had simply told me to stop him. Now, I knew why.

I shared my hypothesis with my companions and they agreed. This ancient artifact might just be the answer to the mysterious death of Cleopatra.

CHAPTER 40

"We need to get the comb analyzed," I said.

I re-zipped the makeup bag after demonstrating how the comb might have been used as a lethal weapon. No, I did not touch it. I only opened the bag to show how sharp the tines were and how easily they could make the identifying marks of a snakebite. The tests required would be to determine whether or not it was tainted with a deadly toxin, and to isolate any traces of DNA.

Luke glanced down at his Breitling Chronospace wristwatch. "The lab won't be open until morning, Lucy. The more urgent task is to stop Abadi from finding Cleopatra's tomb. If she has the cartouche she will use it to pinpoint its location. If she finds Cleopatra's treasure she will use it. She will make it look like the Syrian government is employing terrorists to rob Egypt blind. This find is a national treasure of the utmost value. We cannot allow her to start a war."

"Then you have to go after her."

"No," Aras said. "Luke needs to go to the Egyptian government and tell them what is happening. He is the only one of us who has any credibility. Who is going to believe *me?* To them I am only a Syrian rebel, the exact type of person they want to exterminate. Even as we speak the protests are getting worse in the city. The Egyptian populace wants the Syrian delegation gone." He raised his head from checking out the situation on the Internet. He was the only one of us now who owned a cellphone.

"Ditto that," Norman broke in. "Luke, it's still early evening. I'm sure you can get an audience with the President or one of his high officials. You need to talk to them. If you want me to come with you I will, but I think maybe Aras and I should tackle Abadi and her terrorist thugs."

"What about Basseem?" Luke asked.

"He's probably across the border by now if he had anything to do with that bombing." Norman avoided my eyes as he answered but I knew exactly what he thought of Chas.

I was smart enough to say nothing.

"Lucy, you should go back to the hotel and get some rest. As soon as the lab at the Cairo museum opens I want you to get that comb you have in your purse analyzed for poisons. I am trusting you not to let that priceless artifact out of your sight. I have a feeling if you're right about it, it will be worth a bundle to any host of black market smugglers."

Luke borrowed Aras' phone and made reservations for a five-bedroom suite at the Nile-Ritz-Carlton on the penthouse floor. A bell rang in my memory. Wasn't that where Chas was staying? We had eaten lunch with him on his room's fancy terrace only a short time ago.

It was five minutes past nine. The museum was across the street from the hotel but the museum lab didn't open until 7:00 am. I was too hopped up to sleep. I knew I would be useless accompanying Luke or Norman and Aras on their missions. Luke's task would require charm, eloquence and diplomacy, and Norman and Aras would probably only require their guns and their fists. I was no help there. They were right to leave me in charge of protecting the comb. If it truly belonged to Cleopatra and was the weapon of choice for her death, it would be worth a fortune once word got out. My job was to see to it that word *never* got out, not until it was in the custody of Cairo's Egyptian museum.

When we arrived at the hotel to get cleaned up, rumor had it that the Egyptian president was hosting a gala in honor of the Syrian delegation. The hotel concierge confirmed that the rumor was in fact truth, and he was very eager to get us up to date on all of the current events in the city. The gala just happened to be the most popular talk of the town.

Syria's First Lady was the guest of honor. That meant Rima Abadi would likely have to make a showing as well before she slipped out to follow the symbols on the notorious onyx cartouche that would lead to Cleopatra's tomb. If I knew her type—the ambitious, unconscionable, egotistical, no-holds-barred type—this would take priority. And she would leave to meet her terrorist conspirators as soon as she was able.

"All right. Change of plans," Luke announced after we let ourselves into the luxurious suite. "We are *all* going to the President's gala." He shook the invite that the front desk clerk had accepted for him in his absence. It was a large cream-colored envelope with gold trim. "Apparently, *I've* been invited. Lucy, you will go as my date. Norman and Aras as my security team. Nothing strange about that… Aras, contact Sayid's helicopter. Let him and Piero know what's happening. Okay, everybody, you have thirty minutes to make yourselves presentable."

He smiled and went to the master bedroom to have a shower in his en suite bathroom. Arrangements had been made with the hotel to have appropriate evening clothes sent up to us while we tackled the grime of the day and turned our gorgeous marble shower stalls into muddy waterfalls.

Luke had given Norman and I one of the bigger rooms. I saw Norman's glance take in the king-sized bed and knew what he wanted to do with it, but we had no time. I stripped and went into the blue marble bathroom with its sharp white towels, his eyes following me, before he stepped out onto the balcony to have a smoke.

There was a large, ceiling to floor closet filled with luxury bathrobes, extra towels, blankets and pillows. I noticed the door was slightly ajar and closed it to keep out the steam. The only reason it caught my eye was because this hotel was so immaculately maintained that it seemed anachronistic for anything to be out of place—even a closet door.

I turned on the shower and stepped into the hot falling water. The floor space of this shower stall was enormous. I could easily lie down; it would accommodate my entire length but I had no intention of sleeping here. I still had to wash my hair.

It was not until I had soaped up and was all slippery with lather and shampoo that I felt Norman slip in behind me.

Or maybe I smelled him before I felt him.

The scent of smoke, subtle and masculine reached my nostrils.

He was silent as a jaguar. He guided the glass door shut, and joined me in the blinding steam. I turned to face him and he slid his hands down my shoulders to my back until the palms of his hands rested firmly against the curve of my lower spine. I raised my arms until my fingers cupped the base of his head and neck, and my face, slick with hot rain, reached his lips. He had considerately rinsed with mouthwash before joining me and I eagerly anticipated the taste of spearmint.

The tender touch of his tongue on my nose and lips made me open my mouth for a kiss, and then he lifted me by my butt, and I was sitting on wet air before he snuggled my urgently parted thighs into his lap.

His penetration was easily received. He got no resistance. I tightened my forearms around his shoulders to keep from sliding out of his biceps, as diluted suds slithered down my backside and my legs to my toes. He clung to me and thrust like a highly charged piston, as though his very life depended on it. My soft breasts were squashed against his hard chest in rhythmic movements and now his back was to the stream to protect me from getting water-boarded. I was acutely aware of my nakedness being pressed up against the shower glass as he finished with a final pulse-pounding shove.

We slid to the mosaic floor of the shower gasping and laughing, still joined together. I felt limp from the heat of the shower and the effort of our lovemaking. I was lying with my head and shoulders against the glass door, still straddling him while he hovered over me.

"That was intense, honey. You okay?" He gently slid out of me, and I allowed my hands to collapse to my chest. Our eyes simultaneously caught the glisten of the diamond on my finger, and he raised my left hand to his lips.

"Oh, I probably should have taken that off before getting into the shower," I said.

He kissed me softly on the mouth and replied, "I *never* want you to take it off."

I reached for him and hugged him with all my heart.

"I'm sorry, sweetheart, I was being selfish. Let me make you come."

"I don't need to. That was wonderful. And we don't have time."

"Oh, if I know you, you don't need more than five minutes." He turned around and straddled me and lowered his face between my legs. His tongue began to work its magic and then I felt a finger enter me. He licked and swirled and penetrated until I could no longer focus and still the shower continued to rain on us and neither one of us thought to shut it off. A second finger entered me, and then a third. He stopped for a few seconds and I tried to control the unbearable yearning. Even the ends of my hair and my fingernails felt aroused.

He was teasing me. He knew this brought me higher and he liked to torture me.

Before he allowed me my reward.

Now his fingertip touched the sensitive bud and I jerked with pleasure. "Oh, god, I gasped. "If you make me wait any longer I'll have to finish the job myself."

He chuckled and began to stir the pot again. I arched my

back in anticipatory ecstasy. And then it came. A powerful thrill of nerves tingling from fingertips to toes.

The phone suddenly rang. Yup, the bathroom had a phone in it. I assumed all of them did. Norman got up to turn the taps off and I rose and dragged my limp (but thoroughly satisfied) body out of the shower stall and onto the marble tiled floor. Oddly, the closet door was opened. I thought I had closed it. Oh, well, maybe Norman had opened it when he came into the bathroom. I took out a robe, struggled into it and went like a happy ragdoll to silence the screaming phone.

It was Luke. He was in the lobby waiting for us.

"Get your clothes on, you two. And stop fooling around. We have two nations to save and a queen's tomb to find. Get a move on."

I giggled. We were late. And Luke had guessed exactly what we had been doing. "Be down in twenty," I promised.

"Twenty minutes? Good God, you two are like monkeys. I should have given you separate rooms. Depardieu is an animal."

"Hey, that's my fiancé you're talking about."

He laughed. "Sorry, sweetheart. I know you want to celebrate, and you should… Look you don't have to come—"

"Of course I have to come. You need a date *and* a bodyguard."

"I have Aras."

"He's not enough. We're wasting time talking. Let me dry my hair and get dressed. Oh, about a dress—"

"It's on your bed. The porter left an evening gown for you and a suit for Norman. Get a move on if you're coming."

"Yes, sir!" I hung up.

I shouldn't feel as delirious as I did. I honestly hoped I was pregnant. That was preposterous however. We weren't even married yet. And even if we were, how did having a family and the job with ISORE mesh?

Furthermore, the present mission wasn't over yet. If the president didn't believe Luke there would be severe ramifications.

Norman was already in the bedroom getting dressed. Luckily my hair was fine and dried quickly. No time to give it a classy up-do. A chic side-part would have to suffice.

I went to moisturize my face and make up my eyes when I saw that the ancient comb was still in my makeup bag.

I returned it to my purse and dug into its bottom for my Oil of Olay, mascara and lipstick.

Just as I had promised, twenty minutes later I was downstairs in the lobby dressed in an emerald silk evening gown with slits up both sides, a color that went delightfully with my light brown, copper-highlighted hair. Norman looked dashing in a black suit and tie.

Luke and Aras couldn't have looked more stunning in their formal dark evening attire.

We took a limo to the President's domicile. The Heliopolis Palace is the official home and place of government. At one time it was a four-hundred-room, fifty-five apartment suite hotel for the rich and famous. It was bought by the government in the mid-twentieth century and became the official palace of the president and the headquarters of his administration in the nineteen eighties when it was renovated. Despite the modern conveniences the character of the original hotel remained visible in some parts. The Heliopolis style, a fusion of Persian, Moorish revival, Islamic and European Neoclassical architecture was retained. It continued to exude classical symmetry and elegant beauty.

Outside the enormous structure, protesters with signs were herded onto one side of the drive to allow ingoing and outgoing traffic. At the present time the demonstration seemed peaceful, but armed soldiers were stationed as a security measure, and no one was allowed within the gardens that surrounded the edifice.

I walked into the palatial building on Luke's arm with Norman and Aras behind us. We were led into a grand ballroom decorated with traditional motifs. An enormous dome rose over our heads. Twenty-two Italian marble columns circled the parquet floor up to the elaborate ceilings.

The floors were carpeted with fine Persian rugs and the room had massive mirrored wall panels and an impressive marble fireplace. The furniture was of rare mahogany and sparkling crystal chandeliers hung from various points surrounding the dome.

The guests were all decked out in formal attire. Every designer you could name was represented. Never had I seen so many black gowns and dark suits. Or so many men in traditional dress. Most of these people were political figures and their spouses. Most were strangers to me.

The first person I recognized was Chas.

CHAPTER 41

No one in my party paid attention to him. I was about to nudge Luke, but he was busy making niceties with some government officials. I could hardly interrupt to point out the scoundrel. To make matters worse, Chas had the audacity to touch a finger to his lips to hush me. Clearly, he was expecting to see me here but had no stomach to confront my friends.

Did that mean Chas was innocent of the bombing incident at the Step Pyramid in Saqqara? If it was he who had detonated the explosives, would he have expected to see me here?

I whipped about to see if Norman had noticed. It appeared unlikely. He and Aras were being briefed by palace security.

After Luke introduced me, a number of VIPs came over to absorb his attention. This was my chance to follow Chas. Norman and Aras' jobs as bodyguards was to keep an eye on their boss, and although I knew Norman wanted to accompany me it might look suspicious if the billionaire archaeologist's head of security was canoodling with his boss' date.

This meant I had free reign to find Chas, and I wanted to

face him alone to grill him about the cave-in at the Step Pyramid.

"Ms. Racine? How nice to see you." It was Colonel Rima Abadi's voice, and my heart constricted.

"Colonel Abadi," I said, trying to loosen a very tight jaw. "How *are* you?"

I was acting a little over the top, but what gall she had to provoke me.

"Have you had the chance to think about what I said?" she asked.

What—whether I would spy on Chas for her? So, she was playing the same game was she, still pretending? I felt an urge to warn her that we were on to her, but seeing all the security at this function made me realize that half of them were employed by the Syrian delegation, and *she* was part of the Syrian delegation even though she was a crook. Did the First Lady of Damascus know it? I caught her image out of the corner of my eye—still classy, elegant and stylishly attractive, but she paid no attention to me. I was nobody and she would never remember that she had once met me on her own turf, in her own country, at the Syrian presidential estate.

"Ms. Racine?" Abadi interrupted my flow of thoughts. She was acting all charming and pleasant even though I knew she had the heart of a reptile, and when I hesitated to answer her question she made a pretense at small talk before abandoning me with a "So pleased to see you again" for someone of greater importance.

I was free to seek out my duplicitous ex once more and found him behind a potted palm drinking whiskey from a crystal glass. He'd been expecting me.

"Thank God, you're okay, Racine," he said. Dressed in formal black, it was the first time I had ever seen his beefy frame clad in anything other than his own casual brand. He looked strange, almost unrecognizable without the khakis and bush hat, but ruggedly handsome all the same. "You look gorgeous."

Emerald green was my color. It went best with my mousy brown hair. I had to admit I did look hot in this dress with its slits up the sides and cinched in waist (and believe me I very rarely looked hot). For modesty's sake (after all we were in a Muslim country) the sleeves were long.

I said nothing to the compliment. Instead (and let me just say a little levity was not inappropriate) I asked, "How did you get an invite to this swanky shindig?"

"I didn't."

Well, that accounted for the disguise. Seriously, I wouldn't have recognized him if it wasn't for the fact that I knew him so well. Ramy Basseem never wore black tie. I knew this because I had looked him up on the Internet after being blindsided by him at the ROM's basement lab. The web was flooded with photos of him, through the years, at various VIP functions. Even in those celebrity days when he was at the height of fame he would attend a formal event in the Basseem label. That meant crisp khakis and shirt, iconic safari jacket and bush hat, a brand he flaunted like a badge of honor.

When I remained silent he continued, "I saw on the news, just before I arrived, that the front entrance of Djoser's Step Pyramid collapsed."

"It *didn't* collapse," I snarled. "It was deliberately blown up."

His eyebrows rose in shock, the gold stud flinching. So, he wasn't responsible for the despicable deed? I am not going to say whether I believed him. As a former celebrity and a very public figure Chas was a terrific actor. However, I would reserve judgment until proven otherwise.

As to asking any more questions concerning the incident I put a hard stop to that. Any comments he had to make would be dubious to say the least. If anyone was going to ask questions it was I.

"Why are you here?" I demanded. "Or were you lying again when you claimed to have lost your reputation and your clout. This is a function for VIPs. And, if you were speaking the truth, you, sir, are no longer A-list."

"The truth, Racine," he insisted. "I promise."

We were conversing in shallow whispers. I for one wished to raise my voice, and give him a browbeating he would not soon forget. But that would only draw attention to our presence and that was the last thing I needed. "I would imagine you to have forgone this function after making your brilliant deduction," I accused him. "The old Chas would never let an opportunity like this go by for the sake of a fussy clambake."

"So, you figured it out?"

I scowled. *Always denigrating my sleuthing skills.* I announced in as loud a whisper as I dared: "The cartouche was inside the mummy."

When only his eyebrows arched minutely, I asked, "Did you manage to get at it before Abadi?"

He nodded. Smiled. "That's what I always loved about you, Racine. Only one step behind me."

One step indeed! I snapped, "Where is it?"

"Somewhere safe."

"What did it tell you?"

"Do you really want to know?"

"Yes. Where is Cleopatra buried?"

"For now, I want to keep it a secret."

Oh, right. My monologue was sarcastic. *The big reveal. You don't want anyone to know until you can make the big exposé on network television.*

Well, if he was in possession of the cartouche and had the location of Cleopatra's tomb, maybe we needn't worry if Abadi meant to trigger an international incident. But I still had my doubts. The airport authorities insisted that Colonel Rima Abadi and her men had taken custody of the Screaming Mummy.

Was Chas one of those men?

"Lucy," Chas said.

Lucy? What was he up to? He rarely called me Lucy.

"I want you to see it. I want you to come with me

tonight, and be the first to lay eyes on Cleopatra's tomb."

Was he working with Abadi? This was the question.

"Can't it wait until morning?"

"No," he said. "By first light the place will be swarming with news media."

The look on Chas' face was sincere, earnest. I recalled what he was like those years ago when he spoke of his dreams. The discoveries he would make, the theories he would prove.

His expression was open, eager and almost had me believing his nonsense.

But if he was working for Abadi and Abadi was partnered with Tarek, then it was best to keep ears pricked and eyes peeled.

"I am not working with Abadi," he insisted, reading my expression. "After Abadi took custody of the Screaming Mummy she had to return to the hotel where her delegation is housed to get ready for the gala. The mummy was transported to the Cairo Museum where I still have a friend or two. I got in—no questions asked—and obtained access to the mummy. She had no idea what that mummy held inside its ribcage. I sawed through its chest with a surgical saw, and took it." He stared at me with eyes as brilliant as the chandeliers in this room, appearing almost wild-eyed and crazed. "I have the cartouche, Lucy. I know where Cleopatra is entombed."

"Where?"

"Come with me and I will show you. You won't believe it… All of it is true. The treasure, her sarcophagus, the golden deathbed; the precious jewels and silver, emeralds galore—her favorite gemstone. The cartouche told me where."

I had to see this for myself. I scanned the room for Norman and Aras. Luke was talking to the First Lady of Egypt, who wore a simple floor-length black gown with a gold and black scarf covering her raven hair. Aras, I noticed, was being watched, and so was Norman. Abadi's people had been alerted or had suspicions, and both were aware of the change in circumstances and stood wary.

I went to Luke first, and he gave me a look that meant 'Not now.' I know it was important that he got on the First Lady's good side so I spun to seek out Aras and Norman, but they, too, were still preoccupied.

I returned to the spot where I had left Chas, only to find that he was gone. If I didn't follow him right this minute, I would lose him.

I glanced back at Norman and Aras, thinking frantically: *how could I risk approaching them?* The best thing to do would be to text them later.

No time for waffling. I rushed out the door, the evening bag swinging out behind me.

He had a luxury automobile, and I was too distracted to take note of the make or model. The only thing that registered in my memory was its color. Red. And this time there was no driver.

Chas was unlocking the car door remotely with his key fob when he glanced back to see that I had followed him. "So, you decided to come?"

I nodded gravely. "But you had just better be telling me the truth."

He removed his dinner jacket, plucked his bush hat from the seat and tossed both into the back, before sliding behind the wheel to reach over to unlock the passenger side.

"Where are we going?" I asked getting in beside him.

He punched the ignition. "Wait and see."

It took only fifteen minutes before I recognized the road to Saqqara. By now I had traveled this route multiple times. I had originally intended to inform Norman and Luke of my impromptu excursion via text, but suddenly I remembered I had no phone.

"You mean you were on the right track all this time?" I was making chitchat to take my mind off my stupid cellphone oversight. "Cleopatra really *is* interred in the Saqqara necropolis?"

I was okay. That slight miscalculation was hardly detrimental, and truthfully, Chas did not frighten me because all he wanted was what he thought he was due—fame and fortune. Whatever Abadi and her terrorist partners were up to meant nothing to him. He finally had what he wanted—the cartouche, and hence the location of Cleopatra's tomb.

He nodded, eyes still on the road. There was very little traffic and the night was dark.

"Whereabouts in the necropolis?" I demanded. "The mortuary site sprawls out over thirty-seven acres of land."

"Where I thought it was all along."

His tone was exaggerated, ominous. Breathless. He was getting into character, ready to play the discovery for all it was worth. Me? I was having trouble wrapping my brain around the whole idea. Scientists had been searching for Cleopatra's tomb for decades. None of them ever found her. And Chas had?

I wanted more than ever to see the cartouche with my own eyes.

The car was silent, except for the hum of the engine. I studied my surroundings and eventually recognized that I sat inside a Porsche. Luke had one of these, among his many luxury vehicles. How was it that Chas could afford this car? I thought he had lost almost everything when he lost his cushy government job. Did his designer line really bring in that kind of income?

His voice suddenly cracked the silence:

"*A message then was sent to Antony that she had committed suicide, perhaps to prompt him to do the same... This he did, but the wound was not immediately fatal and, hearing that Cleopatra still was alive, he was taken to her, being hoisted through an upper story window and dying there in her chamber...*"

He turned to glance at me before returning his attention to the road. "Sound familiar?"

I almost gasped aloud. I had read this very passage not too long ago. It had been highlighted in yellow in one of his history books.

"The cartouche verifies it," he added. He reached across my lap to a locked glove compartment and I recoiled. The knee-jerk reaction had nothing to do with fear—or surprise that the cartouche had been travelling with us all along. It had everything to do with the fact that his nearness unnerved me.

His eyes lowered momentarily to my hand that had flown from my lap before his attention jumped back to the road. "That's quite the rock you have on your finger," he remarked cavalierly. "So—the gorilla finally popped the question." He chuckled quietly to himself. "After popping your cherry."

My blush flooded me from head to stilettoed foot. "You are such a jerk," I said.

He shrugged then leaned in and finished tapping the combination to his locked glove box. A quiet click sounded, before the hatch released. "Maybe I was just jealous."

Was? Why was he using the past tense?

"You've gotten a lot more adventurous in the sex department since *our* days."

My head swung in annoyance. How would he know that? If he was trying to push my buttons, attempting to get me to respond to his romantic overtures, this was the wrong way to do it. Besides. His chance was long past. I felt nothing but contempt for him. What's more, that knee jerk reaction that had caused me to withdraw my hand wasn't fear, it was repulsion. Never again did I want this man to touch me.

The only reason I was here was because I was drawn to the tomb of Cleopatra. I was not scared. Not of Chas. And not of Abadi either. Abadi couldn't hurt me. She was safely occupied by the Egyptian president's gala. Norman and Aras had their eyes on her. And if she was headed this way, they would be right behind her. And if she *was* in fact complicit with Tarek, the boys would have their eyes on him as well.

Chas was too much of a coward to be directly involved with a terrorist. Abadi, yes. I could believe that. But not Chas. I had spent enough time with him to see how fast he spooked.

So, if he tried anything I could easily take him. My brief stint at ISORE had taught me how.

And then it struck me. The sex talk. I drew in a breath of disbelief. Then pure disgust. I glanced at his profile. A smug smirk destroyed any pretense of attractiveness. He was downright ugly at this moment.

"Nice complimentary bathrobes they have at our hotel, eh? Nice bathrooms too."

The closet door, it was ajar. He made no attempt to hide the fact that he had been spying on us. He had watched us have sex in the shower. Pervert!

He chuckled when he caught my expression of disdain in his peripheral vision. "You are a randy, unapologetic minx now," he said, eyes refocusing on his driving.

"Hope you enjoyed the show," I replied calmly. "That will *never* be you."

"Think I realized that—when I saw your nether regions gobbling up that gorilla's dick."

We were three quarters of the way to Saqqara. My heart was pounding like an engine, my fists whitened. I swear I nearly whacked him; had I been in possession of a tennis racket I might have. I certainly almost bit through my lip. *Stop the car.*

Demanding he stop the car and let me out was just plain stupid. Did I really want to be abandoned on an empty desert road, in the dead of night—just because of a few vulgar remarks?

My inner, sane voice got control over my gut reactions.

"What happened to you, Chas?" I asked softly. "You used to be so sweet."

Once upon a time he was an idealist with big dreams that he had made come true. Why was he trying so hard to hurt me when it was *he* who had rejected me the first time around?

"Do you want to see the cartouche?" he asked grumpily. "It's in the glove compartment."

Fine. He refused to succumb to true confessions. Sure, life had thrown him a lemon, but his lemons were never totally sour. Good stuff happened for him. Even now. He was going to be declared the discoverer of Cleopatra's tomb and be crowned the twenty-first century's Howard Carter. Did he know how many archaeologists coveted that title? Sometimes you got everything you wanted—just *not* the girl.

I reached into the glove compartment and withdrew the black, onyx, stadium-shaped stone. It was not large, nor terribly heavy, only the span of an average man's hand, and about as thick. Puny as far as Egyptian relics went.

I had a rudimentary knowledge of hieroglyphics and recognized some of the symbols. There was a large triangle shape and two rows of a dozen dots beneath it. Mostly the glyphs were alien to me.

The car rolled to a halt, and I glanced up. We had arrived. The trip was shorter than usual because of the lateness of the day. There had been virtually no traffic.

I had been expecting the ruins to be deserted but a jeep was parked up ahead of us.

"Who is that?" I asked pointing at the dusty vehicle. In an hour or so it would be midnight. Why would anyone be here this time of night?

"Oh, that's just Leon Abraxas, my director and his cameraman. I told them to meet us here."

Why did that not surprise me? The sooner Ramy Basseem got those headlines up on the media, the faster his find would go viral.

Chas had parked as close to the Step Pyramid as he was able. We were once again on the north side where the cave-in to the main entrance had occurred. Then something dawned on me as the headlights struck the terrain where the mummies were partially exposed in the ravaged ground.

Two rows of dried heads.

Twelve round heads in each row.

Looking up.

I realized, too, what I had failed to see, at first, in the

cartouche. The dim lighting inside the car had obscured the details of the triangle. It was stepped. Just like the pyramid. It did not take all that much imagination. With the slightest effort all of the dots could represent heads aimed toward the heavens.

CHAPTER 42

Chas and I exchanged enlightened glances. His eagerness was infectious. We hurried out of the Porsche, he on the driver's side and me jettisoning myself from the passenger seat. We turned our attention up, wind swirling the sand around our feet, and I shielded my eyes from the dust.

The car door slammed, and Chas clamped the bush hat on his head, and then walked around the vehicle until he stood beside me. It was close to midnight now and the sky was black outside the city lights. In the countryside, desert and sky became one. If I was not mistaken there seemed to be a yellow glow around the top step of the pyramid.

The last sentence in the passage Chas had recited while we were still in the car flooded my thoughts. *Hearing that Cleopatra still was alive, he (Antony) was taken to her, being hoisted through an upper story window and dying there in her chamber…*

Chas nodded with excitement as I turned to look at him.

An upper story window? Did that mean what I thought it meant?

His eyes grasped my thoughts. But there was one piece of information he was missing: I knew how Cleopatra had killed herself; he did not. He was ignorant of the comb.

My hand involuntarily went to the evening bag with its gold chain that hung on my right shoulder. The small makeup bag containing the bejeweled ivory comb was still in my care. I should have left it in the hotel safe, but intuition urged me to keep it close. So here it was.

Chas of course was unaware of the fact.

"Truce?" he said, holding out his hand.

"Fine," I agreed without shaking hands. I had no desire to ever make skin contact with him again. The idea revolted me.

"I'm sorry for my bad behavior, Lucy." The apology was timely, and seemed heartfelt. He shuffled his feet nervously and glanced at me from beneath lowered lashes. "When I see you with that god-like bodyguard it makes me realize what I missed. I am just jealous. I really wish you the best."

"It's okay, Chas," I said. I was feeling confident. Nothing he said could hurt me. What he had done was remind me how lucky I was to have Norman. My right hand instinctively clasped over my left to cup the diamond ring that I so cherished. My happiness made me feel generous. I could not hate this man. After all, we did have a history. Maybe I could even help him. I smiled. My voice came out playful and benevolent. "You have to stop with the voyeurism. It really creeps me out. And no woman is going to want to be with you if you continue to act that way."

He hung his head sheepishly. "Honestly, Racine. I never meant to spy on you. I was going to intercept you before you got into the shower, and tell you that I was in possession of the cartouche. After all, you made a great investment into this adventure. You deserve to see the outcome. I *wanted* you to come with me. That's all. But I realized once I was inside your hotel suite that I would have a hard time explaining my presence."

"How did you get into our suite without being seen?" I asked.

"I slipped in after the porter left you people your formal party clothes. Those soft-close doors take a long time about swinging shut. If I saw anyone, I was going to make up some excuse of being concerned for your accident. And, if they didn't believe me I would reveal I had the cartouche. They wouldn't have detained me after that. They all want to know where Cleopatra's tomb is too… Serendipitously, all of your buddies were inside their own private bedrooms cleaning up. The living area was empty. Your—Depardieu was on the balcony having a smoke. I slipped in hoping to find you. You were nowhere in sight when I first came in, so I hid in the bathroom linen closet."

I had one more question that required an answer. "Why didn't you talk to me before I got into the shower and before Norman came in?"

He gave me a helpless look. "I don't know. I just froze. I suddenly realized that you might think I caused the cave-in and start screaming."

"I am not a screamer."

"How could I know that? Fortunately Trevanian and his brother left for the lobby so I could sneak out."

Silence fell hard and fast. "Well, no hard feelings," I admitted. "Let's just forget about it."

"Yeah, let's," he said, and I heard the excitement creep back into his voice. "I can't wait for you to see this." Again his eyes turned up to take in the top of the Step Pyramid.

"Antony was hoisted through an upper story window and died in Cleopatra's chamber," he reiterated. If I hadn't quite caught on to the significance of this line, he was determined to hammer the fact home. His right hand rose to follow the direction of his eyes. A moment of utter quiet descended, as though all of Egypt's gods and demigods were waiting for his great pronouncement. "I swear to God, Lucy. That's where Cleopatra's tomb is. Up there…" He clapped one hand on his hat as we stared up. A palpable hush deadened the night air between us as the wind died, and we both took in the enormity of his statement.

"*This* is what the passage meant," I said. It was what I had independently deduced as well.

His head bobbed enthusiastically. He extended an arm in the direction of the scaffolding that appeared on the side and angled to the rear. "Shall we?"

There was no one around. Any journalists who had come to report the story of the accident at the Step Pyramid of Djoser had long since departed. The only evidence that anyone other than us had ever been here was the extra, yellow caution tape strung around the disaster. It was a story of little significance since no one was trapped inside it, and there was no blow-by-blow Internet video reporting the details of the rescue. No one had known about our part in it and so interest had died even before it started.

What did I say about the desolation of this historical site after hours? It was totally deserted and even during visiting hours it was mostly empty. And that was primarily due to the lack of maintenance. Money was tight and most of it went to supporting the big tourist draws in Giza and the Valley of the Kings in Luxor. God only knows what would have happened if Aras had not found us with the drone. We would probably still be trapped under the pyramid.

The emptiness of the landscape was daunting.

It was just as well because other than his film crew, Chas was happy to make the discovery alone. He *had* to be alone in order to stage the great reveal.

I returned my eyes to the glowing pyramid summit. Had a floodlight been left on for some reason?

"You want us to go up there? I can't climb the scaffolding in these shoes." I glanced annoyingly down at my stilettoes, the heels of which were sinking into the ground.

"Then I guess you go barefoot. Got a problem with that?"

The ground was mostly sand and we were on the other side of the explosion so there was no shrapnel or rubble. The scaffolding consisted of dense layers of steel beams, some were even wooden, and there was rough plywood flooring. But there was very little floor and mostly beams, so many beams in fact that it was hard to see through them. It was a tight weave making for a three-dimensional ladder.

I glanced up at the height. The subtle glow at the summit continued to puzzle me. We would be climbing a small mountain that had to be as tall as a twelve-story building, and I didn't feel like risking a million slivers in my feet, or slipping on the steel rods.

"Yes, I have a problem with that."

He left me standing where I was and returned to the car. When he rejoined me several minutes later, he was holding a pair of black Sketchers dangling from two fingers. The rubbers soles were bright orange. "I remembered your size and purchased you these."

"You bought me shoes? You just assumed I would come with you?"

I made no pretense of my outrage.

He shrugged, spread out his hands to take in the grandness—the unique specialness—of what we were about to experience. The enormous pyramid stood starkly outlined against the night sky, its cap haloed like something supernatural. "I *hoped…*" he explained, "not *assumed.* This is *huge*, Racine. I just could not see you missing out."

Fine, but I still resented his presumption.

I snatched the recreational shoes, stripped my feet bare and tossed the stilettoes willy-nilly onto the ground. The Sketchers fit. Perfectly. Dammit, he knew my shoe size. Why was that cringe-worthy?

Oh hell. What did it matter? Now, I could climb the scaffolding in style *and* comfort.

Unfortunately, I would have to do it in an evening gown. Thank goodness for the side slits, which would enable maneuverability, because I was not about to change clothes in front of him even had he offered me a suit of rugged Basseem duds for free.

I hiked up my skirt and faced the three-dimensional ladder. "Okay, lead the way."

"First, give me your purse."

I instinctively flinched. *Why?*

The words had not left my lips but the question clearly appeared in my expression.

"It will just encumber you. Do you really want that thing swinging around your neck while you climb?" I had slipped the chain over my head to carry the bag across my body; it was quite light. The evening bag was only roomy enough to hold the makeup bag with the precious comb, forcing me to leave my gun behind—which was no big deal. It would have been confiscated at the palace anyway.

"Suit yourself," Chas said, as he rolled up his sleeves and doffed his bush hat cavalierly, as though he were indeed the indomitable Indiana Jones. "Ladies first."

CHAPTER 43

The going was steep. And high. There was a time when I could not have made this climb. My fear of high places would have turned me into a cowering, whimpering puppy. It is amazing what adrenalin, motivation and curiosity will do. What is even more amazing is the power of love. Norman had helped me cross the highest bridges in my life—both metaphorically and in reality. I only wished that he were here with me now. Tomorrow, I, no doubt, would get an earful. I should have told him where I was going.

But this was Chas. I had spent so much time with him lately; it was just like old times.

We climbed side by side, my skirt flapping in the wind until we neared the top. I did not know what to expect, and during our arduous climb he explained to me his hunch.

"The top few steps of the pyramid are hollow," he said, and clutched at his hat as a gust of wind caught at it. "Cleopatra, during her lifetime, rebuilt the summit of Djoser's pyramid to include a chamber."

This made sense. She knew her days as pharaoh were numbered and she had no time to build her own pyramid. She also wished to hide her treasure from Octavian, and what better place than an already existing monument? When her faithful stonemasons finished renovating the pyramid to include her burial chamber, she asked them to cover the entire thing with a veneer of limestone. This made the tampering of the original structure invisible and for two thousand years it was hidden.

Over the past hundred years explorations of the Step Pyramid led to the conclusion that it was rebuilt multiple times. None, however, believed that it was hollow. Before technology enabled investigators to see through stone, it was established that this particular monument was constructed from solid rock. And so for decades the solid part of the Step Pyramid remained unexplored. True, the subterranean maze and the burial chambers belonging to King Djoser were well known. After all, looters, from the time it was built, had shown the way.

Later when advanced imaging technology became available the Step Pyramid stood last in line for investigation. The structure lacked the awesomeness of the Sphinx or the Great Pyramids of Giza and, to most, was a crumbling old ruin that attracted minor interest.

No one had thought to use muon tomography to measure its opacity. Muon Tomography, if you've never heard the term, is a non-invasive method that uses cosmic rays to generate three-dimensional images of the interiors of large monuments. And yes, it can be likened to x-raying a pyramid. So, is this what Chas had done? Had he employed muon tomography to see inside the Step Pyramid without having to drill into the stone?

When I asked him he said no. He had no access to technology because he had no funds with which to pay for it. Besides, before he got hold of the cartouche, what would have made him even think to use the technology on this pyramid? But once he had the cartouche he was able to isolate the exact location of Cleopatra's tomb. Little did he know that all along he was searching the right spot. But the crypt of Cleopatra wasn't in the shafts and galleries burrowed beneath the pyramid. It was located within the pyramid itself.

And when he realized that the queen's tomb was inside the body of the Step Pyramid he had to figure out the exact location of the 'window'. All *this* was, he informed me while waving a hand in the direction of the peak and performing a balancing act on a horizontal beam, was a guess. But he was right.

My goodness was he right!

Tilting my head, I could see where a square of stone had been removed near the pyramid's summit. It had the impression of being a window. And from this window golden light flowed. It explained the yellow halo I had detected from below.

"How did you know where to find the 'window'?" I asked.

"An educated guess—and phenomenally good luck."

He grinned as we both clung to the crossed vertical beams. Our footing was on a plywood plank. The skirt of my gown flapped relentlessly against my legs. I was breathless, not just from the climb but from the whole adventure. As I perched on a steel rod at least forty meters from the ground I felt like I was floating in outer space except that Chas was here with me too, and the night sky was filled with bright stars. Strangely, there was no moon.

Chas' hat suddenly flew off his head and swirled like a flying saucer into the black abyss of the desert. He did not appear particularly concerned, swore once, and then continued as though that gap in our conversation had not occurred: "After I decided on the spot where I guessed the window might be, the bricks were easily removed." He paused for theatrical effect. "Are you ready to see the greatest find of the century?"

I stood balanced precariously for a breath to take in the moment. My rubber soles rolled and I gripped a bar for balance. We were at the level of the window and a few more steps and an awkward crawl on hands and knees would take us inside.

"Okay," I said. "Let's do it."

The opening was just wide enough for Chas to climb through with minimal hindrance, although he had to unhook his shirt from a crag once before he passed freely. For me it was a breeze and I slid into the chamber like wine flowing from a bottle.

The first thing I noticed was the pile of cracked bricks on the stone floor. Had he done this all by himself? And when? When had he removed these bricks? I thought he had only just learned of the tomb's location a few hours ago.

It was obvious that no care had been taken in breaking through to this chamber.

Then the familiar chemical smell made me realize how it had been accomplished so fast. Chas was some kind of demolition's expert and had managed to blast a hole in the thinnest part of the wall (Cleopatra's original window) without damage to the chamber within. And then he had widened the remainder by hand, precisely, by pick and hammer.

I raised my eyes. I should have suspected something sinister on the spot but I was too awed by the scene before me to notice anything odd. The space was lit up with several kerosene lamps, which gave off the soft yellow glow I had noticed from below. That should have been my first clue.

The tomb was a smallish chamber and the far wall seemed foreshortened. From the outside I would have expected this chamber to be larger.

For its purpose however it was quite large enough. The first thing that caught my attention, once my eyes adjusted to the dim light, was the bed of gold—Cleopatra's sarcophagus. Was it real, solid gold? Yes. And beside this sarcophagus carved to resemble an elegant bed frame, two desiccated bodies lay on the floor, one on either side.

My mouth opened to gasp. I had no doubt now. These were the queen's maidservants. Their bodies were withered. Their garments although aged almost to dust remained recognizable as servants clothing and in one piece, but I knew that if I touched the fabric it would explode into powder in my hands. Their clothes were that old.

This was an archaeological site of the highest magnitude, a historical find unparalleled by any other than King Tut's tomb, and nothing must be touched until the experts brought in the proper equipment. I was truly privileged to share this find with Chas.

I moved forward to see more. I must witness the lady pharaoh herself.

I don't know if the golden bedframe, which was really a raised sarcophagus originally had fabric bedding and a mattress. What the body lay on was deteriorated and what I could see appeared to be some kind of luxury material. I was careful not to touch anything as I stood a foot away from the base of her golden bed. She herself was dressed in a sheer, ankle-length dress made of what must have once been pure, fine, white linen, and a silk cloak. Around her throat was a heavy gold necklace embedded with emeralds, lapis lazuli and pearls. On her feet were white papyrus sandals, now aged to brown encrusted with grey pearls. On her arms were gold serpent bracelets, several clasped to her upper arms (loose now due to the atrophy of her muscles and the desiccation of her skin) and fine, filigree bangles around her wrists each decorated with a gemstone eye.

Her face and skin were brown and dried to resemble aged leather. It was impossible to describe her features. Certainly she looked nothing like the granite statue at the Royal Ontario Museum. Nor did she resemble the image on the silver coin Norman and I had found inside pharaoh Djoser's underground, labyrinthine crypt. It was impossible to tell whether she had once been a great beauty.

I hugged my evening bag against my chest, which held the murder weapon that had claimed Cleopatra's life. It dawned on me then that the pattern of jewels in the necklace matched the jewels encrusted on the comb. I moved up until I stood quite close and opened my small, gold-chained purse and removed the makeup bag from within. It did not occur to me at the time to question the whereabouts of Mark Antony's body.

"What are you doing?" Chas asked.

I ignored him and unzipped the plastic zipper, tipped the makeup bag, and watched the comb tumble out and land crookedly on Cleopatra's chest, just above her crossed, shriveled, brown hands. The only part of the comb that might be poisonous were the teeth, and I wouldn't harm myself if I arranged it more precisely between her fingers.

Nevertheless, just to be safe I turned the pliable makeup bag inside out to use like a glove, and I reached out to pick up the comb by the shaft.

"At last," a voice said in a thick Arabic accent.

My knuckles clenched. The voice came from in front of me, not behind me where Chas waited.

I held the comb in a vise grip and tucked my fist protectively against my chest, as I looked up into the fierce gaze of Nizar Tarek.

He stood at the head of the sarcophagus; his dark, piercing brown eyes meant business. He was dressed the way he always dressed, sleeves rolled up in army green, exposing his bare, powerful biceps, an AK-47 semi-automatic rifle slung over his right shoulder. In his right hand was a revolver and it was aimed directly at my heart.

"Did you truly believe that we would never meet again?" he inquired.

His voice was soft, gentle. Chilling.

Instinctively, I jerked backwards, and spun to seek Chas for protection.

CHAPTER 44

He too held a gun. And it was aimed straight at my face.

Et tu Brute?

The famous line from Shakespeare's play *Julius Caesar* rolled off my thoughts but not my tongue as I stood in shock. Caesar's friend Brutus had joined the Romans to assassinate him just as Chas was betraying me now. He might as well shoot me in the head. Because if he didn't God only knew what Tarek had in store for me.

"I am so sorry, Lucy. I did not want it to end like this."

"It doesn't have to, Chas," I whispered in anguish. "Just let me step aside." *And then you can shoot him.* The tears pressed against my lids as I realized wholeheartedly that this man, a man I once trusted was about to toss me away like a half-eaten sandwich.

My voice was so low I was certain Tarek heard nothing. "Please. Think about what you are doing."

Hesitation appeared in Chas' body stance. I had a chance. Maybe. Then his eyes glowered. There was a whole evil organization behind Tarek. Chas was alone.

He became adamant, and waved both arms around to take in Cleopatra's death scene. "If I give you to him, all of this will be mine. Don't you see what it means? I'll have my life back. My reputation, my celebrity *and* my academic status!"

"You'll be a murderer," I accused.

His head shook sadly. "I am not going to shoot you." He indicated with his pistol that the onus would be on the terrorist.

"You're sacrificing me just because I wouldn't be seduced by you?" *Of all the narcissistic, arrogant, idiotic reasons—*

I was shaking in fear but my anger was keeping it in check.

"No. If you had slept with me I would have given you to him anyways… Don't look at me like that. I am only getting back what was mine. It was so unfair… And nobody cared about me when I was rotting in that jail. Can you even imagine what it's like to have your dignity, your freedom and your privacy taken away from you? I had to shit in front of those prison guards. Eat with derelicts and criminals. And live with the threat of being beaten up every day. Even *you* didn't care when I told you about it. *NO*-body cared—except Abadi and her people."

Abadi! The name made me gag. And her people. What people? Did he mean the terrorists like Tarek? Who else could he mean? My heart fell as I sought his eyes for some semblance of compassion, some indication that this man was once a person of principle and conscience. A man I once thought so highly of that I gave myself to him. A man I once thought I loved.

He dragged his head back and forth, as though he could read my thoughts. "I never loved you, Racine. Not then. Not now."

"Think about what you're doing, Basseem. You won't get away with this." Yes, that's right. He was no longer my Chas. He was Dr. Ramy Basseem. Jerk of the first order. I turned to include Tarek in my warning. "*Neither* of you will."

Tarek's muscles pulsed as he responded to my threat. His accent was thick, guttural. "I kill people for a living, *mademoiselle.* No one has caught me yet."

"My friends will come for you. As we speak, they are coming for you *now!*"

My bravado ended with an embarrassing squeak. I had no idea if anyone was coming for me. If anyone even knew I was missing. How could I be so stupid? This was the stupidest move I had ever made. Dammit, the boys were going to kill me.

Despite myself I could not help but laugh. They couldn't do a damn thing to chastise me. I would be dead.

Think Racine. You can get out of this. You've been in worse situations than this.

But I was only fooling myself. Because no, I had not. I had never been in a situation as impossible as this.

Fortunately for me, I no longer had any feelings for Ramy Basseem. He was no longer the young man I had fallen in love with when I was still a naïve teenager. He was a criminal. A crook. A thug.

I no longer had to give any thought to what might happen to him. I only had to save myself. Tarek had proven himself more than once to be a beast. An animal of the desert like a scorpion. No. He was worse than a scorpion. A scorpion only stung out of fear. It did not kill for pleasure or greed or power.

What's more I was privy to something that neither of them was. I was not helpless.

"Stop your chatter, Basseem. And bring her to me," Tarek commanded. He continued to speak in English because he knew my Arabic was poor. And he wanted me to understand every word he uttered. "I have wasted enough time."

Basseem gestured with the nose of his gun. "Don't make this harder then it has to be."

I am not afraid of you. The pathetic man was like a cartoon villain, a coward at heart. He was more of an egotistical, swollen-headed, arrogant headline hunter than anything else. His pseudo persona as swashbuckling hero was laughable. Indiana Jones? Ha!

With that thought I turned my back on him to face my real enemy.

Nizar Tarek was calm. His muscles were tense beneath the army green. He thought of me as a helpless woman. He had once held me prisoner in his terrorist camp. I had posed no threat to him. I had been saved by my friends and by the man that I loved. I willed my thoughts to him—if only he could hear me. *I am so sorry, Norman, for being impulsive.* I understood now why Johnny had flip-flopped on taking me with him to rescue Alessandra.

Impulse might have gotten me into this jam but perhaps it could get me out. I had to get out. I had promised Colleen that I would be there for the birth of her baby.

And nothing. *No-thing* was going to stop me from meeting my niece.

"Come with me," Tarek ordered. He nudged me towards a false wall. Behind the wall, which had two openings to the main chamber, was a well with steps leading down. Oh shit, where did that go?

"Move!" he shouted.

"Wait," Basseem said. He made eye contact with Tarek. "Will you keep your promise and leave me with all of this?" His eyes swept the death chamber and all the riches it held.

An ugly smile curled the terrorist's lips. He nodded. "You've got what you want," he said. "Now give me what *I* want."

He was lying. Any fool could see that.

Basseem stepped past me, cocked his pistol. "Duck, Racine!" And fired.

But he was too slow. The terrorist was a practiced sniper. He dodged aside and the bullet shattered the wall. A split instant later his own bullet escaped the revolver and pierced Basseem in the chest.

At first I was paralyzed with shock. Chas had tried to save me! This unexpected turn of events froze my brain—but not for long. Fury sent adrenalin soaring, and I came to life. I still clasped Cleopatra's comb with my makeup bag. I gave no thought to my subsequent actions. I had to help Chas, and impulse took over.

I lunged at Tarek and slashed his naked arm before he could turn from firing a second and third bullet into my ex. He had no intention of allowing *me* to die so easily. Wound me, he might, just to cause insufferable pain. But give me an instant reprieve from life? Never.

Instead of shooting me, he backhanded me in the face, and I nearly tumbled down the stairwell.

I dropped the comb and the makeup bag, and lay on the ground staring up at him. Rage turned his swarthy face purple. Or maybe it was the poison. Oh, God, I hoped so much that it was the poison. Could it work that fast?

"Get up," he screamed.

He was still standing, ignoring the damage I had done to his arm.

Slowly, I rose to my feet, head throbbing, the powerful revolver following me. Maybe the poison was no longer active; maybe all I had succeeded in accomplishing was signed for myself an even more severe death warrant.

He glanced at the wound I had inflicted on him. The tines of the comb had broken the skin and left four bloody, parallel scrapes. "You thought you could hurt me with that puny trinket?" He kicked it where it lay on the floor into the open chamber and it stopped just short of where Chas lay bleeding, eyes open, gawping at nothing, his gun hanging uselessly at his side, clenched in a dying fist. For the first time I wondered: had he even known how to use the thing?

Tarek scowled as the blood beaded and trickled down his arm. That was my cue to flee and I tried to but he collared me and shoved me until I hit the jamb of the wall. If he was in agony, he showed no signs of it. "I am going to give you the slowest, most excruciating death you can imagine."

An unexpected bullet shot past, and rang against the stone beyond us. I ducked behind the false wall as a second bullet collided with the wall, stopping Tarek in his tracks.

This time the stone broke and crumbled, shattering onto the floor, and then we both turned to see someone climb through the window followed by two others, all armed.

"It's over, Tarek," one of them said, glancing briefly at Chas' prone body. "Put down your weapons."

Oh my god, it was Norman! I started to run toward him but Tarek clawed me around the waist, yanked me up against him to use as a shield, and pressed the revolver to my head. "You shoot me, I shoot her."

I gulped and locked eyes with Norman. *I am so sorry.*

He returned my gaze. *You have nothing to be sorry for.*

We were at a stalemate. Chas' fingers had loosened as he lay dying and the gun thudded out of his hand. Aras picked it up and I felt awful for accusing Chas of blunt cowardice because with his final act he had proven me wrong.

I sent my sight past the deathly still, crumpled archaeologist to the fallen comb. Norman's attention followed, then returned to Tarek where he noticed the scratched arm and how the skin around the wound had turned black.

Norman lowered his revolver and the two men beside him became hyper alert, their weapons still fixed on the terrorist. "If you don't want to die," Norman warned. "I would suggest you let Lucy go."

A simpering curl appeared at the terrorist's bearded mouth, and he laughed as he poked the revolver's nose forcefully against my skull. "And why would I do that? I hold all the cards here. *I* have the woman."

My man smiled in turn, the source of his amusement less obvious. "That may be so but she already gave you the deathblow. You see that jeweled comb on the floor? It is Cleopatra's comb, and the means by which she died. It's filled with poison, and now that poison is inside you. If we don't get you to a poison control center *tout suite*, you are a dead man."

Tarek's face darkened. "Is that true?" His mouth scowled. "I don't believe you. How can a poison still work after thousands of years?"

Norman returned the terrorist's scowl. "That is the dilemma, isn't it? Maybe it can and maybe it can't. Are you willing to take that chance? Some poisons become even more deadly over time."

Tarek swung me violently about, causing my heel to snag on my long evening gown, and I tripped. Before he could catch me and throttle me, or whatever he had planned to do, Norman fired a bullet that punctured him in the head. Norman was a marksman. When he aimed to miss, he missed. When he aimed to hit, he hit. Tarek toppled over, almost landing on me, but I dodged his crumpling body and escaped. Two more shots were fired into the fallen body, and they came from Luke and Aras.

Norman hurried to meet me and I collapsed into his arms, groping at his chest, his arms and his neck, just needing to know he was real.

"Oh, my darling Lucy," he whispered, emotion thickening his French accent. "*Ça va?* Are you okay?"

I nodded without being able to find my voice, tears streaming down my cheeks. My mouth was so very dry, swallowing was difficult, and it was as though I had gulped down a tennis ball wrapped in cotton batten.

A while later my heartbeat slowed, the flood of tears diminished, and I could breathe normally again. I whispered against Norman's throat, "Is he dead?"

Norman did not answer at first, and I realized then he was wondering whom I meant.

There was not only one potential corpse; there were two.

Luke was crouched near the terrorist's motionless form. Under one of the billionaire's arms, something was tucked. He had held onto the thing even while he had employed his gun. At this moment I did not care what it was. All I wanted to know was if the reign of terror had stopped.

Luke remained still for a few more seconds before he moved. He could not have possibly heard my question, but he raised his head and answered, "He's gone."

I stepped back and Norman released me. Aras had gone over to the golden bed. Outside the window I heard the chopping sounds of a helicopter.

I glanced around to find Chas, who was lying on the floor where his nemesis had felled him, a pool of blood seeping out beneath his back. As luck would have it, Tarek's aim was impeccable and the bullet had hit his heart, allowing no chance of resuscitation.

Norman walked over to squat by the body, trying his best to curtail his emotion and show only what he deemed appropriate. "I'm sorry about Basseem," he said.

So was I. Chas was dead. There was no doubt about it. No one had to tell me he was gone. I had seen the face of a dead person before.

I went to his lifeless body and knelt beside it while Norman rose to give me some space. I don't know where he went or for how long but when he returned, he hovered over me until I looked up. He was holding something and now offered it to me, Basseem's trademark bush hat. So they had found it outside.

I accepted the hat and placed it gently on Chas' chest. At the last moment he had proven himself to be the hero I always knew he could be.

There would be plenty of time to reflect and grieve when all of this was over, and I got up to seek the other dead person. Luke was kneeling over him, making sure.

The corpse of the terrorist had me a little spooked. I had never wanted to hurt anyone as much as I had wanted to hurt Nizar Tarek. My conscience was churning. I had acted out of fear and emotion—just like the first time I had pulled the trigger on this brute.

Was this my fault? Was I the perpetrator of this mess?

It seemed no matter how often I got myself into these life and death situations, resorting to violence remained counterintuitive. Shaun just might be right and I should reflect carefully about my future with ISORE. My brother-in-law had an enormous stake in my wellbeing, but perhaps, in this, he was correct.

I watched Luke as he got to his feet after examining the terrorist. I had to know the cause of his death.

Luke came to join us and I nervously asked, "Do you really believe the poison was still effective?" I paused briefly, and dropped my tone until barely audible. "Or was it the bullets that killed him?"

Luke studied me curiously. "We won't know until we have the comb tested, and if we really want to know the cause of death, we will have to wait for a post mortem."

This was the last thing I needed; I felt myself shrink inside. All the questions, the interrogation, the interviews; could my nerves take much more?

"A post mortem?" My voice came out rasp-like as I tried to control the emotion. "But the authorities, they *can't* know—"

"He's a wanted terrorist, Lucy," Norman reproached before he guessed the reason for my anxiety. His expression filled with compassion and his eyes fixed on Luke's as they mutually agreed. "I doubt that they will do a post mortem. He isn't worth it. The Syrian government will pay a king's ransom for getting rid of this savage. So no, we won't tell them about the poison."

I was horrified by what I had done, but Tarek had had no intention of letting me live, and he had killed Chas, Chas, whose last act in life was to save me.

The whole horrible scene replayed itself in my mind. I had been taking a huge chance with the comb, but it was the only hope available to me at the time. I was trying to save Chas, not knowing that it was already too late.

"He was going to kill you, Lucy. And *not* quickly. You had no choice."

"That was *not* why I did it," I said.

The rush of adrenalin dissipated as I felt my muscles relax. I felt limp like I had just completed a triathlon, and believe me I had no idea what that even entailed. My vision wandered lazily over my surroundings. This whole thing was so surreal. A terrorist at the tomb of Cleopatra—inside a pyramid—had nearly killed me, and had it not been for Chas' resurgence of conscience he would have succeeded. Chas was human after all.

It was still hard to believe that if it wasn't for Chas, God knows what would have happened to me. What were the odds of anyone locating this site? It had taken Chas decades to pinpoint, and I could have died in here without anyone ever knowing.

My attention flickered towards the false wall. Tarek could have buried me in a vault, somewhere down those dark stairs. My thoughts returned to the man who had saved me. *Thank you, Chas.*

I almost burst out crying when the realization finally registered, and I forced myself to check the tears. As I said there would be time enough for mourning at his funeral.

I understood now how the team had found me. In Luke's hand was the drone. He had had it tucked under his arm while assessing Tarek's pulse so I had failed to identify it at first. Now its lovely sleek lines drew me like a flower, and I went to him and lifted *Firefly* out of his grip. I stroked it as though it were a puppy and whispered, "I love you, you beautiful thing."

Luke smiled. The relief he felt was palpable. "Better watch it, Lucy. Gushing like that might make your fiancé jealous."

Norman laughed. He too was feeling the weight of the terrorist threat lift. "That piece of metal and plastic is the best piece of luggage we could have brought with us."

Yeah. Amen to that. I was feeling a little better. Thank goodness Johnny had decided to steal it. Because I don't know that Luke would have thought to bring it himself.

I scoured the chamber for Aras, as I hadn't seen him in awhile.

Where the heck was he? "Has anybody seen Aras?" I asked.

"Yo! Aras," Luke shouted. "Where'd you disappear to?"

There was no answer.

Norman scratched his brow. "Last I saw him, he was inspecting Cleopatra's golden sarcophagus."

He had either gone out the window back onto the scaffolding or he had made his way past us down the steps behind the false wall. There was no other way out of this chamber.

We traded concurring glances and nodded.

And opted for exploring the underground stairwell.

CHAPTER 45

Luke and Norman each seized one of the kerosene lamps. I hitched up my long gown and tiptoed down the stairs. The steps were shallow. They angled downwards and then stopped at a wide doorway. I gasped, dropping my skirt, as my vision took in an enormous crypt. Aras was there holding his own kerosene lamp, paralyzed by the splendor of the vault.

"Cleopatra's treasure trove," he said as our eyes met.

None of us had the ability to respond. This discovery was breathtaking. I literally felt as though the air had been vacuumed out of my lungs. We each took in the sight as though we stood alone, totally mesmerized—and speechless.

The first thing that caught my attention was a life-sized granite statue of what had to be Cleopatra herself. And yes, if you asked me, she was beautiful. Her features were fine and regal, and not masculine like those images on the coins that we had discovered earlier in the subterranean tunnels. Luke suggested that the masculine images were to intimidate the populace. Cleopatra had no intention of being treated any differently from her male counterparts and so she probably had the brutish images engraved on the coins to emphasize her power. And if this sculpture was indeed the queen herself, she was a splendid, and terrifying force of nature.

Surrounding the statue were various pieces of furniture: an alabaster throne trimmed with gold and studded with emeralds, amethyst and agates; a chariot of rare, exotic mahogany, also decorated with gold and various gems; a divan so exquisite you would never want to sit on it. The back of the divan was engraved with a royal scene painted in turquoise and orange pigments, inlayed with lapis lazuli and gold. The seat was meant for lounging and the legs resembled serpents ending in viper's heads.

If that wasn't enough, there were alabaster chests filled with jewelry, and gold and silver coins. On a simple wooden table, very much like a lady's vanity, were a makeup kit, an alabaster perfume box, a tarnished, face-sized mirror, and a yellowed but still very lovely set of ivory brushes and combs. Was this hair set a gift from Caesar? The decorative jewels encrusted on the handles and shafts matched that of the poison comb still lying on the floor upstairs.

And that wasn't all that had been buried in her two-story tomb. Several mummified cats lay about on the floor. Scarab beetles accompanied them. And to ensure that she and her companions would be well nourished in the afterlife there was food—oh yes, there was food. Baskets of barley, figs, dates, grapes, and melons, all dehydrated now into seeds, but strangely recognizable. And to keep the party going there were jars of wine. I recognized the style of jar and the residue inside them.

I sought out Luke, the billionaire archaeologist, to whom this find would mean the most. He was staring at something off in the corner below the vanity table. At first I thought it was just a jumble of tarnished metal—silver plates perhaps—but as I approached I realized that this *something* was a suit of fine armor, discolored by time but distinctive all the same. It had the identical emblems that were embossed on the sword and shield discovered earlier, and was of Roman manufacture. Underneath the armor was another desiccated body—that of Mark Antony.

He had fallen while attempting to retrieve something. What was it, an offering for the queen? Was this her final request? I moved up next to Luke and saw that he had removed a small alabaster vial from the deceased soldier's hand. In the light of the kerosene lamp the white opalescent stone of this tiny container glowed ethereally, proof that even as he wrestled with a self-inflicted fatal injury, Mark Antony had tried to fulfill his love's last wish.

It was a bit of a struggle for Luke to pry the vial out from between the shrunken, bony, crooked brown fingers of Octavian's former proconsul, but when at last he attained success I lowered myself to the level of the vial and detected from the rim, the faint scent of orange blossom, Patchouli and honey, purported to be Cleopatra's most cherished fragrance.

I glanced back at the dead soldier, an upwell of emotion filling me. Exactly what had caused the deathblow would have to wait until the mummy was expertly examined sometime in the future—for now we could only guess. Somewhere beneath that armor Mark Antony had sustained a mortal wound, and yet had made the greatest romantic gesture of all. He was dying and was determined to bring Cleopatra her favorite perfume so that she might smell seductively enticing on her journey to the afterworld, but sadly, he had expired before he could make it up those stairs to his lover's side.

As I gazed at the stairs I had a thought. Why did Tarek wish to bring me down here? My eyes scanned the entire room and I noticed a further stairwell, this one descending ever deeper. I was certain that the terrorist had no intention of showering me with gifts from Cleopatra's treasure just as I had no doubts that he had intended to force me below.

What was below? Like a zombie, numbed by the surrealness of it all, I took the kerosene lamp that Aras had left on the floor and walked to the stairwell, hidden in the shadows.

"Where are you going, Lucy?" Norman asked.

"Down there."

"There's another level?"

"Yes." I indicated the hole in the floor. It was hidden in the darkness behind one more false wall, which was why we had not seen it at first. It was wide enough for a man to pass through but it was narrower than the stairwell where we had descended from the upper story of Cleopatra's tomb.

Lamp in fist, I went first while Norman followed with no intention of letting me out of his sight. When we reached bottom after several zigs and zags I knew where we were.

It was the vault where Mark Antony's sarcophagus sat. The shield and sword remained in place; they had not been touched and miscellaneous tools lay scattered about that were absent before. These included a large crowbar, heavier than the one we had used, and scissors, and a bottle of chloroform, plus rolls upon rolls of wide, flesh-colored fabric bandages. Tarek had been here and left these things, and clearly they were meant for me. He had intended to knock me out with the chloroform, wrap me like a mummy and stuff me into the sarcophagus and close the lid.

Involuntarily, I cringed. A flood of adrenalin shot into my system causing my heart to palpitate. Had Tarek succeeded in his insanely cruel plan I would have regained consciousness—just in time to suffocate to death.

"Don't feel bad about what happened upstairs, Lucy. *I* don't. It was self-defense. That man was no man. He was a monster."

He wrapped his arms around me and I felt his heat. He tipped my face up to meet his.

"No one can grieve over a monster."

I gulped and waited for the shiver to pass.

One thing was for certain. I would never have to endure this terrorist's threats again. Norman removed his dinner jacket and draped it around my shoulders. I smiled at him because it was the only thing I could think to do. He felt bad for me because of Chas. He didn't have to. I must remember to reassure him of that when we returned home.

"Let's go back upstairs," I said. "I hate this place."

CHAPTER 46

As far as I was aware, Chas was not particularly religious. But because he was something of an icon for Egypt, he was given a traditional burial. Chas did not have many living members of his immediate or extended family, but he did have a huge supportive community and of course his notoriety had made him a public figure. He had fans.

His funeral was on the scale of what would have been proper for a head of state or a celebrity. It took place in Cairo at the site of the brand new, Grand Egyptian Museum, a state-of-the-art facility that was to replace the old museum where Chas and I first met. After eight years of construction, the facility was almost completed. It was slated to open at the end of the year, but for now the modern glass and concrete building would house the memorial service for one of Egypt's most controversial and celebrated archaeologists.

The seven of us arrived early. Alessandra's ankle was on the mend and she entered on Johnny's arm. Aras and Luke escorted Arianna Chase who had caught a last minute flight in order to pay her respects. Norman and I came last.

The Grand Egyptian Museum is built on a slope on the Giza plateau overlooking the famous pyramids on the edge of the Western Desert. As we passed through the sculpture gardens at valley level, an enormous granite statue of Pharaoh Ramses II, standing at the entrance to the great atrium, accosted our eyes. After learning about the triumphant discovery of Cleopatra's long-looked for tomb, the authorities had dedicated a new wing to Dr. Ramy Basseem. I understood that the experience at this new wing was to replicate Chas—I mean Dr. Ramy Basseem's—journey in uncovering the great tomb.

The team mingled with the guests and mourners of the famous Egyptologist. The public and the media joined together to celebrate the life of a national hero. I had begged the boys to allow Chas this dream—to be remembered, not as a dirty bureaucrat's minion, but as the brilliant archaeologist who had found Cleopatra's tomb.

After all, he *had* discovered it.

With a little encouragement they all agreed, after learning how he had sacrificed fame, fortune, *and* his life—in an attempt to save mine.

Colonel Rima Abadi was noticeably absent. Luke informed me that she was arrested and was awaiting arraignment in the local prison, her bail set at two million dollars. When the Egyptian authorities were informed of Cleopatra's tomb—and Abadi and her terrorist partners' attempt to plunder it—the conspiracy was broken wide open. The Syrians were humiliated by the idea that one of their very own trusted officials had conceived of such a plot. They promised to clean house and crack down on any further illicit activity meant to take advantage of the tensions between the two countries.

There was a formal reconciliation and representatives from both countries were in attendance at this sad and yet glorious occasion.

The service was soon to start and those who wished could afterwards drive to the cemetery where Chas would be interred in his family's mausoleum. Other guests and members of the community were encouraged to stay at the museum for refreshments and mingling.

I left Norman and the team paying condolences and exchanging reminisces of the famous archaeologist with officials and family members. Alone, I meandered to the Grand Staircase, which led from the valley level of the museum to the plateau. As I climbed the marble steps in my black high heels, feeling my knee-length charcoal skirt swish with my movements, I noticed just beyond the railing that it was lined with almost a hundred statues of kings and gods. To show my respect for the old gods and the new, my dress had a high round neckline with black lace across the top of my chest, and wrist-length sheer sleeves.

At the landing, galleries opened from a wide lobby, and at the far end were ceiling-to-floor glass panels that overlooked the magnificent pyramids, a symbol of one of humankind's greatest architectural achievements.

My relationship with Chas had taken place a million years ago, but today it felt fresh, making me wonder: how can you know a person, and not know him at all?

The view was splendid. The three dimensional, triangular structures were monstrously huge, stunning works of design, craftsmanship and engineering. Their peaks rose to the heavens, baking in the sun, casting enormous shadows across numerous visitors—tiny moving dots like ants that swarmed the arid landscape—reminding me once again how such a simple thing like a pyramid could capture the collective imagination.

Chas would have adored this. He would have loved knowing how high in esteem his country held him. He had succeeded where other archaeologists had failed—including Luke Trevanian. He had located Cleopatra's tomb.

The ancient queen had a story to share with the world. The interpretation of that story would be up to Egyptologists, globally. I looked forward to learning—after all the evidence had been recorded, documented, and analyzed—what that official narrative would say. I had my own ideas, but not being considered an expert I doubt that anyone of importance would listen.

Nonetheless, all of Cleopatra's riches, her grave goods, the remains of her servants, her lover Mark Antony, and herself would be conserved and preserved for posterity—thanks to Chas.

Some would say he was a poor excuse for a hero, others would say he was no hero at all. But at his heart Chas had proven to be true. He wasn't evil like those people he had partnered with. He was just weak, and more than a little greedy. But didn't all heroes begin their quest with a weakness?

I knew one thing was for certain. I never loved him back then, and I didn't love him now. And I wasn't even sure if I had forgiven him. He had been willing to sacrifice me for fame and power. And if not for that sudden surge of conscience, he would have handed me over to Tarek like a chip in a poker game.

He wanted to bind himself to my memory? Of that he had succeeded.

He had taken the bullet for me.

I looked down at something my hands had found as I was musing out the sky-facing windows. It was a simple gold plaque mounted on a marble pedestal. There was nothing else on display here except this view. They had not yet time to build the new wing.

The view was dedicated to the memory of Ramy Chas Basseem PHD, university professor, book author, film producer and presenter, clothing designer, past director of the Egyptian Museum and Egyptian Supreme Inspector of Antiquities. That was quite the glory label.

As I mused over his accomplishments I heard the subtle sounds of encroaching footsteps, and turned.

"*Hé*," Norman said, and stopped in front of me in his handsome dark suit.

"Hey," I echoed in English.

"You okay?"

I breathed as he extended both hands, which I took with gratitude. "I will be."

We were silent for a long time, our fingers twined together. There were things we wished to say to each other but this was a difficult time. I brought his attention to the plaque and made an amusing comment about the flamboyant Egyptologist's string of accolades but Norman was in no mood for jokes.

"I am so sorry about Basseem, Lucy," he said softly. "I know he meant a lot to you."

The silence that followed was unexpected, and awkward, and he was unable to meet my gaze. I squeezed his fingers to let him know I was okay, although his expression made me believe he thought otherwise. That thought disturbed me. How could he possibly believe anything had been rekindled between Chas and me?

If I had a soft spot for Chas now, it was only because I had lately realized that he wasn't completely twisted by greed and humiliation. To take a risk to save someone else was unheard of in his world. So for *that* he deserved a nod. But the real heroes still lived, and I was about to reassure one of them that he was the only one that mattered to me when I heard footsteps nearby.

I glanced over his shoulder and saw a woman approach.

My eyes widened. Oh my gosh, could it be?

"Yasmine? Yasmine Lim?" I gasped.

A broad smile illuminated her oval face as she shot Norman a quick nod before saying: "Lucy. Your boss told me I could find you up here."

She wore purple-rimmed glasses and had her long, sleek, black hair parted to one side and hanging loose, and was dressed in a black skirt and matching blazer with a light grey and white, checkered, silk blouse underneath. She looked remarkably well—her ivory complexion enhanced with makeup—for someone who had recently been deathly ill by poison. The only thing that made me think she was still recovering from her ordeal was the extraordinary whiteness of her skin that caused the plum lip color she used to stand out unnaturally.

"When were you released from the hospital?" I asked, making an effort to curb the judgmental scrutiny.

"This morning when I heard about Chas. I insisted. I wanted to attend his funeral."

"So, you two stayed in contact with each other? He never said much."

"We were in touch somewhat; mostly on official business. We weren't what you would call close friends. But *you* two: I had no idea you were still—"

"We *weren't*." I didn't want her to bring up unwanted memories. That stuff with Chas really *was* the past. "You look well," I said. *Considering.*

Did she know who had poisoned her or what the motive might have been? I still refused to believe that it was Chas. Yes, he had motive if anyone did, but this had the handprint of Abadi or Tarek—well, maybe not Tarek—he'd just as soon blow out someone's brains with an Ak-47 as do something so subtle as slip poison into her drink.

Yasmine appeared un-predisposed to pursue the topic, and I was inclined to agree. Best to think about it later, as I had no idea how to bring it up. Now that we had reconnected there was plenty of time to catch up after things had quieted down, and I reached over and gave her a heartfelt hug. "I am so glad to see you, Yas."

"Let's talk later," she suggested, releasing me with a gentle pat on the arm. "I believe the memorial speeches are about to start."

As she stepped back and her arms swung down I noticed a large diamond on her left hand. "Yas. Are—are you engaged?"

She glanced briefly down at her ring and smiled. "Eight months. The lucky guy's a politician running for the senate this coming election but we haven't set a date yet. He's been too busy." Her hand reached mischievously over and lifted mine. "Oh my god, Lucy. You too?"

I grinned, and then turned to introduce Norman. All this time he had been silently watching us, his quiet patience not only a virtue, but also his trademark. "Have you two ever met in your global roaming," I asked them both. "Archaeology can sometimes be a very small world." I had certainly learned that this was true in the past week with Chas' sudden unexpected reappearance in my life.

"I've heard of you, of course," Norman said, extending a hand. He was also a charmer when he chose. "But I don't believe we have ever met in person. *Enchanté*, Yasmine."

"*De même*," she replied, shaking his hand, her French almost as fluid as his. In Arab countries many educated people spoke French and English as well as Arabic. Yasmine just happed to be fluent in all three, as well as in Mandarin. "I certainly would remember you had we ever met." She turned to me with a sly smile.

No need for playful innuendo because she had noticed Norman's gorgeous physique on her own. *But that isn't all he has to offer* I wanted to say, and before I could think how to elaborate without embarrassing the subject of my praise, I realized she had already experienced his charm.

My phone chimed unexpectedly.

I fished it out, glance up and apologized for the interruption. "Just a second, while I shut this off."

My intent was to decline the call, but when my eyes wandered briefly over the name of the caller, my head shot forward and I squealed: "It's Shaun, my brother-in-law. Colleen's in labor!"

***

That put an end to our plans to attend the actual burial. Shortly after the service we took Luke's private jet back to Toronto. It was the longest eleven hours of my life.

When we arrived at the hospital we were still in our mourning clothes. We had gone straight to the airport from the museum leaving it up to the hotel, via Luke's request, to pack our things and ship them to us, expedited, to his mansion. We didn't even stop at our homes to shower and change when we landed. While we were waiting to pass through customs, Shaun had texted that Colleen was asking for me. She had been in labor for twelve hours and the baby could make her entrance into the world any minute. My sister wanted me to be there.

I had promised that I would. Dammit, I had *promised.*

I am not the best sister in the world, but mine is. Colleen is loyal to a fault. She gives me the benefit of the doubt even when it is clear that I am lying through my teeth. But my lies are never harmful and she knows it. So when I told her I was on my way, I meant it. Just because it was going to take me a few more hours than I would have liked did not mean that I didn't mean it. As it was she believed me and she was holding back on bringing baby Madonna into this world until I could share the miracle with her.

Like I said, she is an amazing sister. Not perfect of course. She is too much of a gossip and a meddler to be perfect. She is also divinely vain: constantly worried whether her highlights are the right shade and whether her mani matched her pedi. But she is kind, understanding, responsible, reliable and punctual. She even had the timing of her baby just right. Little Madonna was going to be born, today, in fifteen minutes—because Mama said so.

And by the way, my reference to my future niece as 'Madonna' is a running joke. Colleen does not wish to name her that. And if you know about how I first met Luke Trevanian and Norman you'll smile too. Although Colleen isn't in on the joke, her husband is. We are both just trying to find the right moment to enlighten her.

I glanced at my watch. Fifteen minutes. I was breathless from racing across the underground parking lot and into the elevator, heart thumping.

The door opened on the maternity ward and I catapulted down the corridor to check in with the receptionist. They were waiting for me with cap, mask and gown, an ensemble I was required to struggle into before I was allowed to meet Shaun at the door of the delivery room. Norman and Luke had dropped me off to find a parking space and would join up with us in the waiting area later.

"Where is my sister?" I heard Colleen holler at the nurse.

"She's on her way."

"You said that fifteen minutes ago!"

"I'm here, big sis," I said bursting in through the door, tying the mask behind my head.

Colleen's face was sweaty, but glowing, looking happy and exhausted and in pain."

"One last push," the doctor urged.

Colleen pushed and little Madonna slid out, new and beautiful into the world.

The medical team took the newborn to clean her up while a single attendant remained to mop Colleen down, but after a few seconds of her ministering, Colleen nudged her away. "Let me see my daughter, please."

"Coming right up. The nurse is just swaddling her."

Exhausted, but clearly pleased to see me, my sister extended her arms for a major hug, which I received grudgingly because: Did I really deserve it?

The paper gown crunched as I sat back on the edge of her bed. "What took you so long?" she demanded.

I could hardly tell her that I was in Egypt, that I had linked up with an old boyfriend, was betrayed by him and nearly killed by a vengeful Syrian terrorist, that I had saved two nations from going to war, and had had to attend a last minute funeral. I smiled, and kissed her on her damp forehead, knowing she would never believe me even if I told her the truth.

"Had to work late?" I said, my voice rising to a humorous squeak.

I grinned and she forgave me; she always forgave me.

She grabbed my hand and gave it an affectionate tug. "Well, you're here now. You can tell me your tall tale later." Her hand jerked up to her eyes, still clasping mine, suddenly noticing the latest acquisition to my humble assortment of fashion accessories. "Holy cow, Lucy! Is that an engagement ring on your finger?"

I was jolted back to reality, my Egyptian adventure evaporating into a Toronto hospital delivery room.

"Oh, yeah. Forgot to mention. Norman and I got engaged."

CHAPTER 47

As far as I was concerned, the occasion was a baby shower. As far as Colleen was concerned it was an engagement party. Didn't matter as long as all of our friends and family showed up to the event at the Trevanian mansion.

Shades of *déjà vu.*

Only a short time ago we were all gathered together in this very house honoring Ramy Basseem, Egypt's very own Indiana Jones.

And now he was gone.

So many things had changed in that short time. Colleen and Shaun were parents. Norman and I were going to be married. Although *when* was still up in the air. Johnny and Alessandra no longer felt compelled to hide their feelings from each other or the rest of the world. And Luke and Arianna? Well, time would tell.

My friend Yasmine was in town with her fiancé so they were invited, too. I wasn't able to meet the lucky man yet as she had arrived alone. He was delayed because of some business affair he had to settle first. He meant to meet her here.

I was hoping that Norman and the senator-to-be would hit it off. I had forgotten how much I enjoyed Yasmine's company, and couples dates would be so much fun.

We linked arms, and I gave her a private tour of the Trevanian household. I was as familiar with the updated, French chateau style mansion as though it were my own. We stood at a third story picture window overlooking the sprawling estate, admiring the view, when I adjusted the drapery to fully reveal the two acres of pristine forest bursting with autumn foliage alongside the river. As we watched enraptured by the scenery, guests drove up the grand cedar-lined driveway and disappeared under the *porte cochere* entrance to park in the cobblestone courtyard.

"This would be a great place to have a wedding," Yasmine said.

I drank in the colors of garden, forest and river, nodding. In this light, time froze and the scene might as well have been a watercolor painting—but it wouldn't be ours. Colorful and magnificent as it was the love that dominated this place belonged to Luke Trevanian and Arianna Chase. They just didn't know it yet.

"I think I want to get married overseas," I told Yas. "Italy or Greece or Spain."

"Sounds good to me," she answered. "I'm of the same mind. As a matter of fact, my father is making a movie in Greece next month. I'm on research leave, as of next spring, but before that I have a month's holiday and I'm heading out there to help on production. You should come, Lucy. We could scout out possible venues. Unless you're planning on tying the knot before then?"

"Before *then?* Are you kidding? You do realize you need at least a year's lead time to book venues?"

She laughed. Clearly she had people to do this type of thing for her.

"I'm serious, Lucy. I would love it if you could make the trip. Keep me company while Talbot is in Washington. He'll be tied up with business for most of that time. I'll be lucky if I see him at all. Please say you'll come. All expenses paid. Talbot owns a villa right on the Aegean in the beautiful island of Schinoussa in the Cyclades. You said you might want to get married in Greece. You could make our villa your home base and scout out venues from there."

So tempting, but I would have to run the idea by Norman first.

We turned from the window and I showed Yasmine the spacious home gym, and the home theater. Of course we only poked our heads in through the doors, as we didn't have the time to really explore; people would be looking for us and most of the guests had already arrived.

The *pièce de résistance* on this floor was my favorite, the spa area (you probably know why). In there was a waterfall feature where I had spent the morning indulging in the sound of crashing water and the sensuousness of a bubbling hot, fragrant bath for two.

My plus one, I'm assuming, was obvious.

My friend oohed and ahhed appreciatively, and then we both giggled because we understood that neither of us would ever be in possession of such wealth. Nor would we want it. We would be wealthy enough. We both had good jobs, and fiancés with even better paychecks. Rest assured when you work for billionaire Luke Trevanian the pay is good, not millionaire good, but good. However, our bank accounts notwithstanding, we were still the richest people on the planet, and not because of our monetary worth. We both possessed what many people never would; someone we loved and that loved us—to share our lives with.

Tinkling glassware and china, laughter and conversation rose from below an open window as Yasmine and I returned to the main floor.

We entered through the spacious, grey marble foyer with floor to ceiling glass panes. I showed her the library to the right of us with its iron-railed spiral staircase (where Johnny Sayid had hidden in the shadows only a short while past).

When we found ourselves once more in the main foyer Yasmine remarked on the uniqueness of the sculpture niches with their modern pieces, and then shoved a finger at the gorgeous, crystal and chrome hanging light fixture above our heads, to which I responded: "That chandelier is hand blown."

Who else but Luke Trevanian could own a hand blown chandelier?

It was a glorious, sunshiny afternoon, with just the slightest autumn nip in the air, so the occasion was being celebrated outdoors. Yas and I wandered freely into the black and white living room, and into the formal dining area, past the handmade Spanish-style dining set. At the far end, the French doors to the stone patio were wide open and from our vantage the shallow ravine appeared just overlooking the river.

As we joined the guests mingling among the decorative mums, yews and other autumn foliage, a young woman dressed in black and white offered us a tray of mimosas. I accepted a champagne flute, frosty with the citrusy cocktail, and steered Yasmine in the direction of the vine-covered gazebo. We stopped to admire the curved infinity pool and its lovely turquoise water where it boldly sat on the precipice of the ravine.

Down by the pool's edge my sister and Shaun sat on a plush outdoor sofa with their swaddled newborn in Colleen's lap. Norman and my sister were tight. He was standing over her, engaged in conversation. And if you were unaware that Shaun was the dad, you might have mistaken Norman for that role; he was looking so affectionately at little Madonna.

Oh yeah. Will wonders never cease? Colleen and Shaun decided to name her Madonna. Madonna Ann Templeton.

"I really should look for Talbot," Yasmine said. "He texted me to say he had arrived ten minutes ago. Hope he didn't get lost on this huge estate." She grinned. The soon-to-be senator, James Talbot, was a familiar face in American politics and could hardly go unnoticed even in a crowd. Except by me. I ignored political rhetoric until it was time to vote.

"First let me introduce you to my sister and her

husband," I insisted. "You've already met Norman."

She agreed and trailed me to where the threesome was surrounded by well-wishers and baby gifts. My sister was delighted to meet her. Shaun, oddly, was not. I wanted to question him on his uncharacteristically diffident behavior when Colleen asked me to retrieve her baby bag from one of the guest rooms. I acquiesced good-naturedly, and left to fetch said baby bag.

By now all of the guests had wandered down to the area of the patio where the infinity pool was the centerpiece of the scene because it seemed to flow right into the vibrant, forested riverscape.

I started to pass the gazebo, and although there was no one around I did a double take because I was certain I had heard voices.

"How much?" a voice asked.

"Two million."

My ears perked up. Who was bartering inside the gazebo? Luke had some pretty high-powered business partners but this conversation sounded suspect.

That was probably what made me eavesdrop. Half of the gazebo was enshrouded in vines and hid me from sight. Feeling slightly guilty and more than a little self-conscious I was careful not to make a sound, and peeked through a gap.

Two men were musing over three pieces of jewelry—a necklace, a pair of earrings and a headband, all made of some sort of precious metal and lying on a felt covered board. One thing that was quite noticeable about these pieces, they all had fixation holes, that is: perforations where they were once attached to a statue. The items appeared ancient. Were these men friends of Luke, antique collectors or maybe dealers?

One of the individuals was tall, extremely good-looking and the other was rough and rather shifty in demeanor.

I was about to leave when Yasmine startled me, having appeared out of nowhere unannounced, and I nearly crashed into her as I stepped into the open.

"Lucy! What's taking you so long?"

I shrugged and said nothing, wracked my brain for a reasonable answer and jested. "Just sipping my mimosa. Want to get rid of the thing before I go inside." Why I troubled to invent this yarn I do not know. I was experiencing an odd feeling, an intuitive sensation that she would drop a cloud over my sunny day if we continued in this vein.

Yasmine's painted lips curved into a shallow U as I raised the glass to her and did a convincing demonstration. Glass empty, I set it on a nearby table.

"I'll come with you," she offered, eyes dancing over the patio. "Still searching for my missing fiancé. Maybe he's inside."

We started for the house and passed around the other side of the gazebo where the interior was exposed.

Yasmine stopped.

"James? There you are! I've been looking all over for you. When did you arrive?" She didn't wait for a response before she shoved me up in front of her. "Darling, I want you to meet my dear friend, Lucy Racine. Lucy, this is James Talbot my husband-to-be."

It was all I could do not to let my jaw drop when the good-looking man stepped out to greet me. I knew Yasmine's husband was something of a superstar in Washington, but I was not into politics so I wouldn't have recognized him from pizza. By now his merchandise was safely hidden somewhere, although apparently not on his person as his hands appeared empty. His buddy, the shifty-looking bugger had vanished.

"Pleased to meet you, Lucy," Talbot said. When I heard his voice, its deep seductive tenor drove all of my suspicions out the door. He couldn't possibly be involved in anything improper; he was much too charming.

"Nice to meet you too. I've heard so much about you."

"All good things I hope?"

"Oh, yes. Of course."

He was polite, and charismatic and radiated a powerful but sophisticated masculinity, not unlike Luke. He couldn't however, hold a candle to my Norman—who was coming towards us by the way.

"Lucy," he said, giving a nod to Talbot and Yasmine, but oddly not offering the former a handshake. "Where's the baby bag?"

"Sorry, I got sidetracked," I replied. I sent smiles all around and apologized for having to leave. "Hope to see more of you James. In fact maybe as soon as Easter. Yasmine just invited me up to your Greek villa in the Aegean to keep her company while you're working."

By the confusion on his face this was news to him. It was news to Norman as well and his expression betrayed something more than just annoyance in being excluded from an important decision. Norman gave Talbot the same look Shaun had sent Yasmine when they met. Why?

It disturbed me a little, but I refused to allow their personal pettiness to dampen my mood.

"Excuse us," I said pleasantly, and accompanied Norman almost at a skip, as we made our way up the flagstones to the house.

I was feeling light and happy and nothing was going to ruin it for me. Whatever was bugging Norman and Shaun could wait. I extricated Norman's hand from his pocket to feel his strong grip. Everything was working out just the way I wanted. There was only one thing missing that would make this day perfect.

We reached the house and as we passed by the kitchen, we glimpsed Arianna and Luke alone. The serving staff was outdoors. Luke and Arianna, looking every bit the host and hostess, were standing against the window casement. Outside, their garden party was an obvious success. They were poised in the sunlight, admiring their handiwork and the golden rays touching their hair, transformed their blonde locks into spun gold like the Greek god and goddess Adonis and Aphrodite. Then Luke turned Arianna around to face him, and kissed her.

Not exactly Rhett Butler sweeping Scarlett off her feet

and up the winding staircase to their bedroom, but it would do!

I turned to Norman and he chuckled. "Finally."

"All's well that ends well," I said.

"Does it?" he remarked. "What's this I hear about you heading off to the Greek islands?"

My phone suddenly buzzed—thank goodness, saved by the bell—and I fetched it out of my bag.

Three words appeared in the text from Aras. Where was he anyway? I thought he was supposed to make a showing at the party.

Don't trust Talbot

Oh no. Not this again. I darted my eyes from side to side as though he might suddenly appear, and clicked off my phone, crammed it into my pocket, pushing aside Aras' enigmatic proclamation, and returned my attention to my fiancé. Oh, wow, did I ever love using that word: my *fiancé*. I traced my fingers tantalizingly up and down his chest. "So much more romantic to get married there than here, don't you think?"

"I don't care where we do it. As long as you do it with *me*."

Norman scooped me up off my feet into his masterful arms, and marched up the winding staircase to find the guest room where Colleen had left her baby bag.

He dumped me on the luxurious designer bed, making the myriad stylish pillows jiggle, while I lay on my back, eyes teasing him.

"Seriously?" he said.

I licked my lips and nodded.

"And Colleen?"

Guess my sister will just have to wait a little while longer for the baby bag.

Fresco Nights Saga: mystery, adventure and romance!

Fresco Nights (Book 1)
What could be more fun than mystery and romance on Italy's gorgeous Amalfi Coast? Seduced into a dangerous scheme to recover a priceless Black Madonna, museum illustrator Lucy Racine is deadlocked by her feelings for her co-conspirators—a billionaire archaeologist and his sexy bodyguard.

Pompeii at Dusk (Book 2)
A plane crash turns an innocent archaeology conference into the site of a double-edged mystery when a fresco of a medusa's head leads museum illustrator Lucy Racine to a secret organization called ISORE—and it involves her boss, her billionaire boyfriend and his bodyguard.

Midnight in Palmyra (Book 3)
Museum illustrator Lucy Racine is recruited to help rescue an archaeologist's young daughter only to find herself in the hands of terrorists—a situation that forces her to confront her feelings for her billionaire boyfriend's bodyguard.

Baghdad before Dawn (Book 4)
What are the Winged Bulls of Nineveh and what do they have to do with the legendary Hanging Gardens of Babylon? Museum illustrator Lucy Racine finds out when she sets out to save the man she loves from terrorists determined to loot and destroy priceless archaeological sites.

Cairo by Nightfall (Book 5)

"Do not scream when you see the mummy." With these words museum illustrator Lucy Racine, member of the Save Our Ruins Effort (ISORE), is reunited with an ex-boyfriend, much to the chagrin of her current one, and launched on a rescue mission that ends in the treasure hunt of a lifetime—the hunt for Cleopatra's tomb.

What Readers are saying about the Fresco Nights Saga!

“Excellent! The book was impossible to put down as one was drawn in it by the end of the first page. Fresco Nights was recommended by the magazine ***Archaeology***. I enjoyed it very much, would recommend it to everyone who enjoys history or archeology.”- Amazon reviewer

“A well thought out mystery with a confident and intelligent main character. She proves on numerous occasions that she is resourceful enough to rescue herself AND the men in her life. Though the "bad guy" was obvious to me, it was still very enjoyable to read simply for the character development alone. This is what happens when a truly skilful writer is at work.”- Amazon reviewer

“Absolutely amazing! Great story. While you can predict some of what is coming, there is enough to keep you guessing. Can't wait to read the next one.” – Goodreads reviewer

“Great story. Romance, drama & a mystery.” – Goodreads reviewer

“Oh, I love books like these. Suspense. Love. Two men. Stolen treasure and archeology finds in caves, murder and love.” – Goodreads reviewer

“Deborah’s descriptions of Naples and the surrounding area is so precise that you feel you are actually there... I love the idea of the tunnels beneath the church and other buildings along with the romance of smugglers and pirates.” – Amazon reviewer

“1st book in a 4 book series. I am new to this author. I won this read through a Goodreads giveaway. Nice cover!! My go 2 genre is always anything mystery ... love them!! I wanna read more ... enjoy her writing style.”- Amazon reviewer

"A fun read, romance, mystery, and archaeology." – Goodreads reviewer

"Characters are very realistic. The action never stops." – Goodreads reviewer

"Just BRAVO! This book was great... It was well written, action packed, and with a bit of a romantic triangle... I am hooked and I look forward to reading the other books in this series!" – Goodreads reviewer

"This series of books are very enjoyable. I love the action." – Goodreads reviewer

"Great read. Draws you in and keeps getting better. Love the series." – Goodreads reviewer

"I love the excitement of these books. Antiques and war torn places. Love and kidnapped your man you think is dead. Keeps you reading." – Goodreads reviewer

"Utterly Charming. I loved it, and very much appreciated the language style." – Goodreads reviewer

Acknowledgements

Nothing warms an author's heart more than hearing a reader say, "When is the next book? I *have* to know what happens!" I believe this novel would not have existed if not for some persistent fans insisting on more. So, thank you dear readers. You have made my characters spring to life in ways I never imagined. And Yes, I want to meet *him*, too!

My sincere thanks to the international archaeologists who recover stolen artifacts and thwart their illegal sale, fascinating and important work that inspired the FRESCO NIGHTS series. And as always, a huge thanks to my husband for proofreading the manuscript and reimagining the story in his wonderful cover design.

About the Author

Deborah L. Cannon is a novelist and short story writer. She writes under three names: Deborah L. Cannon under which the Fresco Nights novels are written, Deborah Cannon under which are published The Raven Chronicles series and her Chinese epic fantasy *The Pirate Empress*, and Daphne Lynn Stewart who writes a series of Christmas romances for pet lovers. She is also a contributor to the *Chicken Soup for the Soul* franchise. She lives in Hamilton, Ontario with her archaeologist husband near the Royal Botanical gardens lakeside with her two Mal-shihs Lucy and Luke.

Made in the USA
Monee, IL
22 February 2021

61138830R00223